MISSION

The Birth of California,
The Death of a Nation

MARGARET WYMAN

IDYLLWILD

PUBLISHING CO.™

IDYLLWILD, CALIFORNIA

For Jerry, Scooter, and Kumi

First edition

Published by Idyllwild Publishing Co., a division of Wild Ink Productions, P.O. Box 355, Idyllwild, CA 92549

IDYLLWILD PUBLISHING CO. and the accompanying logo are trademarks of Idyllwild Publishing Co., a division of Wild Ink Productions

Publisher's Cataloging-In-Publication
Wyman, Margaret
    Mission / by Margaret Wyman
        316 p. ; 24 cm.
    ISBN 1-931857-00-8
    1.   Historical Fiction–Kumeyaay Indians of California
    2.   American Literature–Mission Period of California
    3.   California Historical Literature–Missions in 18th Century
    I. Title

PS3573.Y58 M57 2002
813'.54—dc21   LCCN: 2001099471

Printed in the United States of America

Margaret (Peggy) Wyman

Margaret Wyman, after careers as programmer, scientist, and star salesperson, has returned in grand style to her childhood dream—that of writing. She is the author of three historical fiction novels and numerous essays and articles. At her new home in the splendid San Jacinto Mountains of Southern California., she is now hard at work on a trilogy, called String of Pearls, tracing the lives of three generations of women from the famines of Ireland to the wilds of America.

ACKNOWLEDGEMENTS

There are so many people I'd like to thank for helping me over the long, often tortuous path to "birthing" this book, but especially I want to thank:

- My husband—my best friend and companion—who believed in me
- The ladies of the "coven" —Michal Costello, Barbara Dixson, Charlie Sunday, and Tessa McRae—who saw me through some stormy times
- Peggy Kidd, my prayer partner and good friend
- Dorland Mountain Arts Colony, where I wrote the first draft
- The reference librarians at many libraries, but most especially those of the California Room at the San Diego, CA Public Library
- The Kumeyaay, for providing their colorful history and for the inspiration they gave me
- Dr. Florence Shipek, who helped me correct the manuscript
- Mike Connolly, who gave me guidance and encouragement
- The legion of agents and publishers who rejected the manuscript and said this book had no market

I
TWO WORLDS
Fall, 1767—Fall, 1768

Chapter 1—Late Summer, 1767

*The Kumeyaay Desert Village of Hawi in
the Great Desert east of what is now San Diego*

Web lay in a pit on a mat of deer grass and desert mallow spread over heated stones. A similar mat of grass and mallow covered her and the other initiate, Mishtai, her best friend. She was able to ignore the dust the dancers kicked up, but the persistent itch on her lower back tested her control. She bit her lip against the urge to move. The priest had precisely positioned two crescent-shaped stones on her abdomen just above her budding pubic thatch. Any movement might shift the stones before the ceremony ended. A lifetime of criticism awaited the girl who could not withstand the temporary discomfort of the roasting pit during her three-day passage from childhood to womanhood.

Out of the corner of her eye, Web watched her friend Mishtai. The two girls had begun their monthly courses on the same day, the day of the last *hellyach-temur* full moon. While Web and Mishtai had gone into seclusion to prepare themselves for the responsibility that went with their new power to bring forth life, their parents had sent out runners inviting the scattered members of their respective *sh'mulq* sibs to come to Hawi for the girls' initiation ceremony. During their seclusion, Web and Mishtai had spent hours exchanging confidences. As the first members of their sibs began to arrive, they had made a solemn pact to help each other through the ordeal ahead of them in whatever way they could.

The itching on Web's back intensified. *No,* Web thought. *I will not give in to you. I will not move. I have not come this far or endured this much to fail now.*

To keep her mind off the torment, she turned her attention to the crowd dancing around the sand pit. Some of the dancers had traveled many days to reach Hawi in time. So many had come that their numbers strained the resources of the small village.

While Web watched the dancing, the girl Amul pushed through the crowd and came to stand at the pit to smirk down at the two girls. Despite the mesh ceremonial cap that hid her face, Web stared back, matching her nemesis' mocking smile. For as far back as she could remember Amul had been the bane of her existence, teasing her, calling her "Slime-Frog" and making slurping noises that caused the other children to laugh at her, always careful to hide her cruelty from the adults.

After a time, Amul tired of her staring and disappeared into the crowd. The moment she was gone, Web's itching reasserted itself. In order to ignore it, she narrowed her eyes to slits to concentrate on the weave of the mesh that had protected her face and head from the swarming spring flies during her time in the pit.

Her mother had woven the ceremonial cap from juncus grass, spending hours wrapping and stitching to create a piece every bit as beautiful as the baskets she made to trade. Woven into the coils was a unique design of frogs and ducks. The animals had been sacred to their *sh'mulq* since the dawn of time when First Ancestor had seen fit to give certain women of her mother's line webbed hands–hands like Web's–where flaps of skin grew up to the first joints of each finger. Web had been named for her hands. Before her, the last one so endowed was her mother's grand-mother. Yet, despite the many stories of Great-Grandmother's abilities as a healer and maker of baskets so beautiful that even the warlike Quechan people came under the flag of truce to Hawi to trade for them and despite her mother's exhortations to be proud of her hands, Amul's teasing and the stares she drew whenever the people of Hawi traveled to other Kumeyaay villages made Web self-conscious of her hands.

One of the elders of her father's sib now stepped out of the group dancing a shuffling circle around the pit and launched into a harangue about the responsibilities the roasting girls must assume as adult members of the Hawi band. Web tried hard to be attentive, but she was too tired and uncomfortable to absorb much. *So many must-nots. So much to remember. How can I ever live up to the expectations of my parents and my band?*

The delectable perfume of roasting *haakwal* lizard, her favorite, assailed her nostrils. In the last three days she had been allowed to eat only a cup of *shawii* acorn mush at those times she had been allowed to leave the pit so that the cooling rocks could be replaced with hot ones. Now that her monthly courses had begun, she must not eat meat or fish or salt for at least one moon; longer if she intended to follow the tradition of the women of her mother's *sh'mulq*. She knew her mother expected a longer period of abstention, but at that moment, Web could not imagine another hour without a taste of *haakwal*, let alone a full moon cycle.

Steady pressure against her right arm broke through her thoughts. Mishtai had given into the exhaustion of three days without sleep.

"Mishtai," Web hissed softly without moving her lips. "Wake up." Her friend did not respond.

Cognizant of the consequences to Mishtai if someone caught her sleeping, Web checked to be sure no one was paying attention before inching her covered hand slowly toward her friend, praying no one would notice the barely perceptible ripple in the layer of grass.

At that moment, the dancers parted to reveal Amul watching her with unblinking eyes. The sight stopped Web's hand. Pact or not, she refused to give Amul the pleasure of being the one to catch her breaking the rules of initiation.

Suddenly Mishtai snorted and jerked upright, convulsing the entire covering of grass. Instantly the presiding shaman leaped to the side of the pit and launched into a tirade aimed at the offending girl. Disgust painted the faces of the members of Mishtai's extended family, standing with her dismayed parents.

Throughout the harangue, Mishtai kept her eyes lowered and barely breathed. After the priest finished and the adults went back to their dancing, she murmured a hurt, "You promised" to Web.

Web could think of nothing to say that would satisfy the embarrassed Mishtai, especially with Amul still watching her every move. She kept her eyes on the lengthening shadow of the closest *'aanall* mesquite. The roasting would end at sunset. This close to the end, perhaps the adults would not hold Mishtai's slip against her for long. Perhaps she could claim she too had nodded off momentarily. Would a lie help, or make the situation worse?

She hoped the right answer would come to her before they were lifted out of the pit for the last time.

After what seemed an eternity, the singing stopped, leaving a gap of deafening silence. The priest signaled the girls' mothers and aunts forward. While the women rolled back the pit covering, Web leaned toward Mishtai and whispered, "I didn't see you until it was too late."

"Don't lie," Mishtai said coldly. "I can always tell when you don't speak the truth."

"But, I–"

Her mother's touch cut off Web's protest. Mother and two aunts helped her out of the pit. "Oh, my daughter, you have made me so proud. Now you are a woman," her mother said, removing the basket cap and smoothing Web's long hair. Prior to the ceremony, she had cut her daughter's bangs just above her eyebrows in the style of the adult women of the people. Now she cupped Web's cheek and gave her a tremulous smile full of the emotion she did not voice.

"Not quite yet, my sister," said Web's aunt, Button Cactus. "We must first give her the tattoo marks of a woman and then the priest will lead her to the holy place."

"The marking will hurt, my child, but you must not cry out," her mother whispered. "Remember what I have taught you."

Web nodded, sucked in a breath to steel herself against the pain to come and allowed her mother's sisters to lead her to a small boulder. Button Cactus, as the eldest, waved for Web to sit, then took charge. After a quick glance at the prickly-pear cactus thorns, laid out in a row next to the sticks of charcoal, Web closed her eyes, took several deep breaths and retreated to the quiet place within her as her mother had taught. She was only partially aware of the thorns puncturing the skin of her chin and of charcoal being rubbed into the wounds until her mother announced, "Stand, child."

Web came out of her trance to find her mother draping a *hekwiir* blanket of twisted rabbit skins over her shoulders. "Remember how I showed you to hold it?" her mother asked.

Despite the throbbing pain in her chin, Web grasped the edges of the drape together at the neck so that both hands were hidden inside the folds of the *hekwiir*.

Her mother smiled, and the aunts placed garlands made of pliable yucca on her head, then stepped away, leaving her standing by herself. Suddenly she was uneasy about what she would soon witness. Besides making the pact to help each other through the roasting, she and Mishtai had spent endless hours wondering over what the priest would show them in this final stage of their initiation. Was it a hole so deep that it led to the back side of the sky? Or a deep pool in whose depths they would be able to see into the spirit world? Or something even more terrifying?

Suddenly she was not at all sure she wanted to become an adult, burdened with responsibilities and cares. Her chin throbbed from the recent assault of thorns and charcoal. She had one last step to complete her initiation into womanhood. No woman in either parental sib had ever failed any of the ordeals of her initiation, yet her leaden legs refused to move.

"Go, child. The priest awaits," her mother urged.

Web swallowed against the cottony feel in her throat. *I do not want this*, she wanted to scream.

"Daughter?" The exasperation in her mother's tone got Web's feet moving.

Mishtai was already with the priest. She side-stepped away from Web.

An assistant stepped forward to help the priest wrap strips of hide around the girls' eyes as blindfolds. Then the priest commanded, "Come."

Already light-headed from hunger, fatigue and pain, Web stumbled along, blindly following the faint crunch of the priest's steps in the sand. Her senses told her that he led them out from the village toward the hot-springs. Sulfurous smells a short while later confirmed her guess as the little party followed the foot path around the steaming water and headed up the rising pan toward the boundary beyond which ordinary Kumeyaay did not pass. The jumbled rocks that lay beyond that boundary were sacred, reserved for those who possessed the power to enter the world of Spirits. When Web tried to stop, the priest's assistant prodded her to keep moving.

At the edge of the rocks, the branch of a creosote bush caught at Web's ankle. She stumbled and would have fallen if the assistant had not caught her and restored her to her feet. She wanted to turn back, away from the land of Spirits into the land of mortals, but the assistant's grip remained on her arm, guiding her over the rock-strewn path.

On and on they went until Web's legs turned rubbery. She was close to fainting when the priest's voice intoned, "Stop."

The assistant stripped off her blindfold, and the shaman commanded, "Look. There."

Web blinked to adjust to the flickering light of the firebrand the priest carried.

"Behold Mother Goddess," the priest thundered. "Behold Her sacred Self. Look you well upon Her for it is from Her that you gain the power to bring forth life. From this moment you, Web, and you, Mishtai, are no longer children. Now you are women."

While the priest's voice boomed off the wall of boulders before them, relating all that would be expected of her now that she was a woman, Web observed, confused by what she saw. An enormous rock formation rose up before her. An odd formation that looked like a double-yoked egg.

She waited for the priest to explain, to tell her what she was supposed to see, but he had fallen silent. She continued to stare, then suddenly it hit her. Not an egg, the rocks formed the flower petals that a woman—that Web herself—carried tucked between her legs. The two lips that kiss each child as it leaves its mother to join the world, and the door through which a baby passes into life.

With that realization, power seemed to pour forth from the rocks, glittering with the afterglow of Sun. That power washed over her, engulfing her like the wind that precedes the life-giving rains. Awestruck, she nudged Mishtai. "Do you see it, my sister?" she whispered over the sound of the shaman's chanting.

"Do not call me sister. You are no longer my friend," Mishtai hissed.

"Silence!" the priest's assistant ordered.

Under his glare, Mishtai seemed to shrink while Web bit back the urge to defend herself.

The priest finished his song and waved his sacred staff toward the rock formation. "The Mother Goddess shows Herself to you now so that you may bear many strong sons and daughters. Look you and think about the man who will be your husband."

Husband.

In one word, Web's awe for the Mother Goddess and her concern about Mishtai vanished, leaving in her innards a void that had no bottom. She had been so intent on performing her role in the initiation ceremony correctly that she had not thought beyond it. Now that the rites had reached their conclusion, the future yawned before her like a deep, pitch-black cave. She was now a woman. Womanhood meant marriage. Children. And keeping a husband happy.

When she had five summers, her parents had betrothed her to Shadow Dancer, a boy of seven summers, son of the renowned *wekuseyaay* rattlesnake shaman, Casts No Shadow. Casts No Shadow and Shadow Dancer lived in the village of Nipaguay over the mountains in the fertile valley of the river that ran into the *'ehaasilth* ocean far to the west. The betrothal had brought her parents great honor and many wonderful gifts from the *wekuseyaay* and his band. Nipaguay controlled some of the richest planting and hunting land and the best fishing areas along the coast. Web's marriage would tie Nipaguay to Hawi. For the people of Hawi, it meant reserves of food should they face another starving time, and reinforcements should the Quechan people decide to wage war again.

In the eight years since her betrothal, Web had seen Shadow Dancer only once: four years ago, when the winter rains did not come for the fifth straight year and the desert refused to bloom, the hungry people of Hawi undertook the long dangerous journey to the coast for food, and there she had set eyes upon her future husband. He was a tall boy with an intense gaze who seemed to be constantly asking questions about everyone and everything around him. Since the time, she had dreamed about him occasionally, but the dreams were the fantasies of a mere girl. Now the reality hit her with the force of a blow.

Marriage to Shadow Dancer meant leaving Hawi and everyone she loved, forever. Why had she never thought of that before?

A great sadness welled up from the pit of her stomach. She ducked her head and blinked back the tears that threatened to betray her. She must not cry. Whatever happened, she must make her parents proud.

Beside her, Mishtai sniffed. Deep in her own misery, Web ignored her friend and looked again upon the Mother Goddess through the mist of her unshed tears. The force flowing from the rocks changed from an engulfing wave to the tenderest of caresses as if the Spirits of the rocks, as if the Mother Goddess Herself, felt Web's fear and wanted to reassure her.

Web had no time to absorb the sensation. The priest repositioned her blindfold, and her world again went dark.

"You are now women. Come. We will return to the village," the priest said, pebbles clattering under his sandaled steps.

Before she could take a step, a small hand gripped Web's arm. "I hope you will leave Hawi soon," Mishtai said. "You are no friend of mine." Releasing her grip, she stumbled off, leaving Web to return with the assistant priest.

Chapter 2—Fall, 1767

Misión La Purísima Concepción, Lower California, New Spain

José Romero put down his tongs and, swiping the sweat off his brow, admired his work. The altar piece was as good as new. No one could tell it had been mended. No one, except perhaps another blacksmith.

Another blacksmith.

Already Father Xavier had written five letters to the Spanish

Crown, begging for a replacement for the ailing Sanchez, La Purísima's official blacksmith. How many more would he have to write before the King did something?

"José, enough!" Romero muttered to himself with a vehemence that made his helper Tito, a bandy-legged Indian boy, jump.

"Leave me," Romero growled at the boy.

The youngster knew his master's moods well. He darted out of the forge and disappeared through the low opening cut into the back wall surrounding the Misión La Purísima Concepción.

Romero heaved a ragged sigh as he surveyed the pile of work waiting to be done. There was far too much work for one smith, but what else could be done? Between the lack of money and shorted shipments of supplies, Father Xavier had enough worries. Right now, the best service Romero could render the padre was to fill in at the forge when he longed to be back at the missionary's side as his personal servant, the position he had held for a decade ever since coming to La Purísima as a stowaway in the panniers of a donkey.

Romero grunted at the memory, rolling his shoulders to relieve the knot of tension that built up during the painstaking work he had done on the altar piece. He was born to an Indian woman, fathered by a Spanish soldier. After his parents both died within months of each other, Romero had been taken to the orphanage run by the Jesuit brothers at Misión Loreto. With so many children to tend, the monks left the younger ones to their own devices in order to indoctrinate the older children in church teachings. Romero had never been playful, but he relished exploring. He had discovered the wonders of the mission's forge on a solitary adventure. He was barely six years old.

Thereafter, he spent hours squatting in the shadows watching the blacksmith bend metal to his will. To Romero, there was magic in the fire, and he made up his mind to learn the smith's techniques.

The Loreto smith at that time was a silent man with brooding eyes and hands the size and strength of cast-iron tortilla griddles. He was, in fact, named for his hands: Manos. Despite his youth, Romero soon worked himself into the position of Manos's apprentice. It was in that position that he met Father Xavier.

Romero sagged down on a bench and allowed his mind to savor the memory of that momentous day.

Father Xavier had come to Loreto from the mainland of New Spain, a Jesuit missionary bound for Misión La Purísima to the north where he was to replace a retiring priest. Since he could not leave for his post until the annual shipment of supplies for the mission arrived from Spain, Xavier filled his waiting time observing Manos and Romero at their work. His obvious fascination with the miracles produced by the fire and the smith's hammer forged an immediate bond between the priest and the blacksmith's apprentice.

In turn, the Jesuit responded by lavishing attention on the boy; more attention than Romero had had even when his parents were alive.

By the time Xavier was ready to leave for La Purísima, the boy had come to regard the priest as his father. He was determined not to be left behind again, so he did the only thing he could think of. He was still small enough to wiggle into one of the donkey panniers, squeezing his body into a tight ball to hide beneath a sack of planting seed.

The pack train was two day's journey out of Loreto when a sneeze gave him away. The head muleteer was ready to beat the boy when Father Xavier intervened and took Romero to his tent. That night Romero slept at the foot of the priest's pallet, happier than he had ever been.

Remembering all this, his chuckle caused a passing Indian woman to stop and peer into the forge.

"Away!" Romero bellowed.

She scuttled off and he picked up one of the shaping tools that lay beside him on the bench. Closing his eyes, he ran his callused finger around the inside, taking pleasure in the feel of the smooth metal and the absence of a seam.

He had slept at the foot of the priest's bed throughout that long journey north, and, after they reached La Purísima, Father Xavier told the boy he no longer had to sleep on the floor, that he could join him on the pallet. Romero did not hesitate. How could he refuse this holy man who cared for him when no one else did?

Then, three nights later, Xavier told Romero to undress and stand naked before him. Again, the boy complied.

The priest sighed as if in ecstasy. "Ah, such perfection. Let me see you, my son. All of you. Turn. Ah, yes, you are a work of art," Father sighed, holding out his hands.

The look of love in the priest's eyes melted Romero's shyness. He stepped into Xavier's arms to receive a kiss he would never forget.

"My beautiful boy, you are as perfect as God could make you," Father had murmured into Romero's hair. "And I need you so."

Remembering the whispered words caused a shiver to course

the length of Romero's spine, raising gooseflesh on his arms despite the heat from the forge. *I need you so.* No one had ever needed him, not even Manos. No one had ever said those words. To be needed . . . In that moment such love had welled up in Romero that the priest could have asked anything of him, even his very soul.

Sitting on the rough bench in the darkness of the hot forge, he remembered the feel of the priest's hands as they caressed his boyish flesh. He remembered the sigh of "Beautiful, so beautiful." He remembered Father rising off the bed and kneeling on the floor. He felt those beloved hands grasping his own arms and pulling him down to the floor to kneel in front of the priest, facing the bed.

"Perfect boy child," Father had said, his breath hot on the back of Romero's neck while his hands traced a path from the boy's naked chest to his groin.

Fingers touching where no one had ever touched him caused Romero to flinch, but the priest's lips were on his ear, kissing it, caressing it with intoxicating words, crumbling his resistance. He was unaware of Father's bare skin on his, of the hardened knob at his nether opening until . . .

He closed his eyes and gave in to the memory of that moment. The moment when he had given Father his body–and his heart.

A noise outside brought him back to the present, to the bench and the forge, to the ever-growing pile of work to be done. So much work. And someone had to do it. *He* had to do it. But first . . .

"I need to show you to Father," he said aloud, addressing the altar piece, testing the metal to be sure it had cooled before picking it up and heading outside.

At midday the grounds of the mission were quiet. The neophytes had taken to the Spanish custom of siesta. He could see napping figures inside the simple huts the Indian converts occupied. Only the chickens strutted and clucked in their never-ending search for stray kernels of corn.

Behind the mission the monolith of El Pilón rose three hundred meters above the valley floor, and the pale reds, pinks and purples of the walls of the arroyo shown muted in the blaze of the midday sun. The doors to the church were shut against the heat of the day, a sign that Father Xavier was not inside. Romero walked past the church to the adjoining adobe structure where the priest took his meals and slept.

Outside the room, he stopped to smooth down his rumpled hair and tuck the tail of his loose homespun shirt into the faded red tie belt at his waist.

A moan came from inside the padre's room.

Through a crack in the door's planks, Romero could see two people in the little room. Father Xavier and Bartolomé, the orphan Indian boy the priest had recently taken in. Bartolomé was acting as the priest's servant while Romero worked the forge. Curious, Romero leaned closer to the crack to get a better look.

From his angle, he saw that the boy was leaning over the priest's pallet, while the priest stood close behind him. As Romero's eyes adjusted to the gloom of the room, he realized that the priest wasn't just standing. The front of his habit was raised, and each forward thrust of the priest's hips forced a moan from the boy and a grunt from the priest.

Romero pushed away from the door in shock. *It can't be. Can't be.*

He stumbled across the compound on bewildered legs. *No. No.*

Chapter 3

Web stopped to collect herself before approaching the ancient twisted *'aanall* mesquite. She had discovered the tree five summers ago after losing her way returning home from a day of harvesting. Ever since, it had served as her secret refuge. Even Mishtai did not know of this place. Web went to it whenever she felt troubled. Resting her palms on the gnarled bark never failed to give her both solace and solutions to whatever problems plagued her.

Earlier she had told her mother that she needed to replenish her supply of indigo bush stems, desert sage leaves, and cough root before leaving for Nipaguay. She had not lied. She did need the herbs, but, more importantly, she needed the chance to think in solitude. There had to be a way to get out of her forthcoming marriage. A way that would allow her to stay at Hawi with her parents and friends in the desert she knew so well and loved so much. She was full to bursting with her problem. She needed someone to talk to. But who?

She had always gone to her mother for counsel on serious matters. However, since her parents had arranged this marriage, she could not very well ask her mother to break the betrothal contract.

As for Mishtai, Web had been rebuffed every time she tried to reconcile the breach in their friendship. Eliminating Mother and

Mishtai, Web had one last place to turn. This *'aanall.*

Dragging in a ragged breath, she knelt beside the tree and whispered, "Who can I turn to for help, oh Wise One?" Placing her hands on the scarred, twisted bark, she touched her forehead to the tree. Immediately, a cloud swirled over her scattered thoughts, hiding them in an unnerving fog like the one she had experienced on her only journey west to the great sea. She waited, breathing slowly, deeply. After a time, the mind cloud thinned, revealing a blurred figure that gradually came into focus.

It was Autumn Sage, the strange man-who-lives-as-woman who had attached himself to the Hawi band. Autumn Sage was a powerful seer whose spirit guide was the ˉowl, the devil bird created by One Above's Blind Twin to rule the darkness. Everyone knew that an owl's hoot could be a warning that something bad was about to happen, but Autumn Sage disdained convention and even tamed a *shechaak* screech owl to be his companion. The people of Hawi accepted Autumn Sage into their number and provided food for him. To do otherwise would offend the spirits who had given the strange seer the power to speak to owls and to see further into the past and the future than any other shaman or sage.

Is there no one else? she thought to the tree.

The image of Autumn Sage in her mind remained crisp and unwavering.

She released her hold on the tree and dragged herself to her feet. Going to Autumn Sage for advice meant subjecting herself to the witch's unnerving scrutiny. She wasn't sure she could force herself to do so.

"You have no choice," she murmured, "because you can wait no longer."

Like his spirit guide, Autumn Sage slept during the day. Web had to wait until it was dark and the rest of the village was asleep. The seer's *'ewaa* lodge sat in a circular clump of mesquites two hundred paces from the center of the village. The moonless darkness pressed in on Web, amplifying every smell and exaggerating the shadows around her. The croaking of the *hantak* frogs that flourished around the hot-springs seemed louder than usual. In the distance a pack of *hattepaa* coyotes yipped their farewells to each other before setting off for their night's hunting. \

Her eyes strained against the darkness, searching for the familiar among the alien shapes around her until they caught the glow of a small fire ahead and locked onto it.

As she stepped into the ring of firelight, Autumn Sage said, "So you come at last" in a tone that announced that her visit was no surprise.

Reminding herself that such was to be expected from the farthest of far-seers did not keep a shiver from coursing down Web's spine.

"Sit, child."

She did and Autumn Sage's large round eyes regarded her impassively across the fire. Perched on his shoulder, the pet owl did likewise. While Web worked up the courage to speak, the desert night fell into a silence that stretched and deepened.

It was the seer who spoke first. "I know why you are here. You wish to ask the spirits what comes for you on your life's journey. Hark." Slowly lids descended over both pairs of eyes observing Web. For a long time, not even the fire disturbed the quiet. Then Autumn Sage's mouth opened and out poured an eerie vibrating bass voice. "The one with no shadow comes for you. He arrives tomorrow."

The abrupt announcement hit Web like a clap of *shuullaw* thunder. Where she figured to have several suns more to prepare herself to leave the only life and people she had ever known, time had run out. Casts No Shadow, father of her betrothed husband, would be here tomorrow to take her away from Hawi forever. She was too overwhelmed to wonder why Casts No Shadow came instead of Shadow Dancer's mother as Kumeyaay custom dictated.

"Believe in He Who Dances with Shadows," the voice intoned.

Web shoved her trembling hands under her hips. He Who Dances with Shadows could only mean Shadow Dancer, her husband-to-be. But what could the seer mean: Believe in him?

"With him, you will know the greatest joy of your life. And . . . your deepest sorrow."

The voice fell silent then, and moments later, the lids of the seer's eyes slid upward. Panicked, Web blurted, "Will I ever return to Hawi?"

The corner of the witch's mouth twitched. "Part of you will."

"Which part? When?"

With a glower that let her know her questions were inappropriate, Autumn Sage rose, turned away from the fire and entered his *'ewaa*.

For a long time, Web stared at the lodge opening, hoping that the seer would return to answer the jumble of questions churning in her heart. Finally she gave up and trudged back to the old mesquite, seeking answers.

This time the tree remained silent, and she crept back to her parents' *'ewaa* to wait for the coming day and the man without a shadow who was coming to take her away–forever.

Chapter 4

At the sound of footfalls approaching the family's yucca-thatched dome *'ewaa*, Web stiffened but resisted the impulse to wrap her arms around her bare budding breasts for comfort. She was now a woman, and a woman did not resort to such childish acts. Instead, she nervously smoothed her hair and adjusted the waist thong that held in place her *heyuly*, the two-piece skirt of yucca fibers. The *heyuly* was her only adornment except for an iridescent pink seashell dangling from a leather thong tied around her neck.

Earlier that morning her father had given her the shell as a going-away present. She had seen a shell like this one just once before, when a woman from her mother's *sh'mulq* had given six of her best baskets in trade for such a shell. While her father was tying the shell around her neck, Web had searched his face for a sign that he would mourn her leaving. She found none, and it had taken all her control to thank him and walk, rather than run, out of the village to her secret tree where she gave in to her grief. She yearned to go back to being a girl without responsibilities and cares. She wanted Mishtai to be her best friend again. She would even forgive Amul if only she did not have to leave Hawi.

"Stop such thinking," she whispered to herself now as she crouched in the *'ewaa*, waiting, grasping one hand with the other for comfort.

"Daughter, come out," her father announced in a too-loud, formal voice.

Heart pounding, Web closed her eyes and ducked out of the hut's waist-high entrance.

"Daughter, your husband's father comes for you."

A pair of unfamiliar feet stepped into the line of sight of her downcast eyes. The owner of the feet spoke in a voice that was both quiet and commanding. "My woman has joined the Spirits. In her place, I come for you."

Web swallowed and, with difficulty, raised her eyes to meet the gaze of the famous *wekuseyaay* rattlesnake shaman, Casts No

Shadow. She scarcely noticed his brown skin which was the shade of new mesquite bark or the deep creases radiating out from the corners of his eyes, or the eyes the color of smoke that seemed to see far into the distance. Instead, she focused on his hair, which he wore in a knot the height of an outstretched hand on the top of his head. That knot was wrapped in yucca fiber and coated with red mud to resemble a single red horn.

She was unable to take her eyes off that horn, and her voice quavered as she spoke the required words, "Welcome, my father."

Casts No Shadow nodded, then bent to grasp her hands. Gently he opened her clenched fists and examined her outstretched fingers, nodding slightly before releasing her. "We leave at dawn, daughter. Rest well. The journey is long." He turned and paced away, taking Web's parents with him.

Amul's wheedling voice at Web's elbow cut into her thoughts. "Now why would he look at your hands? Surely he already knew that you're a freak."

Web was too tired and distressed to ignore Amul's goading. She put aside her inner turmoil and faced her accuser. "He saw what any wise person would see, Amul."

"And what is that, Slime-Frog?"

"The blessing of the gods."

Amul gave her head an indolent toss. "No, I think he saw trouble."

"You do, do you? And why do you think that?"

The practiced, sullen languidness vanished from Amul's face, replaced by undisguised hatred. "It does not take the gift of far-seeing to recognize that you and your frog hands will never fit anywhere but here at Hawi where your parents protect you so no one dares speak against you, but tell me, who will protect you at Nipaguay?"

Web drew herself up. "The gods will protect me, Amul, as they always have."

"If you believe that, you are a bigger fool than I thought."

"We'll see who is the fool, sister."

"Yes we will, won't we?" With that, Amul strolled away, leaving Web feeling more empty and confused than ever.

Chapter 5

That night, Web chose to stay out under the family's open-sided *wisal* shade bower, rather than in the *'ewaa*. She could not bear to listen to the familiar sounds of her parents in sleep when, in the morning, she would have to leave them. The wind did not rest all night and neither did Web. Too soon it was morning and time to depart.

While Casts No Shadow waited beside her father, studying Web with his smoky eyes, her mother placed the every-day basket hat over Web's hair and secured the ties of the *hatupul* burden net around her head.

Web's heart ached at her mother's touch. She kept her head bowed and her eyes focused on the ground. She dared not look at her mother or the surrounding mesquite thicket or the familiar yucca-thatched lodges that made up the center of the village of Hawi or the people gathered there. One glimpse would undo what little control she had left.

Her mother finished and took a step backward, then her father announced, "It is time, daughter. Go to your husband with a happy heart."

Among the gathered band, Web heard giggles from some of the young girls. The sound made her want to scream, "Cruel ones! How can you laugh when I hurt so?"

As she shifted her eyes, a scowling Mishtai moved into her line of sight at the edge of the assembled throng. Web looked at her, hoping for some sign of forgiveness before she departed. Instead, Amul sidled up to Mishtai's side and whispered something into her ear that made them both laugh in a conspiratorial way.

So Mishtai was now Amul's friend. Mishtai would be sorry because Amul could not be trusted. Amul was mean and Amul was wrong, wrong about Web not belonging anywhere but Hawi. *I'll prove that fact if it's the last thing I do,* Web vowed silently.

Her mother touched her arm. "It is time, my child."

She glanced up to meet her mother's moist eyes. For a moment, she wanted to throw her arms around her mother's strong neck, to feel the comfort of her mother's arms, the warm press of her sagging breasts.

"The father of your husband waits. Go. Go in peace," her mother whispered, nodding.

Web averted her eyes and swallowed. Time to go, to leave here forever, to walk across the mountains to a new village, a new band, to join a man and live a life unknown.

Her mother shifted as if to prompt her into motion. *Whatever happens, I must honor the will of my parents. I must make them proud.*

With that thought, strength flowed into Web's back and legs.

She adjusted the load in her net and walked to the *wekuseyaay*.

He nodded at her and, with thanks to her parents, struck out on the trail that would lead them westward over the mountains where all the Kumeyaay bands met to harvest acorns every fall and down, down into the great valley that ended at the *'ehaasilth* ocean. For once, Web was glad for the weight on her back which forced her to bow her head thereby hiding the tears she could no longer hold back.

They had not gone far when a figure appeared suddenly on the trail in front of Casts No Shadow, causing him to stop abruptly. Behind him, Web gasped.

Though the person was dressed in woman's garb, the structure of his face and the shape of his legs belonged to a man. On his shoulder rode an owl.

The sight of the bird threw Casts No Shadow momentarily off balance until he remembered the seer–a man-who-lived-as-a-woman–who was rumored to be living somewhere in this *matsay* desert.

"I am Autumn Sage," the man-woman announced in the language reserved for shamans.

Casts No Shadow drew himself up to full height and regarded the stranger through narrowed eyes. "Who are you that dares to speak the Sacred Tongue?"

Autumn Sage mimicked the *wekuseyaay's* gestures, aping them exactly. "I bring messages from the gods for you, shaman."

Casts No Shadow held back the sneer that threatened to twist his lips at the man's audacity. "From the gods, you say?"

"Do not mock me, shaman. The gods allow no other to see as far into the future as I do."

"The proof of far-seeing is in what comes to pass. Not in words," Casts No Shadow said.

"Thus, soon you shall see that my gift is as real as I claim," Autumn Sage said.

The *wekuseyaay* held back the impulse to sweep a mocking bow. Instead he nodded. "Then, by all means, proceed with the task with which the gods have charged you."

The seer settled on the ground and, with a sigh, fell into a trance. Casts No Shadow heard the rustling of the girl's skirt behind him. A glance over his shoulder revealed that her small face was blanched and drawn. He had no time to warn her to silence before an eerie, vibrating voice issued from the seer's parted lips. "Strange beasts will come, clothed in mirrors. After you and your son join Those Who Have Gone Before, Nipaguay will cease to exist."

Years of challenges, open and covert, had taught the *wekuseyaay* never to ridicule a rival before he was completely ready to discredit him. Yet now he had to check himself hard not to snort with derision at the preposterous prediction.

The trance voice went on. "Your knowledge will be lost, but part of you will live on–here in this desert."

The owl hooted, sending a chill down Casts No Shadow's spine. Autumn Sage's eyes reopened. He blinked twice as if awakening from sleep. Casts No Shadow studied the man without speaking. The voice, the self-assurance, and the fuzzy prophecies–someone had schooled this witch well. Whoever the teacher, he had done a fine job with his pupil except for one detail: he had taught the seer the sacred language. Violating that taboo would prove costly to Autumn Sage's teacher. Casts No Shadow would see to that.

"You cannot know him. He rests with the spirits now," Autumn Sage said.

Another trick, Casts No Shadow decided. *Appearing to read thoughts.*

"Oh, but I can read thoughts, Shaman. Especially yours," Autumn Sage said.

"Then you know what I think of your claim to power."

"Your thoughts cannot change the present or the future. This girl has been chosen by Grandfather Serpent. She is the future."

With another hoot from the owl, the witch faded into the brush, leaving Casts No Shadow alone with the girl.

"W–what did he say?" Web asked.

"He told us we would have good weather and that we would arrive at Nipaguay by the time Sun reaches His zenith," Casts No Shadow lied. He looked to the clouds building over the massif of mountains to the west. "Still we have a long journey and no time to linger. Come."

Like the dutiful girl that she was, Web did as she was told.

Chapter 6

How much farther? How much farther? The question spun through Web's exhausted brain like a ceremonial chant. The load on her back seemed to grow heavier with each step. No matter how she loaded the burden net, sharp edges dug into her sore back. She was used to carrying heavy loads, but with all of her belongings in the net plus the wedding gifts she was taking to Shadow Dancer and his kin, this was the heaviest. By the time they had reached the foot of the mountains, the straps had rubbed her shoulders raw. During the climb, she had been in too much pain to care how the *wekuseyaay* managed to move under the sun without displaying a shadow.

For a week she had scrambled to keep up with the pace he set. So far she had spent seven nights in strange villages, forced to be friendly with women she did not know when she longed to be sleeping. For seven nights she had witnessed the awe in which the people of each band held Casts No Shadow. For seven nights she had fallen asleep before she had eaten all her food. And for seven mornings she had been ripped out of sleep and forced back onto the trail before her body was ready.

Once they left the acorn-harvesting areas in the mountains, Web recognized nothing familiar. Her heart felt as heavy as the burden on her back, weighted down with sorrow and dread.

How much farther?

Head down, lost in her own misery, she nearly bumped into Casts No Shadow who had knelt on the trail, eyes focused into the distance. She glanced ahead, expecting to see a village or a person.

She saw nothing.

The *wekuseyaay* raised both his hands, palms out, in front of his chest and began to sing words of a chant unlike anything Web had ever heard. Casts No Shadow's voice began in a quavering whisper, rose steadily to a shout, fell off to a whisper, rising yet again. While he chanted, he drew from his pouch a gourd rattle and a fan of sacred *'ihpaa* eagle feathers and began to inscribe circles in the air with them.

Only when his voice fell off a third time did her ears detect the buzzing sound just up the trail ahead. There a pair of *'ewii* rattling serpents coiled side by side, ready to strike.

Casts No Shadow rose and approached the *'ewii*, speaking to them, punctuating his words with shakes of the rattle and sweeps of the fan. Web watched mesmerized as the two creatures simultaneously uncoiled and glided away into the brush.

Casts No Shadow gave the rattle one final shake and turned toward Web. "Come, daughter. Shadow Dancer awaits us."

The name of her future husband hit Web like a blast of winter wind. Panic mounted a fresh assault on her strength.

Casts No Shadow put away his rattle and fan and strode off without waiting to see that she followed.

When he reached the Mission's forge, Romero's grief exploded. "No! No! No!" he screamed, hurling the altar piece against the adobe wall, smashing it beyond recognition.

"Stop!"

Romero whirled to see Nemesio, the corporal of the mission guard, and two of the corporal's men. They fell on Romero and pinned his arms before he could react.

Nemesio scooped up the now-twisted altar piece. "Destroying the King's property, huh? This is a Crown offense, blacksmith. My jurisdiction." He jerked his chin toward the door. "Bring him!"

Nemesio spun on his heel and marched out. The soldiers followed, half-dragging Romero between them. "Corporal, I . . ." Romero pleaded.

"Silence!"

Romero obeyed. Besides being a martinet, Nemesio had a sadistic streak that no sane person would willingly invoke.

The corporal led the way to a rocky slope where a string of storage cellars had been dug into the side of the hill. "There," he said, pointing to one of the smaller caverns. The soldiers forced Romero to his knees, then shoved and kicked him into the hole. They then dragged a heavy cask of brandy over the opening, plunging Romero into total darkness. Instantly, he felt the desperate need for light and air. He kicked and pounded on the barrel. It didn't budge.

Above him, Nemesio snorted scornfully. "It seems that our good priest's old plaything is angry. I wonder why. Could it be that he found out about the priest's new pet?"

Laughing, the three soldiers walked away, leaving Romero alone to face the silence and darkness of his crypt prison.

The trail broke out of the tangled confusion of sage and manzanita, and Web found herself looking down a broad river valley that ended in an expanse of blue water and bluer sky. The air was hazy. It felt heavy to her lungs and smelled of must and brine. It was the smell she remembered from her only previous journey to the ocean. A nose-wrinkling smell, bordering on unpleasant that colored all her memories of that time.

Searching ahead for the *wekuseyaay*, she spotted a village that had to be Nipaguay. A quick glance showed twice as many lodges, shade arbors and cooking fires as Hawi, spreading out from the cluster of huts at the village center and running into the side canyons where the individual families had their huts and gardens. A stout defensive bulwark guarded the village on the vulnerable valley side, while the curve of the river protected its back and one side. Along the other side stood a thicket of sycamores and alders, leafed in the rich green that comes from ample water. Web was tired enough to forget her fear of the unknown and to welcome the thought that she would now be able to rest.

Many figures moved around the village center and, even from a distance, she could hear adult laughter, barking dogs, crying babies, and the sounds of children at play. She remembered Nipaguay as a rich village, but her memories did not stretch far enough to include the reality her eyes now took in. Her nerve might have failed her if Casts No Shadow had not been so far ahead.

By the time she reached the settlement, a crowd surrounded the returning *wekuseyaay*. At the crush of so many strangers, Web hung back next to one of the *'ewaas*. She had never felt so small, so out of place. She kept her head bowed and bit her lower lip to keep it from trembling.

Casts No Shadow's voice rose over the bedlam of unfamiliar voices. "Daughter, come."

Without looking up, she moved forward until she saw the *wekuseyaay's hemenyaaw* yucca sandals, surrounded by dozens of pairs of dusty bare feet. One pair of those feet stepped forward. Web raised her eyes to see a tall nut-brown man, whose strongly-built square upper torso sat atop legs and hips so spare that it seemed impossible for him not to topple over. His head was likewise too small for his chest and for the prominent squared nose that occupied its exact center.

"I am Big Nose, Kwaipai of Nipaguay."

Web nodded in acknowledgment of the village leader but her eyes were drawn to the woman standing to his right and a step behind, the position reserved for the *kwaipai's* wife.

The woman eyed Web haughtily. She had the pert jutting breasts of a childless woman. Black tattooed dots encircled each aureole as if to emphasize the prominent nipple. A line of similar dots wrapped each biceps like a bracelet, and smaller circles of dots decorated both cheeks. Tattoo lines ran from the outer corners of the woman's eyes to her hairline, making her eyes appear wider. The eight lines of tattooed dots radiating from Web's lower lip to the edge of her chin must have seemed sparse and plain in contrast.

Unconsciously, Web raised her hand to cover her chin. When she did, the other woman's nostrils flared and she clutched Big Nose's arm and whispered urgently into his ear.

Big Nose looked from her to Web and murmured something in an irritated tone too low to hear. The woman muttered something under her breath, turned on her heel and shoved her way through the crowd, without greeting Web as formality prescribed.

Without missing a beat, Casts No Shadow went on with the ritual welcome. "My son, your wife has come."

The crowd moved aside, forming an aisle way to one of the *'ewaas*. A man ducked out the lodge opening. He straightened but did not move forward immediately. In height and build, Shadow Dancer was a copy of Casts No Shadow, and, as with him, his hair was his most noticeable feature. Forsaking the bangs of the other men, Shadow Dancer wore it in three equal thick plaits, one on each side of his head braided and wrapped with cords; the third hanging free and long down to his waist in back.

He paced forward, stopping in front of Web. Under the bright midday sun, a reddish aura emanated from his head, the result of the blood-red highlights in his inky hair. "Welcome, wife." His eyes were soft brown and filled with dancing lights. "I have prepared the lodge for us. Come."

"Go with your husband, daughter. May you bring us many strong sons," Casts No Shadow declared.

Husband? Sons? Web's heart began to race, and her lungs did not seem able to draw in enough air. This was all happening too fast. She hardly noticed Shadow Dancer's glance at her hands or the momentary shadow that clouded his eyes before he led the way through the aisle of people and up to the nearest side canyon to a newly constructed *'ewaa*.

She followed on feet she could not feel. As she bent to duck inside, she spotted the *kwaipai's* wife standing partway down the canyon. The look of undisguised hatred on the woman's face made Web shiver involuntarily as she hurried inside.

Something had gone terribly wrong for Romero. There had to be another explanation. Perhaps he had jumped to the wrong conclusion, or perhaps his eyes had deceived him and he had not seen what he thought he saw. Father Xavier loved him. He was sure of that. He would never betray that love. Not Father Xavier. Yet, in a fit of rage over some innocent misunderstanding, Romero had destroyed Father's prized altar piece.

"Have to explain." Romero's voice sounded alien in the smothering confines of the earthen walls.

"Need to get out. Have to dig," he told himself.

He managed to twist his body around so he would not pull dirt down onto his head, then he attacked the earth walls with his hands, hardened from months of smithing. Clawing away dirt and rocks, he ignored the nails that ripped away from their cuticles. There would be time to heal later, but now he had to get out, had to explain his actions to Father and seek his forgiveness.

Dust filled the small chamber, but Romero was only distantly aware of his own coughing. He had to get out to make amends.

At last his fingers punched through into air. It was nearly dark. Father would be at vespers. Rather than disturb the service and risk angering the priest further, Romero decided to wait in Xavier's quarters.

He scratched and shoved his way out the opening in the earth and crept across the grounds, keeping to cover in case Nemesio or one of his men was about.

From the church came the sounds of Father Xavier's voice reciting vespers. The familiar sound reassured Romero. *Father will understand. He will forgive me. He loves me.*

Reaching the adobe hut, he let himself inside.

"You!" Bartolomé gasped from where he stood beside the priest's pallet.

Afraid the boy would alert the guards before he had the chance to talk to Father Xavier, Romero lunged across the room, grabbing the orphan, wrapping one hand across his mouth.

The struggling boy managed to twist his face away from the gag of Romero's hand to cry, "Help, Father!"

Romero's slap cut off the yell. "Don't! I have to see . . ."

Father Xavier burst into the room, cutting Romero short.

He fell to his knees and reached out a beseeching hand to the priest. "Oh, Father, I am so sorry,"

The priest slapped away Romero's hand and shouted, "Guard!"

Nemesio raced into the room, followed by four of his men.

"F–father, please let me explain," Romero stammered.

"Arrest that man!" the priest demanded, pointing an angry finger at Romero.

While the soldiers grabbed Romero, Nemesio yanked Bartolomé out of Romero's grasp. Frantically, Romero sought eye contact with the priest to no avail. He tried to prostrate himself in supplication, but the guards dragged him upright.

"First you commit desecration. Now you attack a helpless child," Father yelled at him.

The priest had never spoken to him in such an angry tone. Bewildered and frightened that he had damaged the only love he had ever known, Romero clutched at the priest's robe.

"Let go of me, you filthy cur," Father Xavier rasped.

Fury contorted the priest's face into an unrecognizable mask. Romero released his hold with a stifled sob.

"Corporal, get him out of my sight. I never want to see him again. Never," Father demanded.

"No, Father. No!" pleaded Romero.

"Out with him," Xavier shouted. "Now!"

"Gladly, Father." Nemesio cocked his head toward the door, his mouth twisting into a sinister smile. The last thing Romero saw as the soldiers pulled him bodily out of the room was Bartolomé folded in Father Xavier's comforting arms.

Shadow Dancer squatted in the rear of the dwelling, preparing an 'emuukwin pipe. Web set her burden net down beside the entrance and laid the cushioning cap on top of it. She did not have a clue what to do next, so she crouched on trembling legs beside her belongings, waiting for him to speak.

He struck a flint to light the tobacco, then sat cross-legged to smoke. He did not look at her. The silence stretched between them.

Exhausted, she sagged against a wall post and closed her eyes. She was unaware that she had fallen asleep until the sound of a male voice commanded, "Come, wife."

Shadow Dancer had moved to a pallet of woven tules covered with hides. Creeping across the floor on unwilling legs, Web could not look at him or draw a full breath. She hesitated beside the pallet, unsure what to do next.

"It is time to mate. Lie down," Shadow Dancer said impatiently.

She lay down on her back on the pallet, arms held rigidly at her sides. She knew about mating from observing animals and from living in the same lodge as her parents, but she had never before performed the act herself. She and Mishtai had spent hours speculating what it would feel like to have a man poke his member inside them, but that had been talk. This was real. And she had never been so afraid. She pressed a hand on her stomach to calm it.

"Put your hand back where it was," Shadow Dancer commanded. "And leave it there."

Web did as she was told. *You and your frog-hands will never belong anywhere but Hawi.* Amul's words surged back into her head full force.

He lifted her skirt. "So little hair." Disappointment flitted across his face.

Web could do nothing but endure his gaze.

He pushed her legs apart. "My father believes that our mating will produce the son who will be shaman after me. It is for you, wife, to make this son."

Web gaped up at him. It had never occurred to her that Shadow Dancer might be his father's apprentice. Heredity did not necessarily endow a son with those attributes a shaman sought in one to teach as a replacement. Yet why would a shaman react with such obvious abhorrence to her hands? Surely he knew the ancient stories better than anyone. Casts No Shadow had had no such negative reaction.

With her mind occupied elsewhere, she did not realize that Shadow Dancer had crawled between her legs and placed the tip of his swollen member against her opening until he shoved his pelvis forward. She was not prepared for the pain that ripped through her insides. She managed to stifle her cries, but tears streamed from her eyes. She lifted a hand to staunch the flow of tears, but Shadow Dancer caught the hand and shoved it back down. "I said keep your hands down. Do you hear me, woman?"

She nodded.

"Then obey me."

He thrust into her again and again. She closed her eyes and retreated into the private place within. As her mother had taught her.

The soldiers dragged Romero across the grounds to the stable where they bound his arms tightly against his body with rope, then dropped him in the dirt like a sack of weevil-infested corn.

Nemesio stood over him with the tip of his razor-sharp sword pressed into Romero's throat. "If Father never wants to see you again, then it is my sworn duty to make certain he does not. Ramos, fetch my horse and rope."

The menace in the corporal's tone cut through Romero's anguish over Father Xavier's rejection. He began to struggle against his restraints.

Crack! The corporal's lash whipped across his face, ripping a scream from his bowels: "Father!" Each fringe of Nemesio's whip was tipped with silver that flayed Romero's cheek. He clamped his eyes shut against the agony.

Nemesio's voice fell to an ominous hiss. "Yelling is no use, blacksmith. He won't come. He has a new pet now. He has put you out like an unwanted dog. For good."

Nemesio mounted his horse and tied to the horn of his saddle the end of the rope binding Romero. "Get up, you pile of filth!" he ordered.

When Romero tried to stand, his knees would not support him so one of the soldiers jerked him up by the back of his shirt and held him upright to face the corporal.

"Look at me!" Nemesio demanded. "Father is throwing you away, blacksmith. He's ordered me to make sure he never sees you again. That's just what I intend to do."

He gave the horse a savage kick. The animal neighed and bucked and took off at a run.

The rope jerked Romero off his stance, pitching him onto his face and dragging him forward. Dirt clogged his ears, nose, mouth. Rocks and spined plants tore at his clothing, shredding it, shredding the flesh from his face, his bones. He was choking. He was bleeding. He felt as if he were being skinned alive.

Again and again, he screamed for mercy through the gag of dirt. With each scream, Nemesio kicked his horse for more speed.

After what seemed like an eternity, Romero's body slammed into a boulder. The force of the blow flipped him onto his back. He opened his eyes to look at the night sky and prayed through lacerated lips, "Dear God, help me."

Then everything went black.

Chapter 7

Four days later Web awoke to find Shadow Dancer gone from the *'ewaa*, a sign that the period of marriage seclusion was over. Alone for the first time since she arrived, she lay on her back, staring up at the tules covering the hut's willow frame, listening to the morning sounds of Nipaguay. A shaft of sunlight pierced the gap along the side of the entrance curtain. She positioned her hands in that light and spread open the fingers of her right hand. In the light the thin membranes of skin that stretched up to the first knuckles of each finger were transparent.

According to the first story her mother had ever told her, long ago in the time before time, One Above created human beings by molding figures from clay. When One Above's blind younger brother attempted, in a fit of jealousy, to match the feat in order to outdo him, in his hurry he had misshaped the figures, leaving their appendages webbed. Angered by his failure, he flung the creatures into the water and there they remained. All but one who struggled out onto land to become human. That one was First Ancestor, the beginning of Web's maternal *sh'mulq*. Because Frog and Duck and Goose were His brothers, First Ancestor forbade all members of the sib to kill or eat those creatures or even to touch the bodies of any such animals downed by hunters.

Through all Amul's cruel teasing, this story had sustained Web. Now, as if beckoned, Amul's face popped into Web's mind wearing a contemptuous smile of triumph. Web blinked the vision away. She did not intend to fail here. Nipaguay was her home now. She would learn to fit in, to be accepted.

Getting up, she untied the comb from the waist thong of her skirt and combed out the tangled mass of her hair. Then she scooped the hides off the pallet and took them outside to shake. Her joints were stiff. Her woman place was raw from three days of mating. Sunlight glinting off the nearby river sparked an idea that made her smile: she would take a bath.

Draping the hides over the top of the lodge for airing, she retrieved from her belongings a net bag containing pieces of the pounded yucca root which served as soap and her best basket, the one so tightly wrapped that it held water without a seal of pitch. She was near the center of the village when the basket was ripped from her grasp.

The wife of Big Nose examined the weave of the basket, turning it over and over in her hands. The bright light of the morning sun emphasized the contrast between the pale beige of the woman's skin and the circles of black dots on her breasts and face.

"Warm sun to you, sister," Web said in formal greeting.

The woman spat back a "Pfaugh!" and heaved the basket into the dirt before stomping away.

Though there were many people in the vicinity, no one seemed to notice the woman's hostile behavior. Web picked up the basket and took the path to the river. There she dipped a basketful of water and sought out a shady spot under a gnarled sycamore where she could bathe in the shade.

"Oh, my, such a beautiful basket," came a female voice.

Web turned to see a head bobbing above the surface of a small pool. The head was attached to the body of a small woman, immersed to the neck in the river.

"You do not have to limit yourself to so little water. Won't you join me?"

The desert had no rivers, and its few pools were reserved for spirits and those who communed with them. Thus, Web had never before been in a pool of water. Hesitantly, she untied her skirt and waded into the pool with the woman. The sensation of the cool water lapping against her skin made the hairs on her neck rise.

"Casts No Shadow says that you come from the land to the east beyond the mountains where there is little water. Here we have plenty all year. This is our bathing place. How do you like it?" the woman asked.

"It–it is wet," Web replied.

The woman laughed, a happy musical trill. "You have much to learn here. I will enjoy teaching you."

Embarrassed by what she heard as ridicule, Web turned to leave the water. The woman's hand on her arm stopped her. "Please, I did not mean to hurt you. I laugh with joy because seven suns ago I dreamed that I would have a new friend soon. And now, here you are!"

Web did not know how to respond.

"I know that you are called Web. I am Halypuusuutt, Hummingbird."

The name fit. Like her namesake, Hummingbird was small and compact with a long, thin nose, bright black eyes and quick, darting hand movements. Even her hair had the shifting metallic highlights of a *halypuusuutt's* gorget.

"I come from the village of Jamo, west beyond the shores of False Bay. I will take you there one day soon. We can gather mussels and oysters."

"What are mussels and oysters?"

A chiming laugh. "Of course, you would not know them. They are shell-covered animals that live in the mud at the bottom of the bay."

Web forced a smile to cover her feeling of ignorance. Hummingbird touched her hair. "I laugh at myself, not you. I have always lived near the ocean." She swept one hand in an arc. "I have never been in a place without water. I have much to learn from you, my sister. Will you teach me what you know?"

Hummingbird's gentle sincerity melted Web's reserve. At last, someone she could talk to. "Have you lived at Nipaguay long?" she asked.

"Six moons ago, I came to Nipaguay as bride to Many Rains. My husband is like a brother to your Shadow Dancer." She leaned closer to Web and whispered, "How is it to mate with a man who talks with Spirits?"

It was the question she would have asked if she were Hummingbird. Web said solemnly, "Sore and sticky."

Hummingbird convulsed in laughter. Web joined in, enjoying her own joke.

When they both recovered, Hummingbird said, "Tell me about your village."

"Hawi is . . ." A sudden lump in her throat would not allow Web to finish the thought.

"Oh, how thoughtless of me. It must have been terrible for you. To leave your people and your ways and to travel so far—" Hummingbird used one hand to form a horn on the top of her head, then pulled her face into a long frown, "—with Casts No Shadow."

Web nodded. "He walked so fast that I had to run sometimes to keep up. He is very–quiet."

"They say he moves too fast for Sun to make a shadow, but I believe he is one of the special ones that does not block the light of Sun."

An involuntary shiver coursed through Web at the memory of the *wekuseyaay* and the two rattlesnakes.

"Ah, I see that you witnessed his way with the rattling serpents. It cannot be easy for you to have such a powerful man as your father."

"I cannot say. This is my first time out of our 'ewaa."

Hummingbird nudged her and winked. "Sore and sticky, you said."

Web smiled, glad to have a confidante to share secrets with.

"I can't stand snakes. At least you won't have to deal with snake things in your lodge," Hummingbird said.

"I do not understand. Where else would my husband keep his sacred objects?"

"Shadow Dancer is an 'aww-kuseyaay, a fire shaman. Didn't you know that?

Again, Web heard ridicule behind the question. And again, Hummingbird hurried to apologize, then told Web the story of the day the young Shadow Dancer had fallen asleep in the area of grains and grasses that was to be burned in preparation for the next planting. "It was only after the fire had begun that anyone thought to miss Shadow Dancer. Someone had seen him sitting in that field earlier, before the burn. At the time he had the habit of lying down and sleeping whenever and wherever he got tired, so when he didn't turn up in a search, everyone feared that no one had seen him asleep in the field and that they would find his body once the smoke cleared. They could hardly believe it when he turned up alive. Somehow the fire jumped right over him without singeing a single hair on his arms. Afterward when the elders questioned him, he could not tell them what had happened. He said he had been asleep. Asleep! Can you imagine? In the middle of an inferno.

"The next day, instead of a rite for the dead, Casts No Shadow conducted the initiation ceremony, making his son an apprentice shaman. It should not be long now before Shadow Dancer finishes his training. When that happens, I will help you prepare the feast." Hummingbird grimaced. "We will be cooking for days."

Mid-chuckle, Web spotted the *kwaipai's* wife on the path from the village.

"Crooked Basket," Hummingbird murmured.

When the interloper caught sight of Web, she spun around and strode away downstream.

"She'll recover," Hummingbird said.

Web crooked a puzzled brow at her new friend.

"She's had her eye on Shadow Dancer for years. Probably from the time before she moved here to marry Big Nose. She comes from Cosoy, the village near the mouth of the river. She is the daughter of another shaman, Red Smoke. She knew that Shadow Dancer was pledged to you, but she has always acted as if she expected him to one day take her away from Big Nose. It is strange, but the only ones who don't see how she behaves are her husband and yours.

"But you need not worry. Shadow Dancer is the true son of his father. Now that you are his wife, he will put Crooked Basket in her place."

Not sure how to react, Web dipped her basket and poured the cool water over her head, luxuriating in the sensation of dripping

wet hair. She was about to dip the basket again when Hummingbird grabbed her right hand and examined the elongated flaps of
skin between the fingers. "Such odd hands." She turned them over.
"Odd–and beautiful. Hands to make beautiful baskets. Is everything you make this perfect?" she asked, turning her examination
to the dipper.

"I think so. Yes." The words were out before Web knew it. Her
mother always cautioned her to be humble about her talents.
Pride was a form of selfishness. Selfishness was expected in
children, but abhorred in adults. Yet Web *knew* that she made the
best baskets. Next to her mother's, didn't they always fetch the
highest exchanges whenever they traded with other bands? Still,
bragging was not the way to keep friends.

"Would you teach me to make designs like that?" Hummingbird asked, appearing not to have heard Web's boast.

Web hesitated. Her designs belonged exclusively to the women
in her mother's *sh'mulq*. Hummingbird was wrong to ask such a
thing. "I can't."

Hummingbird nodded. "I know. I don't know why I asked such
a thing. All I have to do is see Crooked Basket and I start to say
the wrong things."

Web nodded understanding. Hummingbird watched Crooked
Basket's retreating form. "Whoever named her knew what they
were doing. Wait till you see the pitiful baskets she turns out.
They're as homely as her soul. No wonder she didn't want you to
join us. In you, that one's finally met her match, thank One
Above."

Hummingbird moved toward the bank and emerged from the
pool. "But come. We have food to prepare, or we will have to
suffer the anger of our husbands."

Once back in the village, Hummingbird showed her which
hekwiin acorn granary to use. Web drew a supply of acorns,
seated herself at an unoccupied *'ehmuu* mortar in one of the large
flat boulders located at one end of the village. She had ground
acorns and piñon nuts for her family for as long as she could
remember. And, for just as long, she had loved the task. From the
steady movement of her arms and the heft and texture of the
esally stone pestle to the crunching sound of nutmeat against
stone, the act of grinding soothed her, transported her to another
place where time did not exist.

The mortars at Nipaguay were deep and glassy smooth from
long use. Like the ones back at Hawi.

No, I must not think about Hawi. This is my home now.

Putting her head down, Web applied herself to pulverizing the acorns until she had the consistency she wanted. Then she heaped the meal into a shallow twined basket over a pad of twigs and poured water over it to leach out the bitter tannins–first cold water, then hot.

She was at the end of this process when a group of village hunters returned with their days' take. Anxious to make a good impression with her first meal for her new husband, Web left the leaching water to settle and hurried over to get some of the meat.

She came up short at the sight of the pile of lifeless *paat* duck bodies.

"And what do you think you're waiting for: me to hand one to you?" The question came from Crooked Basket.

"I–I don't want one."

"Don't tell me you're afraid of a duck," Crooked Basket said. "Ignorant little desert mouse doesn't know what's good."

At Crooked Basket's smirk, Web's feelings of inadequacy surged back full force. She turned away rather than challenge the *kwaipai's* wife. She had to learn to live here or risk shaming the parents she loved and missed so much.

"Ignorant little desert mouse," Crooked Basket hissed.

It took all Web's control to walk, rather than run, away from those awful cutting words. She was so preoccupied that she nearly collided with someone standing in her path.

Casts No Shadow's gray eyes bored into her as if seeking her most private thoughts. After a long time, he stepped aside, and Web escaped past him to the safety of her own *'ewaa* where she put aside the incident with Crooked Basket and busied herself with fixing the meal.

Chapter 8

Romero hung back in the protection of the rocks, waiting for an opening before he entered the little town. He did not want to be seen. The reactions to his appearance from the few people he had met on the trail to Loreto had made him leery of showing his face to anyone. He needed a safe place to heal his wounds and recover from his ordeal; a place to get back on his feet until he could return to Misión La Purísima and reconcile with Father Xavier. Loreto was the only home he had known besides La Purísima, and Manos the blacksmith was the only person he knew to ask for help.

After dragging Romero from La Purísima, Nemesio and his soldiers had left him for dead in the middle of the trail. However, Romero survived and came to find himself in a partially-collapsed hut where he was tended by an ancient toothless hag. The woman would not say why she helped him. At least, he couldn't remember her giving him a reason–one of the many gaps in his memory between La Purísima and returning to Loreto. All because of Nemesio. Nemesio who had turned him into a vile creature who terrified others. For that, Nemesio would pay!

As he waited, the night deepened. A chill December wind blew off the Gulf. Shivering, Romero watched the movement of torches and caught drifts of voices as the night sentries assumed their posts. To keep warm, he thought about Nemesio and the punishment he, Romero, would dole out once he was strong enough. *I will make you beg–no,* scream *for mercy, Nemesio. And your pleas will fall on ears made deaf by what you did to me,* he silently vowed.

Romero waited until the night guards had nodded off before he limped into the silent town. The forge was in an adobe barn near the wharf. As he moved along the slumbering streets, the familiar smells and night sounds of the place brought back memories of the nights when he used to sneak out of the Loreto orphanage for his best adventures.

Outside the forge, he stopped to listen.

From inside came Manos's murmuring. The only time the blacksmith said much was in his sleep. Many were the nights Romero had fallen asleep to a lullaby of the man's muttering. The familiar sound after so long and painful a journey brought a smile to Romero's lips. The unaccustomed movement caused twinges of pain in his cheek. Touching his mouth, his fingers found the hard ridges of scars. One day he would have the strength to look in a glass, to see what damage being dragged out of the valley behind Nemesio's horse had caused. Some day. But first he needed a place to lick his wounds and plan for the future.

He eased open the door, stepped across the threshold, and filled his lungs with the scents of charcoal and smoke, smells of the forge that he loved.

A dog growled.

"Someone there?" Manos asked

The dog growled again, louder this time. Romero took a deep breath and answered, "It's me. Romero."

"Romero? I don't know anyone by that name. Show yourself."

Romero stepped into the room still lit by the glow from the forge fire. The forge dog yipped, and Manos reached out a restraining hand to keep the animal in check. "Well?"

"Don't you recognize me?" Romero asked.

Eyeing him suspiciously, Manos picked up one of the hammers. "Should I?"

"I'm Romero the orphan. You remember, don't you? From ten years ago?"

"Bosh! You cannot be that boy. José was handsome. You are . . ."

The pity in the smith's eyes proved too much for Romero. He had to know, had to see what had happened to his face. He limped to the slack tub and peered into the mirror of the water's blackened surface.

The monster that looked back at him was hideous. The skin on the left side of his face was gone, replaced by hardened red tissue, mottled with patches of white, purple and blue. The lower lid gaped away from the eye. Most of the outer part of his left ear was gone, and a chunk was missing from his left nostril. It looked as if someone had held his face to a candle until the left side melted.

Romero was too stunned to cry out, too horrified to move. He had felt the scars on his face, but nothing had prepared him for the hideous mask he now wore.

Behind him, the smith cleared his throat. Romero could not bring himself to turn around. He had nowhere else to go. He had to convince Manos to take him in, to give him a place to recuperate, until . . . He focused his energy on keeping his voice even. "I am that José Romero. I had an accident." Behind him, the forge cur snuffled.

"Why do you come here?" Manos asked testily.

Romero turned slowly to face his questioner, ignoring the look of repugnance that flitted across the smith's face, struggling to keep the desperation out of his voice. "I need a place to heal. I need to regain my strength."

For a long time, the smith did not answer. He held the collar of the straining dog and studied Romero.

"I will work," Romero said. "I have worked as a smith at . . ." He cut himself off. He did not intend to tell anyone how or where he had spent the last ten years. He did not want to explain for fear he would give away his motives. That he must never do. Nemesio must not know that he had survived, must never suspect an attack until it came, must not know his fate until Romero handed it to him in person.

At last, the smith spoke. "Two ships will sail for the Filipinas on the Eve of Christ's Mass." He laid aside the hammer, dragged the dog to the door, and booted the animal outside.

Romero waited, afraid to speak or move for fear that he might interrupt the smith at the wrong moment.

Manos walked to the forge and stared into the banked coals for a time before he continued. "Of course, there is much to do to get them ready to go."

Romero refused to acknowledge the glimmer of hope that tried to sprout in his heart at that moment. He held his breath and waited for Manos to deliver his verdict.

"Too much work for one man." The smith looked sideways at Romero. "You can sleep in your old corner. I will see if I can find you some food."

Manos went out the door to the accompaniment of barks from the dismissed cur. Romero sagged forward, catching himself on the sides of the slack tub, closing his eyes against the chance that he might again see his reflection. It was too late to do anything about what he looked like. Now his job was to get revenge.

He started toward his old corner. A growl stopped him.

Somehow the dog had found its way back inside.

"Out!" Romero said.

The dog took a step forward, baring his teeth.

"Stop there," Romero warned.

The dog barked and set himself as if to charge.

Romero's kick caught him squarely on the snout.

The dog squealed.

A second kick caught the animal in the ribs, throwing him against the wall and into a heap.

Whining piteously, the dog picked itself off the floor and slunk outside, never taking his eyes off the hideous mask that was Romero's face.

Chapter 9—Spring, 1768

Once the period of marriage seclusion ended, Web's life became a blur as she struggled to learn the ways of her new husband and the customs of her new village. Besides avoiding Crooked Basket, one of the hardest things for her was getting used to preparing and eating unaccustomed foods, especially fish. Shadow Dancer was Nipaguay's best fisherman. Although custom dictated that he distribute his catch to others, Hummingbird's husband, Many Rains, who always accompanied Shadow Dancer in his reed canoe, made sure that Web got the best of whatever he caught each day.

A steady diet of fish made her secretly long for something more familiar. She was still under the restrictions of her passage into womanhood, but that did not keep her from hungering for meat, especially her favorite lizard. Still, food was but one of the changes Web had to deal with. Another was the fog which rolled up the valley nearly every night, chilling her to the bone, weighing down the air she breathed, and turning familiar things into ghostly shapes. So many adjustments might have defeated her if not for Hummingbird's ability to make her laugh. Laughter eased the frustration of the mistakes she inevitably made.

It was spring when Hummingbird invited Web to go mussel-gathering at False Bay for the first time. They took a path that wound along the high bluffs which defined the river valley on the north. A similar set of bluffs, covered with grains, grasses and other edible plants, ran along the south side of the valley. Hummingbird chattered and laughed as they went. She seemed oblivious of the unpleasant musty smell of the air and the growing rumble coming out of the west. First would come a crash, followed by a bubbling, scouring sound, followed by a lull. Then the sequence would repeat, again and again, louder and louder until Web's nerves were jangling. After a considerable walk, the pair broke out of the chaparral and, for the first time in her life, Web came face to face with *'ehaasilth*, the great sea.

"The gods of the water are angry today," Hummingbird said, sweeping a hand at the wind-whipped waves.

To Web, the churning water seemed like a creature frantic to escape a trap. Her only other exposure to the ocean had been from a distance. Standing so close now, she was terrified of the booming waves and surging surf. She could not move.

"Come, sister. Hurry," Hummingbird urged. "Crooked Basket and two others follow us."

Even the energy in her friend's voice and her own desire to stay away from the *kwaipai's* wife could not overcome the paralyzing effect of the ocean. Crooked Basket came striding up the path at the edge of Web's vision. "Out of my way, desert mouse," she demanded.

With her eyes held by the angry water, Web's legs would not obey.

Crooked Basket's voice went up a notch. "Are you deaf? Out of my way!"

Still Web could not move.

"Leave her alone. Can't you see that the sea frightens her?" Hummingbird said.

Crooked Basket glanced at the two women with her. "Such a shame for her husband to be burdened with this ignorant, backward excuse for a woman."

One of the other women nodded in agreement.

Hummingbird sidled over to Crooked Basket. "How difficult it must be for you, sister."

A question clouded Crooked Basket's haughty expression. Hummingbird continued. "To know that Shadow Dancer now has a wife, and you still have the husband you have always had. The same husband you will continue to have."

"How dare you speak to me like that? Shadow Dancer . . ."

A sharp intake of breath from the *kwaipai's* wife broke the ocean's hold on Web. She turned to see the unmistakable mud-daubed red horn of hair rising over the brow of Casts No Shadow.

Since his wife's death, the *wekuseyaay* had chosen to live alone, a decision the people accepted as the great man's way to strengthen his connections with the spirit world. Since he had no wife to do for him, it fell to Web to feed him. Rather than becoming more comfortable in his presence over time, she had grown more ill at ease. One reason for this was his ability to appear suddenly without warning and to vanish the same way.

Without another word, Crooked Basket and her companions shoved past Web and Hummingbird. When Web looked again for the *wekuseyaay*, he had disappeared.

Hummingbird shrugged. "Sometimes I think he lives already in the land of the spirits."

"Not yet. Not the way he eats," Web said, trying to alleviate the tension with some humor.

Hummingbird smiled, then looked toward the other three women. "If I were Crooked Basket–and thank One Above that I am not–I would learn to accept reality. I certainly wouldn't bother you anymore. Not when Casts No Shadow knows what she's doing the instant she does it. Does he know about the baby?"

"Baby?" Web asked.

"The one that grows in here." Hummingbird patted Web's stomach and cocked her head at a birdlike angle.

Web stared down at her belly. *Baby?*

"You have not gone into seclusion for your courses for the last two moons."

Web's mind stumbled back and forth over the rocky path of her memories of the last two moon cycles until she realized that her friend was right. "I–I . . . ."

"You have been so busy trying to do everything right, trying to fit in here that you haven't had time to think about anything else. Oh, my dear sister! I am so happy for you!" Hummingbird wrapped Web in a hug tight with emotion. "I am so happy you came to Nipaguay. So happy you are my friend!"

When Hummingbird released her, Web had to force a smile. The idea of a baby–her baby–had not yet sunk in.

"You will have a strong son," Hummingbird said. "Just the thing to silence Crooked Basket once and for all. She who has no sons and no daughters. She who is barren as a salt flat. Now, come. We have mussels to gather."

Chapter 10

At first, Romero was too weak to do more for Manos than tend the fire, haul charcoal, and keep the tongs, sledges, swages, fullers, punches and a host of other tools organized. As his strength returned over the next few months, he gradually took over more tasks until he was doing half of the smithing. Except for an occasional nod, Manos never commented on his old apprentice's skill. He never asked where Romero learned so much. Since he also did not ask where Romero had been in the intervening ten years, the story José had invented went untold.

The smith's dog never again growled at him, darting away whenever Romero got too close.

As the capital of Lower California, Loreto was the center of Spanish commerce and military activity. Between shoeing horses for the soldiers, repairing equipment for trading ships and supplying cast iron and copper items to the growing number of permanent residents, the forge was always busy.

Romero was glad to do the work and thankful for the chance to recover, but he refused to run any errands for Manos that would expose him to the reactions of strangers who might glimpse his face. The smith accepted each "no" with a shrug and did the errands himself. Romero looked forward to those times when Manos was gone. He relished the quiet, the smells, the heat. Most of all, he relished the chance to think about his future.

Toward the end of February, he was alone in the forge when it came to him: the perfect revenge for Nemesio. He was shaping a brand on his anvil, when the image of the corporal's smooth, handsome face popped into his head. *Yes, that was what he would do. Brand the man in the one place everyone would see. An eye for an eye, a face for a face.*

At that moment, Manos pushed through the door, flung his cap on the workbench and slammed the door shut. "The King has lost his mind."

Romero put the brand aside and motioned the smith to quiet his voice. The King of Spain might be across the sea, but he had ears and eyes everywhere. Manos's words could land him in terrible trouble. Romero could not afford that; not until he was strong enough to get back to La Purísima.

Manos waved off Romero's warning. "I tell you this time he's lost his mind completely! Imagine expelling the Black Robes."

"What!" gasped Romero.

"The King has ordered all the Jesuits out of California. King or not, that's no way to treat men who have risked their very lives to build missions and bring the heathen Indians to God. They all deserve sainthood, not expulsion."

The Jesuits, leaving New Spain. "No, it can't be."

"It is. The whole lot of them are down on the wharf right now, guarded by soldiers. Soldiers with loaded muskets! As if the holy fathers were criminals. It's not right!"

Father Xavier leaving. No, it's not possible.

Romero bolted out the door. He had to get to the wharf, had to see Father Xavier, had to explain, had to know Father still loved him, had to set things right.

"Halt!" Two soldiers blocked his path.

Romero ducked and feinted to get past them, but the butt of a musket jammed into his gut, felling him.

One of the men kicked the gasping Romero onto his back. "It's him all right. Look at that face."

The other one grunted agreement, and the pair dragged Romero to his feet. "Come along peacefully, and you can walk. Otherwise, we will drag you along at the end of a rope."

"Where am I going?" Romero choked out, holding his throbbing stomach.

"Prison," replied the one who had hit him.

Romero made a lunge for freedom. Nothing could keep him from seeing Father Xavier, from explaining, from . . .

Something hard connected with the back of his head. That was the last thing he remembered.

Chapter 11

The next few days went by in a daze for Web. A new husband, new village, new ways, and, now, a baby growing inside her. Everything was happening too fast. She had never felt more in need of her mother's wisdom, never despaired more of the enormous distance separating them.

Only Hummingbird understood her shaky state. Whenever they were together, she did not try to force conversation. She seemed content to share Web's presence, no matter now distracted or quiet Web was.

One cloudy morning, Hummingbird persuaded Web to leave the village to harvest grass seeds in one of the areas controlled by her family. The grain in the field bent under the weight of its seed. Web was awestruck. She had never seen so much ripe seed in one place.

Hummingbird glanced around approvingly. "The rains have been good this year. My husband will be pleased we are able to put so much in our granary." She pointed toward a ridge of dirt at the western edge of the field. "That is the limit of our family's fields. Beyond lies the fields of the people of Cosoy and they never share their land and grain with anyone. Whatever you do, do not go beyond that line."

Web nodded, and the two of them bent to work, hitting the grain stalks with seed-beaters–cupped baskets with grasping handles–and catching the seeds in flat *hataayily* baskets. Every so often, they would stop collecting to winnow their take, tossing the seeds into the air so that the wind would carry away the chaff, then pouring the cleaned seed into tightly-woven yucca-fiber sacks.

The rhythm of the work lulled Web. Her thoughts were far away when Hummingbird said, "It is time to return to the village."

Web looked around at all the untouched grain. She could not leave. Not with so much bounty left to reap. Not when she was feeling so at peace for a change. "This is such a good place, and I am hungry for seed cakes instead of fish. You go. I will come soon."

"All right, but don't stay too long. It grows late."

Web waved her friend off, then bent back to her task. While her hands worked, her thoughts wandered to memories of Hawi. Her eyes saw the ridge of earth when she passed it, but her mind was too involved to take it in.

A chorus of whoops tore apart her reverie. She found herself encircled by an angry mob of strangers, all men.

"Who are you? Where are your people?" one demanded.

"I–I am W–Web. I come from Hawi, er, Nipaguay," she stammered.

The man jabbed his spear at Web. "Your land is there. This," he stomped the ground, "is Cosoy land, Cosoy grain, Cosoy seed."

"I–I am new here."

"A foreigner," someone sneered. "As if we could not tell from the marks on her face. A desert-dweller. Where are your people?"

"It is true that I come from Hawi, but . . ."

"Lizard eater!" someone yelled.

"I mean no harm. Here, take the seed. Take it all." She thrust her heaped *hataayily* toward the one who seemed to be their leader.

That one slapped the basket out of her hands. "We don't want your seed, Lizard Eater. It is time the people of Cosoy taught you and all Nipaguay a lesson. Tell the men of your village to prepare for war."

Web did not hesitate. She took off running, abandoning the *hataayily* and the sack of seed. She arrived at the village out of breath and furious at herself for not paying better attention to the boundary. She found Big Nose leaning against one upright of his wisal, smoking a pipe of sage-scented tree tobacco. Crooked Basket sat beside him, coiling a new basket that was already misshapen, though she had barely begun to form the sides.

Web knelt and hurriedly explained what happened. Big Nose listened impassively. When Web finished, the *kwaipai* set aside his *'emuukwin* and stood up. "The men must talk." He strode off to gather the adult males for a council, leaving Web alone with his wife.

"So now the stupid little desert mouse brings us into a war," Crooked Basket sneered.

Web had never talked back to the woman, never defended herself against her venom. Now she could not–would not–let the charge go unanswered. "I did nothing."

"Nothing? To you, war is nothing? You brought nothing but bad luck to us. Those things you call hands aren't human. Only a witch has such hands. A witch or one cursed by a witch. Evil comes to Nipaguay with you."

Web bit back the urge to shout her innocence. She returned Crooked Basket's stare. "You don't believe that. Why not say what you really mean? Admit that you're angry because now you cannot have Shadow Dancer."

The hint of a flicker in Crooked Basket's gaze told Web she had hit a tender spot. "You do not belong here. I will not rest until you go back where you came from," Crooked Basket spit.

"I don't think Shadow Dancer wants that, because, if I went, his son would go with me."

"Son?" As she grasped Web's meaning, Crooked Basket appeared to shrink.

Smiling smugly, Web got to her feet and walked back through the village toward her 'ewaa. She had to skirt the cluster of men gathered to discuss the Cosoy challenge. She did not see her husband or Casts No Shadow among them. For that, she was glad.

She busied herself, preparing dinner, while eavesdropping on snatches of the discussions that carried to her on the breeze. The anger she had felt toward Crooked Basket had now turned inward. How could she have been so inattentive, so careless?

As the men's discussion proceeded, she felt increasingly exposed and friendless.

"I wish to speak."

At the sound of Casts No Shadow's voice, Web glanced up to see him move into the center of the circle of seated men. "Where our new daughter comes from, the land is not so productive as here. Her people do not live so close to others as we who live so near to Cosoy and the other villages. Our ways would be as strange to the people of Hawi as theirs are to us. Our new daughter learns quickly, but she has not yet had time to learn all our ways."

Her heart hammered wildly. Casts No Shadow had hardly spoken to her since their arrival here. She often wondered if he regretted marrying his only son to her, instead of a woman from one of the nearby villages. A woman more familiar with local customs. Yet, here he was: defending her forcefully in front of the whole village.

He continued, "We do not want war. I believe that Cosoy does not want war. If you agree, I will go this night to Cosoy and convince them to keep the peace that has been between us for so long."

Around the circle, bobbing heads and grunts signaled agreement. Web turned back to her work to cover her emotions from the dispersing group.

"Daughter."

She hastened to rise as the wekuseyaay approached. "Your eyes tell me what your lips do not." He touched the tip of a finger to her bare midriff. "You grow a baby. Indeed the spirits have told me you will have two sons. This you must tell your husband as soon as he returns."

In the time it took for Web to glance down at her stomach and back up, the *wekuseyaay* vanished into the gathering shadows.

Two sons, she thought. *Ha'waak. Twins.* Then she hugged herself.

Darkness fell. Still Shadow Dancer did not return. Finally, Web went into the *'ewaa* and lay on their pallet, hands tucked out of sight, too keyed up to sleep. How could she explain to her husband all that had happened that day? Would Casts No Shadow be able to head off war with Cosoy?

Shadow Dancer came in sometime later. The scent of deer's blood clung to his skin and hair. She swallowed against the sour taste of bile that rose from her stomach at the smell.

Always meticulous with his things, be they weapons or magic objects, he wrapped his bow in the basketry case Web's mother had made for him as a wedding gift and stowed his arrows in another one Web had made. Then he lay down beside her.

"Welcome, my husband."

"It is late. I did not mean to wake you."

"I was not sleeping."

"Are you ill?"

The note of concern in his voice brought her relief. He had not yet heard of the problem with Cosoy or her part in it. "Not ill. I could not sleep."

An awkward silence fell between them while she searched for a way to begin. Before she found that way, his slow steady breathing announced that he had fallen asleep. She closed her eyes, glad to put off longer what she had to say.

She woke to the morning. The people of the village were already at their daily tasks. Shadow Dancer went off to see to distributing his kill from yesterday to his hunting partners and receiving theirs as was customary, leaving her alone to worry about what she had not yet told him. She sat down under the shade arbor to fret.

A commotion at the other end of the village drew her to her feet in time to see Casts No Shadow enter Nipaguay, leading a tall, strongly-built man. Planting his staff firmly on the packed earth, the *wekuseyaay* stopped near the open area at the heart of the village. The stranger stood beside him.

The stranger began addressing the gathering of villagers as Web approached. "I, Badger, *kwaipai* of Cosoy, come to extend my hand in friendship. There will be no war. My people do not fight with friends over a misunderstanding."

A murmur of approval went through the assembly. More than a few glances shot Web's way, and she quickly retreated to her *'ewaa* where she sagged onto the pallet with a huge sigh of relief. A moment later, Shadow Dancer entered, his face clouded.

She buried her hands in her skirt. "I–I did not know how to tell you."

"How could you be so stupid? Even a child knows better than to cross into the field owned by another family. A child."

He took a step toward her. She raised her arms to ward off the blow she feared was coming.

"Get those hands out of my sight! Now!"

She did as ordered, cowering against the wall.

"My father saved you this time, woman. Next time, you and the rest of us might not be so lucky." He turned abruptly and ducked outside.

Web listened to the crunch of his retreating footsteps. The fainter they grew, the smaller she felt. She had failed. It was just a matter of time before he sent her back to Hawi in disgrace. She curled into a ball and wrapped her arms around herself and waited for the end.

Chapter 12

The moon was waning when Shadow Dancer left on a journey with his father. He left without saying a word to Web about his destination or the length of his absence. It was Hummingbird who told her that the pair had gone to council with shamans from other villages. "They must travel far to the north, a journey of at least six moons."

Web accepted the news with a forced smile. The longer her husband stayed away, the longer her own fate remained undecided.

Misinterpreting her silence, Hummingbird hastened to reassure her, "But you must not worry. Many Rains will provide meat and fish for you."

And that he did. Web had more than enough to eat during Shadow Dancer's absence. When the time came for the people of Nipaguay to make their annual trek to the mountains to harvest acorns, Shadow Dancer and Casts No Shadow had still not returned. Web made the journey with a heavy heart. The people of Hawi would also be in the mountains. Their harvest area was close to Nipaguay's. That meant that she would likely have to face her mother. How would she ever explain to her mother what had happened to her marriage? How could she admit that she had failed where no woman of her *sh'mulq* had ever failed before?

When they arrived at the first harvesting site, her spirits lifted a bit to find no other Kumeyaays in the area and the stands of her favorite *neshaaw* black oak, heavy with nuts. Every day she went out to harvest acorns with Hummingbird, dreading that the people of Hawi would appear during her absence from camp. Yet, every evening she returned to find her fears unrealized.

On the night before they were scheduled to return home, Hummingbird led the way back from their day's work. "I have never seen so many fat acorns, sister! Never have we gathered so many so fast. Already your sons bring us good fortune, and they haven't come out to play yet."

Despite her fatigue, Web had to smile at her friend's merry chirping. She passed her hand over her rounding stomach, feeling the flutters of the lives growing within.

Hummingbird slowed her pace. "We have visitors."

Web used her hands to support the burden net so she could lift her head to see what her friend meant. Another band of Kumeyaays had set up camp across a dry creek bed from Nipaguay's. One woman caught her eye. As if she had felt Web staring at her, the woman straightened and looked her way.

"Mother!" Web slung down her load and bounded forward, sweeping her mother into a fierce hug, filling her lungs with the familiar scent of her skin.

When they parted, her mother looked Web up and down. "You are with child?"

She felt suddenly shy under her mother's gaze. "Two," she whispered.

"Twins? Oh, my daughter, the gods have blessed you."

Web nodded. How much older her mother looked than just seven moons ago.

"You look well, daughter."

The formality of her mother's tone and the impersonality of her sentiment brought Web back to the moment. She longed to tell her mother about all the pain and loneliness she had endured since leaving Hawi. She longed for the comfort of her mother's arms and the wisdom of her advice. She longed to go back to the way life had been before her roasting.

But life did not go back. It moved forever forward. "As do you, mother," she responded.

Her mother nodded. "Have you seen Mishtai yet, daughter?"

Web craned around to look for her old friend.

"No, Web. Mishtai is not with us now. She, too, has married and moved away. Kushtoy is the band of her husband."

Web's smile sank at the news. Kushtoy was a poor band, forced to eke out an existence deep in the desert east of Hawi. A poor marriage into a poor band was the price Mishtai had paid for falling asleep in the roasting pit. A harsh punishment for such a small mistake.

Web stiffened at the thought of punishments and mistakes. Suddenly she felt the need to consult with the seer. "Did Autumn Sage come with you?"

Her mother gave her a suspicious look. "Why do you ask? Is there some problem with the babies?"

"No, nothing like that. It's—it's not for me. I have a friend who needs a seer," she said, hoping her mother would not see through her lie.

"Well, your friend will have to find someone else. The seer has gone to a great gathering of sages."

At the mention of the sages' council, Web felt a flush spreading across her face. To cover it, she fell to helping her mother finish the shelter she was building. When it was done, her mother turned to her. "What troubles you, daughter?"

"It—I . . . Nothing really."

"The first child is never easy. With *ha'waak*, it will be twice as hard."

At her mother's sympathy Web's already shaky control began to unravel. "Mother, I . . ."

Suddenly a group of Hawi women surrounded them, chattering and laughing, throwing questions at her, exclaiming over her pregnancy. In the uproar, Web's confession remained unspoken. By the time Web extricated herself, Sun had already sunk behind the peak called *Poo-kwoo-squuee'*, Crooked Neck, and it was time to return to her own lodge.

She bid her mother goodnight and trudged across the dry creek bed. She had just stepped onto the other bank when Amul emerged from the dusk shadows. Web drew in a deep breath and faced her long-time tormentor.

Amul walked a circle around her, studying her from foot to forehead. "So you breed. Quick work."

For once, Amul left off the hated nickname. Web put a hand

over her stomach. "I bear twins."

"Sons, no doubt. After all, their father is a shaman."

"And you, Amul. Have you married yet?"

At the question, hatred sparked in her rival's gaze. When Amul did not speak, Web pressed her advantage. "A betrothal then?"

"You know the answer. You only ask the questions out of spite. Our little slime-frog never changes, does she?"

"Have you ever considered that you yourself might be the problem, Amul? That your skin does not hide the viciousness within you from the eyes of young men? Why pay bride-price for a virago when there are so many better young women available?"

"You might have a husband, but you will never fit in no matter how hard you try–sons or not."

Web watched Amul stalk away, feeling the muscles of her face bend into a smile of triumph. Turning back to re-enter the Nipaguay camp, she hesitated for a time, allowing her roiling emotions free-play. *I will prove her wrong*, she vowed to herself. *I will fit in. I will not fail.*

Then she straightened her back and marched to her *'ewaa*

Chapter 13

All the long journey back to Nipaguay, bent under her full load of acorns, Web considered the things she could do to win over the people of her new village. By the time the line of walkers crested the ridge above the river valley and she caught sight of the village, she knew what she would do. That very day she enlisted Hummingbird to help her gather willows, then she set to work.

Shadow Dancer and Casts No Shadow were still gone, which allowed her to devote most of every day to the task. Hummingbird helped further by preparing her meals and keeping the curious at bay.

At last the work was done. Web tied the last knot and stepped down from the rack to appraise her effort. The willow basket stood tall and straight and solid. She had had to stand on tiptoe to complete the upper rim. *Hekwiin* storage granaries were usually crudely made since most people saw them as utilitarian. Not this one. The coils of Web's *hekwiin* sported willow coils of even thickness, secured by precise stitches which created a symmetrical diagonal pattern of vertical lines running from bottom to rim. And with every stitch she had taken in the basket, she had sewn in her prayers for acceptance by her new people. She smiled, tired but pleased by the results of seven suns' worth of effort. Hummingbird rushed up beside her. "It is done?"

When Web nodded, Hummingbird cupped her hands around her mouth and shouted for the others to come see what Web had made for them. People poured out of their lodges and gathered around the new *hekwiin*, admiring it and lavishing praise on Web. She basked in their attention, wishing Shadow Dancer had been there to share her moment of triumph.

One of the men climbed atop the rack next to the one Web's new granary occupied and, with a hoot, kicked apart the sagging, misshapen *hekwiin* resting there. A scowling Crooked Basket watched from the edge of the milling crowd. According to Hummingbird, the *kwaipai's* wife had made that basket, but it had never been used because no one trusted that it would stand up under a load of acorns. When she conceived the idea of making her *hekwiin*, Web's concern had been to gain acceptance. Now she realized she had done something even better. Whenever Crooked Basket went to the granaries for acorns, she would have to face the fact that Shadow Dancer was married to someone else, someone capable and accepted.

"It is too beautiful for a mere granary," Hummingbird said, as they watched Big Nose and a pair of elders organize the men into a chain to fill the new granary.

Hand on her stomach, Web turned to her friend. "Nothing is too beautiful for my people. Nothing."

II

HA'WAAK

Spring—Late Summer, 1768

Chapter 1—Spring, 1768
East of the Kumeyaay Village of Nipaguay

A veil of mist drifted over the mountainside where Casts No Shadow sat, but he was not conscious of the wet or anything else except for the hint of coming dawn teasing at the hem of inky blackness along the eastern horizon. The day that was about to be born marked the return of Sun's ascendancy over the forces of Darkness, the time when the grasses sprouted and the trees budded and the land and people awoke from their winter's lethargy to bloom in the light and warmth of Sun. At this moment, across the land of the Kumeyaay, he and all the others who spoke to the Spirits waited in sacred places like the top of this mountain to sing thanks to Sun and urge Him on His way. This was a time of great power, and great responsibility. The songs must be sung correctly, in proper order, in just the right tone, or Sun and all the Spirits would be offended.

Seated on his right side, Shadow Dancer untied his leather medicine bag and removed each object, placing it reverently on the ground before him: the carcass of an animal burned beyond recognition, a clump of blackened grass, and three bones fused together by fire. At either end of the display, he placed two charred stones, the most sacred of all his spiritual objects.

Seeing the stones never failed to take Casts No Shadow back to that terrible day when his only son had miraculously escaped death after falling asleep in a field just before the vegetation was burned off in preparation for replanting. The thought that the boy he so loved could die such a horrible death–would die in the way the Kumeyaay people used to release the souls of the dead from the prisons of their useless bodies–so overwhelmed Casts No Shadow that his mind had ceased to function for many hours.

He had not been aware when he carried Shadow Dancer's things out of the family *'ewaa*. Not aware when he had arranged them on the ground–his son's sling, spear knife, fish-hooks and a crystal. Not aware when he began the death chant, praising his son to the spirits so they would allow him entrance to the land of Those Who Had Gone Before.

He was lost in unawareness when a ghost appeared out of the night. The ghost of Shadow Dancer. Casts No Shadow saw the ghost yet did not see it. Did not see it even while the apparition approached and handed him two smoke-blackened stones. The moment the rocks touched his flesh, the shaman's mind snapped back from its journey into unknowingness. And, as he looked from the stones to the ghost and back to the stones, he began to understand that he was holding a miracle. Those stones were real. As real as the ground under his feet and the air he dragged into his lungs. But no ghost could carry a real rock. Only a human could do that. That was when he knew that what he thought was a ghost was really his son. His son, his precious son had escaped death and had come back to him very much alive and breathing.

Such a miracle could only come from the gods. Could only come from the Spirit of Fire who had chosen Shadow Dancer to speak for Him to the Kumeyaay people. Accordingly, the next day Casts No Shadow performed the rite, anointing Shadow Dancer as *'aww-kuseyaay* fire shaman, one of a long line of such chosen ones stretching far back into Kumeyaay history.

Since then, Casts No Shadow and other local shamans had taken turns instructing the young man in the rituals and knowledge he must have to serve the people. Thus Shadow Dancer had grown in knowledge and stature among the Kumeyaay with every passing seasonal cycle. Already he had led two public ceremonies and taken over responsibility for directing and timing the burning of most of Nipaguay's fields. One day soon his human instruction would end, and he would assume all the responsibilities of a shaman while the spirits continued to teach him what they wanted him to know. Today was preparation for that day. Today Shadow Dancer would learn the proper way to sing Sun into supremacy of the skies.

When he judged the eastern horizon light enough, Casts No Shadow donned his cape of molted rattlesnake skins and retrieved a bundle from among the rocks. He had hidden the bundle there last winter on Longest Night after he had spent the hours of darkness praying that Sun would not forget to return from His long journey, return to bless the land and the people with His life-giving warmth and light.

Now sitting cross-legged, he undid the covering of the bundle to reveal an elaborate staff inscribed with magic spirit symbols. At the first ray of Sun, he presented the staff to the new dawn and chanted in the sacred language:

Grandfather Sun, come this way.
We, your children, need Your light.
Come this way.
Give us Your light.

Shadow Dancer cocked his head in concentration. Casts No Shadow repeated the song a second time, and a third, then nodded at his son.

Shadow Dancer sat tall and began to sing to the rising sun. The chant was perfect, in words and tone.

Casts No Shadow nodded. Again the son sang. Again, perfect.

Without prompting, Shadow Dancer repeated the song a third time, completing the required iterations without a mistake.

Casts No Shadow buried his satisfaction and went on to the next step. Chanting in a whisper, he drew out of the bundle a small gourd containing water from the sacred mirror spring. The gourd was also painted with the symbols of magic. He held it out to his son, who repeated the chant another three times before taking the gourd and drinking a mouthful of the water.

Raising his face to the sky, Shadow Dancer launched into the trance song the spirits had sent to him in a dream during his own initiation:

I am Shadow Dancer.
I seek the spirits
Of the ones who have gone before
And those who have yet to be.
I am a dancer of shadows
Come to join you in your dance,
To dance with shadows
To dance with shadows.
I seek the Land of the Spirits.
I am Shadow Dancer.

The words tapered off in a sigh, and Shadow Dancer's head fell forward. He was off on his journey to the world beyond.

Casts No Shadow set the staff and gourd down and allowed himself to smile. His son learned quickly, and well. At the meeting of shamans from which they had just returned, Shadow Dancer had conducted himself with the poise and assurance of someone who had spent a lifetime, instead of a few years, traveling between the human world and the world of Spirits. One day soon, the father would be able to turn over most of his responsibilities to his son and devote his time to his grandsons instead of seeing to the never-ending ritual needs of the people of Nipaguay.

At the thought of grandsons, Casts No Shadow's mind turned to Web. Seeking a wife for Shadow Dancer among the bands of the desert had been his wife's idea. "The time will come when Nipaguay needs an alliance with the desert people," Crimson Sky had said. Because her ability to see into the future had always proved uncanny, he began to make inquiries. That is how he learned that the leader of Hawi had a daughter who was two summers younger than Shadow Dancer. It did not matter to Crimson Sky that the girl's hands were webbed. She was adamant. "This desert girl is the right wife for our son, husband. I have seen this."

They had made the long journey to Hawi together, shaman and wife, each carrying a heavy load of gifts suitable to such a betrothal: baskets of dried fish, strings of rare coral shells, and ten silky sea otter pelts. With such impressive gifts, the bargain was quickly sealed, and Casts No Shadow and Crimson Sky returned to Nipaguay to wait for the day when the message would arrive that the girl had reached adulthood.

However, a year after that journey, Crimson Sky died.

The loss of his wife had left too large a void in Casts No Shadow's soul to be filled by another woman. He took the choice available to *wekuseyaay* and built an *'ewaa* for himself on the far edge of Nipaguay. He had now lived alone for nine summers; long enough that he could not remember living any other way.

Casts No Shadow's musings were interrupted by Shadow Dancer's murmurs and flapping arms, a sign that he had reached the land of Fire, his spirit protector. Time for Casts No Shadow to begin his own journey. He raised the gourd to his mouth. "I am ready, my Father," Casts No Shadow said to the sky. "Show me what you would have me see. Tell me what you would have me hear." Then he drank from the gourd, placed it carefully on the ground and drew the cape of snake skins around his body.

A moment after he closed his eyes he was flying across the arc

of a rainbow and swooping down into an *'ewaa* where two baby
boys lay side by side. His twin grandsons. Just beyond their
down-covered heads, a thick cloud swirled and undulated. The
veil across their future. Casts No Shadow tried to part the cloud
with his hand, but the mist was too thick and the noxious fumes
it gave off caused his eyes to burn and water.

He wanted to ask, "What do You hide from me, Father?" but
his tongue would not form the words.

The vision released him before he was ready to return. He came
to consciousness filled with frustration and concern. He had
never failed to penetrate the veil of the future. Until now.

Shadow Dancer's eyes opened and he, too, shook himself free
from the last vestiges of his spirit travels. "Father, I saw the most
wonderful thing." His voice was hoarse with excitement. "There
was a fire in a raised pit. From the heart of the flames, a stone
arose. It was a stone unlike anything I have ever seen or imagined."

He grabbed his father's arm. "This stone was thin like an *'epilly*
tule, with an edge sharper than the finest arrowhead. I took this
stone into my hand and, with one swipe, cut down a whole stand
of willows." His voice took on an edge of awe. "This stone was
as thin as a blade of grass, but *nothing* could break it."

He leaped to his feet and began pacing the narrow ledge like a
nervous *nyemetaay* cougar. "Imagine what such a stone would
mean to our people."

Casts No Shadow managed to set aside the residue of feelings
from his experience to ask, "Where was the fire?"

Shadow Dancer planted his feet and pointed west. "On that hill
above Cosoy." He turned to his father. "But that makes no sense.
No one at Cosoy has such a thing."

In his puzzlement, Shadow Dancer's face took the contours of
the boy he had been not so long ago. "To that place the fire will
come, and there you will find such a stone. The spirits do not lie,
my son," Casts No Shadow reassured him.

Shadow Dancer thought about that a moment, then asked,
"What did you see, my father?"

Casts No Shadow needed more time to understand the meaning
of his vision before he spoke about it. "I saw two fine sons waiting
for their father to return. But first he must finish his duties."

Shadow Dancer's smile at the news of the birth of his sons did
not reach the level of his eyes. For months Casts No Shadow had
sensed trouble between his son and Web, but he had refrained
from interfering, assuming that the problems were those of two
strangers learning to live together. Now he saw that there was

something else involved. Something that could threaten the harmony of Nipaguay and the future of their *sh'mulq*. He must investigate. First, however, the ceremony must be completed.

Setting aside his concerns, he resumed his place and sang the rest of the songs in the cycle, listening carefully to his son's repetitions. After the last song, he showed Shadow Dancer how to rewrap the ritual objects and where to hide the bundle. While he removed and folded his snakeskin cape, he let his thoughts return to his trance vision. Was the cloud that he had seen over the future related to the trouble between his son and the girl from the desert? If so, such trouble could threaten the entire village, the whole Kumeyaay nation, and it was his responsibility to find a way to penetrate that cloud. But how? The spirits showed only what they were willing to reveal.

Shadow Dancer stood up. "Come, my father. I must greet my new sons."

Casts No Shadow waved for his son to lead, then fell in behind him, his mind on Spirits and what they hid.

Nothing in Web's life had prepared her for the pain that surged from her lungs to her loins. She bit down on a strip of rawhide in an effort to stifle a scream. Despite her efforts, a muted cry still escaped.

As the pain receded, Hummingbird's arms relaxed their hold around her chest. "Soon, my sister. Soon your sons will come out to see their mother. Soon."

Her friend's murmurs provided small comfort as the next pain began, growing from a twinge to a clench to a stranglehold, until the only reality in Web's world was the terrible all-encompassing agony that had her in its cruel hold.

"Mother!"

The cry seemed to come from far away.

"Mother, help me!"

Hot tears streamed down her face, but she did not have the strength to stanch their flow. Crooning nonsense syllables into her ear, Hummingbird wiped her face with a strip of softened deer hide while the *sinkuseyaay*, the woman-healer, monitored Web's progress.

Web closed her eyes. Her mother's image appeared, smiling in the special way she reserved just for Web. "Mother," Web rasped. The image reached out and stroked her face, the way her mother always used to touch her.

A moment of comfort, then the pain began anew.

Web's eyes shot open to the sight of the threads of a spider web glistening in a shaft of sunlight against the rush roof of the birth lodge. Then the pain grew, absorbing every fiber of her body, blotting out all other sensation. Like the threads of a web entrapping an insect, she felt trapped in a squeezing agony so great that she feared she was about to die.

The next moment her body seemed to split in two and her innards streamed out onto the birth skin beneath her.

Her screams died away, and she felt as if she were drifting, as light as a breath of air, in a pool of peace. *This is Death,* she thought. *I go to join the spirits.*

The silence was broken by crying that grew steadily louder and more persistent. When she tried to open her eyes to see the source of the sound, her lids were too heavy.

A second voice joined the first, bawling plaintively.

She had heard such a sound before, but where?

The *sinkuseyaay's* voice echoed in her ear. "Can you hear your two fine strong sons? They are calling for their mother. Open your eyes, my sister, and meet them."

But I am dead, Web thought. *How can I hear the cries of the living?*

"You must meet your sons, sister," Hummingbird urged. "They need you."

Web mustered the strength to open one eye, then the other. In her arms, Hummingbird cradled two wiggling blurs.

Web blinked to clear the film from her eyes. The two blurs became infants, identical from the black down on their tiny skulls to the demanding set of their jaws.

"*Ha'waak.* Twins," she rasped in wonder.

Hummingbird laughed. "Both the same except for this small spot." She pointed to a black dot on the left baby's earlobe.

"*Ha'waak,*" Web repeated, trying to comprehend what had happened to her.

Hummingbird looked at the bundle in her right arm. "This one reminds me of a sand flea, and this one," she lifted the baby on the left, "a cricket."

Sand Flea and Cricket. Good milk names for little boys. When they were older, the elders of Nipaguay would give them proper names, but, for now, her friend's choices would do nicely.

"And so they shall be called, my sister," Web said, then closed her eyes and drifted back into the pool of peace.

"Wife?" The sound of Shadow Dancer's voice outside the birth lodge woke Web. He could not enter the hut. The powers that bring forth life were too strong; they would destroy his ability to talk to the spirits.

"You have fine, strong sons," answered Hummingbird who kept guard outside the lodge while Web slept.

Web looked down at the pair of identical heads nestled against her chest. A tenderness she had never known welled up in her. "Fine, strong sons," she whispered.

"She is well?" Shadow Dancer asked Hummingbird.

"She is tired. She sleeps," came the reply.

"My sons–are they–do they . . . ?"

"Their hands are like yours," Hummingbird said curtly.

The words felt like a slap to Web. What if the babies had webbed fingers like her own? What would Shadow Dancer do then? Make his sons hide their hands as he insisted she do?

Sand Flea yawned and sought her breast. The tiny mouth clamped over the nipple with surprising strength. A moment later, Cricket found the other nipple.

The tug of the suckling infants pulled Web back from her bitterness. Twins were a special blessing from the gods. The gods had chosen her womb to bear such special fruit. Fruit that meant good fortune to all the people of Nipaguay. Surely now Shadow Dancer would soften toward her. Wouldn't he?

Chapter 2

Web sat in the shade of the *wisal*, cradling her babies and watching the activity ebb and flow around her. Now that she and the twins had completed their period of seclusion, the people of Nipaguay had decided to celebrate the good fortune the birth of the *ha'waak* meant to the village. Several nearby bands had come to join the festivities so the village was crowded and noisy. The twins were oblivious to the fuss made in their honor. When they weren't nursing, they slept.

Casts No Shadow materialized beside Web and gently took Sand Flea into his arms. She smiled, hoping that would mask her surprise. After more than a year at Nipaguay, she was still not used to the ghostly way the wekuseyaay appeared and vanished.

Casts No Shadow, however, had eyes only for his grandson. His joy in the twins touched her. Cooing and making faces at Sand Flea, he seemed far removed from his image as the mysterious, imposing shaman of far-flung renown.

A group of six women approached the shade arbor. Crooked Basket and her closest friends.

"You do us honor, sister," one of the women said to Web.

"Through you, the gods have blessed our village," said another.

The women clustered around the *wekuseyaay* to admire Sand Flea. Crooked Basket took hold of the infant's tiny hand and examined it. Web was tempted to say something sarcastic but held back. Why do more to damage an already shaky relationship?

After the women moved off, Casts No Shadow bent to return Sand Flea to the crook of Web's arm and glanced after the departing group. "She is an unhappy woman who begrudges anyone else joy. Do not allow her anger to touch your heart, daughter. After all, the gods have smiled on you four times. With two sons and your two hands. She has no such blessings, and jealousy consumes her."

Casts No Shadow had never spoken so personally to her before, and it took some moments to absorb his words. By the time Web thought to thank him, he had vanished.

"Jealousy," she murmured into the soft black hair on Sand Flea's head. "Crooked Basket is jealous of us, my sons."

Sand Flea looked up at his mother and yawned.

Chapter 3

After the twins' honoring ceremony, the demands of motherhood, planting, harvesting and food preparation occupied Web's every waking hour. She was too busy to pay more than passing attention to Crooked Basket's glares and whisperings when she chanced to meet her around the village.

The spring rains proved bountiful, followed by a period of unusually warm and sunny weather. The grains and grasses in Nipaguay's fields sprouted quickly and grew thick and lush. Everyone anticipated abundant harvests by Longest Day.

But one morning several suns before that time, a loud commotion in the center of the village drew Web to investigate. She found a crowd gathered at the communal granaries. In their center stood Crooked Basket, brandishing a handful of acorns. "Worms! These nuts are riddled with them."

An apprehensive buzz rippled through the gathering.

Crooked Basket dashed the nuts to the ground and pointed at

the huge basket behind her. "Here! This is the problem. This granary
is defective. All the acorns inside are ruined. All of them!"

Web's jaw dropped. The granary was the one she had made, her
gift to the village, her way to fit in.

Faces swiveled toward her.

Her mouth gaped for words but none came out.

Big Nose pushed through the crowd and scooped another
handful of nuts from the hopper of the huge basket. After a quick
glance, he faced the crowd. "Burn it!"

Someone retrieved a brand from the nearby cooking fire. In an
instant, the dry willow of Web's beautiful, perfect basket caught
fire. She had used fresh green willow throughout, coiling carefully, anchoring each coil exactly. Even if she had not taken such
care, insects would not live in willow. Everyone knew that. What
had gone wrong?

As she turned away from the flaming pillar of the granary, her
eyes met Crooked Basket's. The chief's wife nodded to her. A
nod of gloating and victory that told Web the insects had not
found their way into her beautiful basket by themselves.

Chapter 4

That night a light rain began to fall; a gentle rain that was a
welcome change from the warm spring weather. Web lay
awake next to the sleeping Shadow Dancer, listening to the
gentle patter on the tules of the 'ewaa. It was obvious now that
Crooked Basket was not going to let up. She would continue to
hound Web. Continue to try to make her feel an outcast.

Only, she won't succeed, Web thought to herself. *I am wife to
Shadow Dancer and mother of his sons. Mother of his twin sons.
That is something Crooked Basket can never be. Like Casts No
Shadow said, she has no such blessings and jealousy consumes
her.*

"And jealousy consumes her," Web whispered, turning on her
side and falling to sleep.

The rain had grown in intensity by the next morning when she
and Hummingbird met to weave baskets together. Hummingbird's
wisal was wide enough to keep off the rain, and they settled
under it to work. Web was helping her friend create a new pattern
using dyed grasses, and neither noticed how heavy the rain had
become until the wind began to blow it on them around midday.

By the time Web ducked into her own 'ewaa, the rain was

pelting down, driven by an increasingly strong wind. Neglecting her own drenched condition, she toweled the babies off with a wad of softened yucca fibers and laid them down for a nap, then stretched out next to them to wait for the rain to subside.

Only, the rain didn't subside. Instead, the downpour increased, and, with it, the wind. The longer the storm went on, the more nervous she became. The earth around them could absorb only so much rain. When that limit was reached, there would be flash floods. Floods like the one that nearly trapped her five summers ago. She would never forget the roar of the onrushing water, the panic as she fought desperately to scramble up the crumbling sandstone walls of the wash, the sob that escaped from her lips as she collapsed on the narrow ledge an eye blink before the angry wall of water surged up the wash, drowning everything in its path, crashing against the constricting walls in a fury against being contained. She had never told anyone about what happened. She could never bring herself to talk about how close she had come to dying.

The wind's voice changed and she sat up just as it ripped away a section of tules. Water began to pour into the interior. Heart hammering with remembered fear, Web gathered the twins into her arms, crawled outside and headed up the ravine to take shelter under a spreading mesquite.

The rain was heavy enough to curtain what was going on beyond the 'ewaa, but she could hear shouting from the direction of the village center. The wind gusted an occasional word or phrase in her direction. Those words painted an increasingly alarming situation developing down near the river. She did not need to see to know that rain and runoff from upstream had swelled the river which would soon be overflowing its banks, if it wasn't flooding already.

A gurgle of water drew her attention to the top of the ravine two arm-lengths away. What had been a trickle of water running down the middle of the cleft moments before had now grown into a sizeable stream. A stream that was quickly cutting a deep furrow in the earth. A furrow that was expanding at an unbelievable rate toward the sieving 'ewaa she had just abandoned. Inside that 'ewaa was everything she and Shadow Dancer possessed. Everything. But what could she do? She had her arms full of infants.

With a dull thump, a portion of the new ditch bank as long as a reclining man and as wide as her outstretched arms collapsed into the eroding stream. A breath later, a second bigger section disappeared. It seemed as if the water were intent on consuming the entire ravine.

A third collapse decided her. She hung the twins' cradleboards on the stubs of branches growing out of the mesquite's trunk, testing them for security and draping a rabbit skin blanket across the tops of the boards to keep the rain off the babies. Then she started down the ravine.

The ground was slick with mud and loose rocks. She slipped and slid, nearly going down on her backside twice but catching herself before she fell. By the time she reached it, the 'ewaa's covering was completely stripped away from one quadrant of its frame and the front support had been undermined by the growing trench.

She squatted at the entrance and began pulling out the contents–a nest of her baskets, the pouch of medicines and herbs, an olla, a pile of burden nets. She grabbed everything in sight but could not bring herself to touch her husband's things. A woman's power to bring forth life could nullify the power of the greatest sorcerer, the greatest hunter or fisherman. That was why women were not allowed to touch a man's weapons or a shaman's sacred objects. Yet, if she didn't touch them, they would be swept away by the encroaching water. She knelt with her hand outstretched over his bow and quiver of arrows when . . .

"Wife!"

She jerked back her hand at the sound of her husband's voice.

"The valley floods," Shadow Dancer said urgently, plodding up the ravine. "Big Nose orders all the people to evacuate to higher ground."

She moved aside and allowed him to gather up his things. Only after he had them slung across his back did he appear to take note that she did not have the twins with her. "Where are my sons?" he thundered.

Under his angry gaze Web could only stammer and point. "I–I–up th–there."

Shadow Dancer stared at her outstretched hand. She quickly thrust it behind her. "You stupid little d . . . ." He stopped himself from completing the phrase Web had heard so often from Crooked Basket. Pivoting away from her, he strode up the ravine, leaving her to pick up their belongings and slip and slide after him.

By the time she arrived at the mesquite, he had lifted the babies down from their perches. She was ready to defend her decision to leave the babies for a moment in order to retrieve their belongings, but the words died unspoken as his anger focused on her. She bent her head so she would not have to meet his cold unforgiving eyes. "You will never again let *my* sons out of your sight. *Never!* Do you understand?"

Web nodded but kept her head bowed, her eyes on the muddy earth at her feet.

"Take them," Shadow Dancer ordered, thrusting the babies at her.

She had to put down her burden in order to take the twins. The force of his anger made her clumsy. It took two tries to sling the bulky cradleboards onto her back and several fumbles before she managed to pick up her dropped load.

"Come!" he commanded, marching up out of the ravine and beyond toward the river gorge.

Web did not have time to balance her load so she fell far behind her husband. Shadow Dancer never looked back as he led the way into the rocks that formed the upper reaches of the gorge. The rocks were slick and treacherous and the wind gusted strong enough to halt Web's forward progress on more than one occasion. Yet she struggled onward, planting her feet and shifting her weight carefully to avoid falling and hurting the twins.

By the time she caught up with her husband, he was seated inside a shallow cave little more than a hole carved out of the rock face. He sat with his back against the cave wall, his legs and feet stretched out into the rain. There was barely room for the twins and herself to squeeze in beside him so she left the pile of their possessions out in the elements in the lee of a boulder before crawling in with him.

He stared out at the rain, seemingly oblivious of her presence.

She was thoroughly drenched, but her first concern was for her babies. She dried them off as best she could, then put one to each breast. The pressure of their tiny, insistent mouths on her nipples reassured her. Shadow Dancer might be angry. He might not like her. He might see her hands as deformed. But he could not forsake or abandon the mother of his sons. To do so would bring consequences no sane man would ever consider. She closed her weary eyes and allowed herself to sink into sleep. The rain couldn't last much longer.

Chapter 5

But the storm not only continued, it grew worse. The wind's howl rose to a roar as it drove the rain before it in slanting sheets that seemed determined to scrub the face of the earth clean of all its features. For four suns the rain and wind continued unabated. There was no room in the little cave for a fire even if she had been able to find dry wood for one. She and Shadow Dancer nibbled on rations of the seeds and grain from the food pouch she had rescued from the 'ewaa. Few words passed between them. Though they had been married for fifteen cycles of the moon, they were still strangers. She wondered if this was the way it was with other couples. With Hummingbird and Many Rains? With Crooked Basket and Big Nose?

Such thoughts were churning around in Web's mind when, all of a sudden, the rain and wind ceased. There was no tapering off, no lessening of intensity. The storm just . . . ended.

Neither one of them moved immediately. Then Shadow Dancer crawled stiffly out from under the overhang and rose slowly to his full height. "The storm clears," he said, peering up at the sky with relief obvious in his voice.

Web scooted out of the little cave with the twins in her arms. Shadow Dancer reached down to take the babies and allow her to get to her feet. It was a small kindness, but one that planted a tiny seed of hope in Web's heart.

He continued to hold the babies while she loaded their soaked possessions into a burden net. Then he helped her lift the load and position it for balance.

By the time she fell in behind him on the way back toward Nipaguay, that seed of hope had sprouted and she allowed herself a small relieved smile.

She did not take much notice of the damage the storm had done until they reached the bluff overlooking the village. Stopping at the lip of the bluff, Shadow Dancer made an odd sound, a mixture of surprise and pain. As she walked up next to him, she could not stifle the gasp that rose to her lips at what she beheld.

The valley floor was filled with water from one side to the other. The river was now a lake, stretching from what had been the center of Nipaguay all the way out to the ocean. For the center of Nipaguay was now underwater, leaving no sign of the huts of the kwaipai or the others that had been there just five suns ago. Flooded, too, was the ceremonial center. Only the cremation area was still there, the level of the water reaching just below it.

In the distance the fields that had been growing so lushly were deep under the new lake. Nipaguay's fields and, further to the west, Cosoy's fields—all the fields.

And, if that wasn't enough to take in, the ravines in which most of the people of the village lived had been scoured clean. Gone were the 'ewaas, the wisals, the family granaries. Gone too were the cactus, mesquite, agave and other plants the people grew in the upper reaches of the ravines to be eaten in times of meager harvests and droughts. These insurance plants had been uprooted by the wind and rain and carried into the valley, into the lake. Besides the plants they ate, also destroyed were the plants the people cultivated to draw deer, big horn sheep, bear, antelope and other game out of the lands to the east for hunting. Worse, few of the smaller animals would have survived the inundation.

Gone, all gone, was the only thought Web's mind seemed capable of thinking. What lay at her feet was a catastrophe, a loss of the sources of food the Kumeyaays depended upon for survival.

As if he read her thoughts and sought to reassure her, Shadow Dancer swept out his arm. "So. The ocean comes to us now. Good. The ocean always provides. No one in Nipaguay will go hungry. I will see to that."

His words were bravely spoken, but Web detected the doubt in his voice. Doubt that turned her concern to fear. If Shadow Dancer was uncertain, there was reason to be afraid. What if the sea did not provide? How was she going to feed her babies?

Chapter 6

With hearts burdened by the loss of their homes and the destruction of so much of the natural abundance upon which their lives depended, the people of Nipaguay set about trying to pick up the pieces. Big Nose and the council decided on a plan, establishing shelter and food as the first priorities. They organized one group to locate, cut and haul back the tules necessary for rebuilding 'ewaas and fishing canoes, all of which had been damaged or washed away. Another group of men went out to hunt. The older children scoured the high ground for rabbits, quail, gophers, birds and any other creatures that had escaped drowning.

Web and Hummingbird found themselves in a group of other women with infants and small children to care for. Their task was to collect any food stuffs that had escaped the calamity and to construct new basket granaries to hold what they found.

Although she had no children to care for, Crooked Basket joined this group and immediately assumed control. She pointed an imperious finger at Hummingbird. "You have no children.

You should be off cutting reeds.'"

Before Hummingbird could reply, Web jumped in. "She helps me with my twins. Besides, neither do you have children, sister."

Crooked Basket stiffened at the challenge. "I am the kwaipai's wife. I know how to get things done."

A sly smile painted Hummingbird's lips. "Indeed you do. And we all know what those *things* are, don't we, my sisters?"

Amid nods and titters from those grouped around her, Crooked Basket's face darkened. "I will not be mocked! And I will not lead those who mock me!" she declared, then spun on her heel and stomped off, trailing two of her perennial supporters.

As soon as Crooked Basket was out of earshot, Hummingbird glanced around the group of women, her eyes dancing with merriment. "So much for her. Now where were we?"

Relieved laughter broke the tension and, without anyone assuming leadership, the women agreed on how to do the task they had been given and went off in various directions, trailing their children, to search the village. "You shouldn't have done that," Web said to her friend when no one else could hear their conversation. "Crooked Basket will get even. You know that."

"You started it. I was just following your lead." Hummingbird laughed. "Did you see the look on her face? She's as full of venom as a rattling serpent fresh out of winter hibernation. Big Nose better watch out. She's liable to sink her fangs into him, as angry as she is right now."

Web managed a smile, her first since the storm, but in the back of her mind a grim thought formed. What if the one Crooked Basket bit wasn't her own husband, but Shadow Dancer instead? What then?

Chapter 7

In the aftermath of the deluge and flooding, Casts No Shadow worked tirelessly to restore order in the physical realm and the spiritual realm of the people. He wore himself out giving encouragement and cajoling others to remain optimistic. He pitched in to build 'ewaas, to repair and rebuild reed canoes, to construct a new ceremonial area, to replant willow along the eroded cuts the rain had gashed in the land. Every day he performed the rituals necessary to restore the natural balance the storm had destroyed. He prayed and chanted and danced until his feet were blistered and his voice was hoarse.

By the next fingernail moon, the village had been re-established with its center moved up to higher ground, and daily life began to return to a more normal rhythm. But there was only so much one man could do to counter what the spirits had sent upon the land.

The rain's fury had washed much soil down into the river and the streams feeding into it. The river then carried that soil out to the ocean where it formed a huge fan of muddy water that spread far out to sea. The presence of so much mud in the water drove away the fish and the seabirds that fed on them. The result was that the men had to paddle out much farther than normal once their reed boats had been repaired or rebuilt. Even then, their catches were meager. And, since all the Kumeyaay villages surrounding Nipaguay were in the same situation with regard to food, all the fishermen were competing with each other for what was available. That meant that, in short order, the boats were forced to go farther and farther out each day.

The areas where the Kumeyaay were accustomed to gathering shellfish were the same areas that remained flooded longest. In addition, with all the hunters in all the villages competing for the same game in the immediate area, the numbers of animals–deer, antelope, big-horn sheep, birds, rabbits, quail, bear and the like–began to decrease at a rate that could not be sustained.

By the second quarter moon after the storm, food was growing scarce. Nipaguay's council decreed that food would be rationed. As the situation continued, worry etched deep lines into the faces of the adults of Nipaguay and the faces of the children grew gaunt. It did not take long for the people to begin muttering about leaving the village and heading into the mountains where game could be more plentiful. That talk soon spilled into the council gatherings.

For hours Casts No Shadow sat and listened to arguments for leaving, and for more hours he talked, using his considerable persuasive skills to counter those arguments. Again and again, he reminded the people of times in the past when the people of Nipaguay, facing hunger, had left the village and gone off in search of food. Those departures had inevitably resulted in other bands trying to usurp the village and the fields and hunting areas Nipaguay controlled. Such attempts at trespass always led to war, and war led to deaths, deaths his people could not afford now if they were to recover from the blow the storm had dealt them.

The talk continued, however and after one particularly contentious council session, he decided he needed help. It was time to seek out the Spirit of the Rattling Serpent.

The sacred *llehup* cave was located in a jumble of boulders perched high on the walls of the river gorge above the village. The climb was difficult and, weakened by hunger and by the exhaustion brought on by his contributions to recovery efforts, Casts No Shadow had to stop frequently to wait for the dizziness that clouded his sight and judgment to clear.

When at last he reached the entrance to the *llehup*, he paused to collect himself. The Spirit of the Rattling Serpent was the most powerful of spirits. Because He traveled between the Middle World and the underground realm where Blind Brother lived in the world without light and ruled Things Unseen, the Spirit of the Rattling Serpent had knowledge and access to information that no other god possessed. A mortal dared not enter His presence without focus and confidence.

Again and again, Casts No Shadow drew his lungs full, then emptied them completely before drawing the next breath. With every inhale, his lungs filled with the powerful reptilian scent that emanated from the cave. The scent of the Spirit and His children. Now and then, the rustle of scales sliding against other scales carried up to Casts No Shadow's ears from the impenetrable darkness within the cavern.

When he felt ready, Casts No Shadow draped the sacred cape of serpent skins across his head and shoulders and began his song.

Look into the darkness, my eyes.
Help me see beyond the black.
Step into the darkness, my feet.
Carry me beyond the black.
Eyes and feet, lead this man into the darkness.
Take me beyond the black
Into the world where He awaits,
Into the darkness
Beyond the black
Into the world where the Ancient One awaits.

Wedging through the narrow opening, the wekuseyaay sensed dozens of sinuous bodies gliding out of his path. He had long ago lost his fear of this special place and the creatures who dwelled within its stone confines. Before Casts No Shadow, Earth Thunder had claimed this cave as his most sacred place. It was from Earth Thunder that Casts No Shadow learned the ways of a wekuseyaay. Before that, it belonged to Earth Thunder's mentor, then to his mentor's mentor and so on back through all the generations of memory.

A pang of sadness touched Casts No Shadow when he realized that he was the last who would ever use the *llehup*. He could never bring Shadow Dancer here for this place was the realm of a wekuseyaay, not an 'aww-kuseyaay. It made no difference to the spirits that, from the day of Shadow Dancer's birth, Casts No Shadow had planned for his son to replace him. The spirits had had different plans for Shadow Dancer. Plans that meant no one would take Casts No Shadow's place as wekuseyaay when he died. It took many years to impart the knowledge and wisdom of the Spirit of the Rattling Serpent. More years of life than remained to Casts No Shadow.

He pushed aside those thoughts and moved deep into the cave, relying on his memory to guide him to the right spot. There he knelt and felt for the small basket. Finding it, he extracted an object and held it before his open but unseeing eyes. The words of his most secret song echoed off the rock walls of the cave, phrases colliding, words intertwining until the air filled with sound. At that point he placed the piece of the Far-Seeing Root on his tongue and began to chew, slowly, methodically, conscious of the movement of each muscle in his jaw, of each component of each sensation of the substance's earthy taste and bitterness.

When he had chewed a soft mass, he swallowed and lay on his back, folding his hands across his chest, staring into the darkness.

After a time, a tiny point of light appeared in the darkness above him. The point grew and expanded until it felt as if the sun had dissolved the stone walls over his head. The wekuseyaay held his eyes rigidly open. To blink would show weakness, and Rattling Serpent Spirit would never show Himself to a weak man.

The brightness grew in intensity, forcing Casts No Shadow to struggle to keep his eyes open and focused.

Suddenly a figure loomed out of the light: an enormous rattling serpent wrapped into a glistening coil. Its scales shown like crystals, colors shifting from deep blues to purples to reds to yellows and greens. The serpent's tongue flicked out once, twice, then its rattle shook, sending a rumble through the cave. This was the signal for the wekuseyaay to speak.

Casts No Shadow's mouth felt as dry as a desert sand wash. His first word came out as a croak.

The snake rattled impatiently.

He tried again. "Spirit, the gods have taken away food from my people. What have we done to so displease You and the other Spirits?"

The hint of a smirk crossed the serpent's face before it vanished. In its place appeared a clearing. Two people lay face to face on the ground: Shadow Dancer and Crooked Basket. The woman's face wavered and her body thinned and lengthened until she turned into a snake. With her tongue flicking, she slithered round and round Shadow Dancer's body, wrapping him with her coils.

Behind Shadow Dancer swirled a cloud thicker than the smoke from the fire that had nearly taken his life.

Casts No Shadow held himself in check against the anger the image raised within. "The cloud," he rasped. "What do You hide from me, Spirit?"

"Are you certain you wish to see?" The sibilant 's' sounds hissed off the Serpent's flicking tongue.

Casts No Shadow felt rather than heard the question, and he answered, "I must see the future. It is my duty to my people."

Dozens of beasts burst out of the cloud and hurtled toward Casts No Shadow, throwing up a great cloud of dust. As the first beast drew closer, the wekuseyaay saw that the one creature was really two: one atop the other. The upper creature sat upright. It had lush hair covering its face except for the area around the eyes and nose bridge where the skin gleamed vulnerable in its naked pinkness. Sun glinted off the strange shell that encompassed its head. It balanced on its hind quarters. Hairless leather covered its chest and the lower parts of its longer hind legs while another type of skin, the color of the midnight sky, covered its shorter front legs and upper parts of its hind legs. Around one of these front legs was a round shield of leather that it brandished toward the wekuseyaay.

More fearsome was the beast the first creature rode. Larger, broader and more powerfully built than the largest deer, but without horns growing on its long graceful head, it had a flowing tail, and a ridge of the same hair running down the back of its neck. It walked on four equal-length legs, snorting and making terrifying noises the likes of which the wekuseyaay had never heard.

When the image faded, Casts No Shadow lay still, trying to comprehend the meaning of the beasts. Without reaching any conclusions, he fell into a fitful sleep.

When he awoke hours later, he was still tired, but the upwelling

of anger within would not let him linger. He did not understand
the significance of the two beasts, but he did know the cause of
his people's troubles. He had to set things right again.

Over time the river level fell and the stream returned to its
snaking course along the floor of the valley. A moon's passage
beyond Longest Day, the willow withes planted along the eroded
cuts began to take root. Some of the fields began to sport green
shadows as new seeds sprouted. Yet food remained scarce and all
able-bodied individuals, adults and children spent their days
endlessly searching for something to eat.

Web awoke inside their newly-rebuilt 'ewaa to find that, once
again, Shadow Dancer had not returned to the lodge to sleep. Her
stomach grumbled loudly and she pressed a palm against the bare
flesh of her belly. Would there ever again be enough to eat?
Would she ever again be able to eat her fill?

To keep from dwelling on the gnawing pangs in her gut and
awaking the sleeping twins, she ducked outside and took up a
basket she was in the process of weaving, hoping that the process
of coiling would take her mind off her hunger and soothe her
frazzled nerves.

Lifting the basket, she realized it was too heavy.

She peered inside–and gasped.

There lay a pair of desiccated duck's feet.

She heaved the basket away from her and stumbled off to be
sick.

When she returned, Hummingbird was squatting beside the
'ewaa. She popped to her feet at Web's approach. "You are so
pale, my sister. Are you unwell?"

Web did not trust her voice. She nodded at the discarded
basket. Hummingbird it up and grimaced at the contents. "She
did this! Crooked Basket, she–"

"Take it away, please. Burn it," Web choked on her own words.

Hummingbird looked ready to argue but hurried away to do
Web's bidding. Web sank weakly to her knees and wrapped her
arms tightly around her bare chest to control an ache that went
deeper than hunger. She saw the hand of Crooked Basket behind
both the duck's feet and the insect infestation that caused her
beautiful granary to be burned. Crooked Basket was the daughter
of a shaman. Who knew what she had learned from her father?
Who knew what other tricks she might be capable of?

"Why does she hate me so? I have done nothing to her," Web asked the sky.

No sooner had the words left her lips than she knew the answer. She had done something to Crooked Basket. Two somethings: she had married Shadow Dancer and she had borne him twin sons while Crooked Basket's continued barrenness was the source of hushed but persistent gossip among the women of Nipaguay. Nothing Web could do would change those facts. Crooked Basket hated her. If Web ever wanted to feel at home here, she had to learn to accept that notion and find a way to live with that reality.

By the time Hummingbird returned, Web felt better. The morning was hot as the two of them struck off out of Nipaguay to spend the day foraging on the far side of the sacred mountain to the northeast of the village. Hummingbird claimed she knew of a hidden copse where there were always birds to snare, a place no one else knew about.

Evidence of the flood's effects was apparent as they picked their way to the base of the mountain and skirted around its eastern side. They stopped there and squatted in the shade of a scrawny mesquite to share a small cake of mixed seeds. As the babies suckled, Web ate, taking tiny bites and allowing each morsel to dissolve in her mouth rather than chewing in order to make the food last as long as possible.

Hummingbird finished her portion and pointed up the mountain. "It's up there."

Web squinted against the sun but saw nothing.

"You can't see the trees until you're almost upon them," Hummingbird reassured her. "Come. Today, we will find two nice, plump quail. You will see." She took Sand Flea's cradleboard upon her back and led the way up the mountain.

It occurred to Web that they should not be walking upon the sacred mountain. However, she was too out of breath to say anything while they climbed and too pleasantly surprised to find herself standing at the edge of a beautiful copse of inviting trees when they stopped.

"See!" said Hummingbird delightedly. "Just like I told you." She surveyed the area and waved to the right. "I'll go round this way and you circle around the other. There are quail here. I can feel it in my bones."

Web adjusted Cricket upon her back, then started circling the trees, moving stealthily so as not to spook any birds before she set her snares. She had knelt to set the first snare when her ears caught the sound of murmurs. Intrigued, she crept forward to investigate.

Parting a tangle of vines, she glimpsed two figures in a small clearing in the middle of the grove. Perhaps young lovers frequented this out-of-the-way place. She could not resist the urge to see for herself and to perhaps find something to discuss with Hummingbird besides food and how hungry she was.

She inched closer–and froze at the sound of a woman's laughter. Crooked Basket's laughter. Something urged Web to turn around and leave, but the intimacy implied in the next peal of laughter made her lean slowly around the tree..

A stride away from where Web stood, Shadow Dancer lay on his side, facing Crooked Basket whose bare leg was thrown over his naked hip. While the kwaipai's wife whispered in his ear, he kneaded one of her breasts. The rapt expression on his face told Web all she needed to know about what would soon happen.

"So this is how you look for food for your sons."

The voice belonged to Hummingbird who stepped into the clearing opposite Web bearing Sand Flea in his cradleboard.

Shadow Dancer scrambled to his feet, trying without success to hide his swollen member behind his hands. Crooked Basket didn't bother to stand. She stretched languidly and sat up, leaning against the trunk of the tree that hid Web.

Hummingbird ignored Crooked Basket and addressed Shadow Dancer, her voice quaking with emotion. "This is how you obey the restrictions of a new father?"

Shadow Dancer glanced around sheepishly as if seeking escape.

"Do you wish your sons to die?" Hummingbird asked.

That brought Crooked Basket to her feet. "He wishes nothing of the sort, and you know it. Can you blame him for wanting me? Anyone who's seen his wife's hands would understand. She is a freak."

Web stormed into the clearing. Her sudden appearance startled Crooked Basket, but Web pushed past her to face her husband. "Your sons are hungry. *I* am hungry. Yet here you are, dawdling with another man's wife when you should be out fishing. How could you?"

Crooked Basket grabbed her arm. "Don't blame him, desert mouse. Blame yourself. Since you came to Nipaguay, all we've had is bad luck."

Web pried off the offending hand. "Not true."

Crooked Basket turned confidently to Shadow Dancer. "You

tell her. The words coming from you might sink through her stupidity."

Shadow Dancer opened his mouth, then closed it again.

"Go on. Tell her," Crooked Basket demanded. "She started all this. Send her back to the desert where she belongs."

Web did not wait for her husband to speak. "I did not bring the killing storm. I did not flood the land and drive away the fish and the game. Only the spirits can do such things. A shaman's daughter should know this."

"Don't blame the spirits when it's your webbed freak's hands that started all our problems," Crooked Basket declared.

Web spun to face her adversary. "Why did you put the ducks' feet in my basket?"

"Duck's feet? What is she talking about?" Shadow Dancer asked the kwaipai's wife.

Crooked Basket refused to answer.

"Wife?" Shadow Dancer asked Web.

She answered, "The day our marriage seclusion ended, the hunters brought back ducks. I would not touch them then and I will never touch them. They are my brothers and sisters."

"Ignorant little desert mouse," Crooked Basket crooned.

Shadow Dancer's angry glance shut her up.

Hummingbird jumped into the stony silence. "Ah, so your lover here did not tell you about her little prank. Then, of course, she did not tell you she was planning to steal Web's shell either." She spun to face the kwaipai's wife. "Oh, yes, Crooked Basket. I heard about your little scheme in the women's lodge." She turned to look at Shadow Dancer. "Now why would Crooked Basket want Web's shell? She couldn't wear it. Everyone would recognize it. She couldn't trade it for the same reason."

Hummingbird looked pointedly at Crooked Basket. "There is only one other reason for such an action. She wants the shell so she can harm Web. After all, her father was a shaman. Who knows the evil ways someone like her managed to learn?"

"Is this true?" Shadow Dancer demanded of Crooked Basket.

Crooked Basket tossed her head. "She lies."

Shadow Dancer gripped Crooked Basket's arm, making her grimace. "Many Rains is my best friend. His wife does not lie. I want to hear the truth. From you."

Crooked Basket wrested her arm out of his grasp. "It is you who is the liar. You who told me your wife disgusted you."

At that moment Casts No Shadow materialized in the clearing. "And what exactly did you say about your wife, my son?"

Instead of quailing in the face of his father's obvious anger, Shadow Dancer gave up trying to cover his now-shrunken member. He threw back his shoulders and, in a firm voice, said, "I said that her hands disgusted me. I made her hide them in my presence."

Casts No Shadow's icy voice pierced the tense air in the clearing like a well-aimed arrow. "Do you, an 'aww-kuseyaay, forget the primary truth of the people? If not for Frog and Duck, Cuy-a-ho-marr would have been slain by the friends of His evil grandfather."

"A child's tale that has no bearing on anything," Crooked Basket said. "Shadow Dancer is right to feel the way he does." She pointed a damning finger at Web. "She is not human. She does not belong here."

"No, woman. It is you who do not belong here." Casts No Shadow looked at his son. "It appears that I have made a terrible mistake." His voice took on the edge of finality. "No shaman would behave the way you have."

Shadow Dancer blanched then and fell silent while no one else moved. When next he spoke, his voice was low and apologetic. "You are right, Father. You have made no mistake. I am the one who has erred."

After a long search of his son's face, Casts No Shadow nodded and turned to Web. Regarding her, he asked in a high ritual voice, "My son, who is this woman?"

Confused by the question, Web looked from father to son. In the same formal tone as Casts No Shadow, Shadow Dancer answered, "Father, she is my wife, the woman you have chosen for me, and the mother of my sons."

Casts No Shadow indicated for Web to hold up her hands. "And what do you have to say to her who is your wife and the mother of your sons?"

Shadow Dancer came forward and took both of Web's hands in his. He looked deeply into her eyes. "I was wrong, my wife. I ask for your forgiveness."

She was too stunned to say anything but, "You are forgiven."

"And what do you do to thank her for her forgiveness?" Casts No Shadow demanded of his son.

With no hesitation, Shadow Dancer raised Web's hands and kissed each of the flaps of skin between her fingers, then stood looking at her until she felt his eyes would swallow her.

However, Casts No Shadow was not done. He pointed at Crooked Basket and said, "My son, who is this woman?"

Still holding Web's hands and without turning away, Shadow Dancer said, "The wife of Big Nose."

Crooked Basket glared at Web.

"And what do you have to say to her?" Casts No Shadow asked.

Without turning away from Web, Shadow Dancer said a firm, "Goodbye."

Crooked Basket's eyes shot open. "No!"

"Goodbye," Shadow Dancer repeated, and, without a backward glance, he led Web out of the copse to the accompaniment of Crooked Basket's sobs.

III

VOYAGE

January 1, 1769—April, 1769

Chapter 1

Early January, 1769—Loreto, Lower California

The grating at the bottom of the thick wood door creaked out of the way and the guard shoved two bowls through the gap with the toe of his dung-encrusted boot. Romero crouched in the corner, waiting for his cellmate to rouse himself and take first pick. The only time Romero had made the mistake of taking his food first, Noche, the half-human brute he shared the cell with, had choked him into unconsciousness with his bare hands. When Romero came to, his bowl was empty; his stomach, even emptier. He could still feel Noche's hands at his throat and see the smile that curled the man's purplish lips as Romero thrashed about, struggling for breath against the man's iron hold.

Now several minutes passed. Still Noche did not awaken. Romero crept cautiously over to his cellmate's corner, ready to spring away should this prove to be another of the man's sadistic pranks. Noche's eyes were crusted shut. His face was bloated and the tip of his tongue lolled from the corner of his open mouth. The labored gasps of his breath did not mask the faint rattle in his chest.

Encouraged by these appearances, Romero mustered the courage to touch Noche's arm with an extended finger.

The man did not react, so Romero pinched the blotchy flesh of the man's underarm, then immediately jumped back out of reach of Noche's grasp.

Nothing. Not even a groan.

Rising into a crouch, Romero studied the back of Noche's skull. He wanted to believe that God had heard his prayers and visited sickness on his cellmate, but, since being dragged away from La Purísima, he was no longer certain God bothered to listen to him.

After several tense minutes without a twitch from the downed man, Romero toed Noche's leg, then, emboldened by the lack of response, he launched a kick that connected squarely with the man's lower spine.

This brought a groan from Noche who attempted to raise up on one elbow. Romero kicked away the supporting arm. Noche flopped back onto the slimy stone floor, and Romero leaped for the food, scooping up both bowls, hugging them to his chest. "I better hold onto this before you knock it over," he said to the back of Noche's head.

Noche moaned and muttered something unintelligible into the floor.

Without taking his eyes off the prone figure, Romero emptied the first bowl of its thin gray slop in hurried gulps. He held out the second bowl. "Aren't you going to eat? It's getting cold."

Noche floundered into position to thrust a trembling hand toward Romero who tucked the bowl safely behind his back. "Ah, but you forget the rules, amigo."

Noche mumbled something that sounded like a question.

"Yes, we play by my rules now. And I say that you have to sit up to eat, No-che," he taunted, deliberately slurring the man's name into two distinct syllables.

Noche sputtered and raked the air with clawed fingers.

"I'll count to three. Either you sit up—or—I will have to eat your dinner for you."

Noche's bloated face contorted with fury.

"One . . ."

On rubbery arms, the man raised his chest a few inches off the damp floor.

"Two . . ."

Noche lifted his wobbling head and muttered something that sounded like a curse, punctuated with burbling sounds from deep in his chest.

"Three."

Noche made a weak lunge in the direction of the bowl, but Romero easily eluded him. "Too bad, amigo. It's all mine now."

While Noche crumpled back onto the floor with a drawn-out groan, Romero ate, savoring this sudden turn of fortune more than the gruel. His thoughts turned to his time of imprisonment.

He had spent his first days in this cell frantically combing every inch of the walls, ceiling, and floor for a way out. Noche had laughed at all his efforts. "There is no way out, except for the door—and the only way you'll leave through it again is when you die."

After a week of futile searching, Romero had to admit defeat. Hopelessness replaced his frenzy. That was when Noche started in, turning Romero's days and nights into a living hell of unprovoked beatings and sexual assaults. Many times he considered taking his own life, only to be stopped by his need to track down Father Xavier wherever the King had sent him and correct the misunderstanding between them. Now Noche was . . .

Voices beyond the cell door brought Romero to the alert. No one came to this section of the prison except to deliver food. And food wasn't due again until tomorrow.

Metal scraped on metal, followed by the squeak of a key turning in the rusty lock of Romero's cell. The door opened, hinges grating a complaint of long disuse. Romero put up an arm to shield his eyes from the flood of light as two men entered. One pointed at him, "That's the one we're after."

The men dragged him from the cell and down a long, stone corridor. Outside, the light was too intense for Romero's weakened eyes. He stumbled blindly along, half-carried by the two men.

When at last he could manage a squint, he found himself wedged between two *soldados de cuera*, Leatherjacket soldiers. From his spotty knowledge of Loreto, he guessed that they were taking him to the docks. There was only one reason they would be taking him there: he was being impressed into the crew of some short-handed ship.

The specter of losing Father Xavier's trail forever loomed too large for him to go without a struggle. He planted his feet and simultaneously yanked his arms away from the grip of the soldiers. He ripped free and took off sprinting.

"Shoot but don't kill him!" someone yelled.

Romero swerved left, racing toward the shelter of a group of huts.

A musket exploded behind him. With his heart hammering and his lungs burning from the sudden exertion after months of sitting, he bolted past a two-wheeled *carreta*. A split second later, a rifle ball thudded into the cart, splintering one of its posts.

Another explosion, and a second ball hit the dirt inches from his right foot.

A third rifle boomed.

Romero felt a stinging in his thigh, and the strength suddenly went out of his leg. He went sprawling.

With his mind screaming "Get away!" he clawed at the hard-packed earth, pulling himself toward the huts on his stomach, dragging his wounded leg.

He had nearly reached the first hut when the soldiers caught up. They jerked him to his feet like a sack of grain. "Next time, you die," the one in command growled, shoving a pistol against Romero's throat and holding it there while he and his companion hauled the blacksmith the rest of the way to the docks and across the gangway of a ship.

Onboard, they dumped him at the feet of a man who stood in the doorway of the lone cabin, backlit by a swaying lantern. "Mate, come here!" that one yelled.

Another man leaned over the upper railing. "Aye, Captain?"

"Take charge of this," the first man replied, turning on his heel and slamming the door.

The mate swung down to the main deck. "Take him below."

"You better chain him. He tried to get away," the soldier on Romero's left side said.

The mate glared. "And you shot him, did you? Damn your eyes, man. I had my heart set on one last romp in a certain tart's bed tonight. Instead I have to cut a musket ball out of a man's leg. Christ's wounds, don't just stand there! Take him below, you worthless tin heads!"

Grumbling, the soldiers dragged Romero into the musty hold and chained him against the bulkhead. After they left, the mate yelled up through the hatch, "Hey, boy, bring a lamp."

A moment later, a thin boy with a humped back climbed into the hold with a lamp whose brass twinkled from recent polishing.

"Hold her up so's I can see through this mess o' blood," the mate ordered.

The boy complied while picking his nose with his free hand and staring dully at Romero.

As the mate probed the wound with his callused fingers, Romero barely managed to stifle a yelp of pain.

"Ah, there she is," the mate said, slipping a dirty knife out of a dirtier sheath that hung on his belt.

Romero had no time to prepare for the knife's plunge into his flesh. He gasped, but somehow he managed to swallow the scream that ripped from his innards. He might be chained, but he refused to show pain or weakness to this or any other man.

Mumbling as he worked, the mate dug for the ball as gently as a bear might grub for insects in a rotten log. Romero concentrated all his focus on the thin boy's pitted face. *Show nothing. Feel nothing*, he repeated to himself.

Then the mate muttered, "Ah, here she be," and jabbed the point of the knife into Romero's muscle.

For a moment, Romero feared he would faint. He forced himself to squint at the purplish blotch on the boy's scrawny neck while deliberately ignoring the bead of sweat that trickled down his own forehead onto his nose and dropped onto his tattered shirt.

The knife's pressure let up and the mate stepped back. "A present for ye, lad." He tossed a blood-coated iron ball to the boy who swept it neatly out of the air. The mate wiped the knife blade on his grease-stained pants and addressed Romero. "Takes a tough one not to yell. I'll hand that to ye."

Romero glared back at him. If his mouth had not been so dry, he would have spit in the man's smug face.

The mate leaned down, thrusting his moon-round face at Romero. "Angry, huh? Well, ye best stay that way. If ye want to live, that is."

With that, the mate and boy climbed out of the hold.

Once he was alone, Romero continued to hold himself rigid against the pain that throbbed mercilessly outward from the open wound. Pain. Anymore it seemed the only reality in his life. And all the pain, all the suffering had one source: "Nemesio," he rasped.

Under the pain's assault, the seams between the bulkhead planks wavered before Romero's eyes. His stomach lurched, sending bitter bile into his throat. He clutched at the chains that held him to the wall. "For you, Nemesio, I will stay alive."

Then his thoughts splintered into a million stars.

Chapter 2

The ship weighed anchor the next morning, and, soon after, seasickness hit Romero full force, adding to the misery of his throbbing wound. His stomach rejected everything he swallowed, but in his resolve to stay alive, he forced himself to eat whenever the ship's boy brought it.

The fifth day he awoke to find the nausea gone. Checking his wound, he was relieved to see that it had begun to heal. For the first time since landing in the ship's hold, he considered his situation.

Chains still bound him to the bulkhead and his only contact with the crew, besides the mate, was the sullen, misshapen ship's boy who brought his food. If he had been impressed, as he assumed, he would have been slapped on an oar long before now. Yet he was still in the hold. Why?

For the next four days, he pondered that question without arriving at an answer.

Then, on the ninth day out of Loreto, he was ripped out of a doze by the mate yelling for the crew to lower sails. Moments later came the clanking and metallic screeches of chain playing out as the anchor splashed off the stern.

Romero waited in the dank dimness, straining for clues as to the ship's location. From the few phrases that drifted his way, he learned that they had reached a port and that the crew was going ashore. He counted one, two, three loads of crewmen boarding the ship's launch for the trip to land. The third load had just left when the hatch scraped open and the mate swung down into the hold, followed by three leatherjacket soldiers. The mate undid Romero's chains, and the soldiers manhandled him up onto the deck.

It was night. The moonless sky was overcast. In the distance Romero could just make out a sweep of pale beach and a cluster of huts. Torchlight flickered behind the window openings of two of the huts.

"Where are we?" he asked, his voice hoarse after long disuse.

"We're going in, but you're going there." The mate swept an arm toward the stern. Another larger vessel loomed out of the darkness.

Romero's heart sank. "Where am I going?"

The mate tossed the soldiers a sly look. "What do you say, compadres? Shall I tell him?"

"Where?" Romero demanded.

"Temper, temper." The mate spat on the deck. "Save your energy, amigo. You will need all you have–where you are going." He thumbed toward the soldiers. "Get this bag of dung off my ship!"

Romero was too weak to give the guards much of a struggle. They chained his wrists to his ankles and tossed him into a smelly launch. On the way to the other ship, one of the soldiers used Romero's long hair to wipe his boots. "You don't mind, do you?" he said, drawing laughter from his companions.

The launch drew up alongside the second ship. Two of the soldiers pulled Romero to his feet. Bent in half, wrists anchored to his ankles, Romero had to struggle to keep upright as the little boat rolled and pitched on the sea swells. "What ship is this?" he demanded.

"His Majesty's packet boat *San Carlos*," the leader of the soldiers said.

Romero had not expected an answer. Emboldened, he asked, "Where is it headed?"

The leader gave him a calculating look. "That's a surprise. You like surprises, don't you? As for us, we're headed to the cantina, as soon as we take care of you." He motioned to his men. They lifted Romero across to a trio of men from *San Carlos* who hauled him to an open hatch and threw him bodily into yet another hold.

Romero landed on his shoulder, wrenching it and reopening the wound when his thigh slammed against the corner of a crate. He lay where he landed, biting his tongue to keep from crying out his pain. From now on, no one would ever know he hurt. No one.

The hatch cover dropped and a lock clicked shut. Then came the sounds of soldiers clambering into their launch and the splash of oars moving in the direction of land.

"I'd help you up, but they chained me to the wall."

Romero started at the sound of a voice and searched the blackness for its source.

Chains clanked off to the right. "Over here. My name is Ignacio."

Romero was still in too much pain to speak. He grunted.

"In case you're interested, we're at La Paz," Ignacio volunteered.

La Paz. Romero vaguely remembered that the settlement lay south of Loreto. Could this be where the King had sent Father Xavier? No, he decided, recalling that Manos had told him that the King had expelled the Jesuits from all California.

"I suppose you want to know why you're here," Ignacio said. "Well, go on. Ask me."

Romero was in no shape to play games, but he bit back his frustration and choked out the question, "Why am I here?"

"Well, I'm a carpenter, and I'll bet you're a . . ."

"Blacksmith," Romero said curtly.

Chains clanking, Ignacio clapped his hands. "Just what I was going to say. Had to be. They need me to build, and you to forge."

"Build and forge what?"

"A new mission."

Romero's impatience dissolved. God had heard his prayers! Father Xavier . . .

"A new Franciscan mission," Ignacio said.

"Franciscan? But what about the Jesuits?"

Ignacio's wave caused his chains to rattle. "Holy Mother, the Black Robes left California a year ago. Where have you been?'

A year ago? Father Xavier, gone a year?

"Don't tell me you've been in prison that long? You poor fool. Where?"

"I–I don't know."

"You don't know where you were in prison?"

"Loreto. But I don't know where Fath . . ." He let the sentence die without an end. His problems were his own, not for discussing with strangers.

"Alta California," Ignacio said.

"What?"

"The new mission is in Alta California. That's where we're headed."

Romero stared at the darker shape that was Ignacio. His mouth felt suddenly dry, and he could not move. Whenever Father Xavier's fellow Black Robes had stayed at La Purisíma, invariably the conversation turned to Alta California, that vast, unexplored tract of Spanish territory lying on El Oceano Pacífico far to the north. Father Xavier's dream–indeed the dream of all the Jesuits of New Spain–was to one day push their chain of missions into Alta California, to bring the savage races who dwelt there to the Mother Church and to God's salvation.

With Father Xavier, Romero would have done anything, gone anywhere. But he was alone now, and Alta California was the last place he intended to go. He needed to find his beloved Father Xavier and reconcile with him, not sail off to some outpost from which he might never return.

"We leave at dawn," Ignacio said.

The words levered Romero to his feet.

"Where do you think you're going?'

"Got to get out . . ." His sentence died with a moan as his hurt leg buckled under his weight.

The hatch slammed open. A man peered down, then yelled over his shoulder, "Those damn soldiers never do anything right. They left the new one free. You two, get down there and chain him!"

Before Romero could sit up, a pair of sailors jumped down and took charge of Romero's bonds, yanking him to the bulkhead next to Ignacio and fastening his chains to a stout iron ring.

Once they left, Romero tugged and jerked at his bonds, searching for signs of weakness.

"Don't waste your energy, blacksmith. Believe me, I know."

Ignacio's words goaded Romero. He kicked and yanked to no

avail.

Ignacio clucked. "Me, I've accepted my fate. Alta California, the chance to build a new mission. Who knows? Perhaps I won't end up in Purgatory after all."

"I'd rather rot in Hell," Romero rasped.

From up on deck came a command for the two men in the hold to shut up. Ignacio nodded toward the hatch and whispered, "If you don't quiet down, you'll get your chance to do just that, blacksmith. You won't be the first–or the last–to settle on the seabed in a chain suit."

Romero stopped struggling. He couldn't die. Not yet. Not until he found Father Xavier–and Nemesio.

Chapter 3

Ignacio was right. *San Carlos* set sail the next morning. From the movement of sun across the cracks in the decking over his head, Romero could tell the ship was moving south. From the size of the swells, he guessed the captain was keeping in sight of land.

A series of sudden lurches the next day sent men scrambling up the masts. From the shouts, Romero concluded that the ship had encountered a problem.

Moments later, Romero and Ignacio were released from their chains and dragged up on deck. Ignacio pointed to the cape of land off the stern. "That's the tip of Lower California, Cabo San Lucas. We have to round it to head north to Alta California." He glanced up at the tell-tales in the rigging. "And it looks like we're in for trouble."

Trouble was exactly what they had. As Ignacio, who had sailed for two years, explained it, the winds were wrong. Instead of filling the sails, they were blowing contrary, which would force the ship to tack far to the north and west. "Which means we'll run out of food and water long before we reach Alta California. If you're a praying man, blacksmith, you best start now asking God to turn the wind or . . ." The rest of his sentence went unspoken.

Besides the crew, *San Carlos* carried a Franciscan friar, Brother Parron, a surgeon, Don Pedro Prat, and a squad of twenty-five Catalan soldiers with their leader, Lieutenant Pedro Fages, in addition to a heavy load of supplies bound for the new mission. Despite many prayers, including Romero's, the winds did not change.

By the middle of March, the crew's rations had been cut by three-quarters and the ship was down to two kegs of water. Then the winds died completely with no land in sight. A bad situation turned even worse when the mate tapped one of the last two water barrels to find it empty. Its contents had leaked into the bilges through an undetected crack in its bottom.

The news raced through the crew like fire through dry grass. That night few men slept.

The next day Romero was hanging on the fringes of the Catalans, eavesdropping on their conversations, a practice he had begun after his release from the hold, when one of the soldiers complained that his front teeth felt loose. Immediately Romero moved away to stand near Ignacio. The carpenter habitually occupied a narrow space between the cabin door and a stack of lashed-down boxes. The minute Ignacio vacated the spot to relieve himself over the side, Romero wedged himself into the space and stayed there, keeping as far away from the rest of the crew as he could manage. He had no intention of dying from *escorbuto* scurvy, like his soldier father. Ignacio would have to find another place to be, would have to take his own chances.

Over the next four days, half the crew came down with scurvy symptoms, including two whose legs swelled to the point they could not get up off the deck. From his place apart, Romero watched the Franciscan and the doctor move about, trying to offer comfort. There was precious little they could do. A few might live, but most would die. That was the way of *escorbuto* once it took hold of a ship.

An air of increasing dread shrouded the ship as, daily, their supply of water and healthy crewmen shrank. Everyone knew that if they didn't spot land, soon, the ship and all its crew would be lost.

That was the situation when a shout echoed from the crow's nest, "Land ho!"

From his cramped refuge, Romero squinted in the direction of the watch's pointing arm. There on the horizon off the starboard bow lay the dark hump of an island.

Captain Vila barked out the names of two still-healthy crewmen, then yelled "Romero!" By now, Romero had witnessed too many ship-board lashings to hesitate. He hurried to the captain as fast as his wounded leg would allow.

The mate directed him and the other two crewmen in lowering the launch over the side and loading it with empty water barrels.

Romero had never been at ease around the ocean. Except for *San Carlos* and the ship that transported him to La Paz, he had never left land. Now, facing the prospect of rowing the small launch through seas that rolled and heaved like some agitated beast, he feared that he would not survive the journey to the island.

Cold saltwater splashed over the gunwale of the small boat into his face, bringing him back to reality. "No, by the Virgin, I will survive. And I'll find a way to escape," he muttered.

"What's that, blacksmith?" the mate asked.

Romero answered by taking hold of his oar and falling into cadence with the others.

After so long at sea, Romero's legs had to adapt to being on land again. His first view of the island, called Cedros, squashed the hint of any hope he might have had to escape here from *San Carlos* and Alta California. For as far as he could see, the ground was rocky and barren. The few thin plants that dotted the landscape grew low to the ground. Anything taller would have been sheared off by the blasting wind. The island was a desert, surrounded by sea.

The mate stood with his back to Romero and the two crewmen, hands on hips, surveying their surroundings. He turned to face them. "I was afraid of this. Well, we'll have to make do. Romero, you help me. You other two, scout around and see if you can find any fresh water. Even a trickle." He stabbed the air in two directions to show where he wanted the men to look. "Don't go getting any funny ideas either. The man who isn't here by noon will taste my bullet when I find him. *When*, not if." He patted the pistol stuck in his waistband for emphasis.

The two crewmen took off, and the mate turned back to Romero. "Drag that barrel over here. Let's see if we can find a *batequi*."

Romero followed the mate to a dry stream bed. Just back from the wash of the surf, the two men cleared the rocks from a patch of sand, then dug out handful after handful of earth until, between them, they had excavated a pit into which water began to ooze.

Relief painted the mate's drawn face, and he waved at Romero. "Go on, taste it. It'll be brackish, but it's wet and fresh."

Romero hesitated, sure the mate was pulling some nasty trick on him.

"Go on, damn ye," the mate demanded impatiently. "Got to keep ye alive, Captain's orders."

Romero tentatively scooped a palmful and sipped. His nose

wrinkled involuntarily at the brine smell, but he was too thirsty to care. When the first mouthful proved fresh, he couldn't scoop and drink fast enough.

"Take 'er slow, or she'll come back up on ye," the mate said.

Romero complied. When he had drunk his fill, he stood aside and let the mate drink.

"Nothing to do now but wait," the mate said. "This will take awhile, too. No sense both of us staying here." He glanced up at the position of the sun, then nodded off to the left. "You might as well look over that direction, in case we missed something better. But be back at noon, or else."

Romero limped off before the mate had a chance to change his mind, and he didn't stop until he put a sizable distance between them. Then he swept the terrain, eyes narrowed against the glare, looking for signs of life or a place to hide.

Nothing. Just sand and rocks and the usual desert plants, scoured by a hot dry wind.

Still he would not give up. He limped onward.

Nothing changed. Not the sand or the rocks or the blinding sun or the scorching wind.

He was about to turn back when his ears detected a noise like peas shaken in a gourd. Just in time he leaped backwards, out of reach of the fangs of a striking rattlesnake.

Realizing how close he had come to disaster, Romero limped hurriedly away before the snake had the chance to launch another attack. He was looking over his shoulder when a half-exposed rock caught his right foot, tripped him and sent him sprawling face down into the sand. The fall knocked the air out of his lungs.

There he lay, gasping and coughing until he recovered enough to get to his knees. Out of the corner of his eye he spotted something purplish-red in color partially buried in the sand. The object turned out to be the remnants of the husk of a *pitahaya* cactus fruit. From the hue, he knew the husk was fresh, probably dropped by some small animal, perhaps also fleeing the rattlesnake. That left him puzzled. As close as he could figure, it was now March and *pitahayas* set fruit in the fall. How could such a thing happen?

The question dragged his mind to La Purísima and Father Xavier. It had been Father's conviction that *pitahaya* fruit could cure scurvy, but he had never had the chance to prove it. Still, anything was worth a try at this point.

Scrambling to his feet, he searched the landscape for the spreading arms of the *pitahaya* cactus.

Nothing.

"It has to be here. It has to be!" he muttered, kicking at a clod of dirt in frustration.

At that instant, a cloud crossed the sun. With the bright glare dimmed, he spotted a depression in the terrain off to his left.

Investigating, he found that the depression was, in reality, the lip of a narrow canyon. As he tried to decide whether to chance a descent, the earth gave way under his feet.

A cascade of rocks and sand swept him along, depositing him at the bottom of the ravine. He had to blink the sand out of his eyes before he could see anything, but what he saw made him forget the aches and pains he had accumulated getting to this place.

There, in a shaded notch in the canyon wall, grew three small *pitahayas*, sparsely covered with ripe fruit. He dragged himself hand over hand up the steep canyon wall and wedged his body against a boulder in order to knock the fruit of the first cactus down with a stick.

Denuding the plant, he gorged on the fruit. He was chewing the last bite of the last piece when he glanced up at the sky.

The sun was close to zenith. Time to get back to the mate, or suffer the consequences.

Romero pulled himself up to the next cactus and filled his pockets with as much fruit as he could carry. If anyone asked about it, he would make up some lie, claim the fruit was for a poultice for his leg wound. There was no reason to let anyone else know what he had in mind. He was taking care of himself. Let the others do the same.

IV

FIRST CONTACT
April—August, 1769

Chapter 1
Mid-April, 1769—The Kumeyaay Village of Nipaguay

After a long time of hunger, the elders of Nipaguay at last led their people east to the mountains to gather acorns. Weak as they were, the band took twice as long to make the journey as the year before, yet they survived the trek–all but the two weakest children. Throughout the long walk, Web worried about her own babies, but they fared better than some of the adults.

They arrived in the mountains to find that the *neshaaw* black oaks had failed to set fruit. They had to glean what they could from the less desirable *'esnyaaw* live oaks and *'ehwap* scrub oaks which had already been picked over by other bands whose hunger had driven them to move to the common gathering grounds early.

The sparseness of the harvest and the hunting kept Nipaguay in the mountains many suns longer than usual. To feed everyone, the women turned to digging for grubs and grinding some of their new acorns to supplement the scant amount of meat the hunters managed to bring to the cooking pots. Web and Hummingbird worked side by side every day, each with one of the twins slung across her back. Web longed to show off the *ha'waak* to her parents and the members of her former band. However, the people of Hawi did not appear, and she began to worry that the great storm had also affected the desert regions and her former band. She would not allow herself to think of what might have happened to her parents as a result of the storm. Such thoughts would have been too much to bear along with all the sadness and worry that already weighed upon her.

At last the time came to leave the mountains. When they returned to Nipaguay, the ocean water had washed away the muddy fan and some of the usual fish and seabirds had returned to their local feeding grounds. Just as welcome were the many rabbits and quail the village children caught the day after the people resettled into their 'ewaas. So the mood of the people was up on upswing when Casts No Shadow and Shadow Dancer went off to sing Sun awake from His long winter's journey into the realms of Night. As the two shamans made their way back to Nipaguay, village hunters brought down two deer. The pair arrived to find the band preparing for a celebration, a dance of gratitude to the spirits for these blessings.

Gradually, over the summer, the haunting look of hunger left the peoples' eyes. Eight moons after their return from the mountains, the great storm and the starving time that followed began to move into the realm of memory and story. Most were anxious to forget those hard times.

Not Casts No Shadow.

As wekuseyaay, he had the duty to remember. Like a weaver of baskets adding a strand of deer grass into a coil, he wove the experience of the starving time into the story of the people that he carried in his memory. That tale stretched far back into the mists of time to the days when One Above first formed humans out of the river mud. That tale was the last piece of information he would pass on to Shadow Dancer for his son's shamanic training. It was the most precious of all the knowledge he possessed because it linked the band directly to the gods and contained all the guidance the people needed to lead lives of harmony and respect for all things.

After moons of watching for signs that Shadow Dancer had fallen back under Crooked Basket's spell, Casts No Shadow was convinced that the kwaipai's wife no longer had power over his son. So, he had made a decision while sitting under the new *wisal* at his son's lodge, smoking a pipe of tree tobacco mixed with manzanita, watching Web play with the twins who were now one summer old. He would pass the peoples' story on to Shadow Dancer at *hellyatai*, the summer solstice. The sounds of baby laughter combined with the pleasure of the tobacco to reassure him in his choice.

He smiled now, stretched his legs out in front of him and settled his back against the sun-warmed boulder to prepare another pipe and think about his grandsons. Their curiosity caused him to see everything with new eyes. He wished he could–

"Father!"

Shadow Dancer's shout from the path leading into the main part of Nipaguay dragged Casts No Shadow back from his far-away thoughts.

"Father, the giant canoe! It has come back!" Shadow Dancer yelled.

Casts No Shadow put aside his pipe and got to his feet. One of the tales from the past that the people requested from him most often was the account of a huge canoe that had appeared on the nearby ocean one day long ago. The canoe was filled with men with sand-colored skin and hair thick as beasts on their faces and heads. Some of the men wore on their heads and attached to their sides devices that reflected the sun like still water in the afternoon. According to the story, these hairy men possessed many wondrous things, but they had sailed away before any serious trading could be conducted.

"The canoe has many white wings, each one spreading wider than those of our brother condor," Shadow Dancer said. "Just like the story."

"With the sign of the crossed sticks?" Casts No Shadow asked.

"Yes, in red."

The hair on the wekuseyaay's arms bristled. Since the hungry time, he had made certain the people conducted the proper ceremonies to propitiate the spirits. Perhaps the gods themselves had come as a result.

"I must see this thing," he said. "Come."

Casts No Shadow stopped paddling first. "This is far enough."

Shadow Dancer pulled in his paddle, although the set to his back announced that he wanted to row all the way out to the giant canoe.

Waves lapped against the rush bundles of the tule canoe as the wekuseyaay studied the strange vessel. The odd craft had folded its wings like a bird at rest. It was even larger than he had imagined.

A sudden chill washed over him, bringing with it the image of the Spirit of the Rattling Serpent and the ominous cloud that had hung behind the twins in his vision. The cloud that had hidden the future from his sight.

"You could see better if we moved closer," Shadow Dancer offered.

"No."

Shadow Dancer glanced around.

It required Casts No Shadow's full effort to control the dread that threatened to stifle his voice. "No closer. No."

"But the stories, the things that the hairy men possessed . . ."

"I sense only evil here. Turn back, my son."

Frustration showed in the set of Shadow Dancer's jaw. There was disappointment in his voice as he replied, "Yes, Father."

By the time their craft reached the beach, Casts No Shadow felt calmer. "You go back to the village. I must talk to the spirits."

While his son beached the tule canoe and headed for the village, Casts No Shadow took one last look at the giant canoe. The hairy men had not stayed long before. Perhaps this time they would also leave soon. *Great Serpent, let that be what you will show me.*

Chapter 2

Web eased herself down beside her favorite milling hole. She filled the hole with acorns from her basket and set to work crushing them into flour. Around her the other women chattered endlessly about the giant canoe. Web kept her head down and tried to ignore the conversation.

Since its arrival seven suns back, the giant canoe was all anyone seemed to talk about. No one had seen Casts No Shadow since the canoe came, and Shadow Dancer too had gone off, telling Web, "I will return when I have the answer."

She did not bother to ask what the question was. She didn't have to. The only question anyone seemed to ask anymore was why the giant canoe had come.

The giant canoe. She was sick of the subject. If only the mysterious boat would sail away, then life could return to normal.

Hummingbird's nudge brought her out of her reverie. Hummingbird nodded toward Crooked Basket plodding toward the river with two water ollas in hand. She flapped her elbows. "Quack-quack."

Web stifled a laugh. Crooked Basket's stomach was so swollen with pregnancy that she had to swing her arms wide to the sides for balance. So, from the rear, she resembled a waddling duck.

Hummingbird's grin fell to wistfulness. "Soon her baby will come out to meet its mother."

Web touched her friend's arm. Hummingbird longed for a child of her own, but, so far, none grew in her belly.

At the river Crooked Basket squatted clumsily and, hanging on to the edge of a boulder for balance, filled one olla, then the other. The sight raised sympathy in Web. Since the scene in the hidden copse last summer, Crooked Basket had ceased to make a difference in Web's life, either positive or negative.

Movement among the rocks above the river drew her attention away from the kwaipai's wife. A man sporting a red horn of hair on his head was climbing down to the village. "My father returns. He will be hungry," Web said, hastily gathering up the ground flour.

Hummingbird pointed in the opposite direction. "And so will he."

Web instantly recognized the familiar smooth gait of Shadow Dancer, hurrying along the path from the ocean.

Hummingbird scooped the flour from her grinding hole and put it in Web's basket. "Here. Take this. I can finish grinding the rest of your nuts."

Web gave her a quick hug of thanks, then hurried up the ravine to her lodge. She was busy at the cooking fire when the men arrived.

Casts No Shadow got there first. He sagged wearily down in the shade of the *wisal*. His face looked drawn and haggard. His red horn drooped to one side.

Shadow Dancer looked vibrant by contrast. "Father, I have talked with the spirits. They revealed that the giant canoe comes with many wonders for our people. They told me it is time to meet the men who sail it in order that we might trade with them."

"I too have spoken with the spirits," Casts No Shadow said quietly.

"Then we will go together tomorrow," Shadow Dancer said.

The wekuseyaay shook his head tiredly. "No, my son."

"Then, we go now?"

"Not now. Not tomorrow."

"When?"

Casts No Shadow merely shook his head.

"But the spirits said . . ."

"The hairy men with the pale skins will not stay. Soon they will sail away."

"Then we must go to them, or—"

Casts No Shadow's hand slashed the air. "We must do *nothing* except allow the strange men to leave."

Casts No Shadow's angry tone sent a shiver down Web's spine. Why did he not say outright what he had learned from the spirits?

Shadow Dancer drew himself up to full height, turned on his heel and stomped off without a word. Web looked after him. She had never before witnessed him disagree with his father.

A few moments later the wekuseyaay heaved himself to his feet and stalked away to his lodge.

Web looked from son to father to son in bewilderment. She did not understand what she had just witnessed, but whatever was going on between the two men, she wanted it resolved. And soon.

She rose to her feet and faced west, toward the ocean where the giant canoe lay at anchor, a brooding presence that had brought nothing but upset to her and the village. "Please go back where you came from," she said aloud.

Chapter 3

Romero stood hunched at the railing of *San Carlos* facing into the cold wind in an effort to escape the charnel smells of sickness on the ship. It had been a month since Cedros Island. In that time, scurvy had ravaged the crew. Already two had died and were buried at sea. Sick crewmen littered the deck moaning in pain whenever they had to move. Only a handful remained healthy.

Romero had consumed the last of his concealed pitahaya fruit two days ago. Now nothing stood between him and a hideous death. Shuddering, he lifted his eyes to the tossing waves to avoid seeing the grotesquely swollen legs and the flesh spotted with the purple blotches characteristic of the disease that surrounded him.

"Romero!" The shout belonged to the first mate Jorge Estorace. The blacksmith had to pick his way around a dozen prone men in various stages of scurvy to get to the mate at the wheel.

"Captain wants someone aloft to look for the entrance to the bay. You're it," Estorace said.

One glance up at the crow's nest caused Romero's heart to beat faster. "I–I can't."

"You can and you will."

Romero looked up again. At the top of the main-mast, the small platform swayed and dipped like a butterfly clinging to the end of a reed in a wind storm. He felt beads of sweat break out along his hairline. "M–my leg."

"A little limp won't stop you. Now move!" Estorace ordered.

Looking up at the top of the swaying mast, Romero struggled to swallow. Panic made his legs leaden. He could not move.

The mate drew his pistol. "Now, blacksmith."

With his options cut off, Romero moved to the Jacob's ladder.

Estorace followed, poking the barrel of the pistol into Romero's ribs. "Now."

Romero grabbed the slimy rope with sweaty hands and hauled himself up. On the first rung, his bare foot slipped, and his body slammed into the gunwale.

Estorace jammed the pistol into Romero's buttocks. "Don't you know anything? Use your toes."

Romero started over, this time gripping the rope with his toes. Success.

"Don't just stand there. Move!" The mate cracked the pistol against Romero's ankle bone.

Romero grimaced at the pain but dragged in a ragged breath and climbed up two rungs. The ladder flexed and swayed under each shift of his weight.

Estorace yelled up, "Whatever you do, blacksmith, don't look down."

Romero scrambled up two more rungs. Moving higher, ropes flexing, swaying.

"Faster!" the mate yelled. "We don't have all day."

Three, then four rungs. With each one, Romero repeated a silent admonition. *Use your toes. Don't look down.*

He was halfway up when the freshening wind swung around to the opposite direction. He was in the midst of a step when his whole world tilted on its axis. He reacted by planting his feet.

Both slipped.

His legs plunged through the rope mesh, jamming his crotch painfully against the spines of the rough hemp. Below him, the deck littered with bodies looked impossibly far away, too far to ever reach again in safety. Fear held him rigid, immobilized.

On the deck, the mate took aim on Romero with the pistol and dropped the hammer. When the ball whistled past the blacksmith's ear, the mate swore loudly and started to reload.

Anger replaced Romero's fear. "Oh, no, you don't!" he muttered toward Estorace. "You won't kill me, you bastard. Nothing will kill me. Not after all I've been through."

Despite his quivering knees, he forced himself to stand and started to climb. With every rung, he whispered, "Not me. Not yet."

At last he reached the crow's nest and clambered shakily into the little basket, relieved to have something solid to support him after the constantly flexing ladder. Stinging sweat clouded his vision. He closed his eyes and fought against the temptation to think about the climb down.

A familiar screech startled him into opening his eyes. A seagull wheeled on the wind, eyeing him curiously.

A seagull . . . a seagull . . .

The bird glided away, drawing Romero's gaze with it. It took a few moments for him to comprehend that the gull was headed toward a headland that guarded what looked to be the entrance to a bay. Land meant he could get off this death ship.

"Land ho!" he cried, his voice cracking, and pointed to the headland.

Estorace waved and immediately swung the ship's bow. Then he shouted, "Come on down, blacksmith."

Romero pretended not to hear. He was beyond the range of the pistol. There was no reason to move from such a secure perch until they were in calmer waters. No reason to spend any more time than he had to among all those sick men. He'd go back down when he was ready, and not a minute before.

Although she had lived at Nipaguay for nearly two summers, the ocean still frightened Web. She never approached it alone. Even in the company of others, she had to fight the urge to run away from the thundering waves. She knew, however, that if she ever wanted to feel completely at home here, she must overcome her fear. To that end, she always went along whenever Hummingbird gathered shellfish.

On this day, the two women came to one of Hummingbird's favorite spots. Over time Web had developed a taste for the mussels they found only in that place. That appetite helped quell her discomfort at being so close to the relentless ebb and flow of the foaming surf.

Before she bent to the digging, she looked out toward the giant canoe. The boat lay in the shelter of the rock massif that protected the entrance to the bay, the same place it had sat since it arrived. The sight of the strange vessel troubled Web. Casts No Shadow and Shadow Dancer had not spoken to each other since their quarrel over what the spirits had told them concerning the vessel. "Go away," she muttered at the boat under her breath.

"What did you say, my sister?" Hummingbird asked from the spot where she had erected a low arch of brush to keep the sun off the twins, sleeping in their propped-up cradleboards.

"I am hungry for shelled fish," Web lied.

Hummingbird laughed. "Then we shall dig a basketful or two."
They set to work, digging in the wet sand until Web's burden
basket overflowed. "Is that enough, my sis . . ."

Web turned to see why Hummingbird had stopped talking. She
found her friend staring out at the ocean where a second giant
canoe was gliding through the entrance of the bay toward the
first.

"Wings like a white swan," Hummingbird said, her words colored
with awe.

Web could not take her eyes off the two vessels. Casts No
Shadow had said that the giant canoe would leave, that no
Kumeyaay must approach it, but he had said nothing about a
second boat. She was suddenly afraid. "We have to get back."

"But, my sister, we aren't finished," Hummingbird complained.

"Now. We have to get back now." Web did not wait for her
friend to respond. Looping the burden net around the basket of
mussels, she knotted the ends of the net over her protective cap,
then scooped up Sand Flea's cradleboard and hurried off toward
Nipaguay, leaving Hummingbird and Cricket to catch up.

Chapter 4

Two days after he had sighted the entrance to the bay, Romero
found himself in a launch headed for his second landfall
since leaving La Paz five months before. Behind him, *San Carlos*
lay next to her sister ship, *San Antonio*. With him on the launch
were the last two healthy crewmen from *San Carlos*.

Before they left the ship, Ignacio had looked up at Romero
from where he lay on the deck because his feet were too swollen
from scurvy to support him, and asked accusingly through puffy
lips, "Why you, blacksmith? Why are you spared when I am
struck down?"

Romero did not answer. He had managed to keep his secret this
long, so why give it away now? Especially to a man who would
likely die soon and be thrown into an ocean grave to be forever
forgotten?

"You there! Watch that oar. I won't be splashed!" yelled
Lieutenant Pedro Fages, the haughty leader of a squad of soldiers
who had come north on *San Carlos*. According to the crew, the
soldiers were there to provide military protection for the new
mission. But Romero saw them in a different light. The Society

of Jesus had collected sizable amounts called the Pious Fund to support their missions in New Spain. Over the last few years he had overheard many angry conversations at La Purísima between Father Xavier and visiting Jesuits over the Crown's misappropriation of monies from the Pious Fund to support non-religious efforts, particularly the military. It was Father Xavier's contention that the Spanish King was more interested in establishing military garrisons in New Spain than founding missions. Romero ached to be able to tell the padre in person that he was right.

"Curse you, man! Stop splashing me!" Lieutenant Fages roared at the seaman manning the starboard oar.

The lieutenant was a posturing martinet whose family connections had gotten him this commission. Romero had listened to hours of Father Xavier's rantings against the monarchy and its corruption. Looking at the lieutenant, he began to see what Father meant.

Between *San Carlos* and *San Antonio*, there were not enough healthy crewmen to manage one ship. Romero had learned through eavesdropping that, besides the two ships, there was a third, *San José*, named for the patron saint of the entire undertaking as well as two land expeditions headed to this place. When all those forces reassembled, the expedition would break into two parts. While one group established a mission in this place–to be called San Diego–the second group would continue north to search for a rumored second bay, called Monterey, where they would establish a second mission. So far there was no sign of either *San José* or the land parties.

"I said stop!" Fages shouted, slamming his palm down on the thwart in front of him.

"Sit down, lieutenant!" yelled Costanzo, *San Carlos's* engineer.

Surprisingly, Fages obeyed, though he continued to glare at the offending oarsman.

The closer the launch drew to the beach, the more Romero's mood drooped. It looked as barren as Cedros Island. *For this? I have stayed alive for this?* his soul railed as the launch nosed into the beach and Romero climbed out into the surf to help drag the boat up onto the sand.

The shore party split into two groups, heading in opposite directions to look for water to fill the ship's barrels. Romero found himself in the group with Lieutenant Fages. He grabbed the rear end of one of the empty barrels and stuck to the back of the group in order to stay out of the lieutenant's line of sight.

A long hour's walk later, the group came to a fresh-water creek emptying into the ocean. Putting aside his despair, Romero joined the others, drinking until he could hold no more. In all his life, after so long at sea forced to drink stagnant water, nothing had ever tasted sweeter.

The men filled their barrels and started back to the launch. They had almost reached the launch where the other party was already waiting when the man carrying the front end of Romero's barrel halted abruptly, causing Romero to stumble. "Indios!" the man gasped.

Romero looked over the barrel to see a large group of naked brown-skinned men standing on a knoll of sand perhaps twenty varas away.

Immediately, all conversation ceased.

One of the dark men walked a few steps toward the other barrel-carriers and began shouting. He punctuated his words with jabs from a stone-tipped lance. All the natives were armed. Romero did not even have a knife. He suddenly felt exposed and vulnerable.

Lieutenant Fages stepped forward and assumed a command posture. "From the King of Spain, we bring you greetings."

The dark man's shouts doubled in volume, and he leaped into the air at random intervals, brandishing his lance at the lieutenant.

Fages stood his ground. "This land belongs to the King. You are his subjects."

En masse, the dark men erupted into a screaming, threatening mob. Everywhere Romero looked, he saw weapons poised to strike him.

Fages turned back to the group. There was no hint of fear in his eyes or stance. "Withdraw to the launch."

Romero did not wait for a second command. He hurried to the boat as fast as his burden and partner would allow. He was not aware that he had been holding his breath until the launch was almost back to the ships.

"Close one, eh?" someone said.

A few men laughed. Romero wasn't one of them.

Chapter 5

In the deepening gloom, Casts No Shadow crouched, waiting for darkness. Behind him, the men of Nipaguay also waited in the expectant silence, while beside him, Shadow Dancer shifted impatiently. Since the arrival of the second giant canoe, the wekuseyaay had observed disturbing signs in his son, and impatience was the most troubling. More than any other trait, the man who wishes to carry the messages of the spirits to the people must possess patience, for the gods speak only when they are ready.

Earlier that day Shadow Dancer had hurried back from fishing to report that he had seen a group of the *kwelmisp* hairy men from the two vessels row to the beach. He managed to conceal himself in the sage nearby to watch them dig a large hole with two unusual digging sticks whose heads were fashioned from what he described as thin slabs of hard stone, sharpened to an edge so thin that they reflected the sun's light. The strangers deposited four bundles, each wrapped in some kind of hide, into the hole, then they performed some sort of odd ritual that involved muttering and hand signs before they refilled the hole with sand and left to return to their giant canoes.

The tale galvanized the already-curious men of Nipaguay. Shadow Dancer had no trouble convincing them to help him unearth what the pale men had buried. Casts No Shadow wanted nothing to do with these mysterious newcomers, but his years as a wekuseyaay had taught him to keep his own council until he knew what he was up against.

At last it grew dark enough for Shadow Dancer to lead the group out onto the sand to the spot he had marked with a length of braided yucca rope. Immediately, the silent men fell to scooping away sand using turtle shells and slabs of bark.

Soon they had the four bundles uncovered. Shadow Dancer climbed into the hole and, squatting, touched the hide cover of one. "So soft and pliable," he said wonderingly. "Either this comes from an animal none of us has ever seen, or some woman has more skill weaving than my wife."

"The *kwelmisps* have no women," Casts No Shadow reminded him, but the comment was lost in the buzz of conversation.

Many Rains spoke up. "Let's see what is inside." He jumped into the hole and helped Shadow Dancer unwrap the strange covering. When it came free, both men gasped and threw themselves back against the side of the hole.

It was one of the *kwelmisps*, naked and dead. His limbs and face were bloated. His toothless mouth twisted into an eternal scream. Worst of all, his pale skin had turned black and blistered like meat roasted too long in a fire.

Casts No Shadow had to struggle to keep the horror out of his voice. "Move away," he warned.

No one needed more coaxing. Shadow Dancer and Many Rains scrambled out of the hole.

The wekuseyaay looked toward the forms of the two giant canoes, lifting and swaying on the ocean swells. Only a witch–a sorcerer with great power–could turn a pale man's skin to black. Only an evil witch would bury someone rather than burn the dead husk of the body in order to release the man's soul to rejoin the spirits who dwelled as points of light in the night sky. No wonder the Great Serpent had warned him to stay away from the *kwelmisps*.

He turned back to the group. Although he could not see their faces across the darkness, he could smell their fear. He did not have to announce that there was great evil here. They knew, and they looked to him to know how to counter it.

His mind raced over all his knowledge about such sorcerers of darkness. The situation required the most sacred, the strongest of songs: the *Chaihotai*. He had never sung it in public, never had occasion to sing it, until now. There was not a moment to waste. As soon as they returned to the village, every man must purify himself in sacred smoke against the evil they had been exposed to. When that was done, he must gather all the people and lead them in the *Chaihotai*.

He threw a silent prayer into the canopy of stars. *Oh, spirits, help this one remember*.

Stepping to the lip of the hole, he lifted his voice in song:

May the gods show pity
And release your souls.
To the final village of your spirits,
May your souls find the way.

He repeated the chant three times for each of the four bodies, then stood by while the others refilled the hole. That done, Casts No Shadow led the silent, fearful group back to Nipaguay and the ceremony he prayed would keep the sorcerer's curse from invading his people.

Chapter 6

When Shadow Dancer ducked into the 'ewaa the next morning, Web awoke from a dream about what the hairy ones had buried. From the scent on his skin and hair, she knew he had been purified by smoke from the sacred fire. The tension in his voice was palpable. "Come, wife. We must sing."

She gathered the sleeping twins in their cradleboards, then followed him outside to find the entire village, except for the smallest children, gathered at the *kusich-ne-awa* ceremonial enclosure. There Casts No Shadow led them in a rite unlike any she had ever experienced. For the next three days and nights the people danced and sang, appealing to the gods to spare them from an unnamed evil. Though she wondered about the nature of the evil, she knew better than to ask, for to speak of such a thing was to manifest it.

The ceremony wore everyone out. When it ended, an eerie hush fell over Nipaguay while the people slept off their exhaustion.

The following day, still groggy from the ceremony, Web joined Hummingbird to gather grasses and herbs in the family fields. After the strain of the last several days, she welcomed the freedom to share confidences with her friend.

When they arrived back at the village late that afternoon, Shadow Dancer and Many Rains had not yet returned from their day's fishing. Web put the cooking pot on the fire and sat down to work on a new basket.

She had just wrapped the coils beginning the design when her husband appeared. Instead of a string of fish, he carried what looked like a piece of hide. To her questioning look, he held it out to her. "I traded the *kwelmisps* for it."

She pulled her hand away. "You met them?"

"The hairy ones' canoes are even bigger up close."

"You went out to the bird boats? But your father . . ."

"My father is wrong."

The determination in his eyes and the set to his jaw cut off her protest.

He pressed the hide into her hand. "You make the best baskets of all the women, yet even you cannot make such as this."

Her fingers traced the fine weave. This was no hide, rather a fine net unlike anything she had ever touched. Where did the pale ones find such thin, pliable fiber?

"The *kwelmisps* cover their bodies with this. The wings of their bird boats are made of it, too. Their canoes are filled with such things. Things that our people have never seen or imagined." Shadow Dancer reclaimed the wondrous net from her. "To possess things like this would mean power for our people. Imagine what the bands to the east would trade for such a hide."

He knelt beside her and riveted her with his gaze. "My father tells us to stay away from the hairy ones. He says they bring evil."

Web nodded. "The spirits have told him."

Shadow Dancer grasped her forearm. "Woman, he is wrong! I, too, made a journey into the land of the spirits. It is they who sent me to the giant canoes this day. It is they who told me to trade for this hide."

He tightened his grip. "I am your husband. I am 'aww-kuseyaay. Do you doubt me? Did your parents at Hawi teach you to doubt your husband?" He spat out the name of her birth band like a piece of spoiled meat.

The harshness of his tone frightened her. Ever since the disagreement between Shadow Dancer and Casts No Shadow when the hairy ones arrived, she had feared this moment would come. The moment when she would have to choose one man over the other. How could she do such a thing when she respected both men equally?

"Answer me, woman," he demanded.

She swallowed against the sudden dryness in her mouth. Her future and the future of her sons lay at stake here.

"Woman?"

"No, husband. I do not doubt you. I believe what you say, and I follow where you lead."

The anger drained from Shadow Dancer's face. He released her arm and turned to look at the sleeping babies. Out from under his direct gaze, she let herself breathe again.

"The pale ones are building a village close to Cosoy," he said over his shoulder.

Remembering the trouble she had caused when she accidentally wandered into one of that band's fields, she shifted uneasily. What were those same men liable to do to anyone who tried to establish a village on their land?

Turning back to her, Shadow Dancer yawned and stretched. "There are many sick among the *kwelmisp*. The men of Cosoy are afraid to attack the new village. Afraid there are evil sorcerers among the paleskins."

Witchcraft. That explained Casts No Shadow's sudden ceremony.

"Let them be afraid," he said, brandishing the piece of net. "Let them wait. I will use their delay to discover more secrets like this to bring back to our people."

She forced a smile. "Yes, my husband."

Chapter 7

Two days after Romero's first trip ashore, Ignacio died, delirious and screaming from the pain of the scurvy that ravaged his body. Romero hid in the hold so that he would not have to be part of the burial party. He had vowed not to set foot on the beach again until the third ship, *San José,* or the land parties arrived with reinforcements.

By now, the disease had claimed so many sailors from both ships that there weren't enough healthy men for even one partial crew. Likewise, the disease thinned the ranks of the Catalan soldiers. During this time, Romero became adept at avoiding the sick and staying apart from everyone else. With the cactus fruit gone and no sign of the land parties, he lived in constant dread of contracting the disease. He put off eating his daily ration of moldy sea biscuits until hunger forced him to bite into them. It was the first bite he dreaded for it would reveal any teeth that had come loose, the sure sign that he had the disease.

Five days after Ignacio's death, Captain Vila ordered everyone, sick and healthy, off the boats in order to occupy a fortification that Lieutenant Fages and his remaining troops had built. Romero had to go to shore despite his vow. He found a way to hang back to the last launch so that he shuttled with the captain and officers, none of whom had been touched by scurvy. Romero was too pre-occupied to wonder why this was true.

Fages's fortification turned out to be little more than a low wall of sticks and brush, enclosing a small hillock, a cannonball's shot from the two ships. While he surveyed the flimsy structure, Romero sensed that he was being watched. Turning, he saw a crowd of brown-skinned people, observing the activities of the Spanish. He did not need to count to know that the natives outnumbered them at least ten to one. He hurried into the enclosure to put a wall–any wall–between him and all those hostile eyes.

For the next two weeks, Romero felt like a caged animal. Inside the crude fort, there was no way to avoid the sick who filled the space so that he had to constantly step over bodies. Outside the fort, there was no way to avoid the watching natives.

Then one day a patrol returned from getting water to announce that the Indians had given up watching the fort. "They're used to us. We won't have any trouble from them now," one of the healthy soldiers said. Romero didn't let himself accept the man's assessment until a week passed without natives watching the fort.

Meantime, the scurvy raged on. With every passing day, Romero's desperation grew. Again and again, his mind turned to the *pitahaya* fruit he had found on Cedros Island. His first impression of this place, this San Diego, was that it was as barren as that island. However, being on land here had changed his opinion.

There was fresh water here. Plenty of it–if you knew where to look. Although he had seen no *pitahayas*, he recognized dozens of other plants that used to grow around La Purísima.

He was returning from burying another *San Carlos* sailor a few days later when his thoughts once again turned to La Purísima and Father Xavier. He recalled the conversation in which Father had told him about *pitahaya* fruit as a cure for scurvy. That had come after Romero had told the priest about the deaths of his parents. Before Father, no one had ever asked him about his family. Certainly no one had ever listened to him so intently. Relating how he had lost first his mother, then his father dredged up the pain Romero had kept hidden since he was orphaned. That pain came gushing out in a torrent of tears. Father had held him until he cried himself out, then Father talked about scurvy.

He railed at the ignorance of ship's captains who refused to believe that scurvy could be cured. Cured by plants that were readily available all across New Spain. Plants like *pitahaya* fruit and . . .

Romero's memory faltered. And what? Realizing that his life depended on remembering what the priest had said, he spent the rest of the night straining for the answer, finally falling into an exhausted slumber just before dawn.

Upon waking, he had the answer. Mallow. Pitahaya and mallow. Taking a water bucket, he walked out the gate and set off in search of the plant that would save him. He had never left the fort alone. Now he moved cautiously, alert to any signs of natives. He made his way to the last burial site, sure he had seen mallow plants there, but did not find any.

He walked two wide circles around the area before spotting one plant up a rise at the end of a line of bushes. It wasn't until he was nearly there that he realized the bushes were really domed-shaped huts. "Oh, God," he gasped, turning tail and dashing in the direction of the fort.

The toes on his right foot hooked a tangle of low vines, sending him sprawling. He leaped up and was about to take off again when, at his feet, he spotted what he had been looking for. He was ripping at the plant, tearing away handfuls of branches, when, from behind him, came a half-stifled cry of surprise.

He swung around to see a brown-skinned woman, her hands reaching protectively toward the two infants she carried on her back. She wore a skirt of fiber strings that covered her from waist to knees, but nothing covered her breasts.

Since Father Xavier insisted that the native women of La Purísima be covered from neck to ankle, Romero had not seen naked female breasts at such close proximity.

As he turned toward her, the woman's eyes grew wide and her hand flew to her mouth. For a long minute the woman and Romero stared at each other without moving.

Then a man shouted.

Whirling around, Romero saw men approaching on horseback from the south. He forgot the woman. Horses could mean only one thing: the land expedition was here at last. Now, now he would find a way home!

Web ran faster than she had ever run before. She ran in terror away from the long-legged beasts, taller than two men, that had appeared out of the morning like a terrible dream. And she ran in horror from the hairy one with the mutilated face, a second, worse nightmare.

Only, this was no dream. She had seen both things, she was sure. They were real, and she knew without knowing how that both things threatened her children, her life and her people.

Chapter 8

Terrified, Web dashed into Nipaguay bearing tales of the fantastic long-legged beasts that had come with a new group of hairy ones. Casts No Shadow went immediately to investigate. He arrived at the knoll above the pale ones' crudely built village to find Shadow Dancer and Many Rains already there. From the defiance in his son's greeting, he realized that Shadow Dancer had ignored his counsel to avoid these newcomers. If his own son defied him, his grip on the credibility of the people of Nipaguay was slipping. The day he lost their faith, his life was over.

With such distressing thoughts occupying his mind, Casts No Shadow lingered only long enough to observe that Web's "beasts" were in reality two beings: long-legged creatures, twice the size of deer, ridden by more of the *kwelmisps*. *The creatures of his vision.* He glanced at Shadow Dancer, but his son was too focused on the creatures to see anything else. With his confidence in what the spirits had revealed to him reinforced, Casts No Shadow returned to the village alone.

Throughout the next moon cycle, Shadow Dancer spent more and more time away from the village and away from his responsibilities as an apprentice shaman. Casts No Shadow noted an edginess in Web but blamed that on her husband's frequent absences.

As for his son, the wekuseyaay decided to do nothing. The pale ones would leave. The spirits had said so. And, when that happened, Shadow Dancer would recognize the error he had made. For a son destined to be a leader, such a lesson had more value than any argument from his father.

Then, a fourth group of hairy ones arrived. In addition to more of the long-legged deer-like creatures, they brought a number of shorter, stockier beasts who made loud wounded-animal sounds that carried long distances.

The news threw Casts No Shadow into confusion. More pale ones? How many of these hairy, smelly men were there? How many more would come before the spirits' prediction came true? More important, when would they leave? Questions that only the spirits could answer.

The day after the last group's arrival he was preparing to go at dawn to his sacred cave to seek out the Great Serpent when Shadow Dancer dashed into the village with news that the Brown Robes, who appeared to be shamans to the hairy ones, would conduct a ceremony the next day. Casts No Shadow immediately changed his plans. His visit to the cave would have to wait until he witnessed the pale ones' ceremony. He needed to observe these Brown Robes. Perhaps what he saw would provide clues to the sorcery of the hairy men.

He arrived with Shadow Dancer the next day to find the hairy ones gathered outside the walls of their village, kneeling in an arc before a waist-high wooden structure. The day was clear and sunny. Needlessly clothed in their usual strange and foul-smelling hides, the pale ones sweated profusely. Joining the front ranks of the watching Kumeyaay, Casts No Shadow wrinkled his nose at the repulsive stench of so much unbathed flesh and studied the objects arrayed on the top surface of the wooden structure.

The middle object glinted in the sunlight. It was formed of two long rectangular pieces of what he took to be highly-polished stone attached to a base of black rock. One piece, the width of his outstretched thumb, stood upright on the base to the height of a man's knee. A second piece, half the length of the first, was joined to the upright piece at right angles a third of the distance down from its top. At the point of juncture, a lump of another substance was attached. By squinting, he saw that this last object was shaped like a man with his arms outstretched along the crosspiece and his legs crooked against the vertical support.

The sight dredged up a long-forgotten memory from the depths of Casts No Shadow's mind. Soon after his uncle had taken him to apprentice, they had journeyed deep into the eastern desert for a council of shamans. Thrilled to be allowed to go, he paid little heed to his uncle's warnings about the dangers they would face. The thrill vanished, however, when their path led them into the scene of a recent battle. There, tied onto the upright arms of a giant grandmother cactus was the rotting body of a man, entrails spilling from a gaping slash that ran from his neck to his crotch. Scavenging birds had shredded the man's intestines and pecked out his eyes.

At that one brief glance Casts No Shadow's stomach rebelled. That image had haunted his dreams for dozens of suns until he learned to control the dreamtime. Now the image, and the horror, returned, disconcerting him.

Shadow Dancer nudged him. "The chief of the Brown Robes," he whispered, pointing to the first of two men who emerged from one of the hairy men's sorry huts. Both men were dressed in white, instead of the brown that gave them their name. Casts No Shadow studied the first one.

Unlike the other paleskins, this one's round face was smooth and hairless, making his skin seem even paler. On his head, a short band of hair encircled his skull, leaving the top bald and vulnerably pink.

This leader of the Brown Robes launched into the ceremony. Casts No Shadow studied his every action and listened closely to his songs, taking careful note of the responses of the second Brown Robe and the gathered hairy ones. He was especially intrigued by a hide bundle that also lay on the wooden platform. Several times during the rite, the Brown Robe leader opened the bundle which appeared to be a stack of skins, each as thin and transparent as threads of a spider's web and covered with strange symbols. This stack of skins was bound together on one side between stiff pieces of another kind of hide.

Casts No Shadow suspected that this bundle was the source of the paleskins' witchcraft. Part of him longed to steal the bundle, to study it and absorb its power; but another part of him resisted the urge, at least until he talked with the Spirit of the Rattling Serpent.

"The pale ones still have no women," Shadow Dancer observed.

Casts No Shadow grunted. He had accepted that there were no women on the hairy ones' canoes since women of his own people were forbidden to touch a man's boat and his hunting or fishing tools because the power that belonged to all women–the power to bring forth life–would bring harm to the owner. Yet, the last two groups of paleskins had arrived by land. Surely they needed women to prepare their camps and food and to share their beds. All clans of creatures had both male and female. If these hairy ones did not have women, did that mean that One Above had created some new kind of being?

Another nudge from Shadow Dancer pulled Casts No Shadow's mind back from its thoughts to see that the Brown Robe leader had begun to move out into the assembled group, cradling an object in his arms. As he passed, each of the hairy ones ducked his head, made a sign with his hand and murmured something. Intrigued, Casts No Shadow had to wait for the leader of the Brown Robes to turn around to see what he carried: two figures carved from a single piece of wood: a paleskin mother and her baby.

Between the newcomer's lack of women and their obvious veneration of this carved female figure, the wekuseyaay did not know what to think.

When he got back to Nipaguay, Casts No Shadow had so many bewildering questions that he collected the things he needed to meet with the Great Serpent and hurried for his cave.

Chapter 9

Romero deposited the sack of *pulse* he carried on top of a stack of similar bags of corn and beans. Climbing down into *San Antonio*'s hold had revived his memories of the terrible 110-day voyage aboard *San Carlos* that got him to this god-forsaken place. Regardless, he had the overpowering urge to hide out here in the darkness, to be carried north when *San Antonio* raised anchor later this morning. He fought down the urge. Although San Diego had become a prison worse than the dungeon he had shared with Noche in Loreto, going north took him farther away from his goal. He had to go south. South to Loreto and Father Xavier's trail.

He punched a sack of corn. Patience. I must have patience, he reminded himself.

"Blacksmith? Where are you?" Estorace, the mate, yelled from the deck above.

Romero's shoulders sagged as if he still bore the weight of the pulse. Already he had been missed. There would be no hiding for him. "Patience," he muttered as he started up the ladder for the deck, the sunshine and the launch back to the beach.

Web stood beside Hummingbird on the promontory above the river valley and watched the wings of the *kwelmisps'* giant canoe bear it out into the ocean. At last, some of the pale men were leaving.

Cricket tottered after a lizard. Web watched Hummingbird trail after her energetic son. Cradling the board holding the sleeping Sand Flea against her hip, Web smiled at the sight of her friend and her son. What would she do without Hummingbird to help her with the twins?

For the last two moons–since the night Shadow Dancer had forced her to declare support for his position regarding the hairy ones–he had spent every day, from dawn to dusk, away from the village. Every night he returned with stories about the pale men, instead of fish or game to contribute to the village's larder.

Shadow Dancer had always hunted and fished with Many Rains. That allowed each of them to give his catch or take to the other in accordance with Kumeyaay custom. Many Rains still saw to it that Web always had fish or game, but she worried that her husband was shirking his responsibility toward his best friend and hers. She worried even more about the deep and growing rift between her husband and Casts No Shadow. For two long, exhausting moons she had prayed that the spirits would send the *kwelmisps* away. The sight of the white wings now spreading out to carry the giant canoe into the open sea thrilled her as few things ever had.

"Such a big smile, my sister. Do you have a secret to tell little Hummingbird?" her friend asked, gently depositing Cricket on the ground to chase after the next thing that caught his attention.

Web laughed. Her friend was continually on the watch for signs of a new pregnancy. "No secrets. Just happiness."

Hummingbird smiled back, but disappointment shadowed her eyes. Web reached out to smooth her friend's cheek. Hummingbird yearned for a child of her own. If only the spirits would grant her one.

The moment between them ended when Cricket took off after a grasshopper. In a wink Hummingbird went after him.

Web looked from the disappearing boat to the one that remained. *All of you go. I want my husband, and my life, back. Leave. Go soon.*

Chapter 10

R omero pulled the ragged blanket tighter around his hunched shoulders and sighed for the benefit of anyone watching. He had to keep up the subterfuge of illness for at least one more day. A half dozen convalescing sailors and soldiers slumped all along the outside wall that surrounded the makeshift compound. Romero was not about to give up his spot in the shade. Otherwise, hot as it was, he would have to discard the blanket–and the blanket was key to his performance.

Donkeys' braying and angry shouts drew his attention to the milling crowd of men and animals, preparing for their journey. One of the donkeys had bucked off its pack and two men were scrambling to subdue the protesting animal and restore the load. The rest of the entourage watched in bored amusement but made no move to help.

To the rear of the excitement stood a small group of men–Don Portola, Governor of California and military commander of the expedition now preparing to leave, and his officers. The gleaming buttons and freshly-brushed wool of these men's uniforms stood in sharp contrast to the smudged and fraying dress of their men and the filthy, worn clothing of the muleteers and Christianized Indians from Lower California come to colonize the second Alta California mission who comprised the bulk of the group.

Urselino, a recuperating carpenter, limped out the entrance of the compound and sprawled on the ground next to Romero. "Wish I was healthy enough to go with them," Urselino said.

Romero grunted. The last thing he needed today was conversation.

"Finding the Bay of Monterey. Now that would be a story to tell my grandchildren," continued the carpenter.

Romero grunted again, leaning away from the talkative man, hoping to change the direction of the conversation–better yet, to end it all together.

"Too bad we're both stuck here," Urselino said. "Sure would rather go north with the Governor than sit around this barren sweat-hole for who knows how long."

Romero hunched deeper into his blanket. Staying in San Diego was exactly what he wanted. Even if the new expedition traveled over land rather than by ship, even one day's journey north was one day further from Loreto.

"Months. We might be here for months." Urselino curtailed his sigh when Governor Portola and company broke their huddle at the appearance of the leader of the Franciscans, Father Serra, and the two brothers who were to found a second mission at Monterey.

Serra's hands darted and swooped against the background of his brown robe, illustrating his words, punctuating his points and holding the rapt attention of his two companions and everyone else who got drawn under their spell. The only part of the Franciscan that moved quicker than his hands were his feet. It was rumored that he could outlast and outdistance a horse on a week's trek.

Serra had come to San Diego two weeks ago with the second land expedition. Since then, Romero had seen little of the man. He studied the padre while Serra blessed the men and animals of the departing expedition. Where Father Xavier's face and hands had been long and aristocratic, Serra's face was round and his always-moving hands, stubby. The Franciscan exuded a tranquility that drew others to him, but his face shown with a passion for his task that bordered on zealotry. He had seen such a look before in a Jesuit brother from Lower California whose name he could not remember. That man's fervor hardened into a fanaticism that led to an uprising by the Indians he had gone to minister to. The brother had escaped, but his servant and the handful of neophytes he had converted were hacked to pieces in the resulting melee.

Remembering that incident, Romero made up his mind to steer clear of Father Serra. No zealots or fanatics for him.

The blessing ended, Governor Portola and his officers climbed into their saddles. After scanning the assembly, Portola raised his sword, the signal to move out. A chorus of cheers went up, and the boom of muskets filled the air. Urselino got to his feet, adding his shouts to the bedlam.

Romero remained on the ground. He would save his cheering for the day he left this place. Until then, there was nothing to do but bide his time. He'd wait until tomorrow to "get well." Then he would find a way south. By land.

"Most of the hairy ones left at Sun Above," Badger, chief of the village of Cosoy, said to the listening council. "Only two Brown Robes, seven owners of the thunder sticks and three others remain here in their village besides the nine dark skins from the south."

Badger sat down, and Red Smoke, the Cosoy shaman, rose. Opposite the place where Casts No Shadow stood at the edge of the seated adult men of Nipaguay, Crooked Basket pushed her way to the front of the women to watch the leaders speak. Her new baby son suckled at one swollen breast.

Casts No Shadow stared at her with disapproval. She knew better than to show herself so soon after giving birth. As wife of the kwaipai, she had a duty to adhere strictly to custom. Custom dictated that a new mother keep herself and her new-born apart whenever possible for a period of at least one moon. The restriction also applied to her husband, Big Nose, but, as kwaipai, he had to be here. She did not.

Casts No Shadow made a mental note to reprimand her later and turned his attention back to the Cosoy shaman.

"The bearded ones loosed their beasts in our fields," Red Smoke said. "Our summer grasses are trampled. And it was not just the people of Cosoy who suffered. Boundaries mean nothing to the paleskins. They violated the hunting and fishing rights of five other bands, too."

His face contorted with anger. "We must drive out these hairy ones before they do any more damage."

At that Shadow Dancer rose, catching Casts No Shadow off-guard. "Red Smoke and Badger speak the truth. I saw the damage the bearded ones' beasts did to their fields. I saw them hunt animals that belong to Cosoy and other bands. They even took fish from my people's fishing grounds."

That claim caused a stir among the Nipaguay men.

"But that is not the most important reason to attack them now.

This is." He held out a length of the newcomer's soft, flexible hide.

Casts No Shadow's heart sank a notch. The hide was proof that his son had gone against his counsel to trade with the bearded ones.

"This and their riding beasts and their thunder sticks," Shadow Dancer exclaimed. "The hairy ones have power unlike anything our people have ever seen. Power we need to possess. I say we take it. And take it now."

Before Shadow Dancer sat down, a dozen men leaped up to support his stand. In the tumult, Casts No Shadow glimpsed Web hovering near the back of the watching women. She must have known about the length of hide, too. Had she also been tainted by contact with the hairy ones?

After witnessing the Brown Robes' ceremony, Casts No Shadow had gone straight to the sacred cave. In the four suns he remained there, the Great Serpent painted the blackness with image upon image–so many that they clogged the wekuseyaay's mind with a bewildering jumble. He had left the cave more confused and with more questions than when he entered. After he had time to sort things through, he decided that the confusion was his fault. That the Spirit was telling him to follow the path he had already begun to walk: to continue to avoid the *kwelmisps* and to continue to wait for them to leave the land of Kumeyaay.

Thus he resolved to wait.

Then, five suns back his patience was rewarded when one of the giant canoes left. And, earlier today, a large group of the strangers had headed north with their beasts carrying loads that could only mean permanent relocation.

He glanced around at the men who had risen to their feet. Each one was trying to outshout the others, too worked up to adhere to rules of civilized conduct. He had told them what to do, yet look at them now. A piece of hide had turned them all into fools with Shadow Dancer, his son and apprentice, the biggest fool of all.

Big Nose's voice boomed above the others. "Wekuseyaay, you have not spoken."

Talking died away and all eyes turned to Casts No Shadow. He looked slowly around the circle of familiar faces before he began to speak. "Three moons ago when the pale ones' second canoe appeared, I asked the spirits what we should do with these new-comers. The gods told me–" he deliberately raised his voice, "–to wait. To have nothing to do with these paleskin strangers. The spirits told me that if we waited, the hairy ones would leave our land and never return."

He stared pointedly at his son. "The gods told the truth. The hairy ones are leaving, just as I said they would. Yet, for some of you, my word is not enough. You did not stay away from the paleskins, and now you want to kill the rest."

Shadow Dancer averted his gaze, but Casts No Shadow did not alter the focus of his anger. "So, for those among you who did not hear me the first time or did not believe my words, I repeat: stay away from the paleskins and they will leave!"

A long strained silence followed. Shadow Dancer would not look at his father.

Red Smoke rose to face Casts No Shadow. "We speak to different spirits, Wekuseyaay. Mine said to attack the bearded ones."

"Perhaps you did not listen well enough," Casts No Shadow replied.

At the jibe, Red Smoke drew himself up. "Your son's words tell me he speaks to the same gods I do. Perhaps it is you who do not listen."

Casts No Shadow again scanned his audience. "Perhaps, but I do not believe so."

The two shamans glared at each other until Big Nose rose. "Casts No Shadow speaks for me."

"And me," various voices echoed from the Nipaguay men. In the end no Nipaguay man spoke in favor of joining Cosoy. Shadow Dancer alone did not speak.

Red Smoke and Badger and the Cosoy contingent rose en masse. "We hear your decision, brothers," Badger said. "And you hear ours. Warm sun to you."

As the Cosoy men filed past, Casts No Shadow drew Red Smoke aside. "Leave the hairy ones be, my brother."

Red Smoke yanked his arm out of Casts No Shadow's grip. "That is exactly what I will not do."

Casts No Shadow nodded grimly and stepped back to allow the other shaman to leave. Across the fire, Shadow Dancer's gaze met his, then skipped away. *Leave the hairy ones be,* Casts No Shadow thought. *Leave them be.*

Chapter 11

A bony hand jerked into the air. One of the scurvy-ridden Catalans wanted water.

Romero pretended not to notice and bent over the sleeping form of one of the two remaining *San Carlos* crewmen. The sailor had broken his arm. Romero straightened the man's blanket for the benefit of anyone who might be looking into the hospital hut. He had volunteered to tend the sick so he would not have to attend Father Serra's ceremony dedicating the new mission, but there was no way he would get near anyone with scurvy. They were bound to die anyway. So why bother prolonging the process by caring for them and risk contracting their disease in the bargain?

The familiar sounds of a priest intoning the mass drifted through the hut's open door. Today was the Feast Day of Our Lady of Carmel, and Father Serra was beseeching the Lady for her intercession to bring the natives of San Diego to the true faith.

Romero stifled a snort. From what he had seen of the natives so far, even an army of saints could not pull off such a miracle. There were simply too many heathens in this vast, isolated place to be subdued by a disease-reduced company of Leatherjackets and a trio of missionaries.

This mission of San Diego was bound to fail. Any fool could see that. He had been forced to come here, but no one could force him to believe in the Franciscans or their doomed project. Better to tend the sick–except, of course, those with scurvy–than waste time on a ceremony dedicating a failure.

"Water," the Catalan rasped, his hand clawing the air.

Romero hunched down, keeping his back to the sick man and his demanding hand. Through the door, he could see Serra and the other two Franciscans, Brothers Parron and Viscaino, grouped in front of a large wooden cross that had been planted in the ground in front of a church hut built of stakes and roofed with tules. Gathered in a semicircle facing the padres was the rest of the contingent from Lower California. Behind them, a ring of curious, dark-skinned heathens watched. Seeing how few in number the Spanish were compared to the natives, Romero shivered.

"Water." The plea came again louder.

Romero whirled. "Shut up."

"Water."

"Water, huh?" He seized the dipper from the pail and carried it to the man, slopping most of the liquid on the ground in his fury.

The Catalan's fingers grabbed at air. "Please."

"Here's your water." Romero turned the dipper over.

With his ability to swallow already restricted by the disease, the soldier gagged, vomiting green bile over himself and the man lying next to him.

Romero turned, stalked over to the bucket and stabbed the dipper back into the water.

The Catalan wheezed and coughed. Romero ignored him. He knew that if he did not get his anger under control, he would kill the man. Killing meant touching, and touching meant his own death. *Not after all this*, he thought. *Not me. Not now.*

Web sat on the ground beside Hummingbird at the edge of the cluster of Kumeyaays from various bands who had come to watch the ceremony of the Brown Robe shamans. The sun, the heat, the strange musical language of the paleskins and the comforting tug of Sand Flea's mouth at her nipple all combined to make her drowsy. She stifled a yawn.

Shadow Dancer had insisted on attending this rite despite Casts No Shadow's pointed warning against it at the Cosoy council two days ago. As Shadow Dancer's wife and mother of his sons, it was her duty to follow his lead, not to question his decision to disregard his father's advice. For the same reason, Hummingbird had come with Many Rains.

Both husbands stood on the front ranks of the Kumeyaays. Although she could see only his back, Web knew that Shadow Dancer's full attention was focused on the Brown Robes as he sought to understand their purpose and their power.

Noises issued from a nearby hut. Through the opening she could make out the forms of men lying on the ground. *The sick bearded ones*, she thought.

Casts No Shadow had warned the people not to accept any food from the paleskins. He said that their food was the source of the illness that turned the strangers' pale skin black. If they possessed such powerful medicine, why did these newcomers not fix their food? she wondered.

A strangled scream came from the hut. Moments later a man ducked out the opening. Web flinched involuntarily when she recognized Twisted Face. She had not seen him since that day on the beach when she had fled in terror at the sight of his ravaged face and the huge riding beasts. It had taken many sleeps before the image of the man ceased to trouble her dreams.

"Sister?" Hummingbird asked.

Web forced a smile to assure her friend that nothing was wrong, then shifted so Hummingbird could not see her expression. It took some time before she could bring her attention back to the ceremony. When she did, she was surprised to see one of the Brown Robes walking slowly through the assembled paleskins, cradling in his arms the wooden figure of a light-skinned woman with a baby. As the Brown Robe passed, each bearded one paid the figure homage.

"So beautiful," Hummingbird murmured.

Her friend's tone made the hair on Web's arms stand up. The bearded ones had no women. What had happened to their women? Who was this wooden woman? Why did they bow to her?

"Such a beautiful baby," Hummingbird whispered, tears welling in her eyes.

Web put a comforting arm around her friend's shoulders. Hummingbird sagged against her and hid her face behind her open hand. "I want a baby, too," she whispered, the last word cut short by a sob. Her body shook under the force of her quiet weeping.

Web held on tight, feeling her friend's despair but powerless to give her what she wanted.

Chapter 12

With the majority of the bearded ones gone, life at Nipaguay began to resume its normal rhythm. Shadow Dancer spent less and less time observing the newcomers and more time attending to his sons, his shaman's duties and his hunting and fishing, to Web's relief.

Although he had twice returned from his day's fishing with rumors that Cosoy was ready to attack the remaining paleskins, the attack had not happened. For that, she was thankful. Every day she prayed to One Above to send away the rest of the bearded ones.

Half a moon's cycle after the Brown Robe ceremony, Web had just coaxed the twins to sleep when Shadow Dancer returned at dusk. Seeing that he carried neither bow nor fishing net curtailed her good mood. Keeping her back to him, she spooned the stew of acorn dumplings into a shallow wood bowl, then handed the bowl to him on her way to the *wisal* where she retrieved an unfinished basket and sat down behind him, hoping he would take the hint and eat in silence. She was sick of hearing about the bearded ones' magic, sick of the whole subject of the newcomers.

Instead Shadow Dancer put down his bowl, lifted away the basket and took hold of her hands. "Wife, today I witnessed the gods at work." He lowered his voice. "The paleskin with the twisted face knows how to bend rocks."

The mention of Twisted Face alarmed Web but not as much as the excitement burning in her husband's eyes. When she tried to move away, he pulled her to him. "He bends rocks in fire and then attaches them to the feet of the riding beasts."

Web understood too well the import of his words. It had taken her a long time to adjust to his fascination with '*aww* fire. Now that he had discovered fire magic among the bearded ones, he would stop at nothing to learn their secrets.

"Our people must have this power. I must get it for them." He released her hands and picked up his food.

Web took up the basket again, but her heart was so heavy that weaving could not lighten it. She ducked inside the 'ewaa. In the darkness, she sagged against one of the side supports and closed her eyes. The image of Twisted Face appeared in the void. She groaned.

"Wife?"

"It's just Cricket," she said, blurting out the first excuse that came to mind.

At the sound of his name, Cricket stirred. She bent to smooth a lock of his tousled hair. Turning her face to the roof of the lodge, she aimed a silent plea at the heavens. *One Above, I must stand behind my husband. Please keep us all safe.*

Chapter 13

When Badger's invitation came to Casts No Shadow and Shadow Dancer to come to Cosoy, the moon had completed a full cycle since their last council. Despite their earlier rhetoric, Cosoy had not attacked the newcomer's settlement. Lately even the rumors of an attack had stopped. Why then did Badger want to talk?

After much deliberation over that question, the wekuseyaay decided that the Cosoy chief wanted to soothe relations between the two villages. Red Smoke's accusation still stung. Casts No Shadow was curious how his haughty rival would try to temper the friction between them.

Badger and Red Smoke met Casts No Shadow and Shadow Dancer at the edge of their village and escorted them to places of honor at the kwaipai's fire. During the required preliminaries, Casts No Shadow kept his expression neutral. It would not do to show how much he looked forward to seeing Red Smoke brought down a notch.

Badger launched into a series of pointed questions about the bearded ones that he aimed at Shadow Dancer. At first, Casts No Shadow thought the chief was being deliberately indirect, but he quickly realized that he had guessed wrong about the purpose of the meeting. His feelings of satisfaction dissolved.

"Every seven days, at Sun Above, one of the Brown Robes and two of the keepers of the thunder sticks paddle out to the giant canoe," Shadow Dancer said. "They do not return until Sun makes for His bed. At the same time, the two other Brown Robes hold a murmuring ceremony at their village."

"When do the keepers of the thunder sticks take the riding beasts to the river?" Red Smoke asked impatiently.

"After the murmuring ceremony," Shadow Dancer replied.

"How long are they gone?" Red Smoke asked.

Annoyed, Casts No Shadow broke in. "Is this why you invite us to come to your village–to ask my son questions about the hairy ones?"

"Shadow Dancer has observed the bearded ones and has the knowledge we need," Badger said.

"We asked you to come here as a courtesy to your son," Red Smoke added patronizingly.

Casts No Shadow ignored the other shaman's baiting and locked gazes with Badger until the chief gave him the answer he wanted. "We planned an attack yesterday but the leader of the keepers of the thunder sticks returned to the paleskins' village before we could get into position."

"Our kwaipai here ordered a retreat when we should have gone ahead," Red Smoke said.

Badger's face grew stern. "I will not risk the lives of our people."

"The spirits speak through me, my brother," Red Smoke declared, jabbing the air with his healing stick. "They say 'Drive out the bearded ones now!'"

Angry, Badger turned to Shadow Dancer. "I need to understand the pale ones' ways in order to set a time for a new attack."

Before Casts No Shadow could vent his anger at the two men, Shadow Dancer spoke up. "I regret what I have told you and I will answer no more of your questions. With my own eyes, I have seen the magic of the bearded ones. They know how to use fire to bend rocks. Such medicine can only come from One

Above or Blind Brother Below."

He got to his feet. "The Kumeyaay people must learn about this power. We must take it and make it our own. We must not harm the bearded ones until then."

While Casts No Shadow stared at his son in disbelief, Red Smoke leaped to his feet. "You are wrong, 'Aww-kuseyaay. You and your father are both wrong. The spirits have spoken. Tomorrow Nipaguay will miss a great victory when the men of Cosoy drive out the pale ones once and for all."

Shadow Dancer turned his back on Red Smoke and stalked out of the village. Casts No Shadow followed, sorting out what had happened.

As satisfying as his son's refusal to help Red Smoke and Badger had been, he was troubled by Shadow Dancer's revelation about the bearded ones' fire magic and his intention to obtain that power. Lately, in his dreams, he had seen his son surrounded by fire while a second shadowy figure lurked beyond the flames where he could not be seen clearly. Those dreams always ended with Casts No Shadow waking up, terrified and sweating.

He wanted to tell Shadow Dancer about the dreams, but his son was too far ahead. By the time he reached Nipaguay, Shadow Dancer had disappeared into his 'ewaa. Heaving a sigh, Casts No Shadow decided the conversation could wait until morning.

Chapter 14

Throughout Sunday mass, memories of his life with Father Xavier kept cycling through Romero's mind. By the end of the service, he had sunk into depression and pleaded a headache from the sun as an excuse not to go with the soldiers to water the horses as he usually did. Instead, he retired to his hut.

The mission was quiet with the guards gone and Brother Parron still out at *San Carlos*. The lack of sound deepened Romero's melancholy. Governor Portola's expedition had been gone a month; *San Antonio*, five weeks. There seemed no way for him to ever get back to Loreto.

He rolled onto the pile of willows and old sacks that served as his bed and slung one arm over his eyes. How much longer would he have to wait in this end-of-the-world place?

He closed his eyes and tried to slip into sleep. The moment he did he sensed he was being watched, a feeling that had been growing steadily over the last few weeks.

He forced himself off the bed and looked out the door.

Nothing.

No sooner had he stretched out on the pallet again than a sound caught his ear: a click that did not belong amongst the usual mission noises.

This time he edged to the hut opening, keeping to the shadows. Peering out, he saw Indians filtering between the huts. Their stealth told him that the mission was under attack.

Heart hammering, he pressed against the wall of his hut. Two days ago, the corporal of the guard had galloped into the mission compound, claiming he had seen Indians grouping for an attack. He and his men had ridden out after the supposed raiders but found nothing. Romero had dismissed the incident as the product of the corporal's overactive, underused imagination.

Now, realizing that the corporal had been right sparked all his repressed frustration and anger. His depression vanished, taking his fear with it. He waited for a break in the flow of Indians, then darted out of the hut and raced to his forge.

Yesterday he had mended a fitting on the stock of a musket. The weapon lay on his workbench exactly where he had left it. The heft of it steadied his trembling hands.

Blessing the wisdom of the corporal of the guard who had insisted that ball and powder be hidden in various places throughout the compound, Romero used his powerful hands to unearth the cache secreted in the corner of the open-sided lean-to that housed the forge.

He had nearly finished loading the musket when an arrow whizzed past his ear, grazing his head before thudding into a post. He whirled and took aim on the savage who had reached into his quiver for a new arrow. "Die, bastard!" he cursed, releasing the hammer of the rifle.

The musket exploded and kicked.

The heathen crumpled to the ground, a surprised look on his face.

In an instant, the two Franciscans, Serra and Viscaino, were out of their hut. "What's going on?" Father Serra demanded, slashing the air with both hands.

Romero did not bother to reply. He was not going to waste words when savages were trying to kill him. The padres had eyes. Let them see and understand that this Mission San Diego was doomed.

Reloading, the blacksmith took aim and downed another

Indian.

"Spare them! They know not what they do!" Father Serra's cry mixed with the echoes of the rifle's shot.

Romero ignored the plea. No heathen was going to kill him; not after all he had done to stay alive this long.

"Spare them!" Father Serra shouted a second time.

At that moment the soldiers, alerted by Romero's shots, galloped into the compound. Their appearance threw the Indians into a panicked retreat. Father Serra ran to the soldiers, arms outstretched, pleading for mercy for the attackers, but his words were not in time to stop a withering fusillade from the soldiers.

"Cowards," Romero muttered, leveling the musket at a fleeing brown-skin. Squinting against the smoke, he pulled the trigger and saw the ball hit just below the man's ribs. The savage toppled with a death scream.

"Cease fire!" the corporal shouted, finally heeding Father Serra's impassioned pleas.

The flame of Romero's anger burned too hot to cool yet. He reached for another ball.

"Break off!" the corporal yelled.

Two of the Indians ran back to retrieve the body of the savage the blacksmith had downed.

"Oh, no, you don't!" Romero hurried his load and took aim.

"Blacksmith!" This time it was Father Serra who yelled. His voice at that moment sounded so much like Father Xavier's that Romero hesitated.

Someone grabbed the weapon out of the smith's hands.

In the distance, two Indians dragged the inert body of the third away.

"No!" Romero screamed, starting after the fleeing attackers only to find himself restrained by two of the soldiers.

"Let them be, my son. They must mourn their dead as we must ours."

Father Serra's words cut through the red haze clouding Romero's vision. "Dead?"

The Franciscan nodded sadly. "Our servant."

Father Serra had brought with him from Lower California a young Indian man christened José Maria. José Maria had attended the brown-robed brothers just as Romero had for so long served Father Xavier. The effort to picture the vital young man dead defeated the blacksmith.

"Come. Let me see to your wound," Father Serra said.

Romero had forgotten the arrow crease until the padre touched it.

"And you, my brother," Father Serra said to his fellow missionary. "I must tend your hand."

Brother Viscaino held his bloodied hand by the wrist. His face was white with shock and his eyes were unnaturally wide.

At the sight of the padre's blood, Romero began to tremble. Father Serra laid a hand on his forearm. "You must ask God's forgiveness. All human life is sacred."

Beside him, Brother Viscaino teetered and began to sink in a faint. Lunging, Father Serra managed to catch him before he hit the ground. With the help of one of the soldiers, the Franciscan leader supported his wounded comrade back to their hut.

The other soldiers left, taking the mended musket with them and leaving Romero at the forge. The smith sank down on his workbench and waited for his shaking to pass.

Forgiveness. When it came to killing savages, that was the last thing he would ask from God. His trembling did not come from remorse, as Father Serra assumed, but from the realization that his rashness might have cost him his life. The Franciscans might just as easily be singing a requiem for him as for their servant. If that happened, he would never get the chance to reconcile with Father Xavier.

He pounded the bench with his fists. By God Almighty, from now on, anger would never again take over his common sense. Never, never again.

The night wind carried echoes of mourning along the path where Web hurried to reach Cosoy. Ahead of her the dark silhouettes of Casts No Shadow and Shadow Dancer bobbed against the moonlit landscape. Smoke from the cremation fires hung over Cosoy like a curtain of fog, making her regret the impulse that made her volunteer to come with her husband to see what assistance she could offer.

At the edge of the village, she paused to steel herself, then, readjusting her grip on the bag of herbs she carried, she walked into a scene she would never forget. Each of the men killed in the attack on the bearded ones' settlement lay in a separate fire pit. Surrounding each pit were the man's possessions.

The sight of eight burning bodies stopped Web in her tracks. In the middle pit was the body of Badger, Cosoy's kwaipai, and on either side of his pit, burned the wisest and most important men of the village. She stared in disbelief at the tragedy before her.

The eight dead warriors were the leaders of Cosoy. Among them, they held the knowledge that the village needed to survive. Without them, who would keep order and know the proper time to burn the fields? Who would know where in the mountains to go for the best acorns in the fall? Who would teach the young?

A hand gripped her arm. She managed to take her eyes off the dead long enough to acknowledge Shadow Dancer. Anguish lay deep in his eyes. "Come."

She followed him into another part of the village where a second wrenching scene brought her up short. A man lay on his back under a *wisal*. Beside him knelt Casts No Shadow. The man's wife hovered at his feet, her gaze darting frantically between her husband and the wekuseyaay. The light of a burning torch revealed a hideous wound in the man's chest.

Shadow Dancer's voice was barely louder than a whisper. "The thunder sticks did this."

Web's hand flew to her mouth. All this pain, this loss, from the bearded ones' booming sticks. It was too much for her mind to grasp.

The arrival of Red Smoke aroused the wounded man who rasped, "Not you!"

Red Smoke halted.

"You are no shaman," the wounded man hissed. "Stay away from me!"

In the space of a breath, all the confidence drained out of Red Smoke's demeanor. His shoulders slumped forward; his chest sank; his spine sagged into a pronounced curve; and the smooth skin of his face cracked into a web of creases. The Red Smoke who plodded away looked twenty summers older than the shaman who had appeared out of the night only moments before.

"Red Smoke is no more," Shadow Dancer muttered.

A chill raced through Web. With all the death and pain around her, she had not considered the consequences to Red Smoke for instigating the failed attack. With his credibility destroyed, the Cosoy shaman had one last choice: to take his own life or force the people of his band to take it for him.

The wounded man sank back with a groan. Casts No Shadow laid out his healing objects. Shadow Dancer went forward to help in the rite.

Web's mind was too full of the horror wrought by the thunder sticks to focus on the healing. She moved off in search of a private place to regain some sense of reality.

Rounding a lodge, she nearly collided with Crooked Basket. At seeing the other woman's obvious distress, Web said, "I am sorry about your father."

Crooked Basket drew herself up indignantly. "How dare you!"

The question confused Web. "Dare?"

"You and those hideous hands. Since you came here, nothing but evil has come to our people."

In a heartbeat Web rose to her own defense. "Blame what happened here on your father, not me."

"You don't belong here."

The words that had once stung so much now made Web tired. "You and me, we both belong with our husbands, and our children."

"Go home, desert mouse."

"I no longer bloom in the desert. Nipaguay is my home and my sons'."

"Your sons belong. You do not." With that, Crooked Basket broke away.

Web stood alone, staring at the woman's retreating back. She had lived at Nipaguay for two summers. In all that time she had never exchanged a civil word with Crooked Basket. Would the woman's hatred never end? Would there ever be peace between them?

The odor of charred flesh hung heavy over the huts surrounding her. So much death, so much pain. Where did it end?

Chapter 15

C asts No Shadow watched Red Smoke grind the root into a fine pulp. The wekuseyaay sat to the right of the Cosoy shaman with Shadow Dancer on the left. A hush lay over the village of Cosoy. No one stirred. The exhausted mourners had retired to their lodges to leave this last step to the three shamans.

Red Smoke laid aside the pestle and looked at Casts No Shadow.

Staring back, Casts No Shadow saw a man he no longer recognized. Gone were the confidence and energy of his old rival. In their place, a shriveling husk of flesh and a fading soul.

Casts No Shadow poured water from a gourd over the mashed substance and swirled the ritual mortar to mix the concoction. He had to add a touch more water to achieve the right translucency, then he put the mortar on the ground in front of his rival.

For a long time no one moved. Finally Red Smoke spoke. "I did what the spirits said. The thunder sticks . . ." His voice faltered.

Casts No Shadow felt his jaw tighten at his rival's display of weakness.

Recovering, Red Smoke went on. "No one can fight the thunder sticks. No one. Not even you, mighty wekuseyaay."

Casts No Shadow refused to be baited.

"You think you can ignore the bearded ones, that they will go away," Red Smoke said. "But you are wrong. They will never go away. They will destroy us—you, me, all the Kumeyaay people."

Casts No Shadow was prepared for the accusation that Cosoy's attack failed because Nipaguay refused to join. That indictment did not come. Instead, Red Smoke sighed. "But that you will see for yourself. I am glad that I will not be here for the end." His voice failed again.

Casts No Shadow forced neutrality into his expression. Red Smoke had been a worthy adversary for too many years to shame him with pity.

The failed shaman reached for the mortar. Casts No Shadow looked into the small fire so he would not witness the other man's shaking hands.

Red Smoke lifted the shaped stone vessel to his lips and took a sip.

"Drink deep. It is eas . . ." Casts No Shadow cut himself off but not soon enough.

Hatred flickered in Red Smoke's eyes. He drank the rest of the concoction in one gulp. "Leave me. And take everything with you."

While Shadow Dancer gathered the mortar and pestle and left the lodge, Casts No Shadow tucked the sack of roots into his carrying bag and got up.

"Everything, Wekuseyaay. I want none of this here when my soul soars free." Red Smoke waved at the things arrayed on a bearskin at the back of the lodge. Power objects and implements of the shaman Red Smoke used to be.

Casts No Shadow nodded, wrapped everything into the bearskin and lugged the lot outside.

"Will we wait, my father?" Shadow Dancer asked. "For his death?"

"The man I knew as Red Smoke is already dead," Casts No Shadow said. "Come. We must burn his things, then we can go home."

Shadow Dancer led the way out of the too-quiet village. Casts No Shadow followed, carrying his rival's bearskin and wondering about the bearded ones. How would they react to Cosoy's attack? Clearly, their thunder sticks dealt the worst evil he had ever seen. Whatever happened, the people of Nipaguay must be protected from the destruction he had witnessed here.

As if reading his thoughts, Shadow Dancer said, "Twisted Face knows the secrets of the thunder sticks."

Casts No Shadow grunted, hoping his son would forget his dangerous notions and stay away from the bearded ones' village.

"But I will not go there," Shadow Dancer said firmly.

The wekuseyaay could scarcely believe his ears. Was his son seeing into his mind?

Shadow Dancer went on. "Better to wait a few days; let the excitement settle. Then . . ."

Casts No Shadow held back a retort. Perhaps the paleskins would leave now, prompted by the attack. He kept silent, following his son into the gathering dusk to a place only shamans knew about to burn his rival's things and hope that the bearded ones would leave soon.

Romero huddled against the wall of the willow-thatched hut that served as the Franciscans' church. The door and window had been covered to hide the funeral of the missionary's servant from the curious Indians who had once again begun to hang around the outpost, undeterred by the deaths of their brothers.

Over Father Serra's droning voice and the occasional crunch of sand under the soldiers' boots, Romero's nervous ears strained for any unfamiliar sounds from outside. If it were up to him, they would all be outside right now—even the Brown Robes—slapping up a defensive picket wall so they would be ready for the next attack. Instead, here they were wasting time at a funeral service when who knew how many savages might be getting ready to overrun the post this time.

He shifted restlessly.

Wailing and shouting from the nearest Indian village had kept him awake all night. That, and the smell of roasting human flesh. Cremation went again God's laws. Such pagans were beyond any redemption the Franciscans could hope to offer. Didn't these padres see that?

At last, the interminable service was over, but before Romero could escape the stifling church confines, Father Serra called his name. "Now we must bury the lad. Will you help, José? Tonight after dark?"

To Romero, all this secrecy was useless. Still, Father Serra insisted that the natives must think that the Spanish had escaped the attack. The blacksmith nodded for lack of any other response. The light came back into Father Serra's eyes. "Good, I knew I could count on you. Now let's go help with that wall the corporal insists on building."

The Franciscan leader was out the door before Romero could say anything. He found it impossible to refuse Father Serra. He did not want to be here, but he could not find a way home. Damn it all, nothing ever seemed to work out in his favor anymore.

The corporal stuck his head through the opening in the temporary curtain hanging over the door. "Come on, blacksmith. We need your strong back."

Romero gave the dead servant one last look. "Things could be worse," he whispered. "I could be you." Then he walked outside to help build the wall.

V

FIRE MAGIC
December, 1769—April, 1770

Chapter 1- December, 1769
Near the Kumeyaay Village of Nipaguay

Cricket had been fussy all day. Web rocked him for what seemed like hours until at last his eyelids drooped. She waited until she was sure he was asleep before laying him down beside his brother and ducking noiselessly outside. She sagged down under the *wisal* and looked up at the night sky.

She felt weary to the bone. Weariness that never let up. The strain of keeping up with two active toddlers every day combined with this new pregnancy was hard enough without Shadow Dancer's being gone, too. *Where are you, my husband?* She tossed the question to the stars. *Come home. I need you. Your sons need you.*

Then, tired as she was, she picked up the winnowing basket she had been making and set to work. She liked to spend time at the end of the day weaving baskets. Besides soothing her, basket-making fed her pride. Her skill made the other Nipaguay women envious. With good reason. Web's creations brought high prices in trade. One of them had fetched the bracelet of rare, matched coral-hued shells she now wore.

One of the twins whimpered inside the 'ewaa. Web held her breath, hoping the whimpering was only part of a dream. When there were no more sounds, she relaxed and thought of Hummingbird.

Poor Hummingbird yearned for a baby of her own so much now that she found it hard to be in the company of any woman with child, Web included.

Though she empathized with her friend, Web sorely missed Hummingbird's company and her help with the twins. And Web missed her husband. Ever since Cosoy's ill-fated attack on the paleskins back in the fall, Shadow Dancer had grown increasingly withdrawn. Then half a moon's cycle ago, he had taken his shaman's bundle and gone off without a nod or even a word about where he was going or how long he planned to be gone.

Shamans did such things–Web knew that–but every new day without him stretched her patience and her energy thinner.

At a fluttering sensation in her abdomen, she put one hand over the bulge of her belly. She smiled tiredly. Such an active baby, kicking as if to find an immediate way out. "No, little one. Not yet," she murmured.

"Wife!"

She started at the shout and levered herself to her feet as Shadow Dancer materialized out of the blackness beyond the rim of the fire's light.

"Prepare food. I must fetch my father," he said, striding past her without pausing to put down his burden net or even touch her. He returned shortly with Casts No Shadow in tow.

From the look on Shadow Dancer's face, Web knew better than to ask questions. She dipped gourds of still-warm fish stew for them, then sat down to resume weaving the basket while she eavesdropped on their conversation.

"I have talked with the spirits," Shadow Dancer began. "About the bearded ones."

She sensed, rather than saw, Casts No Shadow stiffen. Since the attack, his counsel to stay away from the paleskins had taken on the stridency of command. Though she had heard grumbling among the villagers about the wekuseyaay's vehemence, no one was willing to test the man or his advice.

Shadow Dancer continued. "The spirits have chosen me for a special task. They directed me to learn the bearded ones' fire magic. To bring it to the people."

Web forgot her basket. "No," she whispered. Twisted Face was the hairy ones' shaman for 'aww fire magic.

"The spirits tell me: become as a friend to the kwelmisps, and they will reveal their power to you," Shadow Dancer said. He gazed up at the star-tossed sky. "To get the fire magic for our people, I must learn the ways of the hairy ones. I must earn the trust of their shaman Brown Robes."

"I forbid it!" Casts No Shadow said.

Web flinched at the wekuseyaay's outburst, but Shadow Dancer reacted as if he expected it. "I must, Father. The future of our people rests on the magic of bending stone in fire."

"Pah on such magic!" Casts No Shadow spat. "If the bearded ones have such power, why do they hide behind a wall? Why do their sick never get well? They are afraid and weak, and they will leave. That is what the spirits have said–to me!"

"All the more reason for me to waste no more time. Tomorrow I go to the pale ones' village to begin my work."

"Tomorrow you will come with me. I have more songs to teach you," Casts No Shadow said.

"Songs can wait. I must learn the magic of bending stones before the hairy ones leave. I must."

Casts No Shadow rose to his feet. "Songs are *our* magic. The *only* magic you must learn!"

Rising, son faced father. "The spirits have spoken. I must obey."

Whimpering inside the 'ewaa announced that the heated exchange had disturbed both twins. Web dared not move for fear that she might cause the tension between the two men to explode.

The firelight illuminated a throbbing vein in the wekuseyaay's neck. "You will learn the songs I have to teach, or you are no longer my son."

Web stifled a gasp at that ultimatum.

"I will learn the fire magic, then your songs, my father," Shadow Dancer said evenly.

Casts No Shadow's voice rasped with fury. "Never call me that again."

The wekuseyaay turned and walked away, leaving behind a terrible silence. Slowly, Shadow Dancer turned his face toward Web. Sorrow etched deep lines on his face. She moved to him in a daze of disbelief.

"The spirits . . ." His voice caught, then trailed off.

She threaded her arms around his waist and hugged him with a fierceness born of her own inner turmoil. "You are my husband. I stand beside you in all that you do."

He returned her embrace. "Oh, wife, the spirits . . ."

She put a finger over his mouth. She wanted to keep him from saying anything else he might regret. "The spirits have chosen you," she whispered.

He nodded sadly.

Inside the 'ewaa, whimpers turned into wails. Shadow Dancer touched her swelling belly. "You see to this little one. I will see to the others." With that, he ducked into the dwelling.

She put her hand where his had been. "He is a great fire shaman, little one," she murmured to the child under her outstretched palm. "You and I, we will stand beside him as long as he needs us, won't we?"

Inside her womb, the baby moved. Web knew it was a nod of agreement.

Chapter 2

For the first time since the Spirit of Fire had chosen his son to be their human messenger, Casts No Shadow sat on the sacred mountain alone waiting for the *maaykaa* dawn. The biting winter wind off the ocean cut through his wekuseyaay's cape of serpent skins, adding to his desolation.

Every year for as far back as he could remember, he had anticipated coming to this mountain to mark the Longest Night, to call to Sun and ask Him to begin His return from Darkness. The shaman's first climb to this summit had been with his uncle, the one who had taught him the ways of the spirit world. On that day he had learned the sacred songs and had stood sentinel as Sun traced an arc from one side of Sky to the other. He and his uncle had repeated that journey together for fifteen winters until his uncle's soul passed into the realm of Those Who Had Gone Before and Casts No Shadow became wekuseyaay in his place. He came alone then until the spirits picked Shadow Dancer to be 'aww-kuseyaay. Thereafter father and son made the annual climb. Until this year.

Today, Shadow Dancer had chosen to be at the bearded ones' settlement instead of doing his duty to the gods and the Kumeyaay people, and Casts No Shadow had come alone to the mountaintop with his heart as heavy as the boulders that held the mountain in place.

A fork of *shuuluk* lightning split the sky, revealing ominous clouds piled against the peaks to the east, and spreading rapidly toward the sea. The gathering storm deepened his despondency.

Among those his age, Shadow Dancer had always been the curious one, investigating, studying, questioning. Casts No Shadow had always encouraged his son's restlessness, his seeking. Now, though, he wished he had been more cautious. Perhaps if he had held Shadow Dancer back more, he would not have been so quick to be drawn in by the paleskins and there would be no split between them.

A pulse of *shuullaw* thunder washed over him. The wind drove rain mist against his back. At the edges of the clouds to the east, the sky grew a little less black, a signal of daybreak. Soon he must begin the songs.

On the next gust of wind Red Smoke's image popped into his mind and, along with it, the Cosoy shaman's last words: "The bearded ones will never go away. They will destroy us."

"No!" he shouted into the clouds. "The paleskins will leave.

They must. The spirits have spoken. You, Red Smoke, and you, Shadow Dancer–you are both wrong."

More lightning flashed in the near distance. In the silence before the thunder, he raised his voice in a prayer:

One Above gives life to all.
He makes the people.
We are his children.
Like a father who keeps his children from harm,
One Above protects us.
One Above who gives us life.

Shuullaw rolled across the sacred peak, engulfing the shaman's words. In the din, he whispered a private prayer. "One Above, protect my son."

It was the first time since his split with Shadow Dancer that he had uttered the phrase "my son." Now spoken, the words felt like an accusation. He had reacted too quickly to Shadow Dancer's revelations. Instead of reasoning with his son and getting him to admit that he had misinterpreted what the spirits had said, Casts No Shadow had let anger at being contradicted by his own flesh and blood overrule his control, severing his relationship with the most important person in his life, the one who would carry not only his blood into the future but also all his knowledge of the world and the Kumeyaay people.

"But my son is wrong," he cried at the heavy clouds.

A sudden lull in the storm amplified his voice and made him feel foolish. Here he was shouting at the sky instead of focusing on the important task at hand.

The eastern horizon had grown lighter, but, this day, the storm would obscure Sun's awakening. No matter. The songs must be sung, whether or not he could see Sun and whether or not his apprentice sang them with him. That was the way of life. That was his way. That was the right way.

Chapter 3

T he mid-January rain lashed against the tule roof of the Mission San Diego's church. Romero huddled into his grimy torn blanket, his mood as dark and heavy as the lowering clouds that had hung over the region for the last month. The mass had barely begun, and already his knees ached from contact with the cold earth.

The uncovered side window looked out on the picket wall erected after last August's Indian attack. Through gaps in the pickets, he spotted something moving. Immediately, his senses snapped to the alert.

Whatever it was, the shape disappeared. However, Romero could not relax. Months of tension had taken its toll on him and every other man in the mission. Even Father Serra.

There was unmistakable strain in the Franciscan leader's voice as he read the first selection of scripture. No doubt today's homily would be the same as every other mass since the attack: forgive the heathens for their actions and help bring them to God before any more souls died unshriven. It was a message that fell on ears made deaf by fear of another attack and by hunger as the mission's supplies dwindled daily.

Food. That's what Father Serra ought to be praying for. Food and reinforcements; not converts.

But there would be no food. Not for at least a month, until the contrary winds that plagued the western coast of the Pacific shifted so that ships had a chance of reaching this outpost on the edge of the world. Until then the mission's best hope for new supplies lay in the return of Governor Portola's expedition from whom no one had heard since it left for Monterey back in August.

The men around Romero launched into half-hearted unison on the psalm Father Serra had chosen for the service. The blacksmith did not join in, preferring to ponder his favorite topic: getting back to Loreto.

The psalm ended and Father Serra moved into the prayer. Bowing his head, Romero thought a fervent prayer of his own: *Oh, Lord, please help me get to Loreto—all in one piece—by land and then help me find Father Xavier.*

Father Serra ended the prayer with a resonant "Amen." Before he could begin the Liturgy of the Eucharist, his face broke into a beneficent smile, and he motioned toward the door. "Come in, my son."

Romero turned to see someone duck away from the door. Leaving the altar, Father Serra rushed to the back of the room. "Please, come in."

With the priest's coaxing a man took a hesitant step into view. Romero recognized him as the young Indian who hung around the forge, the one he had come to call Three Parts for the unusual way he wore his hair.

"Come, join us. You are most welcome," Father Serra urged.
Three Parts moved hesitantly into the church. Father Serra held
out a hand. "Come to God, my child."

After several moments Three Parts took the offered hand, and
the priest's smile changed to reflect equal parts of relief and
delight. Serra glanced at Romero. "José, isn't this the man I've
seen at your forge?"

Unused to being addressed by anything other than "Romero" or
"blacksmith", Romero was too surprised to answer right away.
The soldier next to him elbowed him in the ribs. "Answer the
padre."

"Y–yes, Father," Romero stammered.

"Then he will kneel beside you, and you will make him welcome."

Father Serra pointed the Indian to the place beside Romero and
motioned for Three Parts to squat down, then he returned to the
altar with new life in his step. He launched into the Eucharist
with more vigor than anyone had witnessed since the attack.
However, Romero was too aware of the savage next to him to
notice.

Three Parts had been at the forge all day every day for a solid
month, watching Romero shoe the horses and mend harnesses.
Annoyed at first, he shooed him away, but, after a time, with the
press of other concerns, he had ceased to notice the heathen's
presence. Now, though, he was not at all sure he wanted to be the
one involved in Father Serra's first possibility of a native
conversion. Serra had prayed continuously for all these months
for just such an opening, and Romero guessed that the Franciscan
would use every means he had to bring Three Parts into his
mission fold. *Every* means, starting with Romero who wanted
nothing to do with this place or the Franciscans. He had been
forced to come here. He would rather risk eternity in purgatory
than associate with the savages who inhabited this god-forsaken
place.

Father Serra bowed his head for the Eucharistic Prayer. The
savage leaned forward, his face a study in concentration. All at
once, Romero could not stand another minute so close to the
Indian. He rose, kneeing the soldier in front of him by accident.
When the soldier grunted loudly in complaint, Romero found
himself momentarily locked by Father Serra's unnerving gaze.

Clutching at his stomach and pretending to be gripped by
diarrheal cramps, he stepped across the men seated between him
and the door and limped outside.

After the close confines of the mass and the turmoil Three

Parts' proximity had caused him, the clouds and rain seemed bright. Back at the forge, Romero tossed a handful of charcoal on the banked coals and pumped the bellows until the eye of the fire was just large and hot enough. Grabbing a half-finished horseshoe with his tongs, he plunged it into the fire and watched the metal heat.

Some day his chance would come. A land party would head south. When that day came, by God, he would be ready. No Indian, no Franciscan, nothing would stop him. All he needed was the chance.

"Make it soon," he muttered at the glowing eye of the fire. "Make it soon."

Chapter 4

The bearded ones had moved their village to the top of a knoll to the south and west of the village of Cosoy. From the main foot path along the south bluff of the valley, a second, newer trail led off to the opening in the wall of close-set sharpened poles that the paleskins had placed around their huts. Web paused at the fork of the trails to rest before continuing on. She slipped the burden net from her back and set her two sons down to work off some of their energy while she sat on the ground to think about what she was about to do.

For over a moon now, except for two visits to the 'ewaa, Shadow Dancer had been gone from Nipaguay. The longer his absence, the wider the split between him and Casts No Shadow and the more grumbling among the people of their village who expected the men they looked to as shaman to be available for advice and guidance.

The situation had grown so tense for her that, last night, she decided to try to discuss it with Shadow Dancer. Now, however, with the wall of the hairy ones' town looming so close by, her courage began to drain away.

Loud shouts startled her to her feet. Bearded ones armed with thunder sticks appeared at the gates of the wall. Quickly she grabbed her sons and, hugging them to her, darted into the cover of some brush.

At the first boom of thunder from the sticks, she forced the twins to the ground and shielded them with her body, praying frantically, "One Above, protect my children."

"Wife?"

She chanced a glance over her shoulder. There on the path a few steps away stood Shadow Dancer.

"Don't be afraid. The Spanish are celebrating the return of their brothers," Shadow Dancer said.

She looked toward the wall to confirm his words before she raised up enough to release the twins. The boys toddled to their father, laughing and holding their arms out to him.

Shadow Dancer scooped them both into a hug, holding them until they squirmed to be put down. He watched them explore their surroundings, smiling indulgently, while he explained, "Spanish is the name the bearded ones call themselves. See, their brothers return from the north."

She followed his pointing finger to see a column of the *kwelmisps* mounted on their riding beasts crossing the river which was swollen from recent rains.

"The man in the lead is their war chief Por-to-la," Shadow Dancer said. "He and his men traveled north many suns' journey to find something called Mont-er-ey. I wonder, what is this thing they seek?"

"How do you know all this, my husband?" she ventured.

"Every day I watch and listen. After a time, I began to understand their tongue." He thrust his hand forward. "Here. This is for you."

She took the object he held out to her. In shape, it resembled a thick 'epilly tule bent into an arc. In weight, it was as heavy as stone. In texture, it felt to her fingers like a grinding hole that had been used for only a moon or two.

"Twisted Face made it," Shadow Dancer said.

At the mention of the *kwelmisp* with the scarred face, she quickly handed the object back. Shadow Dancer placed it in her palm again. "This is not stone as I thought at first. It is called iron. The Spanish nail it to the feet of their riding beasts. The thunder sticks are made of it also." His enthusiasm did not mask his drawn look.

"You are thin," she said, touching the hollow of his cheek.

"It is the Spanish food. Strange tastes and textures. I am not used to it yet. Even so, there never seems to be enough. Though I do not understand their words, the *kwelmisps* always complain about their food."

He lowered his voice. She could scarcely hear him over the Spanish din. "Their food supplies are low to the point of starvation. I fear they will leave before I can learn their fire magic. I *must* learn it. I must."

He turned away from her to watch the arriving Spanish. His fervor had robbed her of all argument. He had to stay, and she had to allow him to, no matter how tense the situation for her at Nipaguay.

The first Spanish reached the bottom of the hill. The sight of their riding beasts sent a chill coursing up her spine. She did not want to get any closer to them than necessary. "I must go, my husband."

He looked at her as if to ask why she had come in the first place. She ignored the look and hefted the twins onto her back. "Learn the magic of fire, then come home."

Shadow Dancer smiled, but she was too tired to return the favor. She turned and headed off to Nipaguay with the noise of the bearded ones' celebration ringing in her ears.

Chapter 5

The return of Governor Portola's expedition swamped Romero with repair work. He was too busy to think about Three Parts, who hung around the forge, watching every move he made. Likewise, Father Serra was too busy to continue his efforts to coerce him into helping convert the Indian. For that, Romero was doubly grateful.

He had just finished welding a new link in a broken chain when two Leatherjackets showed up. One, named Artiaga, shoved a broken bridle at Romero as if he expected the smith to interrupt everything else to fix it. Romero considered repaying the soldier's haughtiness in kind, until the men's conversation grabbed his attention. He swallowed his pique and invited them to wait for the repair so he could hear more.

The men stretched out in a spot of shade and went on talking without missing a beat. "I've never seen him so angry. Even when we turned back without finding the Bay of Monterey," Artiaga said.

"Can you blame him?" Talavera, the second soldier, asked. "Except for the picket wall, nothing's been done here since we left."

"Nothing but eating from the looks of the foodstores," Artiaga said. "I suppose the Indian attack's the reason for the delay in building."

"That was in August. Five months ago," Talavera said. "Five months and all the progress they have to show is that wall. Don

Portola has every right to be angry. Not even one convert!"

Romero glanced toward Three Parts. As always, the Indian seemed mesmerized by the fire. What did he see there? What was he thinking?

Artiaga scratched his crotch. "It's not converts I care about. It's my belly. I don't intend to go hungry. Unless we see a supply ship soon, we'll all be starving."

"No, we won't," Talavera said. "We'll be long gone before that happens."

Artiaga started to protest, but Talavera cut him off. "Don Portola's given the padres an ultimatum: either a ship shows up by March 19, or we leave Alta California to the savages."

At that moment Father Serra emerged from the mission and hurried across the compound to his quarters. His pale, grim face confirmed what the Leatherjacket had said.

March 19. Less than two months away. Romero felt the first stirrings of hope sprouting in the void of despair that had occupied his heart for so long.

"Well, we know where we can find the Franciscan the next two months, don't we?" Talavera said. "On his knees, praying for a ship."

"Let's hope God's gone deaf," Artiaga said.

"Amen," Romero whispered. "Amen."

Chapter 6

Through a thin stream of smoke from the fire, Casts No Shadow gazed intently at Many Rains as the rain pattered on the tules of the 'ewaa. The young man had come seeking advice. Trouble clouded his face. The wekuseyaay waited for him to speak first.

"My woman–lately she has been acting strangely. Today, I–I followed her." Sadness flickered in Many Rains' eyes. Casts No Shadow steeled himself for news that the young woman had taken a lover.

"She went to the bearded ones' village. I hid where she could not see me and watched while she–she prayed to the paleskin woman god. She prayed for–" The sadness in his eyes deepened into pain. "–for a baby."

Such problems were outside the scope of the wekuseyaay's interest or powers. Many Rains knew that. Why, then, had he come here?

Many Rains stared into the fire a long time before continuing. "While I was there, I spoke to Shadow Dancer."

Hearing his son's name spoken aloud for the first time in three moons caught Casts No Shadow by surprise. He struggled to keep that surprise out of his expression.

"He says that, for the last six days, the Brown Robe leader conducts a ceremony. The same one over and over. He says that the paleskins are preparing to leave." A twinkle replaced the sadness in the young man's eyes. "All the paleskins."

Casts No Shadow threw off his practiced calm. "Even the Brown Robes?"

Many Rains nodded.

"How long till they go?" the shaman asked.

"Four suns," came the answer.

Casts No Shadow gazed out the opening of his hut at the mist. After such a long, trying wait, just four suns more until the kwelmisps left and Shadow Dancer returned to Nipaguay.

"Will you take Shadow Dancer with you to the sacred mountain?" Many Rains asked.

Six suns from now, Casts No Shadow must climb to the top of the mountain to perform the rite of Sun's Ascendance after winter. He had taught his son the songs last spring, but with all the turmoil at the coming of the paleskins, that time seemed long ago.

"He did not mean to hurt you. I know that," Many Rains said.

"It is not me he hurt with his foolish notions. His people look to Shadow Dancer to act wisely in all things. It is them he forgot. It is them he must never forget again."

"Then you will not take him with you to the mountain?" Many Rains asked worriedly.

More than anything, Casts No Shadow wanted his son beside him singing Sun into the sky six days hence, but he would wait to talk with Shadow Dancer before he made his decision. "That is something for us to discuss when he returns. Meantime, do not worry about your wife. No matter that she prays to the paleskin mother god, the spirits will hear her prayers. May they grant her wishes and may she soon give you a strong son."

With a nod of gratitude, Many Rains rose and ducked out into the rain.

Casts No Shadow stared into the fire, mulling what he had heard. The hairy ones had brought so much sadness and pain to the Kumeyaay people that it would take a long time for life in this valley to resume its normal course. Since he had been right about the paleskins, after the strangers left, the people would turn to him for the right direction to take. He must be ready. Tomorrow he would go to his sacred cave. Tomorrow he would see the future.

Chapter 7

As the mission bell tolled sext, Romero scarcely breathed. The cheering began before the bell stopped clanging. The smith added his voice to those of the rest of the Spanish who had waited for this moment on tenterhooks, afraid that Father Serra's novena would work, that God would send a supply ship, forcing them to prolong their stay in San Diego.

Earlier that day, Serra had celebrated High Mass in honor of Saint Joseph, patron saint of the expedition to Alta California. Romero had fidgeted throughout the service. He wasn't alone. The congregation, Governor Portola included, shifted and twitched the entire time. No one wanted to stay here. No one, except the Franciscans.

After the Mass, rather than concede that God had not answered his prayers, the stubborn Serra had stationed himself where he could watch the mouth of the bay for sails. From the end of the Mass until the bell began to toll sext, time seemed to stand still for Romero while he held in tight check his hopes for an end to his exile.

As the bell's ringing died away, happiness surged through Romero's body. *Home! I'm going home!*

He raced to the forge to begin dismantling it for the trip back. When he arrived, Three Parts–whom Father Serra called 'Carlos'–was squatting in his usual place near the bellows. Despite all Father Serra's attempts to teach Carlos about the Church, it was clear that the Indian's interest lay in smithing, not religion.

At Romero's arrival Carlos rose to his feet.

"You're always acting like you want to help," Romero said to him.. "Well, here's your chance. We're leaving, you bloody savage."

Carlos cocked his head as if to understand the Spanish words.

Romero beckoned. "Well, come on."

The Indian came to stand across the hearth from the smith just as a cry went up.

Romero tensed, fearing another attack.

"Sails!" came the shout. "A ship! At the mouth of the harbor!"

"No," Romero gasped. "No, not now. Please."

A Leatherjacket sprinted past the forge, spouting profanity, heading for the lookout post in the center of the fort.

Stunned, Romero forgot Carlos and stumbled after the man to find a crowd gathered around Father Serra and Governor Portola. "The Lord has heard our prayers!" the Franciscan proclaimed. "He sent a ship! Our mission is saved!"

"Where? I see no ship, Father," Governor Portola demanded.

"It was there. I saw its sails with my own eyes," Father Serra said. "It sailed north, past the entrance to the bay."

Although he said nothing, no one could miss the skepticism in the governor's posture.

"It's easy to miss the entrance. Captain Vila will tell you," Father Serra said.

Neither Serra nor Portola nor anyone else spoke for a long time. In the yawning silence everyone stared out at the empty sea. Then, drawing himself up to full height, Father Serra raised his hands to the scudding clouds. "It is a miracle wrought by the hand of the Holy of Holies. God sent the ship, and it will return as soon as the crew discover their error. We must wait here until they do."

Romero wanted to scream at the Governor to shut his ears to the Franciscan's persuasion, but his mouth refused to work.

Portola did not respond immediately. He continued to stare at the bay. "Five days. If this ship of yours does not appear by noon on the fifth day, Father, we will leave. All of us, Father. *All* of us."

Father Serra nodded agreement, but said, "The ship will be here before then. You will see. God will not have us fail in this holy task He has laid before us."

The silent crowd dispersed. Romero plodded back to the forge in a daze. He did not believe that Father Serra would lie, but now, just when everyone was ready to leave, they faced five more days of agonized waiting. For Romero, the change of fortune had come hard on the heels of surviving two years by clinging to a dream of getting back to Loreto and one day finding Father Xavier. Now this. It wasn't fair. God was playing some kind of cruel game with him.

He shook his fist at the sky and yelled, "I hate you!"

Just then Carlos stepped out of the forge hut. The sight of the savage sparked the fury roiling inside the smith. He lunged at the Indian, grappling with him, then pulling him to the ground.

When Carlos tried to roll away, his action merely added fuel to the fire raging inside Romero. He grabbed the Indian around the neck and bore down with all his power.

Carlos gagged and struggled.

Romero tightened his grip.

Carlos bucked, trying to force his attacker's grip loose.

Romero dug his knees into the savage's sides and rode out the moves.

The Indian's leg lashed out, catching a cooking pot that had been brought in for mending, causing it to bang down hard onto Romero's elbow. The force of the blow loosened the smith's grip.

Carlos immediately rolled free, scrambled to his feet and stumbled away before Romero could recover.

The blacksmith got up but decided against a chase. Why bother? Perhaps the savage would stay away from now on.

He leaned wearily against the workbench. Five more days. How would he endure it? How could anyone believe in a God that played such cruel tricks? What had he ever done to deserve all the bad things that had happened to him?

He glared at the ashes heaped on the forge. "Why me?"

No one answered.

With a break in the rain, Sand Flea and Cricket spent the day splashing in puddles and digging in mud, burning off the excess energy they had built up during days of confinement in the 'ewaa. By late afternoon they had wound down enough to accept dinner and an early bedtime without complaint.

Once they were asleep, an exhausted Web plodded out to the wisal. She lowered herself awkwardly down onto a pile of damp carrying nets and tried to get comfortable. With the bulk of the new baby, no position seemed to work. Her back ached. Random pains shot up her legs. The skin of her abdomen itched constantly.

She unhooked the wooden scratcher from her waist thong and dug at the worst of the itches, then reached for her pouch of medicines. Extracting a small hide container of salve, she rubbed the thickened concoction into the stretched skin of her stomach. The familiar odors of creosote and crushed chia seeds brought to mind her mother.

The recipe for this ointment was her mother's closely-guarded secret. The mixture worked for any number of skin irritations.

Web had turned to it when nothing else soothed her itching. Although it did not entirely eliminate the problem, the aroma always made her feel better.

Breathing in the scent, she closed her eyes. Many Rains had come to her four days back with the happiest news she had heard in moons. Tomorrow the Spanish would be leaving. All of them. For good. For her, that meant Shadow Dancer would be home again not just to sleep here occasionally, but permanently. She drifted off into sleep and a dream about him.

Sometime later, a sound startled her awake. She turned to see her husband staggering toward her out of the gathering dusk. Her bulging belly made it hard to get to her feet. She used the roof support for leverage and hurried forward as fast as her swollen body would allow.

He faltered and nearly fell. She caught him, sliding an arm around his waist and supporting him to the *wisal*.

He sank onto the cushion of nets. It took several minutes before he could speak. "He–he tried to choke me," he rasped. "T–twisted Face."

At the memory of that man's hideous face, goose bumps erupted along Web's arms.

"H–he t–tried to kill me," her husband croaked.

Web lowered herself down beside her husband. She wrapped him in her arms and held him until he stopped trembling. He felt like a miracle after such a long absence, but concern for him would not allow her to enjoy the moment.

After a time Shadow Dancer sat up and gathered her to him. Up close she could see the welts on his neck. She did not trust her voice not to betray her emotion.

"He flew into a rage after the Brown Robe chief Serra saw the big canoe," Shadow Dancer said in a husky voice.

She searched his face for signs of a wound that would account for his confusion. Seeing none, she said as gently as possible, "The big canoe has been there since the Spanish arrived."

"Another one. The Brown Robe Serra has been praying every day to the Spanish gods for its arrival. And today it came." His eyes took on a respectful cast. "I did not see it, but Brown Robe Serra does not lie."

A second, stronger chill coursed down Web's spine at the note of awe in her husband's tone. Her lower lip threatened to quiver when she spoke. "Many Rains said the Spanish leave tomorrow."

"This new canoe missed the entrance to the bay and sailed on north, so now the Spanish will wait five more suns to see if it returns."

"You will stay at home now, husband?" she asked hopefully.

"I need sleep before I decide." He smiled at her and helped her to her feet. "Come, wife. Lie with me."

She followed him into the 'ewaa and stretched out beside him, but, between worrying about him and the difficulty of finding a comfortable position, she got little sleep.

In the morning, Shadow Dancer awoke bright and cheerful. He played with the twins while she dragged herself through preparing breakfast. Grateful for a chance to sit but nervous to learn what he had decided, she settled herself across from him and waited for him to speak first.

"This day I must go to the sacred mountain. Tomorrow I must sing Sun on His journey toward summer."

"Then you go with your father?"

He stiffened. "I have no father."

After that, he said no more to her. He gathered his shaman's pouch and headed out of the village.

Not long afterward, Casts No Shadow appeared in his eerie, too-quiet way. "I heard that he was here." Since the day of their argument, the wekuseyaay had not spoken Shadow Dancer's name or referred to him except as 'he'. The rigidity of the older shaman's posture provoked pity in Web. Like any concerned parent, he had acted out of love for his son only to have that love brushed aside by Shadow Dancer's need to stand alone as a man with his own mind, his own wisdom. The longer the rift existed between them, the more inflexible their respective positions. She was caught in the middle.

"Shadow Dancer was here," she answered, hoping the name would soften the wekuseyaay.

"And now?"

"He went to the sacred mountain. To call Sun."

Although he did not show it, she sensed Casts No Shadow's disappointment. In the space of a breath, his reaction passed. In its place were a mask and manner even more implacable.

"He . . ." she began.

Casts No Shadow's hand sliced the air, silencing her. Stiffly, he turned and walked away. She wanted to call him back, to plead for a reconciliation, but that was not her place. The two men had to work this out between them. Until then, she would have to wait, and hope.

In her belly, the new baby kicked and wiggled with a force that made her forget the two men and their problems.

She held her stomach. The baby had moved down.

Another kick.

Such an active baby! Always moving. She would be glad when it was time to give birth.

A ripple moved from the bottom to the top of her stomach bulge. The baby turning a somersault.

She smiled wearily. Soon this ordeal would end, and she would hold a new life in her arms. If only the trouble between her husband and his father could end on such a happy note.

Chapter 8

On March 23, 1770, the packet ship *San Antonio*, whose sails Serra had seen on Saint Joseph's Day, glided into the bay. It had returned to San Diego after losing its anchor on the voyage back to Lower California after the failure of Portola's party to find Monterey. With the exception of the five Franciscan missionaries, the crowd that gathered to watch the spectacle was subdued. For most of them, the arrival of the supply ship meant a few days delay in their return to Lower California with Governor Portola. For Romero, *San Antonio* meant the death of hope.

Father Serra's novena had wrought a miracle for some, a disaster for others. With the supplies from the *San Antonio*, the Mission San Diego could continue and Romero would face a measureless sentence in exile. With scars and a limp that made him instantly recognizable, he would never be able to hide away among the men of Portola's group in order to escape by land. The only other way back to Loreto was *San Antonio* or, if and when they could find the crew, *San Carlos*. For a brief time, he entertained the idea of stowing away on *San Antonio* but his memories of the scurvy immediately quashed that idea.

As the supply ship dropped anchor, Father Serra led the Franciscans in a hymn of thanks. The Latin words drove Romero further into the mire of despair. There was no hope. He would never again see Father Xavier, never again taste love. He would rot here until an Indian arrow killed him or they all starved to death.

Seeing the joy in Father Serra's face proved too much to bear. The smith trudged slowly back to the fort. At the forge he picked up the only thing still left on his workbench to mend: a pistol that Lieutenant Fages had brought in that morning for repair.

What's the use? he thought. *Why not end it here and now?*

Melancholy made him clumsy. The gun slipped from his grip. He made a swipe for it but missed. Upon impacting the ground, an old powder charge in the chamber exploded, burning Romero's outstretched hand.

He staggered backward, shrieking with pain.

The noise brought Fages with a handful of soldiers and Don Pedro Prat, the expedition's lone physician.

The doctor tried to examine Romero's wound, but, agony or not, the smith had seen too many men die to trust Prat with any medical problem. "Father Serra," he croaked.

"Send for the padre," Prat ordered one of the soldiers.

Lieutenant Fages picked the gun off the ground. "My pistol." The censure in his voice was unmistakable even through Romero's pain. "You clumsy oaf," Fages said, then stomped away.

Despite his wound, Romero started after the haughty officer. The doctor grabbed to restrain him, accidentally brushing his coat across the fresh burn.

Pain shot up the blacksmith's arm, stopping him in his tracks, then crumpling him to the ground in a dead faint.

Chapter 9

After celebrating Sun's return to primacy in the heavens, Shadow Dancer returned to Nipaguay and took up life where he had left off. Then the kwelmisps' giant canoe–the one that had left last summer–returned. Web feared that her husband would go back to the paleskins' village. When he did not, she took it to mean that he had decided to abandon his quest to learn the Spanish fire magic.

Seven days after the second boat returned, Web awoke at first light with a cramp. She brushed the back of her hand across the cheek of her sleeping husband, kissed the slumbering twins, gathered her birthing things and lumbered to Hummingbird's lodge. Despite the strain between them over her pregnancy, her friend had insisted on helping with this birth.

Hummingbird was already awake. She supported Web the rest of the way to the birth lodge set at the far edge of the village. Outside the lodge, Web paused. "I have missed you, my sister."

"And I, you," Hummingbird replied, her voice cracking.

Web started to say more, but a new pain wrenched away her ability to speak. Hummingbird held her upright until the pain passed, then helped her inside where she spread the birthing hide, helped Web squat over it, and went to call the village birthing woman.

The cramps soon gave way to pains that grew in frequency and intensity throughout the day. Hummingbird knelt behind Web, supporting her and whispering encouragement through the duration of each pain, mopping her brow and rubbing her back in the interim.

That night, the pain seemed to level off. "My baby?" Web rasped fearfully.

Hummingbird sponged the perspiration from her brow. "The baby is fine, my sister. Do not talk. You need all your strength."

In the gap between the lodge opening and its covering mat of woven grass, stars shone like signal fires against the indigo sky.

"No moon," Hummingbird observed.

A sudden fierce pain gripped Web with an intensity that would have toppled her onto her back if Hummingbird had not been braced for it. The pain forced Web beyond her ability to stifle her screams.

The next pain came on top of the last. By now, Hummingbird's arms around her chest were all that held Web to reality. With the twins' birth, she had experienced nothing like this ripping agony. Nothing.

The birthing woman peered between Web's quivering legs. "It comes."

Another pain seized Web. This time she did not have the strength to scream. *I'm dying*, she thought.

As soon as that idea swirled out of the fog in her mind, Web decided to welcome death as a release from the unendurable agony.

An instant before the next pain, the small wedge of indigo sky that she could see turned to a brilliant, blinding white.

Death? she wondered as more pain exploded in her loins.

Then, as suddenly as it came, the pain vanished, leaving her to float in what felt like a warm pool of still water.

Her lids were too heavy to lift. She lay still, content to let her other senses see for her eyes while she tried to remember how she had come to this world of spirits where there was such peace, and she was so tired.

An infant's cries interrupted that peace. It was a baby, a new one. Why did its mother not comfort it?

The cries grew more insistent.

Hush, little one, she thought. *Go to sleep*.

Hummingbird's voice came from somewhere nearby. "She is

beautiful, my sister. Open your eyes. Look at your daughter."

Web struggled to lift her heavy eyelids. Her ordeal had clouded her vision. She had to blink in order to see a tiny infant with a face that seemed to be all mouth. Then she remembered. "My baby?"

Cradling the child in her arms, Hummingbird nodded. "A beautiful daughter." She nodded at the birthing woman who ducked out of the lodge.

As Web took the child into her arms, gratitude pushed aside all other feeling. "My daughter," she whispered.

The baby broke off crying and stared up at Web.

"She knows her mother," Hummingbird said. "Look, see her hands."

Web took the baby's tiny hands in hers. Between the fingers of both hands, flaps of translucent skin stretched up to the first joints, just like her own hands and those of her maternal grandmother. The mark of First Ancestor. She was too filled with joy to be able to speak.

Hummingbird leaned over the pallet. "You should know, too, my sister, that at the very moment this little one was born, the gods sent a star shooting across the heavens."

A shooting star. That explained what had lit up the night sky before pain overwhelmed her.

Hummingbird gently touched the top of the baby's head. "This little one is meant for greatness."

"Greatness," Web murmured sleepily.

"You must rest now, my sister. Rest and think about a name for the little one." Hummingbird cleaned up the last evidences of the birth and left the lodge.

The baby wiggled in her swaddling of soft deer hide, then settled into sleep. Looking at the tiny wrinkled face, Web suddenly knew what to call her. "Sleep well, little Shooting Star."

Chapter 10

The bright spring sunshine and soft blue April sky were lost on Romero. While everyone else attached to the mission and presidio of San Diego gathered outside the walls of the fort to wish Governor Portola's group farewell on their journey back to Lower California, he sat in the hut that served as a forge, nursing his burned hand, sunk in deepest melancholy over his situation.

The sounds of the crowd drifted to him on the spring breeze.

Each note of laughter, every word of banter drove him deeper into depression. He sighed and shifted. The movement caused his damaged hand to throb.

Gritting his teeth, he cradled the injured hand in the open palm of the other until the pain subsided. It was all so unfair. During the attack last August, an Indian arrow had struck Brother Viscaino in the hand. Now that wound was sending the priest back to Lower California while Romero had to stay in San Diego nursing an injury that was, to his mind, far more serious than the priest's.

He had learned about Brother Viscaino's reprieve yesterday and immediately went in search of Father Serra to ask to return south with the expedition also. He had found the leader of the Franciscans in his quarters busily scratching out letters to send back to Lower California with Portola. Serra had barely looked up from his writing while Romero pled his case. After a cursory examination of the smith's wound, the priest declared, "You'll be back to work in no time, my son," and dismissed Romero with a wave.

Angered by the memory, the smith hawked a wad of spit into the dirt. "In no time, he says. Damn worthless brown robe!"

Chirping drew his gaze to a nest of sparrows tucked under the roof thatch. One of the parents had returned with food for the hatchlings.

The peeping of the baby birds rankled Romero. He grabbed a poker and used it to pry the nest from its ledge. The three naked baby sparrows spilled into the dirt. With one swing of the poker, he crushed their tiny bodies into a bloody pulp.

The effort left his hurt hand throbbing. He dropped the poker and clutched the hand waiting for the pain to pass.

It was then he sensed someone watching.

Craning around, he spotted Carlos standing beside one of the storage huts across the footpath. He had not seen the Indian since the day *San Antonio* arrived to end his dream of escaping this awful place. Seeing the Indian at that moment re-ignited Romero's rage.

Forgetting his injury, he scooped up the poker and flung it at the Indian.

Carlos slid sideways, avoiding the iron rod.

"Filthy savage!" Romero hissed, looking around for another weapon.

Carlos wagged his head. "No savage. Me Carlos."

Hearing understandable Spanish come out of the Indian's mouth knocked the wind out of the smith's fury. As his anger abated, the pulsing in his hand increased to an intensity that made him bite his lip.

Carlos picked up the poker and walked slowly toward him.

Romero backed up. "Just like a savage to kill a man who can't defend himself."

Carlos stopped in front of the smith and looked pointedly at the broken nest and the remains of the sparrows. "Twisted Face savage. Me Carlos."

"Why you . . ."

Romero lunged at the Indian, but Carlos easily deflected the move and shoved him backward.

Windmilling his arms to stop his fall, Romero slammed his injured hand against the workbench. The explosion of pain robbed him of breath and motion.

When he could talk again, Romero looked up at the Indian. "Go ahead. Kill me and get it over with."

"No kill."

"Do it!" Romero yelled. "Give me peace!"

Carlos squatted beside him. "Carlos not kill. Not give Romero peace." He stretched the blacksmith's name into three distinct words: Ro Mer O.

The smith knew then that he had met his match. When he could move, he rolled away from the Indian and got to his feet. Carlos also rose.

From the distance Governor Portola boomed the order to move out. A chorus of cheers and rifle fire followed.

"You stay?" Carlos asked.

Romero nodded. "I stay."

"Bueno." The Indian turned and slipped away.

Romero sank onto the workbench. Amid the sounds of Portola's group heading south, he buried his face in his good hand. *I am doomed*, he thought. *Doomed.*

Chapter 11

C asts No Shadow crested the top of the bluff and paused to survey the valley below. The river was in spate from a month of rain. It had overrun its banks in the usual places so that spring sunlight shown like a hundred mirrors off the resulting overflow ponds. That brightness made him squint.

He looked down on the village of Nipaguay. The sight of his home always made him smile with pleasure.

Two small figures tumbled out of one of the lodges and raced to the river. At the sight of his twin grandsons, the wekuseyaay smiled through his weariness. Though gratifying, his journey had been a long one, and all because of a dream.

In that dream he had been in the desert far to the south, standing in the center of a circle of four strange men when the empty land beyond the circle filled with thousands of rattlesnakes emerging from hibernation. He tried to warn the men to turn, but no words would come out of his mouth. Four of the snakes separated from the rest, slithered forward and struck the men simultaneously. Those men had crumpled to the ground, and he himself jerked awake. Immediately, he gathered his shaman's things into a bundle and set out for the desert to the south.

He had walked south for eleven days, and, on the eleventh night, an old woman appeared at his campfire. She led him to a poor village deep in the dry dun-colored hills. In her hovel lay one of the men from his dream.

Casts No Shadow did not have to look to know about the puncture wounds in the man's calf. He set to work without delay, entering the spirit world to talk with the Great Serpent and His children. In that place where time has no meaning, he argued as forcefully as he knew how to convince the Snake Spirits to release their hold on the young man's soul. In the end, they agreed, and Casts No Shadow returned from his spirit journey to find the old woman weeping for joy and the young man on the mend.

A similar scene repeated three more times. Only with the last did the rattling serpent band shun the arguments of Casts No Shadow, keeping the man's soul for themselves. The effort left the wekuseyaay more tired than he could ever remember, but, with his work over, he did not dawdle. He headed for home.

Home. How he had missed his grandsons!

By now Web would have passed the period of birth taboos and she and Shooting Star would be free to take part in the normal life of the village.

He had seen his granddaughter only briefly before he left. Throughout his entire journey he had not been able to forget the sight of those tiny webbed fingers. Twin boys and now Shooting Star. Blessings that the gods had bestowed on the people of Nipaguay through Web, the desert girl.

He lifted his hands to the sky and prayed, "Thank you, One Above, for Web. Keep her and the children safe from want and harm."

He could not bring himself to include Shadow Dancer in the prayer although the image of his son and the memory of their argument haunted him constantly. He had not uttered Shadow Dancer's name or the words 'my son' since that day. "May he come to his senses," he said to the sky.

A glance up the valley showed a haze of smoke hanging over the place where the bearded ones had built their village. Casts No Shadow's jaw tightened. The gods had not sent the newcomers away. How much longer would the Kumeyaay people have to endure their presence?

Patience, he thought. *Time has no meaning in the world of the spirits. The hairy ones will leave when the spirits decree.* Readjusting his burden, he headed down the steep trail into the valley.

He had to try three paths before he found a safe crossing of the river, high with rain run-off. To his satisfaction, he slipped into Nipaguay without detection. He dropped his things inside his 'ewaa, noting that it had been freshly swept, thanks to Web, then he went to see her and his grandchildren.

His fatigue dissolved at the twins' squeals of welcome. He scooped them into his arms and danced in a circle, bouncing them, marveling at how much they had grown. Too soon they were demanding to be put down. Reluctantly, he watched as they raced away to find a new delight to enjoy.

"Welcome, my father." Web came up behind him cradling Shooting Star in her arms.

The baby reached out a hand to him. He gave her his finger to clutch. "She is as beautiful as her mother."

Web blushed at the compliment. Her heightened color made him aware of how thin and drawn she looked. A quick glance around the lodge site told him why. He could feel a flush of anger spread upward from his neck. "He went back to the bearded ones?"

Web ducked her face as if checking the baby.

"He leaves you alone," he hissed.

"He . . ."

"He abandons his children," Casts No Shadow said angrily.

"We . . ."

"He is wrong."

"No!" Web said, drawing herself up and staring him in the eye. "He is 'aww-kuseyaay. He does what the spirits have told him to do. I am his wife. I follow him."

This time it was Casts No Shadow who looked away while he

got his temper under control.

"He is your son," she went on. "He is the father of your grandchildren. Please end this break between you. For the sake of us all."

"I cannot."

"Please."

"It is he who must end it."

She looked ready to say something more but did not. She turned away from him and plodded back into the lodge.

For a long time he stood alone looking at the dwelling. It had been wrong—no, it had been cruel to show her his anger. She had to support her husband, no matter how foolish the path. From now on, he would not discuss Shadow Dancer with her.

That decided, he squared his shoulders and went to his 'ewaa to unpack.

As the sound of Casts No Shadow's footsteps faded into the distance, Web remained in the gloom of the 'ewaa, sorting through the tangle of her emotions. Conviction had ripped apart the two men she loved. Now stubborn pride kept them apart, and she was trapped in the middle. Someone had to bend. But who? And when?

Shooting Star's hands jabbed the air, the baby's way of searching for a breast to suckle. Web guided the small mouth to a nipple and leaned back against the pile of dressed rabbit skins she planned to join into a blanket when she had the time.

She smiled ruefully. *If* she had the time was more the issue. With a new baby and with Shadow Dancer back to spending most of his time at the Spanish village, her energy had sunk below her ability to replenish it with rest or food. The twins now had two summers. The only thing that stood between her and collapse was Hummingbird.

Since Shooting Star's birth, Hummingbird spent more time at Web's lodge than her own. She had assumed the care of the twins while Web waited out the prescribed after-birth period. Between the blessing of Shooting Star and the return of her friend, Web's life had begun to return to the form she had longed for when Shadow Dancer announced that he was resuming his quest to learn fire magic from the Spanish. Web wanted to plead with him to reconsider, but could not bring herself to speak against the advice of the spirits.

The day he left she managed to hold back her tears until he was across the rain-swollen river. Hummingbird arrived moments later. She took Web in her arms and let her cry herself out. Hummingbird had been there with Web every day since, bringing food and helping with the children.

Thoughts of her friend made Web aware that she had not yet seen her today. Already it was Sun-Above. Where could Hummingbird be?

Imagining all kinds of mishaps, Web ducked out of the lodge and headed toward her friend's. She found Hummingbird kneeling in front of her hut, packing a burden net.

At Web's approach, Hummingbird whirled as if caught doing something wrong. She scrambled to her feet with a nervous smile.

"Is something wrong, sister?" Web asked.

Hummingbird came toward her, moving woodenly as if unsure of the ground. "I–I was going to come to your 'ewaa next."

"What has happened? Tell me."

"Nothing has happened, sister. I was coming to say goodbye."

"Goodbye? Where are you going?"

At the rise in her mother's voice, Shooting Star broke off suckling and began to whimper. Hummingbird reached out to stroke the baby. Her voice was barely audible. "I go to stay in the village of the Spanish."

Web did not need to ask the reason. Hummingbird had finally succumbed to the lures of the Brown Robes. She was going in order to be near to the paleskin mother god whom she believed could help her conceive a baby of her own. Knowing how much her friend longed for a child, Web bit back a protest. She embraced Hummingbird. "May One Above bless you then, my sister."

Hummingbird's shoulders shook with silent weeping. Web held her without speaking.

When her tears were over, Hummingbird extracted herself from Web's embrace, picked up her burden net and hurried away. Web watched her go. First Shadow Dancer. Now Hummingbird. One by one the Spanish seemed to be robbing her of everyone she loved most. "No more. Please take no more of the ones I love away from me. I . . . ." Her whispering died away, choked by a sob.

VI

DESERTION

Spring—Fall, 1771

Chapter 1
Beginning of March, 1771

A t the place on the path to the ocean where a second trail
broke off toward the Spanish fort, Web took leave of Casts
No Shadow and her sons. The twins had nearly three summers'
growth and the physical coordination of boys twice their age. Their
grandfather had agreed to take them fishing for the day so Web
could go to the mission to see why Hummingbird had summoned
her.

Although the wekuseyaay said nothing, Web knew that he
disapproved of both Hummingbird and the summons. He led the
boys away after a curt nod, leaving Web to watch their retreating
figures with a mixture of sadness and pleasure. The sadness
stemmed from Casts No Shadow's continued refusal to discuss
Shadow Dancer or a reconciliation between the two of them. The
pleasure came in seeing the normally dour wekuseyaay take such
delight in the rambunctious little boys.

She glanced warily toward the Spanish encampment. She had
avoided the place since before Shooting Star's birth over a year
ago when the group of paleskins had returned from their northern
journey.

Web sighed. If back then she had gone through with her
intention to persuade Shadow Dancer to give up his notions
about learning the Spanish fire magic, perhaps Shooting Star
would recognize her own father instead of wailing whenever he
tried to hold her during his infrequent visits to Nipaguay.

She adjusted the cradleboard strapped to her back. Shooting
Star's little hands reached out and grabbed hold of Web's hair.
Web reached back and tickled the baby's fat arm, eliciting a
gurgle of nonsense syllables. "Yes, little one, we're going."

Despite the trepidation she always felt around the Spanish, Web was anxious to see Hummingbird. Her friend had come back to Nipaguay only twice since moving to the mission. What had prompted her to send for Web? And why had she requested that Web bring a rabbit-skin blanket? Was she sick like so many of the Kumeyaay who had gone to live with the bearded ones?

The closer she drew to the picket wall, the stronger the mixture of odors she had come to associate with the Spanish: an offensive combination of dung from their riding beasts, unwashed flesh, their strange foods and human excrement. She breathed through her mouth to keep from gagging.

She had to pass between two paleskin guards to enter the fort. Their bold gazes unnerved her. She hesitated and was about to turn back when Hummingbird appeared. "Oh, my sister, you did come. And you brought the blanket. Good. Here, I will hold the baby while you put it on."

"But the day is so warm. There is no need for a blanket," Web protested.

Hummingbird glanced nervously at the watching soldiers. "The Brown Robes require that women cover their upper bodies."

Web searched her friend's face for signs that she was playing one of her usual jokes. Finding no humor, she draped the blanket to cover her front.

Hummingbird was dressed in a sack-like garment that covered her from neck to ankles. Its shapelessness emphasized the gauntness of her face and the lack of sparkle in her eyes.

Following her friend into the mission compound, Web came up short at the sight of Many Rains. He was dressed in garments like those worn by the men who tended the beasts the Spanish let loose in the Kumeyaay fields. One piece was made to wrap around his legs, while the other, a shorter version of Hummingbird's, covered his chest and hips. It was tied at the waist with a short rope of braided yucca. He came toward them smiling. When Hummingbird first moved to the mission, Many Rains had been distraught. Over time, however, his agitation faded, and he was left dazed and disoriented. Web had tried to offer comfort but decided to leave him alone when he showed no response. To see him here, dressed as he was, rendered her speechless. What was going on?

When he reached them, Web saw that Many Rains' mouth smiled, but his eyes were full of sadness. Hummingbird touched her husband on the wrist. "Today the Brown Robes hold a ceremony for us. It is their ritual for joining woman to man. It will allow Many Rains to live here at the mission with me."

The news stunned Web. Of all people, Many Rains was the last one she expected to succumb to the Spanish lure.

Many Rains spoke up. "The Brown Robes will not allow us to lie together until we have this ceremony."

"The Spanish Holy Mother will bring us a child," Hummingbird declared with her thin jaw set in a stubborn line. "A child as beautiful as your little Shooting Star."

Web swallowed the retort that rose to her lips and mustered a tight smile. Just then, she spotted Shadow Dancer across the compound. He waved and started toward her only to have a Brown Robe, the one called Serra, stop him. Web watched as her husband exchanged words with the leader of the bearded ones' shamans. When had he learned the paleskins' language?

The conversation ended and he joined Web and the others. He swept an arm toward a cluster of Brown Robes gathered near the hut marked by the crossed sticks of the paleskin god. "Father Serra, he asks me to help with the wedding," he said to Web.

She wanted to know what the words "father" and "wedding" meant, but surprise made her blurt out, "And you will?"

"It is the way I am winning their trust," he answered. For the first time Web sensed discouragement in her husband's demeanor, but before she could pursue the issue, the Brown Robe Serra beckoned Many Rains and Hummingbird. They hurried off, leaving Web alone with Shadow Dancer. "You are well, my husband?" she ventured.

"The learning goes slowly, very slowly."

She did not press. The last time he came to Nipaguay, he had complained that he could not convince Twisted Face to show him how to handle the objects of the fire magic. She interpreted his current dejection as a sign that Twisted Face was still not cooperating. She took heart from this but was careful not to let it show. A sudden clanging startled her.

"That is the mission bell, wife," Shadow Dancer explained. "It means I must go to help Father Serra for the wedding."

He rushed off, leaving her alone and feeling exposed. She drew the rabbit skin blanket more tightly around her, glad for its comfort despite the day's warmth.

The ceremony began with chants from the shaman Serra. Web could make no sense out of the words and actions of the Brown Robe leader even with Shadow Dancer's translation. She soon gave up trying to understand the rite and shifted to studying her husband.

How handsome he was! And how clever to have already learned the language of the paleskins. As she watched him, she allowed herself to begin to hope that he would soon be back in their 'ewaa. A hope that she had denied herself since the last time she came to this fort.

Movement out of the corner of her eye drew her attention. She turned to find herself the object of scrutiny by eyes set into the scarred and twisted visage of Twisted Face.

His attention unnerved her, and she moved to get out of his sight. She skirted the nearby hut and made for the gate, slowed by the bulky cradleboard that she had taken off her back. She was about to step through the unguarded opening when someone grabbed her arm, jerking her to a stop, nearly causing her to drop Shooting Star.

"Well, well. What do we have here?" The gaze of a Spanish guard ran from her neck to her knees. His breath reeked of decay. The stench from his body made her gorge rise.

She bent her head and stared at the ground rather than look into those probing eyes.

"A shy one, huh?" the paleskin said, forcibly lifting her chin.

Avoiding his eyes, she hugged the baby to her chest and fought to keep the fear out of her face.

The soldier walked around her, spreading his stench until she thought her stomach would rebel. Finally he stepped back. "You'd do—if I was desperate. Only I'm not that far gone yet."

Shooting Star began to whimper. Web clutched the cradleboard, praying that the sound would not prompt the paleskin to do anything to her or the baby. Especially the baby.

"Go on. Get out of here," he said.

Because she could not understand the words, she tried without success to sense the meaning from the man's facial expression.

"You better go, woman," he growled, "before I change my mind."

The man's angry tone got her moving. She ran up the trail as fast as her burden allowed, not slowing until she reached the main path. She continued along the bluff top, stopping only when she reached a secluded spot along the river. There she knelt until her panic subsided and her breathing returned to normal.

The guard's grip had left a red mark on her wrist, but his leer had left a deeper mark that made her feel unclean. Hanging the cradleboard from a tree branch, she disrobed and plunged into the water, immersing herself in the cold river, cleansing herself of the Spanish filth, until her teeth began to chatter.

Emerging from the water, she tied on her skirt and took Shooting Star down from her perch. The baby sucked on her fat little fingers and gurgled happily. Web kissed her daughter's forehead and looked back at the fort. "Never again will I go to that awful place," she vowed, then headed for Nipaguay.

She did not stop shaking until the next day.

Chapter 2

B rother Gomez stood outside the hut that housed the forge, peering in. He had been there all morning, silent and watching, and his presence rattled Romero. What did the man want?

Once the noon bell finished tolling, Brother Gomez finally broke his silence. "Carlos."

At the sound of his name the Indian bounced to his feet. A year had passed since Carlos had surprised Romero by calling him a savage in Spanish. Since then, the Indian had become the Franciscans' translator. When they had no need for him–which was most of the time given that they had managed to win so few converts–he hung around the forge becoming such a fixture that he had become virtually invisible to Romero.

"Carlos, you are always here with the blacksmith. Why?" Brother Gomez asked.

"I wish to learn the fire magic," Carlos said.

"Oh, no!" Romero said. "No savage touches my tools."

"Blacksmith, watch yourself," warned Brother Gomez.

"Converting savages is your job, Padre. My job's to smith. Period."

"The Lord rewards those who bring new lambs to His flock."

At the mention of rewards, Romero put down his hammer and looked directly at the missionary. "The only reward I want is a way back to Loreto. I want to go by land, and I want to go a free man."

The missionary had come to San Diego aboard *San Antonio*. He was one of the Franciscans meant for Monterey but returned to San Diego when Portola's expedition had failed to find the place. Like Romero, he had escaped scurvy, but the deprivations of his voyage and the subsequent journey north with Portola had weakened him so that he had never fully recovered. Now the day's bright sun accentuated the deep creases that patterned his face when he said, "That seems an equitable trade."

"W–what do you mean?" Romero stammered.

"Your return to Loreto for teaching Carlos here how to smith."

Romero searched the priest's face for a sign that the Franciscan was trying to trick him. When he found no such indication, he ventured, "What exactly are you saying, Padre?"

"To use Carlos' words, he wants to learn your magic. If you agree to make such a contribution to our cause, José, Father Serra will reward you. I will see to it."

"And just how will you do that, Padre?" Romero pressed.

"I will write to Father Serra asking for your release from this mission and for your return to Loreto."

Serra had gone north again with another group to try to find Monterey. A letter would take months to get to him–if it ever did. Still . . . . "By land?" Romero asked.

"By land."

Romero looked from Brother Gomez to Carlos. The speed with which the Indian had learned Spanish astonished everyone. That meant there was intelligence behind those cunning brown eyes. And Carlos was strong. Romero had learned that first hand. With intelligence and strength, Carlos–and Romero–were already ahead of the game. "Agreed."

Brother Gomez nodded, then addressed the Indian. "Well, Carlos, you have your wish. José will teach you the magic of his fire, but–" he held up a finger, "–you must agree to two conditions. First, you will receive religious instruction with the goal to one day becoming a member of the Holy Mother Church. Second, you must move to the mission permanently and agree to follow the rules we require of all neophytes."

Romero held his breath while Carlos considered the offer.

"I agree," Carlos said at last. "I will go to my village for my things."

Trapped air rushed out of Romero's lungs in an audible grunt. He watched the Indian head out through the mission gates.

"Bless you, blacksmith!" Brother Gomez said. He raised his face to the sky. "And thank you, Virgin Mother, for answering my prayers at last. We promise to protect this precious soul You have entrusted to us, to instruct Carlos in Your wonders and to deliver him to Your son as a Christian and a devout member of His Holy Flock."

Romero watched the padre as he prayed. He himself had ceased praying the day *San Antonio* had sailed into the bay and saved the mission, dashing his hopes of returning to Loreto. Why bother to pray when the only thing you wanted had been snatched away from you?

He had lived without any hope for so long that he had forgotten how hope felt.

"Keep me informed of his progress, blacksmith," Brother Gomez said.

"Of course."

If the Franciscan heard the irony in Romero's voice, he did not show it. He walked off and Romero turned back to the forge. There was so much to know, so much to teach the heathen. Where would he start?

Shadow Dancer caught Web in a jubilant embrace, lifting her off the ground and swinging her in a circle. "At last I am to learn the fire magic of the Spanish." He set her down. "The Brown Robe Gomez got Romero to agree to teach me."

Out of the welter of mixed emotions that the news raised in her, the only detail her mind grasped was that Twisted Face had a name: Romero.

"The spirits heard my songs," Shadow Dancer said. "Soon I will bring the paleskins' power to all the Kumeyaay people."

When her feelings finally sorted out, Web felt joy and relief in equal measure. Joy that her husband was about to realize his dream; relief that there would soon be an end to the extra burden his absence had put on her.

But when she smiled at him, he looked away too quickly. She did not have time to steel herself for what he said next. "In return, I must live at the mission."

Her jaw dropped. How could he agree to such a thing? Had he forgotten that Twisted Face had tried to strangle him? Didn't he realize that he could die from the mysterious sickness that had taken the lives of so many of the Kumeyaays after contact with the Spanish? Once he moved to the mission, he would never get to come to Nipaguay. The Brown Robes would punish him if he tried, and she had seen enough of the beatings and other horrors the Spanish used for punishment to know that his first try would be his last. Did he not understand that his children needed their father? That she needed a husband?

He gripped her shoulders. "I must do this, wife. I have to learn the bearded ones' secrets. For my sons. For my people." Undisguised rancor roughened his voice. "I am no longer an apprentice. It is time to be a real 'aww-kuseyaay, to stand apart from my father."

He had not mentioned Casts No Shadow since the two men had argued. She fought the urge to remind him that he had not finished his shaman's training, that the people needed that knowledge as much as the Spanish fire magic.

He went on. "My father is neither right nor wrong. After I know the secrets of the fire, I will go to him and make peace between us once again."

The eyes he turned to her begged for understanding. "Soon, I will return to you, my wife."

At the love in his tone her doubt vanished. Since the day she had caught him with Crooked Basket, she had witnessed his disgust toward her change slowly to tolerance and then to admiration and love. And as his love for her had grown, so had hers for him. He was her husband. He knew what was best. He had to do this. And she had to help him do it.

He gathered his things into her best carrying net. She watched him, memorizing every move and angle of his body. Too soon, he was gone without saying goodbye to the twins who had again gone off with their grandfather for the day. She hugged herself against a yawning gulf of grief.

Shooting Star awoke from a nap and began to fuss to be fed. As Web bent to pick her up, one of the baby's hands brushed her cheek. She felt the touch all the way to her heart. She gathered the little one to her. "Oh, my precious baby, he is gone."

Shooting Star's face crumpled and her whimpering turned to wails. The baby's cries dissolved Web's restraint. Her own eyes stung with tears. "Gone," she whispered. "Gone."

Chapter 3

At the beginning of July, Brother Gomez's shaky physical condition began to deteriorate. Intent as he was to teach smithing to Carlos and thereby escape San Diego, Romero did not find out about the situation until the ship *San Antonio* showed up unexpectedly.

The arrival of the ship pulled him away from the forge when nothing else could. He stood with the other Spanish from the fort watching two new Franciscan brothers come ashore in the first launch. When only Brother Parron came out to greet them, Romero joked to one of the guards, "Brother Gomez must be sleeping again."

"It's not right to joke about such things, blacksmith," the

soldier shot back.

"What things?"

The soldier looked at him as if he could not believe the question. "Where have you been? Everyone knows the padre is sick unto death."

"Sick? When?" Romero stammered.

"Since two weeks back." The soldier jabbed a thumb at the launch. "And those two are our new padres."

Romero was too stunned to even manage a nod. *No, not Brother Gomez. It can't be. Not now.*

He rushed to the padre's quarters, but two guards kept him from entering. Frantic for a chance to talk with the priest, he took up a vigil outside the hut. He had to find out if Brother Gomez had kept his end of their bargain.

All day and night he sat there, waiting for an opening. He was still in place early the next morning when a squad of soldiers showed up to carry the sick priest's litter to the launch. With every nerve rubbed raw by fear that hope was about to be snatched from his grasp yet again, he pushed his way into the group of soldiers and grabbed up the ailing priest's hand. "Did you write the letter, Padre?"

When the soldiers tried to drag him away, Romero shoved them aside and squeezed the hand harder. "Did you?"

The priest's eyes fluttered open, then shut.

"Out of the way, blacksmith," the corporal yelled.

"Help me, Father," Romero pleaded, uncaring who heard him. "Answer me."

The lids lifted, revealing blue eyes that had trouble focusing.

"Padre, please."

"Romero," Brother Gomez rasped.

"Yes, Padre. It's me, Romero. Did you write the letter like you said you would?"

The missionary managed to lift one hand off his sunken chest. He brushed Romero's scars with a fingertip. "Such a tragedy, my son."

"Romero!" the corporal warned.

"The letter, Padre. The letter," Romero urged.

The missionary's eyes took on a puzzled cast.

Romero leaned closer in order to hold their focus. "The letter to Father Serra. Did you write it?"

"Serra. He is a saint," Gomez whispered.

Hands grabbed Romero and yanked him away from the priest. "Get out of here, blacksmith. Now!" the corporal ordered.

When the blacksmith tried to get back to the padre, two soldiers dragged Romero out the gates and hurtled him face-first into the dirt outside. He picked himself up in time to see the soldiers bearing the priest's litter down the hill to the launch.

"No," he shouted. "No!"

"Can I help you, my son?"

The voice belonged to one of the new missionaries, Brother Dumetz. Romero's will refused to let go of the last slender thread of hope offered by that voice. Brother Gomez had given a promise. If he had not written to Father Serra, then Romero had to make sure someone did. Someone like this new padre Dumetz. Taking a breath to calm his anxiety, he began by saying, "I am the mission blacksmith, Romero."

Brother Dumetz nodded. "Mission San Diego could not exist without you."

"For three months now, I have been teaching the Indian—the one called Carlos—how to smith."

"Excellent. Is he learning?"

"All heathens are slow-witted. I have to work very hard to teach him even the simplest things. Eventually he catches on."

"The Lord will bless you for making such a contribution to our mission."

Contribution. Brother Gomez had used that very word when they made their original bargain. The coincidence gave Romero heart. "Then Brother Gomez told you."

"Told me?"

"About our bargain."

"My son, Brother Gomez has been out of his mind with fever since I arrived here."

Romero sucked in another breath to steady himself, then told the padre about his agreement with Brother Gomez.

"You say you did not choose to come to San Diego. How is it then that you are here?" Brother Dumetz asked.

He could see no way out of telling the truth, but he abbreviated it as much as he dared. "I left Mexico chained in the hold of *San Carlos.*"

"I see. A prisoner. What was your crime?"

"I—I don't know," Romero lied.

The missionary eyed him sharply. "My son, our King would never imprison anyone without cause. If you do not admit your guilt, you can never receive God's forgiveness. Until you do, you should be thankful for this chance to expiate your sin."

"But our agreement . . . ." Romero pleaded.

"Continue your teaching, my son. In that way, you can make amends for your crime. Remember: Heaven awaits those who repent."

The missionary walked away, leaving Romero with an unobstructed view of the rolling green water of the ocean. As he limped down to the beach, every step added fuel to his feelings of betrayal.

By the time he reached the surf, he was angry enough to lash out at someone. A short distance down the beach Dumetz stood next to Brother Jayme, the other new missionary surrounded by the rest of the population of the mission, watching the launch carry Brother Gomez out to *San Antonio*. Romero was fed up with priests and their lies. He spun around and headed the opposite direction as fast as his limp and the loose sand would allow. Since he was out of shape from months of inactivity and poor food, he quickly ran out of breath.

The moment he stopped to rest, laughter sounded behind him. He turned to see two Indians standing a few feet up the slope of the beach. The man and woman wore the shapeless garments the padres required of their neophytes. The man held a string of fish. The woman, a shallow basket heaped with just-gathered shell-fish.

The man spoke to the woman in Indian gibberish, eliciting a giggle. All at once Romero knew that they were laughing at him—at his limp and his disfigured face.

Forgetting his fatigue, he ran at the woman, grabbed her by the hair and slung her to the sand. When the man tried to intervene, Romero caught his leg and kneed him in the groin.

The man shrieked and crumpled to the sand.

Meantime the woman scuttled to her feet and tried to run down the beach.

With little effort Romero tackled her, knocking the air from her lungs with a satisfying "umph." Leaping to his feet, he aimed an angry kick at her bare midriff. "I'll teach you."

She screamed.

Another kick. "Filthy–" a third kick "–savage."

Without warning someone shoved him back. A man darted between the blacksmith and the downed woman. "Stop this instant!"

Romero found himself staring into the anger-mottled face of the second new missionary, Brother Jayme. Behind the priest trailed three soldiers from the mission garrison.

"Help this woman up," the priest ordered.

The soldiers did not seem inclined to obey until they saw Captain Fages hurrying toward them. Fages had been away from San Diego for most of the last two years, a situation that agreed with Romero and all the soldiers. Two weeks ago, however, he had returned to San Diego, bringing two nasty surprises: Lieutenant Fages was now Captain Fages, and he had replaced as military commander of Upper California the capable and respected Captain Rivera y Moncada who had led the first land expedition to San Diego. As lieutenant, Fages had won the enmity of all the men in his command for his inflexibility and harsh punishments. As a captain, he had grown even more cruel and rigid.

"What's the problem, Padre?" Fages asked.

"This man was beating these Indians," Brother Jayme said.

Under the captain's glare, Romero knew he had better speak up in his defense. "The filthy savages bumped into me."

The missionary's voice rose in disbelief. "You kicked this woman! I saw you."

"Then the *puta* asked for it," one of the soldiers said.

Fages whirled on the soldier. "Twenty lashes!" He pointed at the men flanking the offender. "You two take this man up to the fort and tie him to the whipping post. I will deliver his punishment in person."

The offending soldier made the mistake of begging for mercy.

"Thirty lashes, then!" Fages thundered. "One more sound out of you, private, and it will be fifty."

The captain possessed a special whip, a dozen thick rawhide strands with one end gathered into a heavy but finely-balanced lead handle, and the tails weighted with lethal pieces of the same lead. With his own eyes, Romero had seen that whip kill one man and maim two more. He had no desire to taste its sting. He clamped his mouth shut against the urge to speak in his defense.

The soldiers marched off with their cohort, and the two Indians stumbled off, groaning and supporting each other. *Just like whipped dogs*, Romero thought.

"And this man, Captain?" Brother Jayme asked, pointing at Romero.

By now, except for the Franciscan, Romero and the captain, the beach was deserted. "He is your problem, Padre," Fages said haughtily. "I have quite enough to handle with my soldiers."

"But he beat up two of my converts. After such treatment, how can I hope to bring more of these children to the Church?"

Romero did not dare speak or return the padre's gaze. He

looked at the ground, as sweat from the sultry July air trickled down his face.

"Your responsibility, Padre," Fages said. "But I'd think twice if I were you before doing anything rash. He's the only blacksmith you are bound to have for a good long time."

With his anger fading, Romero wished he had some way to hide from the new padre's accusing eyes.

Brother Jayme glared at the blacksmith. After a long silence, he declared, "Fifty Hail Marys, blacksmith."

Romero had to fight the impulse to laugh aloud at the ridiculous sentence. But, as the padre walked away, he remained, eyes on the ground, listening to the sounds of sand crunching under the man's sandals. When he finally looked up, he found Captain Fages studying him.

"Be thankful you're not mine, blacksmith," Fages said. "I would kill you."

The captain wheeled and strutted back toward the fort. Romero watched his retreating back. No wonder the soldiers hated the man. No wonder he had heard so much desertion talk.

Wait a minute. Desertion. Why haven't I thought of that before?
One night, he had eavesdropped as Dominguez and others talked of their plans. At the time, he dismissed it as bravado, but what if they were truly serious?

The moment his feet started walking, they knew exactly where to go.

The whipping was underway when Romero reached the mission compound. Dominguez, the man he sought, stood with a clump of his fellow soldiers, glumly watching the lash fall on their comrade's naked back. Romero wedged himself into that group as unobtrusively as possible.

By the time he had gained a position next to Dominguez, the errant private had passed out from the pain of the beating. Still the flogging continued. With each sickening *thwack* the captain's whip stripped more flesh from the unconscious man's body.

Between blows, Captain Fages scanned the gathered troops as if searching for his next victim.

The final blow fell, removing the last strip of recognizable skin from the private's back. When the wrist ropes, binding the man to the post, were cut, the unconscious man crumpled in a heap.

"Leave him!" Fages ordered. Turning on his heel, he marched

into the hut that served as his quarters and slammed the door.

Romero chanced a sideways glance at Dominguez. The normally swarthy skin along the man's jawbone shown white. Romero leaned toward him and muttered, "I see what you mean."

Dominguez looked suspiciously at Romero.

"Fages," the blacksmith said. "He is a cruel one."

Dominguez snorted. "He is a *brujo*."

Romero pierced the soldier with his eyes. "When are you leaving?"

Dominguez whirled and grasped Romero by his biceps. "What do you mean by that, blacksmith?"

Romero answered in a calm near-whisper, "I know you and some of your friends are planning to desert." He continued to stare into the soldier's eyes, as he added, "Can we talk of this? In private?"

Dominguez glanced sideways at the others who had watched the whipping, as if aware that he was drawing attention to himself. Quickly, he released Romero. "Where can we talk?"

Romero jerked his head in the direction of his forge. He moved away and strode to his hut. Fortunately, Carlos was gone. Moments later, Dominguez's form filled the doorway.

"How do you know about my plans?" he demanded.

"Keep your voice down," Romero warned. "Never mind that. I'm not your enemy." He moved closer. "When are you going?"

Dominguez hesitated a split-second, but did not try to deny Romero's assertion. "We're fed up," he said. "We're leaving tonight."

"Tonight?" Romero said, exhilaration bubbling into his voice.

"Two years in this place with no end in sight. And now Fages gets made a captain." Dominguez swung a length of pipe against one of the poles holding up the roof. Vibrations brought down a shower of dust and tule pieces. "I'm married, but I haven't seen my wife or son in two years. Without wives and families, how are we supposed to stay sane? Most days there's not enough to do to bother waking up."

Dominguez heaved the pipe at the workbench. "Hang Fages! My first duty's to my family, then comes the King."

Romero saw his opening. "It's a long way to Lower California. You and your friends, you'll need a blacksmith."

"You'd leave?" Dominguez asked, surprised.

Romero threw off all caution. "Take me with you."

"I have to ask the others."

Romero could not trust his voice to say anything else. After Dominguez left, he looked at the work piled on his bench. None of it mattered as much as Dominguez's approval.

He went to his room but could not sit still, so he returned to the forge and paced back and forth behind the enclosed side of the hut where no one could see him.

Time crept by even more slowly than usual. *What could be taking so long? What if they said no?*

At one point another soldier came by the forge and yelled for Romero. The smith stopped pacing and hid behind the wall until the man gave up and went away.

It was late afternoon when Dominguez returned, but before he could reveal the decision, Carlos reappeared, bent nearly double under a load of wood. Romero had to wait what seemed like an eternity for the Indian to drop the load before he could send him off again.

As soon as Carlos was out of sight, the blacksmith turned to the soldier.

"Midnight, at the river where we water the horses. Make no noise," Dominguez said.

Romero's heart was beating so fiercely he could hardly hear himself. "I'll need a horse."

"We don't have enough horses. You'll have to use a donkey. The muleteer's with us, too."

A donkey would be no help if Fages sent Leatherjackets after them, but Romero saw no other choice.

"The midnight guard's going, too," Dominguez instructed. "Wait until he's on duty and the guard he relieves is well out of sight before you leave your hut."

Romero could not keep the grin off his face. "Gracias, amigo."

"Don't thank me until we're gone. And remember: no noise."

After Dominguez left, the smith turned to the workbench and picked up a knife with a broken blade. Fages' knife. And it would stay broken, wouldn't it? And so would all the rest of this pile. He was on his way back to his life. This time nothing would get in his way. Nothing.

Chapter 4

R omero was too overwrought to hide his agitation. He skipped the evening meal and retired to his hut before dusk to begin the long wait for midnight. He would not allow himself to think beyond meeting the others. He had suffered the consequences of dashed hopes too often to give himself completely to the emotion again until he was actually on the trail heading south.

Finally, after an interminable wait, the last of the mission inhabitants went to bed and a hush fell over the compound. Romero lay on his pallet, staring out at the star-flung summer sky, waiting for the sounds that would signal the changing of the guard. He passed the time by trying to pick out figures among the stars. No matter where he looked, his eyes seemed to trace the robe and cowl of a priest, of Father Xavier. *No, I must not think such things. Not until I am away from this place.* He turned his back to the doorway, so he would not be tempted to think about anything but the next few hours.

At long last, the creak of leather and a few words of muffled speech from the direction of the gate announced the change of guard. Romero counted slowly to thirty, as high as he knew the numbers in succession, five times, then rose off his pallet. The relieved guard moved so slowly to the barracks that Romero felt his heart would burst from impatience.

Once the door closed behind the man, Romero scooped up the roll containing his blanket and the few tools he dared take along and sprang free from his hut. He crept across the compound to the gates, holding his breath out of fear of being discovered so close to escaping. The complicitous guard waved him through the gap in the gates, then fell in behind.

This path was not used as much as the others so it was rough and overgrown. As he shifted his awkward load, Romero's bare right foot stubbed against an embedded rock. "Oow!" he yelped.

Instantly the guard's hand clamped tightly over his mouth. Together they stood like a pair of interlocked statues, waiting for the shouts that would signal they had been discovered.

After a long unnerving interval, the soldier released Romero. "Quiet," he cautioned in a taut, angry whisper and led off down the path.

Dominguez and eight others were already gathered beside the river. Romero knew all of the men but one. A whiff of the stranger identified him as the muleteer who had recently driven a herd of livestock to San Diego from Lower California. The knowledge that one of their number had already traveled the trail they would take made Romero relax a bit.

The mule driver gave the blacksmith the reins to a mule, but when Romero tried to mount it, the animal skittered sideways. Two hard jerks on the reins put a stop to that.

No sooner had the blacksmith settled into the saddle than Dominguez took off with a wave for the group to follow. At the blacksmith's kick, the mule resisted, but a harder kick aimed at the animal's lower stomach got it moving.

The mule refused all efforts to move up in the line of march, and Romero found himself bringing up the rear, a position made doubly precarious since he possessed no weapon other than his bare hands.

Once past the Indian village of Cosoy, Romero looked back at the fort. A crescent moon cast silvery light on the picket wall, leaving deep elongated shadows on the nearest side. There was no hint of movement, no whisper of sound. For the first time all day he let himself hope that he was finally on his way home.

His mule chose that moment to snort. The noise sounded like an explosion in the stillness.

Whipping back the ends of the reins intending to punish the animal with a slash across the eyes, Romero stopped himself before he could deliver the blow. The punishment would make him feel better, but it might cause the animal to bray, or worse.

"I'll take care of you later," he whispered, giving the mule a swift kick.

The animal grunted its discomfort, and for the first time in months, Romero smiled.

Chapter 5

Web hurried past the barren place where the Spanish had churned up the earth and stuck in seeds. Of the few seedlings that had sprouted, few remained, and most of those had withered under the summer sun.

If the Spanish have so much magic, why do their plantings die? The question popped unbidden into her mind, and she immediately shoved it aside. She was on her way again to the mission to see her husband despite her vow not to return. The Spanish had exhausted their food supplies, and every three days for the last moon she had carried *shawii* acorn gruel to Shadow Dancer rather than force him to forage for food like the other Kumeyaays who had moved to the mission. Foraging would take him away from learning the bearded ones' fire magic. Faced with the choice between making frequent trips back and forth to the mission or prolonging her husband's stay among the Spanish, she picked the former though each visit meant seeing Twisted Face and enduring more of the soldiers' leers.

On this day, however, she found the gates unguarded. She

hesitated to enter, but, seeing nothing out of the ordinary, she proceeded to pass inside. There she saw the reason for the lack of guards: all the soldiers were gathered around what Shadow Dancer called the flogging pole watching one of their own receive a whipping. Covering her ears against the cracks of the lash and the cries of the man being beaten, she turned away from the sight of his bloody lacerated skin.

Such cruelty to one of their own kind was unthinkable to the Kumeyaay people, but these Spanish did such things, and worse, to each other as a matter of course. The more she saw of these strange paleskins, the more she believed they were evil spirits sent by a wicked sorcerer bent on forcing the Kumeyaay people of the coast off their bounteous lands. That was the only explanation that made sense out of their sudden appearance and the pull they exerted on both Shadow Dancer and Hummingbird.

Before she reached the area her husband called the forge, Shooting Star began to whimper to be fed. "Hush, little one," she coaxed, hoping to calm the baby until she could find a private place to feed her daughter, away from the soldiers who constantly stared at her breasts.

Shooting Star stopped complaining, but Web knew the silence would not last for long. At the forge she found Shadow Dancer alone and obviously upset. "You are troubled, my husband?"

He accepted the basket of gruel from her. "Romero ran away."

"You mean, the Spanish are prisoners here, also?" The question came out before she realized what she had said.

If Shadow Dancer heard her, he gave no indication. "The soldiers have a new war chief, Captain Fages. He is a cruel man who has his followers flogged for the smallest reason. This is the second day in a row he has had one of his own men beaten."

She waited for him to eat some of the food before asking, "Why do they not choose a new war chief?"

"The soldiers do not choose their leaders. The one they call the King chooses them."

The baby began to cry again. Checking to see that no soldiers were in the area, Web unwrapped the infant from the cradleboard and put her to her right breast. "That makes no sense, my husband."

"It is their way, though our way is better." He forced a half-smile. "During the night, Romero left with nine soldiers and the keeper of the carrying beasts. They went south, back to where they once lived."

The baby sucked greedily at Web's nipple. She looked down at the small webbed hands kneading her breast, gathering the courage to say what she had to. In the silence Shadow Dancer slurped the gruel she had brought for him. She watched him for a time before speaking. "So now will you return to our village?"

Shadow Dancer gave her a long look. "This war chief Fages sent one of the new Brown Robes after Romero and the others."

"He did not go himself?"

"Those men would never surrender to him. They hate him. He did not go because he is too proud."

Web could not comprehend such foreign thinking. A Kumeyaay leader led by consensus. No one would agree to follow a man they did not respect.

Shadow Dancer leaped up and began pacing back and forth. "Romero, he *must* return. He must. There is still so much for me to learn."

In the face of his intensity, she kept quiet but issued her own silent plea to the gods that Romero never return so that her husband would come home.

Shadow Dancer stopped pacing. "You ought to see Hummingbird before you leave, wife."

Web shifted the baby to her other breast. "Is she ill?"

He hesitated as if deciding what to say. "Not her. Many Rains is."

She waited for him to continue, but he said no more. Satisfied, the baby spit out the nipple and looked placidly up at her mother. "Will you return to Nipaguay with me now, husband?"

"The new Brown Robe will bring Romero back. I must be here when he does."

Frustrated that her husband so stubbornly clung to his beliefs, Web secured the baby on the cradleboard and hurried away from the forge before her frustration could ooze out in accusations she would regret.

Hummingbird and Many Rains lived in a poor hut near the south wall of the mission compound. At her approach, Hummingbird rose from the ground outside the hut where she had been sitting. Worry had etched deep grooves in her forehead and around her eyes. "My husband is sleeping," she said quietly.

"What is wrong?" Web asked in a hoarse whisper.

"His man parts have been injured."

"What happened?" Web asked.

"Twisted Face kicked him there. On the beach five suns ago."

"What?" The word exploded out of her. "Does my husband know this?"

Hummingbird nodded.

"And yet he stays here," Web muttered angrily under her breath.

She handed the baby to Hummingbird and ducked inside the hut. Many Rains lay on a pallet, eyes closed, his face pale against the dimness.

When Web touched his arm, the man's eyes fluttered open. They were filled with such sorrow that Web had to look away. "My wife wants a baby, but I do not know if I can give her one now."

Web did not know what to say.

"He was kicking her. And I–Twisted Face . . . ."

Web put a finger to his lips. "That one is gone. He ran away with some soldiers last night."

"May he die on the journey," Many Rains said, his voice tight with hatred.

Web nodded. "And may you recover and may the magic of the Paleskin Mother work for you and your wife."

Many Rains managed a wan smile. "Thank you, my sister."

Web backed out into the sunlight and reclaimed the baby. "He sleeps now."

Hummingbird nodded sadly and sagged down next to the hut entrance. Web walked away, keeping her angry thoughts to herself. Shadow Dancer's quest for the Spanish fire magic was beginning to warp his judgment. For all of this, the best thing that could happen now was for Twisted Face to make good his escape, one way or another.

"May he die on the journey," she said aloud to the sky.

"Ba-ba?" Shooting Star said.

Web swung the cradleboard into her arms and kissed her daughter. "Shall we go home, little one?"

Shooting Star grinned and laughed and babbled a baby-talk version of her mother's question.

"Sand Flea and Cricket?" Web said.

At the mention of her brothers' names, the baby's eyes lit up. Web caught her little hands and kissed them, then looked toward the mission. "Come home, my husband. Please come home."

Chapter 6

Romero sat in the sandy dirt, too exhausted to lift his head to see who owned the hand that held out the moldy sea biscuit to him. He made a tired grab for the food, too hungry to ignore it, no matter how rotten.

"Make it last," Dominguez growled. "That's all there is."

Romero nibbled on the edge of the biscuit and held the pieces in his mouth for a time before chewing. Little saliva flowed into his cottony mouth. He reached for his water tin, but Dominguez's hand stopped him. "Save it."

The smith had no energy left for argument. No one had figured the hot dry summer weather into their plans. The farther south they moved, the drier and rougher the terrain. The game they had counted on to sustain them had never materialized. After five days' travel, their food was gone.

The only abundant thing about the country they were passing through was Indians. There were hundreds of them against just ten poorly-armed men, besides Romero, in their small party.

"We'll stop here for the night," Dominguez said.

Romero roused himself. "But Fages . . ."

"Fages be damned! If we don't rest our mounts, they'll die underneath us."

A glance around the ring of men showed a nod or two of agreement, and not one of dissent. The idea that that martinet of a captain was tracking them had driven Romero beyond the point of exhaustion, but he could not go on without the others. Not when savages surrounded them on all sides.

Their leader by default, Dominguez ordered two men to stand watches. For once he did not choose Romero. The smith nibbled his biscuit and watched one of the men, a squat surly private nicknamed "Pax" for no discernible reason, scuttle up a rise that had a view to the north.

Too soon Romero finished his food. Too done in to retrieve his blanket, he curled onto his side and fell immediately to sleep.

He was deep into a dream featuring a table laden with roasts and meats and fruits of all kinds when someone yelled, "Riders!"

By the time he wavered to his feet, Pax had skidded down the slope to report, "It's Brother Paterna with a white flag."

"How many Leatherjackets?" Dominguez asked.

"A dozen," Pax said.

"And Fages?"

"Didn't see him."

Dominguez stared into the distance before speaking. "Let's see what the padre has to say."

Several men protested.

"You have a better idea?" Dominguez demanded.

No one did. Pax climbed the rise and disappeared. He returned a few minutes later with Brother Paterna who walked, leading his horse.

The Franciscan was one of a group of missionaries who were at San Diego awaiting assignments to come from the absent Father Serra. Romero had been too preoccupied teaching smithing to Carlos to pay much attention to the visitors. He recognized Brother Paterna, but that was the extent of his knowledge of the man.

Calmly, the dusty priest looked around the circle of men. "The trail from San Diego has been long."

"Is that what you come to tell us?" Dominguez demanded.

The priest ignored him. "You are all so tired."

"And hungry," someone behind Romero volunteered. Dominguez glared at the man.

Brother Paterna held out his hands as if bestowing a blessing. "You can all rest and eat now. Captain Fages offers each of you a full pardon."

"Sure he does. And I'm the next Pope," Dominguez snarled.

"As God is my witness," Paterna said.

"Who was Fages' witness, Padre?" Dominguez asked.

"God—and three other priests."

A hundred witnesses would not convince Romero to trust Fages, not where deserters were concerned. Deserters reflected negatively on the captain's authority, a fact that the man's inflated ego would never allow.

When no one spoke for a long time, Paterna said, "The trail to Misión Velicatá grows even more difficult beyond this point."

"He would never pardon us, Padre," Dominguez said.

"There is no water, no game and no grass for your animals," the priest went on.

"We're deserters. He'll shoot us—or worse," said Dominguez.

Brother Paterna looked at Pax. "Are you hungry, my son?"

Head hanging, Pax shifted nervously. "Yes, Padre."

"I have food. Would you like some?"

Pax's voice cracked. "Oh, yes, Padre."

"Do you want to come back to San Diego?"

Eyes shining, Pax nodded. "Oh, yes, Padre."

"Pax!" Dominguez yelled.

Brother Paterna untied a large sack from his saddle. "I have food for everyone who wants to go back with me."

Romero stood his ground while all the deserters except Dominguez surged forward for the priest's handout. After a time, even Dominguez joined them.

Romero strode to his mule. "Witnesses or not, I don't trust Fages. I'm for heading south. Who is with me?"

No one would look at him.

"I know the trail, blacksmith," Brother Paterna said. "It's suicide to try it alone."

"I'm going," Romero declared.

Romero swung onto the mule, but, before he had gone twenty paces, soldiers surrounded him. One took the reins. Another tied his hands together. He struggled, but he was too weak to escape the bonds or the men.

"This is for your own good, my son," the priest intoned. "My conscience will not allow me to let you put your life in such jeopardy."

"It's my life," Romero growled.

"No, son. It is God's."

"There is no God."

Brother Paterna drew back as if Romero had hit him. "Guard!"

Two more soldiers rode over.

"This man will walk back."

The soldiers shoved Romero bodily off his mule. His hands were tied. He could not break his fall. He landed on his face in the dirt, knocking the breath out of his lungs.

"God gave you life, blacksmith. You owe Him your thanks," Brother Paterna said.

Faced with the prospect of walking back to San Diego, Romero held his peace, but inside he shouted, "There is no God!" Then hands jerked him to his feet, and he found himself on his way north. On foot.

VII

BROTHER FUSTER

August, 1773—April, 1774

Chapter 1—August 1, 1773

Misión San Fernando Velicatá, Lower California

"Padre, Padre! Here they come!"

At the shouts, Brother Vicente Fuster raised his head toward the crucifix nailed to the adobe wall of his room. "So, my Savior, the time has come at last," he whispered.

A boy burst through the doorless opening. "Padre! They come!"

"Yes, Miguelito. I heard you."

The Indian boy's mischievous grin and the energy radiating from his small frame brought a smile to the priest's lips despite the bad news.

The boy turned serious. "But you are sad, Padre. Why?"

Ducking Miguelito's penetrating gaze, Brother Fuster busied himself with the straps on his saddlebag. The message from Father Palou, the presidente of the missions of the Order of Friars Minor in Lower California, had come weeks ago. Every day since, he had left his room with the intention of telling his flock the news, and every night he returned with the words still unspoken. "Why don't you run out to meet them? Perhaps one of the soldiers will let you ride on his horse," he said to the boy.

As the priest hoped, Miguelito sprinted away, forgetting his question. Alone again, Brother Fuster sagged onto his pallet with a defeated sigh. Just when he was making such progress, when he was finally experiencing a sense of accomplishment here at this northernmost of the missions of Lower California, he was being ordered away. Worse, he had not even told his loyal converts.

He dug his fists into his temples. *Failure. You are a failure, Vicente. Give up. You don't have the calling. Amalia . . .*

The name came unbidden, slicing through his silent recrim-
inations. Unconsciously, his hand sought the pocket stitched
inside his sleeve and drew out a single lace glove. Amalia's
glove, the one she had dropped in her hurry to leave him the last
time they had been together. Along with the memory came her
words: "I have decided to join the Poor Claires." She had
repeated the phrase again and again until she cut through his
disbelief.

"But what about our love?" he had finally stammered.

"Love for God is the only pure love," she declared.

In all the years he had known her, he had never once over-
stepped the bounds of decorum with her, but, at that moment he
was seized with the urge to gather her in his arms, to kiss the
hurtful words from her lips, to force her to abandon her foolish
notion and run off with him. In the end he could not bring
himself to touch her for she was his heart's true love, his reason
for breathing. Yet all he could manage to do was stutter, "P–
pure?"

"I will devote my life to serving Him," she said, tossing her
thick curling hair defiantly.

"But the Poor Claires are–poor," he threw back at her.

"The better to serve Him," she said firmly. "You must leave
now. I enter the convent at dawn."

In a last-ditch effort to bridge the yawning gulf that had opened
between them without his realizing how, he reached for her arm,
but she pulled out of his grasp and hurried off, dropping her
glove in her haste. This glove. The only tangible thing he had of
her besides the longing that still haunted him.

True to her word, Amalia had entered the convent the next day.
Afterwards, he had spent a year trying fruitlessly to piece his life
back together. His plight led him to the solace of religion and the
Convento de San Francisco at Zaragosa, the archdiocese for his
home village of Alcaniz in the Spanish province of Aragón. A
year after that, at age 17, he took his final vows. Now, a decade
later, he found himself in New Spain, assigned to this Misión San
Fernando Velicatá.

Velicatá. He had been a Franciscan for a dozen years before he
arrived here, but in this place he began to feel for the first time
that he was more than an impostor running away from a broken
heart. Before Velicatá, he had often pondered leaving the Order
of Friars Minor. Yet after he arrived here, such thoughts ceased to
cross his mind. That is, until Father Palou's message had come.

Brother Fuster drew the lace of the glove through his fingers. In his vows, he had promised to forsake all personal possessions. Yet he could never bring himself to discard this glove. He had never told anyone about it, but God knew he had it. And that tormented Fuster.

Why am I so weak? What can't I just throw it away now and make a clean start?

An irregular opening cut beneath the sloping flat roof of the hut served as the room's lone window. Through it, the dry wind now bore a cloud of dust. The sounds of creaking leather and clanging traces in the distance announced horsemen arriving. Those sounds brought the priest out of his reverie. *I must pray*, he thought. He tucked the glove back into its hidden pocket and hurried out of his hut to the building that served as the mission church.

Coming into the shadowed interior from the brilliant beating August sun, he had to stand still until his eyes adjusted to the gloom. Except for a lone candle burning on the altar, the small room was empty. He began to kneel at the altar, but, with his fingers still sensing the lace of Amalia's glove, he stretched out face down on the hard-packed dirt floor and, with his arms stretched out to the sides, pressed his nose into the earth. "Forgive me, Father, for I have sinned."

He stopped.

God had heard all his excuses dozens of times before. Yet still he possessed the glove. Still he lived in violation of his solemn oath.

His right hand clenched into a fist, ready to pound the floor. He took a deep breath and forced his hand to relax until its palm cupped the ground. "Help me, Lord, to obey my superior, Father Palou. Help me . . ." He swallowed, "To leave this place and go where the Reverend Father sends me. Help me do so without regrets for this place I have grown to love so much."

He stopped himself in order to get control of the sudden emotion that threatened to spill out of him. When he could trust his voice again, he continued. "I have tried to be a good shepherd to the flock of your red children here. Please guide me so that I may continue to do your work in Upper California."

The words "Upper California" flooded his mind with images. The first tales he had heard about the northern missions were of the Indian attack on Misión San Diego four years ago. Since then, several parties of San Diego priests had come south to Velicatá seeking food and livestock when their crops failed to grow and the supply ships failed to appear. As a consequence,

Brother Fuster had come to think of Misión San Diego as a waterless, barren place surrounded by hostile natives.

Publicly he supported his superiors' heroic attempts to shore up the first Upper California mission, but, in private, he considered such efforts wasted. Without water, there could be no crops. No crops meant no way to feed converts and, eventually, there would be no converts.

Leaving Velicatá was one thing. Going to a mission that had no chance of surviving, quite another. But how could he ask God to grant him a reprieve from the assignment he had been given when he could not even part with Amalia's glove?

He turned the question over in his mind until excited voices outside signaled that Reverend Father Palou's party was about to arrive. He closed his eyes and put aside his inner turmoil long enough to pray, "Plant me where I may serve You best. Amen."

Getting to his feet, Fuster brushed dirt from the front of his worn robe, touched his sleeve to be sure the glove was still in its hiding place, then squared his shoulders and walked out to greet his visitors.

Chapter 2

The corporal in charge of the squad escorting Father Palou's party reined in his horse and pointed. "There it is, Padre. The mission and new Royal Presidio of San Diego."

Brother Fuster squinted against the glare of the late August sun. What he saw hardly fit his idea of a Royal Presidio. Squat tule-roofed pole huts surrounded by a stockade the height of a man. Inside the compound a cross of rough-hewn timbers stood before one of the huts signifying the mission church.

A cluster of rush-covered domes that housed the mission's neophytes stood outside the wall. The few Indians in evidence wore a haphazard collection of cast-off Spanish clothing, evidence either that the native women had not yet learned to weave or, worse, that the mission flocks could not provide the necessary wool.

A natural bay lay to Fuster's left. Its rippling blue-green water in the shape of a giant's crooked finger reaching several leagues to the south was contained on the west by a strip of sand that varied in width from a few varas to half a league. The mouth of the bay was protected by a rib of rock that rose abruptly from the ocean to a height of over a hundred varas, then tapered down to the level of the sea as it ran northward.

Opposite this rock, which had been christened Point Guijarros on nautical charts, and across the expanse of the bay, the mission occupied the next highest piece of land, good for defense, not good for growing crops. Crops needed fresh water, but the only water Fuster could see was salt.

By the time the column reached the native huts, a welcoming party had congregated outside the stockade gates. Among the listless faces, Brother Fuster counted surprisingly few brown ones for a mission established four years ago. Closer, the mission buildings looked more squalid than at a distance.

He touched his sleeve for the glove's reassurance. *Not here, Lord. Please don't put me here.*

Brother Fuster had to work to hide his dismay at the sparse meal the two San Diego missionaries served. He took small bites of the *gacha* corn gruel and set down his spoon between each one to make it last longer. Too soon, his bowl was empty, yet he was still famished.

An Indian woman in a shapeless brown robe that emphasized her small frame cleared away the bowls. After she left, Father Palou dismissed all the brothers except for Fuster and the two San Diego missionaries. With the others gone, the more serious of the two missionaries, Brother Luis Jayme, leaned forward. "We apologize to Your Reverence for the meal." He darted a glance at his missionary companion, Brother Peña. "The rains did not come and our seed withered in the fields."

His hand rose from his lap, then dropped back as if the effort cost too much. "Our supplies—we have to ration—only the Divine Father knows when the next ship will come."

"Last year there was too much rain," Peña inserted. "It washed away our seed, and we had no more to plant. This year, no rain."

"The mission register shows seventy converts, Brother Jayme, but I have seen no more than ten," Father Palou said.

Brother Jayme looked squarely at the mission president. "We cannot feed them, Father. We had to let them leave. To forage for food. If we don't move the mission soon, our efforts here are doomed."

"You have discussed the matter with Captain Fages?" Palou asked.

The San Diego missionaries exchanged another look, then Jayme answered in a low voice, "The Presidio and its soldiers ought to stay here, Father."

"What, and leave the mission unprotected?" Palou demanded.

Brother Jayme cleared his throat and shifted on his bench. "There have been—incidents, Father. Between the soldiers and our converts."

"Were the soldiers punished?" Palou asked.

"No, Father. No punishment. Nothing. Despite letters and pleas of protest from both of us," Jayme said.

"It is Captain Fages' view that he controls all things temporal, including discipline for soldiers and Indians, whereas we Franciscans control only the spiritual," Peña said.

"Misión Carmel has experienced similar problems, Father," Jayme said. "Captain Fages also refuses to provide men to establish new missions. It is for both those reasons that Father Serra went to Mexico City a year ago—to put our case before the new Viceroy."

Father Palou closed his eyes and crossed himself. "May God speed Father Serra's return and grant the Viceroy the wisdom to honor his requests." He looked back at the two San Diego missionaries. "I won't ask you for details of these problems between the soldiers and your converts, Brother Jayme. I have been on this frontier too long not to know what they are."

The missionary sat up a bit straighter as if Father Palou's empathy had tapped some hidden spring of internal strength. "Reverend Father, there are hundreds of potential converts just in this river valley alone. Souls awaiting the word of God, ready for the sheltering arms of the Holy Mother Church if only we can feed them."

"Brother Jayme has already written to Father Serra in Mexico City requesting permission to move the mission to a place further up the river where rainfall is more dependable," Brother Peña offered.

"Have you received a reply?" Palou asked.

"No, Father," Jayme said. "And it could take months to get one. Months we don't have if we are to have a crop next year."

"Or if we want to have any converts left," Peña added.

Father Palou pushed back from the table and walked to the hut's open door where he stood looking out for a long time, hands clasped behind his back. At last he turned to face the two San Diego missionaries. "In Father Serra's absence, I suppose the decision rests with me. First thing tomorrow, I want to survey the river valley."

"So you agree?" Brother Jayme asked.

Father Palou nodded. "San Diego is our first mission. It must not fail. Tomorrow we will find land with adequate water for crops."

Brothers Jayme and Peña both slumped with relief.

"And regarding your request, Brother Peña," Palou went on.

Peña's surprised look announced he had momentarily forgotten whatever he had asked for.

"Brother Fuster?" Palou said.

The conversation had lulled Fuster. Hunger pangs had sent his mind off into visions of the meals his mother used to prepare every Sunday after the family returned from Mass. At the mention of his name, his attention snapped back to the moment and his superior. "Yes, Father?"

"Tomorrow you will assume Brother Peña's duties."

"Here?" he blurted.

Father Palou answered with a reprimanding glare. "Brother Peña has asked for relief."

Fuster bowed his head.

Palou's voice lost some of its edge. "You are being rewarded for your success at Velicatá."

Fuster nodded, keeping his eyes focused on the dirt floor. God had given him the one thing he did not want. There was nothing left to do but make the best of it. "Thank you, Father."

Chapter 3

Romero slumped against the back wall of the forge hut. A film of sleep blurred his vision, but he did not have the will or the energy to blink it away. Why bother? Today would be the same as all the days before it: not enough food, brackish water too disgusting to drink and too many hours to fill, stretching ahead into an endless chasm of boredom. Always before, he had been able to lose himself in his work, but, since returning from the aborted desertion attempt a year ago, he had lost interest in everything, even smithing.

Surprisingly, Captain Fages had kept his word. None of the men was punished for his role in the desertion attempt. All had returned to their normal duties as if nothing had happened. However, for Romero, returning proved worse than any physical punishment. The moment he turned back to San Diego, he gave up all hope of ever leaving the place.

Sleep provided his only escape from the endless boredom. Every night he fell asleep willing his body to die. Yet every morning he found himself still alive and faced with the prospect of another day in this living hell.

From the other side of the hut, Carlos turned toward him, holding out a pistol. "Master, how shall I fix this?"

Master. What a joke! I am master of nothing, not even my own life, Romero thought, beckoning the Indian to bring the weapon to him.

Carlos came to him, moving like a cat, silent and fluid. Romero had returned from the foiled escape to find Carlos at the forge as if he knew the smith would return. When Romero had ordered him to leave, Carlos had smiled, a crafty, mocking smile, the first and only smile the blacksmith had ever seen cross that acorn brown face.

For the past year, the Indian had left the forge only to serve as translator for the padres. He had stayed even when the padres, faced with dwindling supplies and a second failed crop, excused the other Indian converts to leave the mission in order to search for food.

Twice Romero had seen Carlos eating something out of a basket. On the first occasion the Indian had held out the basket to him. "Here, master, eat."

At the time, the Spanish rations had been cut to one-third of normal and Romero's belly ached constantly to be filled, but he drew back from the offer in revulsion. "Insects and lizards. The filth you eat will not pass my lips, savage."

The Indian's eyes had narrowed, but his face remained noncommittal. "Starve then, master. Carlos will eat it all."

Now, the Indian handed Romero the pistol. The hammer had cracked. The blacksmith heaved a sigh. A year ago he would have been eager to tackle such an intricate job. Now, just standing required more energy than he had. Although Carlos had proved a quick study, performing most of the smithing work for the past year with little help from Romero, gunsmithing was one of the skills the blacksmith had no intention of ever teaching him.

"It belongs to the new *tendiente*, master. You must fix it," Carlos said.

"Not *'tendiente'*, you dullard. *Teniente.*" Romero's ire began to rise at the mention of the new officer who had arrived from Lower California yesterday, escorting a group of Franciscans. Ortega was new to San Diego only in his recent promotion to lieutenant. He had been merely a sergeant when he commanded the garrison that was left at San Diego when Governor Portola and Father Serra set out in April of 1770 to search for the Bay of Monterey.

It was rumored that Ortega had come to San Diego with news that the hated Captain Fages had been replaced. Although such news would be reason for joy, Romero chose not to find out if the rumors were true. To do so would force him to talk to these men who had so easily given up on freedom and caved into Fages' pardon. Romero regarded those men as traitors and as enemies. Someday they would pay for betraying him. Until then, he refused to have anything to do with them.

"How do I fix it, master?" Carlos asked.

"*You* won't. I'll fix it. Out of my way."

With effort, Romero pulled himself to his feet, then had to lean against the wall while a bout of dizziness passed.

"Good morning."

At the unfamiliar voice, Romero craned around to find one of the new missionaries who had arrived the day before.

"I'm Brother Fuster," the Franciscan said. "Brother Peña's replacement."

So, yet another priest gets to leave this hateful place. "I didn't know he was sick."

"He isn't. He is to go north with Father Palou."

At least Peña wasn't going south. Romero trudged to the forge and tossed charcoal onto the fire, then motioned Carlos to work the bellows.

He put the new missionary out of his mind until the man spoke again. "Who is your apprentice, blacksmith?"

The Indian answered. "I am Carlos."

"You speak Spanish?" Fuster asked.

"I speak good Spanish," Carlos boasted. "I translate for the padres."

"And you're learning to smith, too. Wonderful!" Brother Fuster clapped his hands together in delight. "The Dominican Las Casas was right. The proof stands here before me."

"What is this thing 'proof'?" Carlos asked.

The priest threw back his head and hooted a laugh. "Intelligence; creativity; the ability to learn. Your skin might be brown, but you are no less human, no less advanced than I."

"Don't be so sure, Brother Fuster."

The voice belonged to the arriving Brother Jayme. "Do not presume to judge the natives of this place by Carlos's standards. Believe me, he is unique. These others," his hands swept a futile arc toward the compound, "They range in intelligence from brutal animals up to the level of trainable children."

"How can you be so sure, Brother, with so few converts?"

Fuster asked.

"Two years' worth of dealing with them. That's how I know, Brother. Two long years with Carlos here the lone beacon to guide me when I needed it." Jayme rested a proprietary hand on the Indian's shoulder, then tapped the other priest's arm. "But come. I must show you the rest of our mission."

Romero watched the two men walk away. This new man's ideas weren't just wrong; they were dangerous.

"What is this word 'proof,' master?" Carlos asked.

Romero shot him an angry glance. "Ask the Brown Robe, not me. Now get to work. Air!"

A momentary shadow crossed the Indian's face before he applied himself to the bellows.

Sagging against the wall, Romero waited for the heart of the fire to glow the right color. *Dangerous ideas*, he thought. *Dangerous man. Dangerous savages.*

Chapter 4

Standing beside Casts No Shadow, Web watched a dozen men from Nipaguay move into position around the perimeter of one of the fields controlled by the village. With hand signals, the wekuseyaay adjusted the men's positions until they were an equal distance apart. Then he motioned for them to stay in place while he turned his attention to the direction of the wind.

The people of Nipaguay had just returned from the mountains. The granaries bulged with acorns. Now it was time to burn the fields before the coming of the rains.

Web studied the sky and the wind, trying to see what the shaman saw. However, she had no more success this time than in the past.

His hand sliced the air. The men on the left end of the field touched their fire-brands to the autumn-dry vegetation. One after another, the clumps of sere grass caught fire until the entire length of the field was delimited by fire. Driven by the light wind, the burning line advanced forward until it hit the rocks that lined the river. With no more fuel, the flames extinguished to smoke, eventually dying out altogether.

Web watched in wonder. No matter how many times she witnessed Casts No Shadow or her husband direct the burning of the village fields, she stood in awe of the men and their knowledge. In all the time she had lived at Nipaguay, never once had fire jumped the field or failed to burn completely. No other village could boast such a record. The two men possessed more wisdom and knowledge than other shamans–knowledge and wisdom Casts No Shadow had begun to teach in small doses to the twins who were now of an age to learn.

Movement on the path on the other side of the river caught her attention. A group of Spanish mounted on their riding beasts rode slowly eastward beneath the bluff that bounded the valley on the south. The paleskins appeared to be searching for something.

The sight of Shadow Dancer riding behind one of the Brown Robes took her by surprise. He rode stiffly as if unsure about being atop one of the fearsome creatures. When had he learned to ride them?

Because he lived at the mission, he had not been able to accompany the village to gather acorns this year. Besides dealing with the loneliness caused by his absence, she had worried the entire time. What would he do without the food she brought him? *You are too thin*, she thought in his direction. *Oh, my husband, when will you return to your family?*

She watched until the mounted group disappeared from view, then she turned back to the wekuseyaay and the blackened field. If Casts No Shadow had seen Shadow Dancer, he gave no sign. In all the months that she had been going to the mission to deliver food to her husband in defiance of the wekuseyaay's counsel, she had never resolved the guilt she felt. Guilt that doubled when she started carrying food to Many Rains and Hummingbird also. Compassion would not allow her to forsake those she loved when they needed help even when that compassion forced her to disobey the one man, besides her husband, she respected above all others. She had paid for her choice with emotional turmoil that ate at her contentment and her sleep.

"Web!"

The shout came from the footpath that led westward to the ocean. Hummingbird emerged from the smoke wearing a broad grin in place of the dour expression that usually graced her face anymore. Since moving to the mission, Hummingbird had returned to Nipaguay only once–for the death rites of her grandmother. She had come despite the Brown Robes' rule against such visits, and, when she had returned to the mission, the Brown Robes punished her by chaining her to a post for three days.

Web found out about her friend's ordeal when she went to the mission to see her husband. She had stepped through the gates to the sight of a soldier cutting the rope that bound Hummingbird to the post. Weak from hunger and pain, Hummingbird slumped down into a puddle of her own excrement. When she tried to get up, the Spaniard deliberately knocked her down and left her lying where she fell.

Outraged to see her friend so abused, Web had lifted her friend up and dragged her to the small dark hut where she and Many Rains lived. There, Web bathed her and treated the wrist wounds left by the ropes. All Hummingbird could say was "I was wrong," a phrase she repeated over and over until she finally fell asleep.

While Many Rains explained what had happened, Web struggled to keep from screaming that he ought to have done something to help his wife rather than accepting the Brown Robes' punishment. She had to remind herself that it was Hummingbird who had chosen to move to the mission, that Many Rains had followed only in order to be with his wife, that Many Rains himself had also suffered terribly at the hands of the Spanish.

While Web was there, Many Rains fed to Hummingbird his own pitiful ration of the disgusting corn gruel the Spanish lived on. As she left to return to Nipaguay, Web decided that from then on, whenever she visited Shadow Dancer, she would carry food to her friends also. She wanted to believe that it was her way of hastening the day when all of them would be together once again in Nipaguay.

"Oh, my sister!" Hummingbird now exclaimed breathlessly, wrapping Web in an energetic embrace. "The Holy Mother of the Brown Robes has heard my prayers at last."

Web pulled away to look at her glowing friend. "A baby?"

"A baby," Hummingbird said. "For four moons now, no blood comes to me. I wanted to be sure before I told you."

It was Web's turn to gather Hummingbird into a hug of joy. Her voice was husky with emotion. "When the baby comes out to see his mother, I will be there with you, just as you have been with me both times."

"Oh, yes, my sister. Please, yes."

A sob of joy choked off Web's reply, and, for a moment, she knew only the pleasure at her friend's good fortune.

Chapter 5

B rother Fuster rubbed his strained eyes and leaned back, eliciting an ominous creak from the splintery wooden bench upon which he sat. On the pitted tabletop in front of him lay a sheet of parchment and a writing quill. Outside the rain puddled beneath the hut's overhang. Behind him, Father Serra paced the small cell as he read another of the stack of letters. They had been waiting for him upon his return to San Diego two days ago from an arduous seventeen-month journey to Mexico City to see the King's new Viceroy about the needs of the missions in Upper California. Although the Franciscan leader's journey had taken a physical toll on Serra, he brought the wonderful news that the Viceroy had approved all but a few minor points on his list of requests.

While everyone at San Diego rejoiced to hear that Captain Fages had been replaced as military commander of Upper California by a new man, Captain Rivera, Fuster was more interested to learn that the Viceroy had agreed to expand the number of missions. In the six months he had been at Misión San Diego, he had spent countless hours on his knees, begging God for the wisdom to accept his posting. He had thrown himself into his missionary work in the hope that satisfaction of bringing natives to God and the Church would mitigate his sense that God had brought him here as punishment for his inability to give up his connection to Amalia.

While the mission rolls at the end of 1773 showed 83 converts and twelve marriages–sizable increases directly traceable to his efforts–his aversion to the place had grown increasingly intolerable.

Now here he was, acting as scribe for the president of the Franciscan missions, the very man who could reassign him, and he did not know how to broach the subject.

A knock sounded at the door. Fuster went to see who it was. Cracking the door, he glimpsed the scarred face of Romero the blacksmith.

"I need to see Father Serra," the smith said.

"He is busy. Come back later," Fuster said, pushing the door closed.

The smith shoved back on the door. "Not later. Now. It can't wait."

"Who is it, Brother?" Serra asked.

"The mission blacksmith, Father."

"Ah, yes, Romero."

Upon hearing his name, the blacksmith shouldered his way into the room. "Father Serra, I need to talk with you."

"Then sit, my son, and tell me how I can help you."

When Romero slid onto the bench, Fuster discreetly removed from the table the precious piece of parchment and the pot of ink to prevent any accidents, then stood in the corner to hear what the blacksmith had to say.

"I have to get back to New Spain, Father. I have to." Romero's voice rose and took on an hysterical edge. "I've been here in San Diego for five years. Five long years."

He reached out to clutch Serra's pale thin hands in his dark thick ones. "I can't take any more. Please, Father. Please."

"God will bless you, my son, for all the hard work you have done for the cause of our mission, especially for teaching your trade to our Carlos."

"Then you will send me back?"

Serra extricated his hands from Romero's grasp and sat down on the pallet. "I'm afraid that is not possible."

"Not possible? Why?"

"We simply have no one to replace you."

"The savage! He's my replacement!" Romero spat. "That was my agreement with Brother Gomez. I kept my end of the bargain. Now you keep yours."

"I know nothing of such an agreement," Father Serra said.

"That's it? That's your answer?"

The Franciscan leader stretched to put a calming hand on the blacksmith's taut shoulder. "You are too important to us to lose you, my son."

Romero slapped away the priest's hand and stood up, felling the bench in the process. "Damn you, Father. Damn you for your lies. I'll find a way out, even if I have to kill someone to do it."

He batted a brass pitcher against the wall and tipped over the table barely missing Fuster's foot before slamming out the door.

Fuster started after him, but Father Serra restrained him. "Let him go, Brother. He needs to cool off alone."

"But he cursed you, Reverend Father."

"Words, Brother, can never harm me. I forgive him. Let him go. Now help me right this table so we can get back to work."

Fuster curtailed more protests and did as requested. The smith's outburst had preempted his own plan to request a transfer to another mission from Father Serra. Now he would have to wait for another opening at another time–and hope when that time came, he would know what to say to get him out of this wretched place.

Outside, the March rain aggravated Romero's anger. "Lying sons of whores!" he bellowed toward the mission church. "Damn the lot of you!"

Opposite where he stood, adobe bricks lay in a stack against the wall of the storeroom, shielded from the rain by the overhang of the roof. Roaring curses, he set upon the pile, hurling the bricks indiscriminately at the surrounding huts.

In front of the church stood the cross Father Serra had erected at the mission's dedication nearly five years ago. To Romero, that cross had come to symbolize a God of betrayal who promised paradise but delivered hell. More, it was the sign of all the lying, conniving priests who claimed to be God's messengers to the masses.

"Spawn of Satan," he growled, taking aim on the center of the cross with the last adobe.

Just as he let fly, an Indian man came out of the church. The throw went wide, and the brick struck the Indian on the side of his head.

The man collapsed into the mud with a grunt.

Romero lurched over to the fallen man and fell on him with pummeling fists.

The Indian rolled into a ball to protect himself from the rain of blows, an action that compounded the smith's anger.

Romero reached for the brick that had fallen an arm's length away. Just as he did, the Indian bucked and Romero's blow glanced off its mark. The friable brick fell into a puddle and crumbled into a hundred pieces.

"Kill you," Romero growled, looking around for something deadly to use on the pinned man.

The Indian's balled fist caught the smith in the throat. Instead of unseating Romero, the blow pushed him beyond rage. He wrapped his hands around the brown neck and squeezed.

The man's struggles increased and so did the hatred in his eyes.

One of the blacksmith's hands let go its stranglehold and moved to the Indian's face where one enormous thumb dug into the right eye socket–harder, deeper until the eyeball popped out, geysering blood.

With a gasp the savage fainted.

Romero glared down at the evidence of his handiwork. "There, you son of a whore. That'll teach you to meddle." He rose, kicked the man in the back for good measure and strolled to the river to wash the blood off his hands.

It was late in the day when Father Serra finally ran out of energy. "That's enough for today, Brother Fuster. I'm tired. We can finish the rest tomorrow."

"Why don't you rest until dinner, Father?" Fuster said. "I'll come wake you."

For a change, the Franciscan leader did not offer resistance to the suggestion of a nap. By the time Fuster had put the vial of ink, blotter and spare quills into their box, Serra was already fast asleep.

Outside, Brother Fuster paused under the dripping overhang to put up his cowl. Out of habit, he scanned the mission compound left and right before heading for the church. A mound the size and shape of a man lay on the ground near the cross. Filled with sudden foreboding, Fuster ran to the mound.

It was the neophyte Paz, husband to the woman Corazón. The pair was the first native couple to be married at the mission. Fuster knelt and gently rolled the unconscious man onto his back. "Oh, dear God!" he cried at the sight of the blood-pooled hole where Paz's eye had been.

Feeling someone watching him, he craned around to see a trio of soldiers staring out at him from the open door of their barracks hut.

"Who did this?" he demanded.

The soldiers stared at him but did not speak.

"One of you fetch Carlos."

None of the men moved.

Fuster pointed at one of the three. "You. Now."

The soldier got up slowly and sauntered off toward the forge. Fuster swallowed his annoyance at the soldier's defiant attitude and focused on the injured man who was just coming around.

Paz moaned and lifted a hand to his face.

Fuster grasped the Indian's hands. "No, my son. No."

Paz writhed in pain, moaning piteously. The noise attracted the soldiers' corporal who arrived at the same moment as Carlos.

Carlos squatted beside Paz and said something in the incomprehensible native tongue. Paz answered in a husky whisper.

Carlos turned to Brother Fuster, his face clouded with anger. "Many Rains says the blacksmith did this."

"Not Many Rains, Carlos. His name is Paz now," Brother Jayme said, coming up from behind the group.

The inappropriate comment given the gravity of the Indian's injury caused Fuster to blurt, "God's mercy, Brother. Can't you see that someone gouged out this poor soul's eye?"

"Who did this?" Jayme demanded of the soldiers.

"The blacksmith," Fuster said, then turned to the soldiers. "Where did he go?"

One of the men cocked his chin toward the gate.

The men's apathy tweaked the missionary's ire. "Didn't anyone try to stop him?"

"That's not our job," the corporal said.

Before Fuster could retort, Brother Jayme stepped between them. "First things first. Let's get Paz into the church where I can tend his wound."

"But what about the blacksmith?" Fuster demanded.

"Into the church, Brother. Do you want to disturb Father Serra?" Jayme demanded.

Since Brother Jayme was the senior missionary, Fuster had to obey. Supporting Paz's legs, he helped Carlos and the other missionary carry the Indian into the church. He held his tongue while Brother Jayme tried unsuccessfully to stanch the bleeding.

Carlos watched for a time, then stepped forward. "I fix."

Reluctantly, Brother Jayme moved over to give Carlos access to Paz.

With the senior missionary hovering over his shoulder, the translator pulled a leather pouch out of his baggy shirt and set to work. In no time, he stopped the blood, then mixed up a poultice of dried weeds and other ingredients from the pouch, all the while murmuring in the Indian tongue.

He retied the pouch and tucked it back into his shirt. "Two days, he must not move." He stalked out the door and Fuster turned to leave also.

"Where are you going, Brother?" Jayme asked.

"After the blacksmith," he replied.

"What did the soldiers say happened?"

"They didn't say anything. Paz said it was the blacksmith."

"And you believe him?"

"Of course I do. He's the one who got hurt. Why would he lie?"

"Because he's an Indian. A lower life form."

Fuster was too astounded by the comment to speak. Jayme went on. "Except for that desertion attempt last fall–for which he received a full pardon–Romero has never caused a moment's trouble in nearly five years here at the mission. Unless those soldiers saw something, it's the smith's word against this savage's."

At mention of the aborted desertion, Fuster knew he would never get the soldiers—all three of whom were among those same deserters—to incriminate Romero.

"Let it go, Brother," Jayme said. "After all, there are a hundred savages like Paz out there but we have only one blacksmith. Do I need to remind you what this place would be like if we had no one to mend our guns and knives?"

"No," Fuster muttered. "You don't have to remind me." He glanced at the sleeping Paz. Brother Jayme could believe what he wished about these brown-skinned people, but he would never buy into the theory that they were any less intelligent or worthy of God's love and protection than white-skinned people. Witness or not, he knew in his heart that Romero had done this awful thing.

Someday he will pay. Someday. And I pray that I am here to witness that moment.

The tangled branches of the willows at the edge of the bay protected the bower from the shower of rain. Inside, Web, Shooting Star and Hummingbird sat dry and comfortable. While they waited for the rain to stop so they could get on with gathering shellfish, the two women plaited tule baskets in companionable silence. With food chronically short at the mission, Hummingbird had been allowed out to search for food. Thus Web had enjoyed her friend's company for eight of the last ten days.

Shooting Star was now three summers old. She played awhile with a floppy doll Web had fashioned out of yucca fiber, then curled next to her mother and fell immediately to sleep.

Glancing at her sleeping daughter, Web had to smile.

"She is beautiful," Hummingbird said, as if reading Web's thoughts.

"As your daughter will be," Web responded looking pointedly at her friend's swollen stomach.

"Or my son, handsome." Hummingbird smiled wearily. "Son or daughter, I hope that the baby comes out soon. So much extra weight to bear. Why did One Above not let us women grow babies on our backs where they would be easier to carry?"

Web reached out to touch her friend's belly. "Then, my sister, you would not be able to hug the child as it grows in your stomach or stroke it with your hands when it is restless."

"Does it hurt?" Hummingbird asked. "When the baby comes?"

"Only for a time. Then you hold your baby, and you forget. I will be there with you–to share the pain."

The two women exchanged an intimate smile.

"Ah," Web said. "The rain has stopped. My boys will be hungry after a day with their grandfather. It grows late. Let us gather our shellfish."

She helped the awkward Hummingbird to her feet, scooped up their gathering baskets and led the way onto the mud.

The receding tide revealed colonies of mussels and oysters. In no time Web had as many as she could carry and set about helping her friend whose pregnancy made bending down difficult.

All of a sudden, five Spanish soldiers materialized out of the brush a few feet away. Their stealth made Web instantly wary. She had heard dozens of stories about soldiers attacking Kumeyaay women without provocation. "Sister," she said quietly, struggling to keep the fear out of her voice.

When Hummingbird saw the soldiers, she shrieked and started toward the brush. The mud compounded her awkwardness and slowed her down.

One of the soldiers gave chase, tackling her from behind.

Hummingbird fell hard onto the mud. An audible exhalation of air cut off her screams.

The soldier flopped her onto her back and said something to his companions.

Web did not need to understand their language to hear the menace in his tone and in the snickers of the others. She held her breath and darted a glance toward the bower where Shooting Star still slept.

"Sister!" Hummingbird cried, reaching out toward Web who dared not move for fear of what the soldiers might do to her and Shooting Star. *Go, paleskins,* she prayed. *Leave us alone.*

The soldier yanked Hummingbird's arm down and rolled her back onto her swollen stomach.

"Sister, help me," Hummingbird sobbed.

The soldier barked a single syllable and threw Hummingbird's skirt over her bare back.

"Sister! Sist . . ."

A scream curtailed her plea as the soldier opened the front of his lower garment, heaved her hips upward, forced apart her thighs and thrust his swollen member into her woman's opening to the urging of the other soldiers.

Covering her ears against those terrible sounds, Web turned away so that she would not have to witness the assault. Her hands, however, did not block out all the sound. She heard two other soldiers join in the attack on Hummingbird and then whimpers began to issue from Shooting Star's bower.

Concern for her child forced her into immediate action.

She plunged out of the water in the opposite direction, hoping to lead any pursuers away from her baby. She ran as fast as she could, but the two unoccupied soldiers caught her easily.

She lashed out at them with kicks and scratches and snapping teeth. Her efforts only served to tighten their grips as they dragged her back to the others.

Hummingbird no longer screamed. She lay naked and unmoving on her back in the mud, surrounded by her three attackers. Bright red blood trickled from her woman place and pooled on the mud beneath her.

Web bit back the scream that rose into her throat for fear that it would frighten Shooting Star awake. No matter what happened to her, she could not, she *would* not allow these monsters to harm her child.

She ceased struggling with her captors. She let them push her to the ground and spread her legs. Closing her eyes, she willed her spirit to fly to the mesquite thicket of Hawi, her childhood home, away from the violation of these cruel man-beasts. She stayed in that place until someone grabbed her hand.

She was vaguely aware of one of the soldiers examining the webs of skin between her fingers. He turned to his companions and made quacking sounds. The others laughed.

Letting her hand drop, her attacker reached into his pocket and drew out a handful of bead strings which he tossed between her sprawled legs. Then, with much laughter and loud talk that could only be boasting, the five men left.

For a long time Web did not have the will or strength to move. She lay staring at the heavy gray clouds, trying to understand what had happened to her.

At last she mustered the strength to sit up.

Hummingbird lay a few paces away, still motionless and bleeding.

Web crawled to her. "Sister?"

Hummingbird's eyes fluttered open and she tried to speak. Grasping her hand, Web put her ear to her friend's mouth in order to hear.

"Son–dead–I am–dead."

"Oh, no, sister. No."

"Dead . . ."

Hummingbird's eyes drifted shut, and a moment later, Web heard the rattle, signifying that her friend's spirit had begun its journey into the Land of Those Who Went Before.

There was no time for mourning. She had to get away from here, had to get Shooting Star to safety. She swayed to her feet and stumbled into the willows with the earth tilting under each step.

"Mother?" Shooting Star piped.

The sound of her daughter's voice kept Web from fainting. She gathered the child into her weakened arms.

"Where is auntie?" Shooting Star asked.

Web had to swallow twice before she could answer. "Auntie has gone away."

"Where?" the child demanded.

Web pressed her precious daughter to her bruised breasts and looked up at the sky through welling tears. "She–she has gone to live with the spirits."

"Can I go, too?"

"Someday, little one. Someday."

Chapter 6

Under a clear star-flung sky the people of Nipaguay chanted and danced around the bonfire whose smoke carried the ashes of Hummingbird's body heavenward to join her spirit in the Land of Those Who Went Before. Inside his 'ewaa, with his sacred objects carefully spread around him, Casts No Shadow prepared to enter that trance that would carry him on the journey he would make this night.

In the brief span from one Sun to the next, events had scrambled his notions of life and the world like the wind scrambles the bird's egg it flings out of the nest. Yesterday Many Rains had two eyes. Today he had only one. Yesterday Web, the mother of his grandchildren, had lain with only one man, Shadow Dancer. Today she had been taken by force by a gang of Spanish. And little Hummingbird. Both she and the child that had been growing in her womb had been murdered by the same men who brutalized Web. Any one of these happenings was almost too horrible to contemplate. Put together, they defied understanding. *Why did I not see these things?* The question echoed again and again in the wekuseyaay's mind.

On the edge of his thoughts lurked a fear–the first he had ever known–that the spirits had found him wanting and no longer spoke to him.

Overlaying the question was the image of Web, her eyes filled with the deadness of one who has witnessed the death of her dreams. It was as if the bearded ones had mortally wounded her soul as much as battered and violated her body. Anger welled into Casts No Shadow's heart, but, with effort, he forced it down and cleared his thoughts in order to proceed with the ceremony.

He breathed deeply ten times, holding each breath before exhaling through his mouth and emptying his lungs completely. Once calmed, he picked up his sacred rattle, offered it to the four directions, the earth and the sky, then held it in the smoke of the small fire. "Oh, Spirits, accept this seeker into Your presence, and show him what he needs to know to guide his people."

As the smoke of the fire drifted around him, he closed his eyes and began to sing the songs that would lead his mind into the place where the veil between this world and that of the spirits parted. He chanted, focusing his full attention on the ancient words, drawing them deep into his bones, filling his body with their power. He chanted and waited for his journey to begin.

Chapter 7

B rother Fuster spent the night in prayer, seeking God's wisdom in the matter of Romero and the unfortunate Indian Paz. At dawn, still without answers or clarity, he rose from his knees to begin his daily duties. His first task was tolling the bell as a signal for the neophytes to gather in the church for Mass.

A thick layer of fog lay along the river that flowed around the base of the hill upon which the mission compound stood. The fog below them gave the illusion that he and the other Spanish were on an island, floating on clouds. In any other mental state, that image might have pleased him. Not this morning.

He pulled on the bell rope, squinting hard against the glare of the gray sky. He felt each vibration of the bell like a mallet hammering the inside of his skull while the guard opened the gates to the just-awakened neophytes. As they shuffled past

Fuster into the church, Brother Jayme left his cell and came to stand next to him.

Fuster nodded but avoided looking at his fellow missionary. His mind was on his dilemma over the blacksmith when Jayme said, "Where is Carlos? I need him to explain today's lesson." He buttonholed a passing soldier. "Run to the forge, Dominguez, and fetch Carlos for services."

The surly soldier trudged off to do the priest's bidding. Inside the church, while the two Franciscans waited, the sleepy converts shifted and murmured.

Dominguez returned alone. "He was not there, Padre."

"Not there. Not here. Where on earth can he be?" Jayme asked.

At that moment Sergeant Ortega happened by. "That one is from the Indian *ranchería* two leagues up the valley, is he not?"

Fuster nodded.

"That village had quite a celebration last night. You could hear them chanting all the way down here. No doubt that's where we'll find him."

Brother Jayme muttered something under his breath.

The sergeant continued. "Wasn't Paz married?"

"His was our first marriage," Jayme answered. "His wife is Corazón, the pregnant woman. Her child will be our first baptism."

The sergeant stuck his head into the church as if to scan the crowd. When he returned to the missionaries, he looked upset. "Don't count on that. She's gone, too. Besides their chanting, there were bonfires burning at that village all night, you know."

Brother Jayme's usual calm vanished. His face contorted with rage. "Bonfires can mean only one thing: cremations. And, if Carlos and Corazón attended, not only have they disobeyed my orders, but they have also sinned against God! Go after them, sergeant. Find them and bring them back. By force, if necessary!"

Fuster laid a restraining hand on his fellow priest's shoulder. "Don't you think . . ."

Jayme brushed it off. "We'll put a stop to their disobedience for good with a taste of the whip and time in the stocks."

The sergeant quickly gathered his men and went after their horses. Seeing the soldiers in a group tweaked Fuster's memory. He grabbed Brother Jayme's arm. "You're jumping to conclusions, Brother."

"I am, am I?"

"Fires and singing could mean any number of things. Besides, I think we have a bigger problem than missing neophytes."

"Such as?"

"Attacks on the Indians by the very soldiers you are now sending out. Yesterday afternoon, I saw five of them come back from patrol. They all smelled of–sex."

"And how would you know about that, Brother?"

Fuster felt a flush creeping across his face. "I–know. Those men–their legs were covered in mud. Mud, Brother."

"Mud?" Brother Jayme asked scornfully. "Of course their legs were muddy. It's been raining. Or perhaps you hadn't noticed?"

"Just their knees and the fronts of their lower legs?" Fuster said. "Brother, those men committed rape! I know it! For the sake of the Almighty, they must be punished."

"No matter what you saw or smelled, Brother Fuster, mud is not proof. Without proof, I–we can do nothing. Nothing, except pray that no women were harmed and that Father Serra will allow us to move the mission away from the soldiers soon."

As much as he wished different, Fuster could not argue with the truth in his fellow missionary's words, so he tried another path. "Surely you won't flog the woman, Brother?"

"Surely I will–if the sergeant finds her at the *ranchería.*"

Fuster riveted his gaze on the other man's rigid face. "Then I will pray they do not find her."

Casts No Shadow paused outside Web's 'ewaa to steel himself for what he would find. His journey into the spirit world had brought him only the singular repeating image of Red Smoke, the former Cosoy shaman, drinking the poison that had ended his life. Instead of answers, he had returned from his journey with more questions, more confusion, more doubt.

Inside the lodge, Web lay on her sleeping pallet, knees drawn to her chest, her hands covering her face. She flinched at the sound of his entry. "No, no," she whimpered.

He knelt beside her. "There, there, my daughter. I am here."

Her eyelids fluttered opened, then fell again.

"I am here," he murmured, taking her hand.

She returned his grip with surprising fierceness. Her shoulders began to shake with silent sobs that quickly became audible. "The blood–all the blood. Hummingbird–her baby. Blood."

He let her cry and ramble without interruption. Tears were the first positive sign he had seen from her since she stumbled into the village yesterday. She had related the story of her attack and Hummingbird's death in a monotone, her eyes flat and vacant as a burned-off field, her emotions numbed by shock, her spirit unable or unwilling to return from the place it had fled during the assault.

Now Shadow Dancer burst into the 'ewaa. He sank onto his knees next to Web's pallet. "Oh, my wife. What have they done to you?"

After four years of estrangement, Casts No Shadow was momentarily shocked by his son's haggard appearance, but he quickly recovered and rose to his feet. "*They* attacked her. *They* killed Hummingbird. They. Your paleskin friends!"

"They are no friends of mine, Father."

At Shadow Dancer's backtalk, Casts No Shadow's anger overcame his self-control. "You have no right to call me that. You are not my son. No son of mine would ever abandon his woman, his children, his people!"

"Hush, Father. You frighten her."

"You are to blame. You and your absurd notions."

Anger flashed in the gaze Shadow Dancer directed at him. "I followed the path of the spirits, Father. Just as I have always done. Just as you taught me. I am learning the fire magic of the Spanish. Soon I will know the secrets of their thunder sticks. Then . . ."

A cry from Web cut him off. She had levered herself painfully into a sitting position. "Stop," she croaked. "Both of you. No one could have helped us. No one."

She turned to Casts No Shadow. "The Kumeyaay people must learn about the Spanish thunder sticks. We *must*. Father, I believe in what my husband does."

Seeing a spark of life return to her eyes, Casts No Shadow put aside his differences with his son in favor of her well-being and stayed his argument.

From outside the lodge came a commotion. Casts No Shadow left Web's side to peek out. "Bearded ones. Why are they here?"

Shadow Dancer blanched. "I did not ask permission to come here."

"You must hide, my husband," Web pleaded.

"Ask for permission to come to your home, to see to your wife?" Casts No Shadow asked incredulously.

Shadow Dancer motioned for the wekuseyaay to lower his voice. "It is one of the rules of the padres."

"What are padres?" Casts No Shadow rasped, trying to curb the loudness of his voice.

"The Brown Robes. 'Padres' means 'Fathers' in their language."

"Hide, Husband!" Web urged. "Don't let them whip y . . . ."

A stifled scream cut off her words. A bearded one looked into the 'ewaa, yelling something to the others.

"They have found me," Shadow Dancer said resignedly. He ducked outside, followed by Casts No Shadow and Web.

Web stood clutching at her husband's arm, her body wracked with huge, gasping sobs. Two more of the hairy, foul-smelling men joined the first.

Casts No Shadow put himself squarely in their path. "Leave us!"

One of the men jammed the butt of his thunder stick into the wekuseyaay's stomach and drove him backward into the 'ewaa.

Casts No Shadow crumpled to the ground, helpless to stop the bearded ones from dragging his son away.

Web staggered after her husband, pleading for the soldiers to let him go. Fearing that the soldiers would do her more harm, Casts No Shadow picked himself off the ground and went after her. Folding her into his arms, he held her until she ran out of tears. When he next looked into her face, the spark of life that had so recently flickered there was gone.

Carlos stood facing the sergeant with his hands bound behind his back but his head held high. "Soldiers attacked my wife. I went to my village to see her."

Sergeant Ortega shot to his feet, upsetting his chair. "Attacked? By soldiers? When?"

Afraid that Ortega meant to strike the Indian, Brother Fuster started forward only to be pulled back by Brother Jayme.

"Last sun," Carlos replied.

"Where?" Ortega demanded.

"What you call False Bay."

"And exactly what are these soldiers supposed to have done to your–wife?"

Carlos's jaw tightened visibly. "They–they took her–as a man takes a woman."

Fuster stared at the five soldiers clumped together at the rear of the room. The same five upon whom he had smelled woman-scent yesterday. Even with their faces in shadow, he saw the smirks they exchanged among themselves.

"Corporal, who was on patrol yesterday in the vicinity of False Bay?" Ortega asked.

The corporal named the five men who immediately went stone-faced. Pacing to them, Ortega faced the first. "Did you rape an Indian woman, Private?"

"No, Sergeant," the man answered.

The sergeant moved to the next. "And you?"

Same answer to the same question for all five men.

The sergeant came back to face Carlos. "Whatever happened to your–wife, my men were not involved."

"Just one minute!" Fuster demanded. "Unlike those five, this man has no reason to lie. Why would he make up such a story if it weren't true?"

Instead of Ortega, Jayme answered. "I disagree, Brother. Carlos has an excellent reason to lie." He moved in front of the Indian. "You know the punishment for going to your village without permission, don't you, my son?"

Carlos did not answer.

The senior missionary's voice lost its softness. "Then let me refresh your memory. Those who choose to disobey the mission rules receive a flogging and a week in the stocks."

"The soldiers attacked my wife, Father," Carlos said.

"Take him, Sergeant," Jayme said.

"She was hurt. I had to go see her," Carlos insisted.

"Sergeant!"

The corporal swung the stock of his rifle into the back of the Indian's skull. Carlos staggered forward and collapsed unconscious on the floor. Fuster hurried to him. "This is wrong, Brother Jayme. He should not be punished," Fuster said.

Jayme looked down his nose at his fellow missionary. "No, *you* are wrong, Brother. He disobeyed. Therefore he will be punished. Believe me, it is for his own good. Reward and punishment are the only sure ways to educate these–these people."

The soldiers pulled Fuster away and dragged Carlos's inert body out of the room where Romero hung at the back of the gathered crowd.

Fuster turned on Jayme. "How can you punish Carlos when you spare the blacksmith? How can you live with your conscience?"

Jayme gave him an appraising look. "What a presumptuous question coming from one who vowed obedience, yet refuses to obey."

Fuster felt shame searing his soul. He hung his head. "Yes, Brother."

Chapter 8

S even days after the soldiers ripped Shadow Dancer from their 'ewaa, Web remained inside, quaking at every noise, too afraid that the soldiers would come again to venture outside for even a moment, too terrified of nightmares to allow herself to sleep. Finally Casts No Shadow could stand no more. The situation called for a special ceremony to help her spirit find its way back from the chaos and darkness to her earthly body. Red Smoke had specialized in such curing, but Red Smoke was dead, so the task fell to Casts No Shadow.

He gathered his shaman's things and forced himself to walk to her lodge with deliberate slowness, fighting down the nervousness that unfamiliar ceremonies always caused him.

Web looked up in fright at his entrance. "I come to sing for you, my daughter," he reassured her.

"I need nothing. Go away."

Ignoring her refusal, he bundled the twins and their baby sister off to the kwaipai's 'ewaa where he asked Crooked Basket to watch them during the rite.

"I'll take the boys but not her," Crooked Basket said, nodding at Shooting Star.

Big Nose did not override his wife and the wekuseyaay was too concerned about Web to argue. Instead, he took the little girl to the next family where the woman Burning Grass agreed to watch the child as long as he needed.

By the time he returned to Web's 'ewaa, word had passed around the village and people had begun to gather. He spread a circular hide on the floor and coaxed Web to sit in the middle of it. She sat staring straight ahead with wide unblinking eyes while people from the village filtered into the 'ewaa until it could hold no more.

He allowed the people to settle and quiet down, then, in the expectant hush, he began. He arranged his sacred objects carefully around her, chanting the prescribed song for each one, placing it on the hide according to the pattern he had seen in a dream the night before.

Once all the objects were in place, he began the curing dance.

For hours he circled her, sometimes passing a fan of eagle feathers over her bowed head. Other times jabbing the end of his staff at the evil ones who lurked in the shadows waiting for a chance to snatch her soul before it found its way back to her body.

He danced and sang long past the time his limbs were numbed with exhaustion. He danced and sang until his head ached. Still he continued. When at last his voice failed, he knelt behind Web, placed the end of his healing pipe against her bare back and began to suck. He moved the pipe along her spine and drew in breath after breath until he felt something give. Then he raised the pipe high in the air for all to see. As he turned the pipe over, a ball of light brown hair fell from its end onto the hide. Hair drawn from within her body by the power of the Spirits.

Murmurs of surprise erupted from the spectators. He ignored them, keeping his attention completely focused on Web.

"Turn, Daughter, and look," he rasped.

Slowly she twisted around and drew back in horror at the sight of the mass of hair. "Take it away," she whispered. "Please."

"You must touch it, Daughter."

"No—I . . ."

"Once you touch it, it can have no more power over you."

She reached out tentatively.

"Touch it, my daughter."

She did, then quickly pulled back her hand.

"Pick it up. Hold it," he commanded.

"I . . ."

"Hold it."

Hesitating, she finally picked it up.

He closed her fingers tightly around the ball of hair. "As long as you keep this, no bearded one can ever harm you again."

She looked at him for reassurance.

The fear of trusting that shown in her eyes tugged at his soul, causing an unexpected upwelling of emotion, adding huskiness to his strained voice. "Never again, Daughter. Never again."

Around them people coughed and shifted, yet he would not allow his gaze to waver from hers. Her reaction was the only thing that counted now.

After a long silence, she blinked. And belief replaced the fear in her gaze.

"Never again," he whispered.

She nodded.

Relief flooded through him. Although he suddenly felt beyond exhaustion, he managed to muster the strength to get to his feet and walk out of the lodge, a signal to the onlookers that the ceremony was over.

Voices erupted inside, everyone chattering at once.

Casts No Shadow paused to steady himself against the roof support of a *wisal*. He looked west toward the bearded ones' settlement. "Never again," he said aloud. "Never again."

Chapter 9

W eb awoke with a start. Heart thumping, she strained her ears for clues of something amiss outside the 'ewaa. Soft, regular breathing issued from the other two pallets where the twins and Shooting Star slept.

Then she remembered her dream, and all possibility of sleep vanished.

Outside, a full moon presided over a clear night sky. Tonight she took no pleasure in the silvery shadows of the night made day. For tonight, she could no longer deny the truth that she carried the child of the Spanish soldier who had assaulted her.

That knowledge brought back the numbing void that had filled her before Casts No Shadow performed the ceremony that guided her spirit back into the light.

Instinctively, she reached for the leather pouch dangling between her breasts. Inside the bag lay the wad of light brown hair that the wekuseyaay had extracted from her body. She had struggled hard to overcome her loathing in order to keep it. One day, in the hands of the right sorcerer, the hair would become the spell that would destroy her attacker. Before that time, however, she had a grave decision to make: to allow the child to grow or to stop it.

Back in Hawi her mother had talked to her about the ways of ending pregnancy. The concoctions had to be mixed precisely to match the size and age of the woman and the baby. The wrong proportions could kill the mother along with the child. Even the right mixture produced side-effects harrowing enough to deter most women from such an option.

Web looked down the center of the sleeping village. Bathed in the silver-white moonlight, the neat lodges of the kwaipai and his assistants stood like humped sentinels. Ghostly stick legs held up the shaggy roofs of wisals. The boulders with their communal grinding holes loomed like giant crouching animals at the edge of the village. In the distance, the figures of the night guards moved silently along the village's strong defensive wall. In the other direction moonlight glittered on the rippling surface of the river.

Nipaguay. The village she had learned to love. Home of her husband and her children. She looked up at the moon and whispered, "This is no child of mine or my people." It was then that she decided, remembering her mother's words. Only one man could help her now.

Turning on her heel, she strode beyond the edge of the village to the lone 'ewaa set apart. Inside Casts No Shadow sat cross-legged before a small fire. He started at her approach.

She faltered. In all the years she had lived at Nipaguay she had never come to his lodge without his expecting her. Never, until now.

Recovering, he motioned her to the place opposite him and waited for her to speak. Thrown off-balance because she had startled him, she did not know where to begin so she blurted, "I am with child, Father. The soldier–I need your help, my father."

"To stop the child," he said slowly.

"I know the danger. My mother . . ."

The wekuseyaay nodded. He would not meet her gaze, but that did not prevent her from seeing the disquiet her announcement had raised behind his eyes. Had he not foreseen this? Had the Spirits not told him?

She watched in silence while he located the ingredients from among his sizable collection of medicine herbs and plants. His movements seemed stiff, forced. When he ground the various twigs and leaves, his hand shook.

"Are you ill, Father?"

"The Spirits–I–it is nothing. Here." She took the horn cup from him. "You must drink it all."

She looked at the liquid in the cup. "This is no child of mine or my people," she said, raising the cup to her lips and drinking. The liquid reached her stomach before the taste registered: bitter and salty, it reminded her of maggoty fish. She clamped her hand over her mouth to keep from vomiting it back up.

"I must go to the moon lodge," she gasped.

Casts No Shadow helped her to stand. She walked, leaning on him to the point beyond which he could not continue. Although he said nothing, she sensed some kind of doubt growing within him. She wanted to ask him what bothered him, but a wave of nausea stifled her intentions.

She stumbled forward under her own power, reaching the women's isolation lodge just as the first cramps hit.

She had only enough time to see that the lodge was empty before the second wave broke upon her.

The pain drove her to the ground. She clutched her belly and rolled into a tight ball.

The third wave crashed in on top of the second, followed by the fourth and fifth.

The sixth pried open her clenched teeth, freeing her screams.

The seventh deafened her to everything but the roar of the agony within her loins.

The eighth, ninth, tenth all blended into one long continuous jagged ripping.

Then, on the eleventh surge, Web's thoughts broke into yellow spots of light scattered across a black landscape.

VIII

ATTACK

October, 1774—November, 1775

Chapter 1—Late October, 1774

W eb's burden net bulged with acorns, adding to the effort of every step and compounding the difficulty of keeping her balance on the rough downward path. After more than two moons away in the mountains gathering acorns, she longed for sight of Nipaguay, yearned for the comfort of her own 'ewaa.

Casts No Shadow's medicine had rid her of the soldier's child. With each day that passed, the memories of that baby, the assault, and Hummingbird's death moved farther into the realm of forgetting, allowing the slow return of hope that someday her life would return to its normal rhythms.

Walking in front of Web, Crooked Basket gave a small cry and stopped short. She stood staring into the distance with a stricken expression painting her face. "Brown Robes–our village . . ."

Web followed the woman's gaze. What she saw caused her to nearly drop her load.

Where Nipaguay had stood less than two moons ago now rose the huts and walls of a Spanish settlement. In the ravine where the kwaipai's 'ewaa had once been, two Brown Robes stood conversing with a brown-skinned man. Despite her shock, her heart leapt when she recognized that third man as Shadow Dancer.

Sand Flea and Cricket also recognized their father and broke away from her, heading toward the old village. Crooked Basket managed to grab them both before they escaped. She pushed the protesting youngsters at Web. "You're to blame for this," she hissed, her mouth twisted in anger. "Just look at Shadow Dancer. Once he was a proud man, but now he is nothing but a slave to the Brown Robes. A slave instead of an 'aww-kuseyaay–all because of you. You drove him away. You and your freak's hands."

"Go find your grandfather," Web told the twins. As she watched them scamper up the line of march, she composed her face, then turned back to her adversary, forcing her voice to remain low and calm. "To cling to hope that my husband will ever be yours will only cause you pain. Forget him."

"I intend to see that someday you feel such pain, little desert mouse," Crooked Basket hissed. "That I promise." She whirled away and stalked off, leaving Web to look at the village that no longer belonged to her and the other people of Nipaguay.

Big Nose's voice thundered over the heads of the seated village men. "Shadow Dancer did this to us. He knew that we would be gone, and he brought the Brown Robes to our village so that they could take it for their own."

He jabbed an accusing finger at Casts No Shadow. "Shadow Dancer has betrayed us. The wekuseyaay must answer for his son!"

Casts No Shadow rose to his feet, burying his fury beneath the dignity of his position. He gazed around the circle of seated men and let the silence build before he began to speak. "Long ago Shadow Dancer ceased to be my son." He paused to let the words sink in. "And I will not waste words on him or his actions when our people are faced with the loss of their homes."

He looked at the kwaipai. "In all this land there is no place to match Nipaguay. The river gives us water even in the dry times. The valley depth shelters us from the ocean wind. Ours are the best fields, the most fertile fields. And no enemy dares attack such a protected site."

With bobbing heads and murmuring, the majority of the audience agreed. He lowered his voice to force the gathered men to listen hard. "We cannot allow the paleskins to take our land. We must take Nipaguay back."

Surprise lit the dozens of pairs of eyes that riveted on him.

"These bearded ones are not the first of their kind to come here. There is not one of us who does not know the old stories by heart. In those tales, the paleskins left as mysteriously as they came. And so I thought it would be when this group came. But they did not go, and out of concern for our people, I journeyed far, far into the land of the spirits to seek the wisdom of the gods."

He paused again, reliving the memories of that journey that flashed through his mind. "When I returned, I counseled our people to stay clear of all the paleskins." He raised his eyes to focus directly on Big Nose. "For five summers I have not deviated from that warning. But now I do. Now I tell you that we must drive the Brown Robes out of our village and out of our land! Forever!"

The audience erupted in multiple conversations. Big Nose had difficulty regaining order. "Cosoy tried to do that very thing, Wekuseyaay, and failed."

"Our village cannot–we *must* not do this alone," Casts No Shadow declared. "All the Kumeyaay people will lose if the bearded ones remain here. All the Kumeyaay people must help drive them out."

Many heads nodded in agreement. The kwaipai's was not one of them. He asked, "And how will that happen, Wekuseyaay?"

It was the question Casts No Shadow had been waiting for. He threw back his shoulders and lifted his chin. "Today, I undertake another journey. To all the villages of the Kumeyaay to tell them what the paleskins have done and ask for their promise to help us when the time comes to launch an attack."

"All Kumeyaay villages, Wekuseyaay?" Big Nose asked skeptically. "That will take you many moons."

Casts No Shadow nodded.

"With no guarantee that anyone will join us," the kwaipai said.

"The spirits have shown me that it is what I must do," countered the wekuseyaay.

While the kwaipai conferred with a trio of Nipaguay's elders, Casts No Shadow looked out across the river at the bent figures of Indian converts working to build the adobe walls of one of the Brown Robes' new huts. First Web's rape, now their appropriation of Nipaguay had hardened his bitterness toward the bearded ones into raw hatred. That hatred that would not let him rest until he saw the paleskins driven once and for all time back into the sea.

Big Nose rose and signaled for attention from the seated men. His face was grim and the set of his jaw showed that he was not wholly behind what he had to say. "When you say it is time, Wekuseyaay, we of Nipaguay will be ready to fight. May the spirits protect you on your journey."

Casts No Shadow acknowledged the blessing of the village council with the merest nod before he turned and walked away from the gathering with the stride that befits a man about to undertake a task entrusted to him by the gods.

Chapter 2

As soon as Carlos finished tapping the adobe brick into place, Romero ordered, "We need more bricks. Go make some."

Carlos looked from him to the remaining stack of adobes and back again.

"Go. Now," Romero barked. "I want this done today or I'll . . ."

The Indian trudged away, cutting off the blacksmith's threat. No matter how many times Romero told himself that Carlos was afraid of him, afraid he would gouge out an eye like he had done for Paz, he knew he was only fooling himself. The reality was that Carlos wanted something that only he, Romero the blacksmith, could give: the knowledge of how to make and repair guns. Knowledge Romero was determined Carlos would never learn, not even if his life depended on it. The Indian had not figured that out yet, and until he did, Romero intended to use him to do every dirty, unpleasant task he could find.

With Carlos out of sight, Romero pulled the jug out of its hiding place and poured a healthy slug of the contents down his throat. The liquor sank into his stomach, taking the edge off the anxiety he never seemed to be able to completely shake anymore. He closed his eyes to better savor the sensation.

Last year he had dreamed his own death. Death that had come at the hands of an Indian. A horrible death amidst flames and smoke and screams of terror. The dream had returned again and again, twisting Romero's nights into torture sessions–until he found liquor. Sweet liquor that blocked the dream and held at bay the fear that threatened to drive him mad. Liquor that Morilla, one of the privates, had figured out how to distill from agave last spring. It had taken just one cup for Romero to decide to put aside his anger at the other deserters and join in protecting the still and its precious product from the soldiers' superiors and the padres. For the blacksmith, the liquor made the endless days of his endless sentence in this place bearable. The alcohol provided sweet oblivion from the deadly monotony of San Diego. Liquor was his only solace. His only escape from the nightmare memories of the Indian attack and the constant fear–the growing fear that another attack could come at any time. And, as such, Romero was determined not to have his one pleasure taken away from him. He hid his drinking, kept the jug out of sight when anyone else was around, and since Carlos was always around, Romero had to invent errands for him whenever he needed a drink. And, lately, he needed a drink more and more often.

Now Carlos returned unexpectedly, forcing Romero to quickly shield the jug with his body. "Well, where are the bricks?"

"No bricks," Carlos said.

Miffed by Carlos's untimely appearance, Romero did not bother to correct the Indian for not ending his sentence with 'master.' "Son of a fitchet bitch, get me some bricks, or I'll . . ."

Once again Carlos walked away before the smith could finish. This time Romero did not wait for the Indian to be out of sight before he took another pull. He needed liquor to ease the queasiness in his stomach; queasiness he blamed on Sergeant Ortega.

When word came that Father Serra had approved moving the mission two leagues east up the river valley from its original site, the sergeant had told Romero that the forge would remain at the Presidio which would occupy the site of the old mission. That suited Romero. Ever since Father Serra had crushed his hopes for ever leaving San Diego, Romero's life had only two goals: to remain under the direct protection of the military, and to stay close to his liquor supply.

Everything was going along fine until yesterday, when Ortega changed his mind and ordered Romero to move to the new mission immediately. Romero argued and pleaded to remain where he was–to no avail. Ortega would not say why he changed his mind. All he would say was, "You're moving, blacksmith. And that's final."

Sentenced to live without the security of soldiers to defend him, Romero dealt with his panic by going straight to Morilla. The private listened to the smith's tale of woe and said he would be willing to fill Romero's empty jugs for the usual price if Romero brought them to the Presidio. Knowing that his trips away from the mission would be few and far between, Romero tried to convince Morilla to deliver liquor to the mission on his weekly patrols. Morilla balked, so, in desperation, the smith resorted to a bribe. In return for Morilla's deliveries, Romero would pay him in advance in silver. Silver that he would have to steal from the mission's treasury.

With that accomplished, Romero had been all right–until darkness fell. The night always brought memories of the Indian attack four years ago. To keep the terrible images and feelings at bay, Romero drank steadily, emptying one jug and starting on the second until he passed out.

He had awakened this morning to the angry shaking of Private Dominguez. "You oaf! You passed out and left this where anyone could see it! You want us all to lose our fun?" The soldier brandished the unfinished jug before shoving it out of sight. "Now get up. The rest of us have been waiting for you for an hour."

The smith had trouble lifting his pounding head off the ground. When he had finally managed to get to his feet, he clung to Dominguez's arm to keep the swaying ground from dumping him back into the dirt. Then, all the way up the river valley to the new mission site, he had been too preoccupied with his own misery to pay attention to anything else.

By the time the group reached the mission, he was feeling better–until he learned that the missionaries expected him to work, live and sleep in the open until the neophytes completed the church. Romero had exploded. "Two leagues from the Presidio! Two leagues, and you expect me to trust that these savages won't kill me in my sleep!"

"There, there, my son," Brother Jayme had said.

He had swiped the padre's hand off his arm. "I'm no one's son! And, if you won't do it, I'll build my quarters myself!"

"Myself," he muttered now, gulping two swallows from the jug before re-corking it and shoving it back behind his tools.

"Myself," he rasped again. "No cursed savages are going to get m . . ." A hiccup cut him off.

He moved to the remaining pile of adobes for another brick. As he bent to pick one up, the world seemed to tilt. He grabbed for the nearest roof support, roaring "Stop that!" at the ground. "No more tricks. Understand?"

The ground finally stopped moving, and he decided it was safe to walk. Immediately his feet tangled and he fell against the wall he and Carlos had been working on.

The mud between the adobes at the upper part of the wall had not yet hardened. The force of his fall jarred loose bricks at the top. They fell, pinning one of his legs.

"Master!"

Romero could not get his mind to grasp what had happened to him. He looked up with bleary eyes to see Carlos staring at him from under a load of bricks.

The next thing he knew the Indian had dropped his load and sprinted off. Romero was trying to figure out why he wasn't feeling anything in his legs when Carlos returned with the two missionaries. While Brother Jayme started wringing his hands and exclaiming, "Oh, dear God," Brother Fuster bent to see to the blacksmith's leg.

Fuster flinched away from Romero. "Liquor. I can smell it all over him, Brother. This man is drunk."

"Nonsense," Brother Jayme said. "Where would he get liquor? We don't even have wine for the Eucharist."

"Where did you get it, José?" Fuster asked.

Romero managed to get his mouth to form the words. "What, Padre?"

"The liquor, José," Fuster demanded angrily.

"I–don't know what you're talking about, Padre," Romero slurred.

"Don't lie to m . . ."

Brother Jayme elbowed Fuster aside to examine the smith's leg. "Leave him be, Brother. Can't you see he's hurt? That leg is broken," Jayme said. "In a bad place, too. Splintered the bone."

A concerned look passed between the two missionaries, while Romero struggled to connect in the murk of his mind the pain he was now feeling with the bricks tumbled across his leg.

"I'll try to set it, my son," Jayme said. "But it might not work."

Once he recognized the pain for what it was, it grew in intensity until it filled his complete awareness–until the only thing he wanted was for it to stop. "Please, Padre, fix it," he croaked.

"All right, my son. Are you ready, Brother Fuster?" asked Jayme.

Brother Fuster grabbed the smith under the armpits, and Brother Jayme grasped the ankle of the broken leg. "This will hurt, José," Jayme warned. "Are you prepared?"

Romero gritted his teeth. "Yes, Father."

The grips of both men tightened simultaneously and they pulled in opposite directions. The leg bone popped, and a pain beyond his worst imaginings of the fires of hell ripped through his body. He fell through a hole in the earth to the sound of his own screaming.

Chapter 3

B rown-skinned neophytes filled the church at the new mission. They knelt on the hard-packed earth in rows with their hands clasped in front of them, heads bowed, as they had been taught. From a rear corner Brother Fuster half-listened to Brother Jayme chant the familiar words of the mass. The rest of his attention was focused faraway on the memory of another Christmas mass and a girl who had knelt across the aisle. Even in the gloom of that long-ago church, the lace mantilla could not hide the glorious tumble of the raven hair that obscured her bowed face. "Amalia, my love," Fuster's heart whispered.

He passed his hand over his eyes and the vision vanished, replaced by the reality of this mission church countless leagues removed from the one in his memory. Brother Jayme moved into the rite of communion. Carlos stood to the side of the altar translating the priest's Latin into the natives' tongue.

Even after nearly a year at San Diego, the language of the Indians still baffled Fuster. His failure to learn it weighed on him as heavily as the sin of omission that he committed every time he left the confessional without admitting that he had Amalia's glove and that it caused him carnal thoughts.

Whenever he brought up his concern that neither of them could directly instruct their catechumens, Brother Jayme said the same thing: "The Lord has sent us Carlos to use until our flock can learn our language."

Every time he heard that, Fuster was tempted to blurt, "Don't be so sure about Carlos." Yet those words never reached the air. Instead he swallowed them and struggled to adhere to his vow of obedience. He had no proof that their Indian interpreter was untrustworthy; only a feeling that Carlos wanted something from them other than religion.

Outside, a cold driving wind howled around the church's adobe walls. Fuster shivered involuntarily. While those Indians who had been baptized shuffled forward to receive communion, his thoughts turned to this mission, to this experiment in the remotest of wildernesses.

Since separating the mission from the Presidio, the number of complaints against the soldiers for assault against the natives had plummeted. More encouraging was the increase in the number of converts who had been brought into the new mission. Brother Jayme had waved off the risk of being so far from the Presidio. "Why do we need more than the guards we have? The Indians are completely subdued."

Fuster had no answer; again only a feeling that trouble was brewing.

He bowed his head and looked at the cross on his rosary. *Most Holy Father, I pray that Brother Jayme is right. Amen.*

Chapter 4

At the west end of the river valley, Sun finally sank into the sea, ending this, the day of His longest journey across Sky. From her place under the shade arbor, Web kept one eye on the sunset, the other on her three children busy at a game Cricket had invented. She hoped that Casts No Shadow would return from the sacred mountain soon. Shooting Star was growing too cranky to stay awake much longer.

The wekuseyaay had been gone from the village for eight moons. He had left the same day the people returned from acorn gathering to discover that the Spanish had occupied the site of their old village. With winter coming, the people had been forced to build another village in another location. The elders had chosen a bench across the river from the old Nipaguay as the new site of its center.

Casts No Shadow had not been there to help her construct a new 'ewaa or feed her hungry brood all these many moons, but she had managed to struggle by without him. While the effort had sapped her in strength and spirit, she refused to complain. She believed too strongly in his task for that.

Then, yesterday he had returned home.

Word of his coming flashed through the village like a wind-driven fire. She had watched his arrival from the back of the welcoming throng. Though he answered the peoples' questions about the results of his efforts with assurances that most of the other Kumeyaay villages were ready to rally to Nipaguay's cause, she alone recognized the doubt deep in his eyes.

No one had thought to build an 'ewaa for the wekuseyaay, so she took him to hers. Rather than pepper him with questions, she left him to brood in silence. His hunched shoulders told her everything she needed to know.

This morning he had arisen well before first light in order to go to the sacred mountain to perform the necessary rites for *hellyatai* summer solstice. He should be back by now, however. What could be keeping him so late?

"Grandfather!" Shooting Star cried, scampering to meet the figure that emerged from the evening shadows.

For an instant, Web thought she saw Shadow Dancer instead of his father. In that moment, yearning flooded through her. Since the soldier's attack, she had rarely seen her husband. She could not bring herself to be in any place where there were Spanish soldiers, and the Brown Robes no longer allowed him to visit the relocated Nipaguay. After so long without him, she had begun to despair of ever getting him back. Though she tried to push aside such thoughts, they would not be denied.

Chattering in her high-pitched voice, Shooting Star led the wekuseyaay to the cooking fire and dipped a cup of stew for him. He took it with an affectionate smile and drew the little girl down next to him. Shooting Star nestled against him and was soon fast asleep.

The doubt that Web had seen in the wekuseyaay's eyes the day before was gone. Suddenly all the questions she had held back demanded answers. She sent the twins off to bed and waited impatiently for Casts No Shadow to finish eating. While she waited, a second man appeared at the edge of the fire's light. Web recognized him as a resident of the village, situated near the place where she and Hummingbird used to gather shellfish. The man's face was twisted in worry. He was out of breath from running. "Wekuseyaay, we have need of you," the man panted. "A rattling serpent has bitten one of the children."

Casts No Shadow popped to his feet despite his obvious fatigue and ducked into the lodge to get the things he needed to cure serpent bites. Web picked up a basket and began weaving in order to quell her impatience over this interruption.

"I ran all the way. My friend . . ." The worried man's voice trailed off.

She nodded curtly at him, upset that she would have to wait still longer to find out from Casts No Shadow what had really happened in his visits to the other villages.

"So many serpents this year," the man went on.

Annoyed by the man's prattling, she pulled too hard on the weaving fibers and broke them. She tossed away the now-useless ends and reached for another strand.

The man's voice fell to a whisper, "My son died one moon ago. From such a bite."

For the first time, she really looked at the stranger. The grief obvious in his face banished her annoyance. What right did she have to be angry over a delay in satisfying her curiosity when this man had lost a child? She herself had seen more rattling serpents this spring than ever before. With Casts No Shadow gone, there had been no wekuseyaay to intervene with the spirits, no one to help the souls of those bitten find their way back to the bodies from which they had fled. In the past two moons, she had heard reports from other villages in the nearby area of at least six people dying from snakebites. No day passed during which she did not worry about her own three active children.

Casts No Shadow emerged now from the lodge. She said, "May the spirits hear your words, my father."

He nodded tiredly to her and went off, with the stranger hurrying to keep up.

She looked to the star-splashed night sky. "And may the spirits keep my children safe from harm," she whispered.

When one of the stars winked at her, she shivered.

Chapter 5

R omero dashed the earthen jar against the wall of his hut. "Damn you, Morilla! You cheated me. Two jugs short. Damn you!"

Drawn by Romero's curses, one of the mission neophytes peeked cautiously through the open door of the smith's hut. Romero flung another empty jug at the man, who fled, narrowly dodging the jar that smashed against the frame of the door.

The smith sagged onto his pallet, the only furnishing in the narrow room he called home, and buried his face in his hands. His liquor was all gone, and Morilla wasn't due at the mission for two more days. Morilla. The man was toying with him and that made Romero furious. He had lived up to his end of their bargain. He had paid in advance and now this–this betrayal. He would never survive two more days. Never. Somehow he had to find a way to get to the Presidio, and fast.

Romero held his throbbing head and tried to think. There had to be a way. Had to be.

To leave the mission, he needed Brother Jayme's permission. That meant coming up with a plausible excuse and approaching the Franciscan when he was most distracted, say just before early mass when his mind was on the service.

Yet that meant enduring a night without liquor to deaden his senses and keep the nightmares at bay. A night when every shadow looked to be an attacker and every stir of wind sounded like an Indian arrow. A night when anything could happen. Anything–all of it bad.

At long last, dawn came. Romero caught Brother Jayme outside the church. He stumbled over his excuse, but Jayme waved him aside and pushed into the church with a distracted, "If you need to go, go."

The blacksmith wasted no time. He grabbed the handiest mule and hobbled away from the mission as fast as his crooked leg, the result of the Franciscans' unsuccessful attempt to reset the break, would carry him. It wasn't until he crossed the river that he realized he had rushed off without his knife.

By the time he reached the place where the trail up to the fort angled off the main path, his head and his leg were both aching and he was out of breath from the anxiety of being unarmed. He paused to catch his breath and massage his leg. Rubbing at the soreness, anger flooded over him. The Franciscans had set his leg wrong, and now he would never walk right again. He looked back in the direction of the mission and cursed, "Whoresons! They'll send a Brown Robe home for a hangnail. But not me who can't even run away from a savage who's trying to kill me. Oh, no. Not me. Can't send me home. I'm too valuable. Yah!"

He gave the donkey's lead a vexed jerk.

The animal snorted and tugged back, pulling the blacksmith off his stance.

Before he could kick the balky animal, a group of soldiers rode out of the fort's gates and headed single-file down the path toward him.

Sergeant Ortega rode in the lead. Romero scrambled off the trail to let them pass. He held his breath for fear that Morilla might be among the riders going out on patrol.

Not seeing the private, Romero continued up the trail once the horses passed. Inside the gates, the Presidio compound buzzed with activity. Spotting new faces among the soldiers, Romero checked the bay. A ship, one he did not recognize, lay at anchor just off shore.

Morilla separated from a group and motioned for Romero to follow him into a quiet corner. The blacksmith decided it was not in his best interest to accuse the soldier of cheating him. Even so, Morilla acted put out by the smith's request and demanded, "Let me see the color of your silver."

Romero pulled out a small sack and opened it.

"Not enough, smith. The price has gone up," Morilla said.

Romero was in no position to argue. He pulled out another sack, the one containing all the silver he had stolen to use for future purchases.

"That's more like it," Morilla said, sweeping both bags into his shirt before taking the donkey's lead and disappearing among the storerooms set to one side of the fort. Romero limped back into the main compound to wait. He settled on the ground next to a wall to study the newcomers while he waited.

One of these men laughed, an odd wheezing chuckle that awakened a memory in the smith. His heart stuttered for several beats. It was Nemesio, the former mission guard from Misión La Purísima.

When Nemesio turned his direction, Romero ducked his head so as not to be recognized.

Again, Nemesio laughed. This time the sound broke through the wall behind which Romero had buried all the hatred he had ever felt toward the man who had dragged him away from Misión La Purísima and his beloved Father Xavier. That hatred overcame his fear of the man. He lifted his face and stared brazenly at Nemesio.

The old mission guard stopped laughing then and said something to his companions, nodding in Romero's direction. All the smith heard of that conversation were the words "deformed" and "ugly".

The words stung like a whiplash across his soul. He had once been handsome. Hadn't Father Xavier called him "my beautiful one"? But that beauty was long gone, scoured from his face by the sand and rocks of a faraway trail. Dragging Romero behind his horse had been all Nemesio's idea. It was Nemesio who had ruined Romero's face and turned him into a monster who made people flinch away. Nemesio who left him for dead.

Only he didn't die. He lived, scarred and angry and ripe to wreak revenge for the seven years of wrongs he had endured since that terrible day when the world he had known was stripped away with the flesh from his face.

Romero watched Nemesio and his companions stroll off to their quarters. Death was too good for a man like Nemesio. He had a better idea. An idea he would put into action as soon as he got back to the mission.

Chapter 6

Brother Fuster was three paces away from his room when an unfamiliar sound coming from the forge stopped him. He listened intently, then moved closer to investigate.

Romero was alone at the forge, bent over the glowing bed of coals. And he was humming! He was so focused on his work that he failed to notice the missionary's approach. Fuster considered leaving but could not resist discovering the source of the smith's uncharacteristically good mood. "Special project, blacksmith?"

Romero glanced up but did not offer a response.

Fuster stepped closer.

"What do you want, Padre?" the smith asked.

Fuster was too used to such brusqueness from the man to react. "What are you making?"

"A brand."

"May I see it?"

Romero appeared to hesitate before complying. He set the piece on the top of his anvil. "Look, but don't touch. It's still hot."

A bar was welded between the three forks of one end of a long metal handle. Attached to that bar were the letters "J" and "R" intertwined.

"Beautiful work, José, but may I suggest adding a cross to it?" Fuster offered.

"No cross," Romero said quickly.

"It's the perfect solution to our problem of how to keep the mission's livestock separate from the Presidio's, but . . ."

"No crosses! No animals!" Romero said, raising his voice. He swept the object out of Fuster's reach. "This is not for an animal."

The bells tolled, calling Fuster to teach catechism class. He did not have the time to pursue the issue further. With a puzzled shrug, he put aside the incident and headed toward the church.

Chapter 7

In a small clearing among tall creosote bushes along the riverbank, Romero added more wood to the little fire and fanned the flames with a piece of stiff hide until the new pieces caught. Waiting for the fire to burn down to the coals he needed, he went over his plan one last time. Every now and then, his hand strayed to his carrying bag only to draw back. The jug was for later. Drinking now might slow his reflexes, and after six weeks of waiting, holding his anger in check until he had the information he needed about Nemesio, nothing, nothing must go wrong.

When the wood reduced to embers, he positioned the head of the branding iron carefully in the heart of the glowing mass, then sat back on his haunches to watch the iron letters of the brand absorb the heat.

His ears pricked up at the sounds of splashing from the nearby river pool. He crept to a concealed vantage point and parted the bushes. Four paces away a naked Nemesio sat neck-deep in the pool, eyes closed, head thrown back in pleasure. Of all the Spanish at the fort, only Nemesio made a habit of bathing regularly. A habit he had not been able to follow since the dry season began. But now here he was, right on schedule, thanks to a late-season rain squall.

Romero's stomach knotted from tension. What was taking the man so long today? Had he decided to soak longer and skip his usual after-bath nap? That would blow apart all Romero's careful preparations and force him to wait for weeks, possibly months, before he'd have another chance like this one.

The smith was drenched in nervous sweat by the time the

soldier stood up to leave the pool. While Nemesio stepped onto the sand and stretched lazily, Romero held his breath in fear that the man would reach for his clothes.

Instead, Nemesio yawned broadly and stretched out on the sand, throwing one arm over his eyes to block the glare of the hazy sun. Romero stole back to the fire. This time, when his shaking hand reached for the jug, he did not pull it back. *Just a swallow to steady the nerves*, he told himself.

One swallow turned into three long gulps before he returned the jar to his sack, grabbed the brand and crept back to the bushes. Loud snoring accompanied the steady rise and fall of Nemesio's chest.

Romero took a deep breath to calm his fluttering stomach, firmed his grip on the brand and stepped from cover. "How was the bath, amigo?"

The soldier sat up.

Before he could blink the sleep out of his eyes, Romero lunged at him, aiming the red-hot brand at the center of the man's face.

Nemesio rolled left, and Romero barreled into him, pinwheeling over his body, slamming onto the wet sand at the edge of the river. In a breath-space, Nemesio pounced on him, delivering a solid punch into Romero's left temple, then driving his knee into Romero's unprotected crotch.

Pain collapsed the smith into a groaning ball. While he retched bile into the sand, the soldier pummeled him with one damaging blow after another.

At one point, Romero managed to croak, "Mercy, Nemesio."

The soldier paused in his beating. "How do you know my name, whoever you are?"

"Purísima," Romero rasped.

Nemesio bent down for a closer look at the smith's face. "Romero. But it can't be. You're supposed to be in Loreto. Father Xavier . . ."

The mention of the Jesuit's name forced Romero's pain aside. "You know where he is?"

Nemesio sat back and looked at the smith with a calculating expression.

Romero clutched at the soldier's arm. "You do, don't you? Where is he? You must tell me."

"Why do you want to know?"

"Because I have to find him. I have to explain about Bartolomé. I have to . . ."

Nemesio's hooting laughter cut him off. "What if Father Xavier doesn't want you to find him?"

"I have to find him. I have to explain that I did what I did out of love."

More laughter with a mocking edge. When Romero tried to struggle up to his knees, the soldier shoved him back and pinned him to the sand. "Is that what you call it? Love? Why, you poor, confused fool. That wasn't love between you and the Father, and neither is this."

With surprising strength and speed, in one motion Nemesio flipped Romero over, ripped his pants down to his knees, raised his rear end and entered him. After years of disuse, the smith's nether opening was unprepared for the assault. He felt flesh rip. He shrieked in pain.

His cries increased Nemesio's ardor. He jammed into Romero again and again, grunting louder and pounding harder with each thrust until, at last, his body went rigid. He climaxed with a strangled cry and fell forward onto Romero's back.

He lay that way for a long time. Pinned under his attacker's body, the smith could not move. The only thing his mind seemed able to grasp was the reality of the branding iron, lying useless in the wet sand beyond his reach.

After what seemed an eternity, Nemesio pushed away and got to his feet. "Now I see why the Jesuit wanted Bartolomé. You're nothing special. Not at all." He pulled on his trousers. "You're wrong, you know, blacksmith. If the Jesuit ever loved anyone, it was Bartolomé, not you."

Through his pain and humiliation, all Romero could muster was a half-snort of derision.

Nemesio stopped in the process of putting on his shirt. "You don't know, do you?"

Romero levered himself up on one elbow and faced his attacker. "Know what?"

"I thought you would figure it out right away, but you didn't, did you? It was Father Xavier who had you arrested in Loreto."

The smith slammed his fist into the sand. "Lies!"

Nemesio finished pulling on his shirt and reached for his belt, then turned back to face Romero. "The same day Father Xavier received the King's order expelling the Jesuits from New Spain, word came to Purísima that you were alive in Loreto. Father needed a way to make sure you couldn't hurt Bartolomé, so he bribed the military commander of Loreto into throwing you into prison."

"No! You lie!"

The soldier squatted next to the smith and lowered his voice conspiratorially. "Oh, no, amigo. It's God's own truth, spoken by the very one who personally placed Father's letter and sack of gold into the commander's hands."

Romero rolled away from Nemesio and covered his ears to block out the words. Chuckling cruelly, the soldier frog-stepped to the smith's side and ripped one hand away from the ear it covered. "And if you ever try to hurt me again, it will be the barrel of my rifle I shove up your asshole. *Comprende?*"

Romero refused to answer.

Nemesio torqued his wrist. "*Comprende?*"

Romero managed a choked "yes", and the soldier let him go.

The smith turned his head so he would not have to witness his attacker walking away. Once he was alone, he continued to stay where he was, too humiliated to cover himself, too distraught by what Nemesio had told him to move.

The longer he stayed on the ground, the more certain he was that the man had told the truth. Bartolomé had caused all this. Bartolomé had stolen Father Xavier's love. Bartolomé was the reason he had been driven from La Purísima and imprisoned in Loreto. Bartolomé owned responsibility for these scars that had destroyed his face and for these seven years in the living hell of San Diego.

Bartolomé. The image of the Indian boy flashed into Romero's mind, propelling him to his feet. After tying his pants into place, he retrieved the branding iron from the shallows. He held it up to the clouds. "Bartolomé, this is for you, if it's the last thing I do."

Clutching the brand, he staggered back into the brush to the ring of still-hot coals and his jug. He downed the liquor in huge gulps, desperate for a way to cleanse himself of the filth Nemesio had deposited in both his body and his mind.

Bartolomé and Nemesio. Two reasons for living. Two reasons for hating. *Nemesio and Bartolomé.* The names were moths chewing through the fabric of his mind, unraveling the cloth of his sanity one strand at a time. All the way to the mission, he muttered the names over and over as if they were the chant of a petitioner seeking the intervention of the Most Holy.

At the mission, he limped straight to the forge, directly to a fresh jug. Carlos was nowhere in evidence, and the fire on the hearth had been banked.

Between swallows from the jar, Romero managed to reactivate the fire until the coals glowed cherry red. Into them, he placed the brand. He watched the metal heat without really seeing it. His mind would not allow him to think about Nemesio and what happened earlier. Instead, he saw himself at La Purísima, standing outside the door to Father Xavier's room. Cradling the carefully-mended altar piece in the crook of one elbow, he raised his hand to knock on the door. But the hand never touched the door. Rather, it stopped in mid-air at the sight of Father Xavier standing behind the naked figure of an Indian boy. The skirt of Father's habit was raised and Father's hips were thrusting forward and back, forward and back, each thrust driving his rampant manhood into the boy's rear opening.

"Bartolomé!" Romero said aloud, yanking the sledge out of its crib and slamming it into the wall. Pieces of adobe fell in a cascade of dust.

"Love!" He swung a second time, hitting another part of the wall. More dust and brick showered onto the hut's floor.

"Purísima!" This time he swung at his work table. The head of the sledge caught the front leg. The wood splintered readily, throwing the smith off-balance. He staggered into Carlos's pallet, barking both his shins.

Crying out, he fell heavily onto the bed on his side, knocking the wind out of his lungs. While he gasped for air, a sudden yearning for Father Xavier welled up from his bowels. "Oh, Father, why? Why did you forsake me?"

The response came as a whisper out of the thatch above his head. "Bartolomé."

Romero reeled up off the pallet. "No! I don't believe you! You love me. Me."

Again the whisper. "Bartolomé."

He fell against the wall and slid down to the floor, cupping his ears against the assault of that voice, that name. "No, no. Me. Romero. You love me."

The whisper came through his hands, louder. "Bartolomé."

Romero pounded his fists against the trampled earth of the forge's floor. "Me," he sobbed.

"Bartolomé."

As the voice grew more insistent, Romero's ability to respond to it faded. He stopped pounding and stared at the floor where the image of Bartolomé appeared to rise out of the dirt, taking human form.

The specter stared at Romero and spoke a garble of gibberish instead of the Spanish the unseen voice had spoken.

Romero shook his head to clear his ears.

A second specter appeared beside the first, identical to it.

The smith rubbed his eyes to clear his vision, but the two Bartolomés remained. The first one spoke more gibberish.

"Speak Spanish, orphan!" he demanded.

The specters exchanged a worried look and moved back a step.

"You're afraid of me?" Romero asked, emboldened enough to lean forward.

The ghosts moved back again.

On the hearth, the head of the branding iron glowed red with heat. The sight fueled Romero's courage. "Come closer," he coaxed. "There's nothing to be afraid of, little one."

While the second image kept on backing away, the first hesitated.

In that instant, the smith leaped and caught it. With a yelp, the second image turned and sprinted away.

"You're re–" He did not get the chance to finish his sentence because the first Bartolomé began immediately to try to escape his grasp.

The boy was no match for Romero whose iron grip came from years at the forge. The smith subdued him with one hand and reached for the hot brand with the other. "An eye for an eye, orphan. A face for a face."

Bartolomé struggled and kicked furiously. To no avail.

Grinning, Romero jammed the hot iron to the one face he hated more than any in the world.

A child's screams rent the quiet of the mission, stopping Brother Fuster mid-sentence. Dropping his missal, he raced out of the church, leaving Carlos and the neophytes in the midst of the day's lesson. He reached open air in time to see a terrified Indian boy streak out of the gates. Since the youngster did not appear hurt, Fuster turned in the direction of the sound and headed for the forge.

What he saw there stopped him in his tracks: The blacksmith, pants puddled at his ankles, buggering a little Indian boy.

"Blacksmith!" he yelled.

Romero turned at the shout. His eyes were glazed and his mouth flapped open and shut as if he were incapable of speaking.

"Unhand him! Now!" Fuster ordered.

The smith looked bewildered by the order but complied, releasing the boy who dropped to the ground like an old rag.

Fuster dashed to the child. The boy was unconscious; his breathing, regular; his heartbeat, strong; but what was wrong with his face? It took a moment to recognize that something had seriously burned the child on the face as well as the buttocks. Raised welts of blackened flesh that spelled out "JR".

Then he understood: the blacksmith had used his brand–the one he would not use on an animal–on this poor child.

The priest was not aware that his hand had covered his mouth in horror until someone behind him gasped, "Oh, my gracious Lord!"

He turned to see Brother Jayme a few paces away. Fuster's tongue came unglued. "Guard!"

Brother Jayme grabbed his arm. "What are you doing, Brother?"

"Arresting this–this monster. Putting him in chains."

The senior missionary put back his hands as if to shield the blacksmith. "No, Brother. I can't allow that. Not the blacksmith. Not now."

Fuster's voice rose with his anger. "Yes, the blacksmith! Yes, now! He branded that boy. Branded him! And I caught him in the act of . . ." He stopped himself before the profane words could pass his lips. "In the act of doing unnatural things to the child."

A dazed Romero looked from one missionary to the other as if they were speaking in tongues.

"I cannot allow such an arrest, Brother," Brother Jayme said. "No matter what he's done, Romero is our only blacksmith. We need him as much as we need food."

Fuster laid the boy carefully on the ground and stood up. "I will go to the Presidio for soldiers. Our guards can hold him until then. Guard!" He headed for the door.

"Brother!" Jayme warned. "I order you to stop your disobedience this instant."

Fuster stopped and turned to face his fellow missionary. "You would let him go unpunished after–after this, this atrocity. By the Virgin, Brother, look at the child. Look!"

Jayme's eyes never moved from Fuster's face. "Obey me. Stop this instant."

"He branded the boy. Branded him. Look, for God's sake. Look!" Fuster shouted.

"How dare you take the Lord's name in vain!" Jayme roared. "This boy is not one of our charges. He is a savage, not our responsibility."

Fuster had to fight to contain his anger. "He is a human being. A child. This one," He pointed a trembling finger at Romero. "He's the savage. How many times does he have to prove that fact before you acknowledge it, and do something?"

"You leave me no choice, Brother Fuster. I must report your insubordination to Father Serra."

"Brother Jayme, I . . ."

"Enough! If you care so much for this child, see to his wounds."

Without ever looking at the boy, Jayme guided a shuffling Romero out of the forge.

In the oppressive silence after their departure, the boy began to moan. Carefully, Fuster picked him up and carried him to his room, his heart sick at all that had happened and his powerlessness to set things right.

It was dusk when shrieks in the near distance brought Web to her feet. On the path leading up the ravine from the river, a small figure staggered toward her. She threw down the hide she had been working and ran forward, catching Sand Flea in her arms as he collapsed.

It took a moment for her to realize that something was wrong with his face. By the time she did, Casts No Shadow was beside her.

"Burns," he said angrily.

"Twisted Face hurt me," Sand Flea sobbed.

Web sought to speak words of comfort to her son but no words would issue from her suddenly-constricted throat.

"Two burns," Casts No Shadow said, his face taut with fury. "Bad ones. On his face and his rear." His tone took on a lethal edge. "The same burns."

Web looked in shock at her son's scarred flesh. She had sent the boys to the mission with food for their father. "Where is Cricket?"

Sand Flea managed to whisper between sobs, "A snake bit him."

Her heart began to race. "Where?"

"Below the mission."

Casts No Shadow was on his feet and hurrying away toward the mission and her other son before Web could react. The wekuseyaay had returned to Nipaguay that morning, exhausted and dispirited after another six moons spent trying to rouse the Kumeyaay against the Spanish. Despite the fatigue that was so obvious in his movements, he raced off now, leaving Web alone to face the horror of what Twisted Face had done to her precious son, not knowing what might have happened to his twin.

She rushed to prepare poultices for the burns from wild swamp roots and applied them gingerly to Sand Flea's wounds. All the while, she had the sensation that part of her had left her body to watch the rest of her go through the motions of helping her son. Nothing else seemed real but his pain.

It took a long time for Sand Flea to quiet, and an even longer time for him to fall into a fitful sleep. Web sat beside her muttering, tossing child, afraid to leave him but increasingly frantic about Cricket. The disembodied feeling stayed with her, and, with it, came a numbness that permeated her every nerve and muscle. Every breath, every moment dragged by endlessly.

Sand Flea moaned and thrashed his arms as if trying to ward off dream demons. Web laid her hand on his unharmed cheek to soothe him.

At that moment, a shadow fell across the lodge entrance. She jumped before she recognized Casts No Shadow's familiar figure. He held Cricket in his arms.

The sight of her precious son levered her to her feet. She plunged out to him with a cry of joy.

Before she could touch the boy, the wekuseyaay stopped her. "He no longer walks among us."

"He is only sleeping," she argued. "I can see . . ."

Casts No Shadow grasped her reaching hand. "No, daughter. Not sleeping. It–it was too late for me to call his soul back from the gods."

She stared at Cricket in disbelief. "No, Father. Look. He sleeps."

The shaman's voice lowered. "The Great Serpent has claimed him. We must release his spirit to join the ancestors. I will prepare the fire."

The part of her that looked on heard her say, "Fire?"

Sorrow clouded the old man's eyes. Slowly, realization pierced her stupor. She fell to her knees with a wail. "No, it cannot be. I sent them to the mission–with food–for their father. I–I can not go there. The soldiers . . ." Her throat ached too much to say more.

The wekuseyaay knelt beside her, still cradling Cricket's body. "The blame is not yours, Daughter. Twisted Face and the Spanish, they killed my grandson. They hurt Sand Flea."

Immobilized by sorrow so profound that it left no room for any other emotion, she looked from Cricket to his brother.

"You must go for your husband," Casts No Shadow said. "Bring him back to his people."

"I cannot go to the mission, Father. The soldiers . . ."

"Ayieee!" came a woman's scream.

Web turned to see Crooked Basket, eyes wide with shock, staring at Cricket, hands over her mouth.

The cry cut through Web's haze. Deep in her a spark ignited. Within the space of a heartbeat, she was on her feet, determined to right this terrible wrong. "Yes, Father, I will go to the mission, and I will bring my husband back. For good."

That night Brother Fuster knelt on the floor of his room before the crucifix and struggled to shut out the disturbing noises coming from the nearby native village in order to concentrate on his nightly devotions.

Then someone knocked.

Fuster rose and opened the door to find Brother Jayme. "Is Carlos with you?"

"I'm alone," Fuster said.

"Have you seen him?"

"Is there trouble?"

"It's those savages across the river." The low clouds above the native village glowed red. "Cremation fires," Brother Jayme said. "That and all the caterwauling are liable to stir up our neophytes. I need Carlos to help me calm things down."

At the mention of cremation, Fuster tensed. Before the other missionary had knocked, Fuster had been praying to God to spare the wounded Indian child's life. He had left the injured boy alone in his quarters for only a moment in order to fetch bandages, but when he returned, the boy had vanished. Although Fuster had searched the mission compound, he came up empty-handed. "I haven't seen Carlos since this afternoon," he said.

Brother Jayme stalked off without another word. Fuster looked in the direction of the Indian village. "Please, God. Take mercy on the child, and help me find the strength to not hate the blacksmith."

The night wind carried an eerie keening to his ears from the native village. He did not need to understand the words to hear the sorrow in the sound. His fingers found his rosary. He turned his back on the red-tinged clouds, closed the door and went back to his prayers.

Chapter 8

Romero closed one eye in order to peer into the jug. The liquor was almost gone. This was his last jug. Where had the rest gone? Was someone stealing his supply while he was sleeping? What day was this anyway?

He clenched his teeth with the strain of trying to figure when Morilla was due at the mission. He did not hear Brother Fuster's approach until someone tore the jar out of his surprised hands.

"You drunk!" the Franciscan bellowed, flinging the jug to the ground.

The jar shattered, spilling its precious remains onto the earth. Romero fell to his knees and fruitlessly tried to scoop up the liquid treasure.

"So this is how you excuse your sins, blacksmith," Fuster thundered.

"Sins? What sins?" the blacksmith slurred indignantly.

"You know and God knows. You cannot hide from the Almighty."

Faced with the missionary's anger, Romero chose not to argue. He gathered up the jug pieces and teetered to his feet.

"Where did you get that?" Fuster demanded.

Romero swept everything off his workbench in order to make a place for the shards. He had no choice now–he had to go to the fort, and knowing that made him furious.

"Tell me, blacksmith," Fuster said.

Romero glared at the missionary. "I can do anything I want, Padre. Anything–and neither you nor anybody else in this hell-hole can touch me. I'm the only blacksmith you've got, so don't threaten me."

With his anger slowly defusing, Fuster crossed himself. "May God have mercy on your soul."

"God? What God?" Romero asked. "Look around you, Padre. There's no God here. This is hell."

Fuster turned away. No sense arguing with a brute, even if he did agree that this place was a kind of hell.

Chapter 9

Except for a faint shadow on one edge, the early November moon was full. It hung like a false sun above Web, casting surreal silvery shadows that made her skittish.

Shadow Dancer had been gone for over a moon. He and the one-eyed Many Rains had left Nipaguay the day after Cricket's cremation. They had gone with Casts No Shadow to try once again to rouse the other Kumeyaay villages against the Spanish. From the reports that filtered back to her, their efforts were at last bearing fruit.

A tendril of chill night wind touched her bare shoulders. Shivering, she drew up the fur blanket. Since the *hellyaach-sekap-tewaa* half moon, she had taken to sitting outside under the wisal after tucking in Sand Flea and Shooting Star. She would stare at the moon and commit her thoughts to the passing breeze, believing that the wind would then carry those thoughts to her husband wherever he happened to be.

Unlike the hole gouged in her heart by Cricket's loss, Sand Flea's burns were healing. As his skin mended, his nightmares lessened. Not so with hers.

Increasingly, the night became a time of dread for Web. Darkness wrested from her the ability to keep locked away all the terrible images from the Spanish attacks on her and those she loved. Scenes swirled through her mind, shifting in sequence, horror building on horror until she was drenched in cold sweat and shaking. Night after night she had to fight down the urge to take her children and flee into the desert, back to Hawi, her birth village, where there were no Spanish.

A branch cracked under someone's weight behind her. She whirled to see three figures emerging from the clutch of mesquites along the top of the ravine to the east.

The sight of her husband's familiar gait instantly erased her fears. With a small cry she ran to meet him, flinging her arms around his neck without regard to conventional propriety, reveling in the feel of his arms encircling her waist and the strength of the chest he crushed her to. She buried her nose in his neck and clung to him until he released her.

Standing back, she saw a new fire burning in his eyes. "When?" she asked.

"Tomorrow night," he said in a low tight voice.

"Men from many villages will join us, thanks to my son," Casts No Shadow said, looking at Shadow Dancer.

My son. Web thrilled to hear those words again from the weku-seyaay.

"We must go to prepare," Casts No Shadow said, nodding to Many Rains who followed the wekuseyaay off into the night, leaving Web alone with her husband.

Shadow Dancer touched her wrist. She felt suddenly shy. She had not been completely alone with him since he moved to the mission, and she had not lain with him since the soldier's attack.

"Come, my wife." He took her hand and led her into the lodge where he stooped to look at his sleeping children. He smoothed back a lock of Shooting Star's hair. "She is so beautiful," he whispered. "Like her mother."

Web felt herself blush at the compliment and the precious love that was behind it.

He examined Sand Flea's wounds. Though he said nothing, his eyes glistened with unshed tears of anguish for the ordeal his son had gone through.

Tenderness for her husband surged into Web's heart. She put a comforting hand on his shoulder. He clasped the hand and turned to her. "I have been so blind."

"You did as the spirits commanded," she murmured.

"I feel such pain, Wife, but it can never begin to match yours. Will you forgive me?"

His eyes searched her face. She stroked his fatigue-etched cheek. "There is nothing to forgive, my husband. My dream has come true. You are here again, to stay. We have new memories to make while we watch our children grow up and while we grow old together."

"Yes," he rasped. "Oh, yes."

He raised her hands to his lips and tenderly kissed each of the extended flaps of skin between her fingers–the same webs he had insisted she hide when they were first married. Then he drew her onto the pallet where she had slept alone for so many moons.

He cupped her face between his hands and turned it to him. "We will grow old together, my wife, without the Spanish in our midst."

This time it was her eyes where the tears welled. "Oh, yes, my husband. Yes."

Chapter 10

The flap across the entrance to the hastily-built war lodge swept aside. Many Rains, Shadow Dancer, and Casts No Shadow emerged into the crisp fall air, their faces taut, their eyes focused on the coming battle.

Seeing her father, Shooting Star whined and struggled against Web's hold. Web shushed the child and held fast. There would be time enough for family later, after the Spanish were destroyed.

The afternoon wind swirled the smoke from dozens of cooking fires where stews bubbled, meat roasted and seed cakes sizzled. Food for the dozens of Kumeyaay men from outlying villages–men from over forty *sh'mulqs*–who, since dawn, had been massing in the river bottom for tonight's attack.

Web had lain awake all night beside Shadow Dancer, listening to the rhythm of his breathing, rejoicing in the comfort of his closeness, memorizing the feel and smell of him.

He had awakened just before dawn, elated by the attack plan that had come to him in his dreams. "We will divide into two groups. Many Rains will lead one to attack the fort first. I will lead the second group against the mission once I see fires from the fort." He had explained this to her hurriedly, then left to put the plan into action.

Between lack of sleep and fear that something might happen to her husband, Web was as nervous as a mother dog when someone is handling her pups. She watched Shadow Dancer and Many Rains exchange a few last words, then Many Rains raced off toward the fort to gather the men hidden near there and prepare to make the first thrust.

The sight filled Web with a mixture of relief and dread. Relief that Many Rains would finally get revenge on the Spanish for robbing him of his eye and the woman he had loved so much. Dread about all the things that could go wrong tonight.

Following after Many Rains was a tall boy near the age of initiation aptly named Antelope. Shadow Dancer had picked him to be the runner who would carry word to Nipaguay when the group left their place of concealment to move on the Spanish fort.

Now Shadow Dancer took the seat of leadership at the council fire, followed by the kwaipais, shamans and most important men from all the *sh'mulqs* who had come to participate in tonight's attack. Web's heart beat faster as her husband lit the council pipe, offered the smoke to the six directions and passed it to his father.

Casts No Shadow accepted the *'emuukwin* gravely, took a slow puff and handed it on to Big Nose who continued the process. Warrior after warrior, the pipe made the rounds of the assembly. With each puff of smoke, Web's fears waned, and her confidence grew.

The attack would work. By this time tomorrow all the Spanish would either be dead or driven off. Then the people of Nipaguay could take back their old village site. The people of Cosoy could reclaim the land the Spanish had taken from them. Those Kumeyaays who had been drawn in by the lies of the Brown Robes would return to their homes. And life could get back to normal at long, long last. *That is, as normal as life could be without my precious little Cricket or my beloved Hummingbird*

*and with a disfigured Sand Flea and the terrifying memories of
the soldier's attack,* she thought.

Earlier she had overheard Crooked Basket convincing a group
of village women to join the attack on the mission. Because
hunting and weapons were the domain of men, not women, Web
had walked away from the group rather than get into a
disagreement with her old nemesis. Now, however, renewed
confidence made her reconsider her opinions. By the time the
'emuukwin returned to her husband's hands, she decided to join
Crooked Basket's women.

Shadow Dancer glanced over at her. Web immediately lowered
her eyes. She would not tell him of her decision until the attack
was over. Otherwise he might try to forbid her participation. She
did not know exactly what she could accomplish during the
attack. All she knew was that she had to participate, had to right
the wrongs that had been done to her and her loved ones by the
Spanish. Tonight she intended to do just that.

Realizing that it was November 5 prompted Brother Fuster to
pull the glove out of its secret pocket and spread it out on his
blanket. Light from the full moon pierced the cracks in the
rough-hewn planks of the door to his cell, casting daggers of
silver illumination across the lace.

The moon had also been full on that other November 5, the
night Amalia had broken his heart. Back then, the light of that
moon had buoyed his steps on the way to meet her. In its light
she had never looked more beautiful. Then a few words from her
lips had driven all the magic out of the night and all the magic
from his heart, leaving him with a yawning emptiness inside and
only one fragile lace glove to prove it had not been just a dream.

Fuster looked up at the crucifix. Keeping the glove was wrong,
but keeping silent about his undying longing for Amalia was far
worse. He was a sinner and a hypocrite; a liar who used silence
to hide his weakness.

"Father, please help me," he prayed. "Help me have the strength to
put an end to my subterfuge. Help me expunge her from my heart
and mind."

He picked up the glove. "Help me cast off this–this anchor that
holds me fast in the mire of sin. Help me to admit my weakness.
Lead my soul to truth and peace."

Sudden weariness overwhelmed him, lowering his voice to a

faint whisper. "Please, my Father. Please."

He curled onto the pallet, drawing the blanket over him against the night's chill and pressing the glove to his heart. He was nearly asleep when a noise outside roused him to wakefulness. He tensed, straining to hear more.

Silence.

He relaxed, assigning the blame to the still-settling walls of the new mission's structures.

The next moment, he dropped into sleep, deep and dreamless, with the glove still clutched between his fingers.

The damp of the river bottom magnified the night's chill, though none of the tense, silent Kumeyaay warriors seemed to notice. Casts No Shadow surveyed the men and the scene. Strength coursed through his veins, making him feel more alive than at any other time in his thirty-nine summers.

Off to his right Shadow Dancer conversed in whispers with two kwaipais from a village a day's walk to the east. He watched his son with a swell of pride that such a strong, capable man–a powerful and esteemed 'aww-kuseyaay who would follow in his footsteps when the time came–had sprung from his loins.

Along with the pride he also felt gratitude that the split between them was now mended. However much he regretted the tragic circumstances of their reconciliation, what was done could not be undone. Cricket's soul lived in the Land of Those Who Went Before. Sand Flea would always wear the scars of Twisted Face's brutal attack. And memories of her rape and Hummingbird's murder would haunt Web all her days. What remained was to go on from here, free of the evil Spanish plague that had spread across the land and the people.

Casts No Shadow looked up at the *hellyach-temur* full moon. Shadow Dancer had chosen this night well. It was cold enough to force the Spanish sentries at the fort to seek the warmth of a fire rather than watching for intruders. It was clear enough so that the gods could witness the final defeat of the Spanish and their evil sorcerers.

The moon was approaching zenith when Casts No Shadow walked away from the main gathering into a copse of sycamores. There, in privacy, he settled onto the ground, closed his eyes and began to breath deeply, filling his lungs with air, holding each breath for a time, then slowly releasing it until his lungs were completely empty. Once, twice, three times he breathed. Six, eight, twelve until the familiar floating feeling overtook him, easing him into a trance. Out of the darkness, a curtain of mist swirled up, parting to reveal the Great Serpent who focused one questioning eye on Casts No Shadow.

"Tonight we attack the bearded ones who have bewitched so many of my people," the wekuseyaay said.

The Serpent's head cocked to the right.

"I come seeking Your strength for all the brave warriors who have put aside their fear to help drive out the evil ones, to end the sorcery that fouls our land and to reclaim the land and the loved ones these bearded witches have taken from them. Will You help us?"

For a time the Rattling Serpent Spirit did not move. Then the snake body stretched, rising into the air until the wekuseyaay had to lean back to see Its great head.

The Serpent poised there as if deciding something. Then the massive body began to ripple, wrapping into coils of shimmering scales until the hooded eyes came back down to Casts No Shadow's level.

The wekuseyaay felt the flick of the Snake's tongue against his cheek.

"I will help, if you start the attack now," the Snake hissed.

As the tongue touched his cheek again, the shaman held himself rigid against the urge to draw back.

"Attack now, Shaman." The words trailed off in a sibilant whisper. The image vanished and Casts No Shadow awoke. He picked himself off the ground and walked back to the rest of the gathered men. He found Shadow Dancer in the middle of a group of warriors and pulled him away. "Start the attack now, my son."

"No, Father. Many Rains has not yet reached the fort."

Casts No Shadow drew himself up. "The Great Serpent has spoken. Attack now!"

Shadow Dancer peered toward the Presidio.

"Now!" the wekuseyaay insisted. "The spirits command it."

Shadow Dancer hesitated another moment before nodding resignedly. He raised his arm, and a hush fell over the throng of Indians.

When all was still, the arm fell, and the first warriors started toward the mission.

From the start the attack had met no resistance. As leaders, Casts No Shadow and Shadow Dancer were the first through the mission gates. They found the night guard asleep beside a small fire. As agreed, Big Nose led part of the group into the compound to carry off anything they could find. Shadow Dancer and Casts No Shadow held back the remainder of the restive Kumeyaay warriors for a time to give the others a head start.

Then Shadow Dancer ordered his forward rank to light brands from the guard's blaze and begin setting fire to the thatched roofs. He and the rest of the warriors stayed with Casts No Shadow until the first roofs were ablaze, then, with a war cry, he led the main charge.

The war cries awoke the sleeping guard. His eyes immediately widened to the size of clam shells. Casts No Shadow looked down at the man, enjoying the sight of his fear.

A Brown Robe emerged from one of the now-burning buildings, momentarily drawing the wekuseyaay's attention away from the guard. The Brown Robe looked around as if stunned by what he saw. The man's gaze met Casts No Shadow's. He held out his arms as if beckoning the shaman to him.

Casts No Shadow returned the man's stare, sizing up his foe.

The Brown Robe shouted over the sounds of the attack. The words washed over the wekuseyaay and were lost to the night wind.

The Brown Robe began to walk toward Casts No Shadow, still speaking whatever spell he was attempting to cast.

Casts No Shadow did not move. He felt a smile playing at his lips. This was as it should be: shaman against sorcerer.

His smile faded and his eyes narrowed in hatred as he watched the Brown Robe's approach. These Brown Robes were the worst witches he had ever come up against. They thought of no one but themselves. They had harmed many Kumeyaay people, including his son, with their spells. They and the paleskin warriors had destroyed the once-proud village of Cosoy and usurped Nipaguay's site from his own people. Because of them, Hummingbird and Cricket now lived among the ancestors, his once-handsome grandson would live out his days scarred, and Web would forever have to endure the torment of memories from her attack.

Without taking his eyes off the advancing Brown Robe, Casts No Shadow nocked an arrow, drew back the bowstring, took aim and let it fly.

When the arrow hit, the Brown Robe staggered and clutched his chest. He raised his face to the sky and spoke what sounded like a prayer to the bearded ones' evil god.

"Silence!" Casts No Shadow ordered.

Because the Brown Robe continued to speak, the wekuseyaay aimed a second arrow between the sorcerer's lips.

The arrow hit its mark, and immediately a crowd of Kumeyaay warriors pounced on the downed man. Big Nose emerged from the melee and yelled, "What shall we do with him, Wekuseyaay? Take him to the village?"

"Not the village. His power might contaminate us all," Casts No Shadow said.

"Where then?"

"Take his body to the river bottom. Leave it and his soul to rot."

Big Nose nodded and turned back to the Brown Robe.

Casts No Shadow raised his staff to the *hellyaach-temur* full moon. "May his spirit wander forever alone and with no place to rest."

A thin cloud drifted across the face of the moon, momentarily obscuring its light before passing away. Casts No Shadow shivered and turned back to the noise and confusion of the attack.

A burst of whoops and shouts shattered the night's silence. The assault on the Spanish mission had begun. Web glanced at the women around her as they waited for Crooked Basket to give the signal for them to join their men in the attack. Each woman stood to lose someone she loved this night, yet determination painted every face. Determination to drive away the Spanish and cast out the evil that had forced its way into all their lives.

As the noise of the fighting grew, Web wished she had been born male and had grown up using weapons. Her clenched fists longed to clutch a spear or a bow–anything besides air.

At last Crooked Basket gave the signal. Web and the other women surged toward the mission. The tule roofs of the buildings closest to the entrance were now ablaze. The crackling of those fires added to the shouting and screaming, grunting and moaning of the fight. Web hesitated at the mission's open gates. Smoke and confusion of motion blocked her view of all but what lay closest to her. She edged around a group of warriors to get to the church.

The doors of the building stood open. In the flickering light of burning roof thatch on the structure behind her, she saw overturned benches and smashed cabinets inside the church. For a moment, her confidence faltered. She was too late.

Then adrenaline pushed her forward and she saw what she had come for: the wooden statue of the paleskin mother and baby, upright and unharmed at the front of the room.

With a cry of triumph, she ran forward and grabbed the statue, wrapping it securely in both arms.

From behind her someone yelled, "Stop!"

She turned to face a young Kumeyaay convert from Hummingbird's birth village, whose name she could not recall. Shadow Dancer and Casts No Shadow had spent hours huddled with the kwaipais of the other villages devising a way to protect and neutralize the converts who lived at the mission during the attack. Obviously that plan had not been completely successful.

"No," Web said, hugging the wooden figure to her and starting out the door.

"Where are you taking her?" the convert demanded.

"I mean to destroy it once and for all," Web answered.

He grabbed her arm. "You cannot destroy her. She is the Holy Mother, chosen by One Above."

Web spun out of his grasp. "Fool. There is nothing holy about this thing–this curse which the Brown Robe sorcerers of the bearded ones thrust among us. After they have destroyed this cursed place, the great wekuseyaay and my husband, Shadow Dancer, will destroy this figure, and, when it is gone, the Spanish will at last be driven from our land, never to return."

"Don't, sister," he begged. "One Above . . ."

"Silence! One Above is *my* God. You have betrayed Him. You are no longer worthy to speak His name."

At that, the man dropped his hands as if defeated by Web's anger. She rushed into the night, the hateful statue tight in her grasp.

A thick cloud of smoke immediately engulfed her. With her eyes tearing, she had to stop moving.

Boom! The nearby retort from a Spanish thunder stick startled her. She whirled around to see an unfamiliar Kumeyaay warrior coming up behind her. His mouth dropped open as if to speak. Instead, he grunted and pitched forward, barely missing her.

Blood oozed from a blackened hole in his back. *He is dead*, she thought. *The thunder stick has stolen his spirit*. The realization paralyzed her.

Through the smoke, a figure appeared in the doorway to one of the huts. Web did not need clear vision to recognize Twisted

Face. He had appeared in too many of her nightmares for her to mistake him for anyone else.

He reeled over the threshold, arms flailing wildly, muttering a stream of slurred words. He grabbed a post for support and stood facing her, stance wavering, head weaving as if disconnected from his body.

Her anger flared. This was the monster who mutilated Sand Flea and caused the death of Cricket. He deserved to die. Yet, she had nothing to kill him with.

She glanced around, hoping one of the warriors saw the hideous man.

There was no one close. No one except the dead Kumeyaay and the bow he dropped when he fell.

She hesitated. A woman must never touch a man's weapons. The taboo had been ingrained in her since she was old enough to understand language.

Twisted Face snarled something at her.

At the sound of his hated voice, her anger became fury. This man *must* die for all the pain he had caused. He must die and she must kill him. She bent for the fallen bow but stopped short of touching it. She could not. The dead warrior would need his bow in order to hunt for food when he reached the spirit world. If she used it . . .

Twisted Face lurched toward her, brandishing a knife.

Dropping the statue, Web grabbed up the warrior's bow and last arrow, but her inexperienced hands were trembling too much for her to position the arrow against the string.

Twisted Face yelled at her and took a wild stab toward her.

The sight of the slashing blade steadied her. She got the arrow nocked, then pulled back on the string.

The string barely moved.

She tried again harder.

This time the sinew moved a finger's length, then popped out of her grasp.

Twisted Face slashed again, eyes wild and unfocused. On his down thrust, the knife caught a railing to Web's left, slicing off a chunk of wood.

Web skittered backward to give herself time and room. Her heel caught and she felt herself falling, yet somehow she managed to catch herself and also hold onto the bow.

Twisted Face laughed, a coarse hacking sound that gave her sudden strength. Setting her feet, she tugged back on the string with all her power. It yielded to her. She took aim and released.

With a dull twang, the arrow stuck in the ground short of Twisted Face. Frantically she scanned the area for another arrow, finally spotting one stuck in a post.

Sputtering at her, Twisted Face stumbled and fell heavily down.

As he attempted to get up, she braced her feet to pull the arrow out of the post. It came out with its head intact.

While she nocked the arrow, the blacksmith growled and launched himself at her from a squat. This time her arrow caught him in the thigh, taking his leg out from under him. He crashed to the ground, bellowing, clutching the pierced thigh.

Web cast around for another arrow.

Nothing.

Suddenly Shadow Dancer was beside her, bow raised, arrow pointed at the blacksmith. She stayed her husband's hand before he could shoot. "Twisted Face is mine to kill. Give me an arrow."

He looked at her askance.

"An arrow, Husband."

He un-nocked the one in his bow and handed it to her. She positioned it, aimed and released.

This third arrow flew straight and true, hitting the blacksmith in the chest, piercing his heart.

His bellowing ceased and he slumped over on his face.

"He is dead," Shadow Dancer said.

"Good."

Web threw down the bow, picked up the statue of the paleskin mother and headed out of the mission gates without a backward look.

For hours, arrows and stones rained over the three waist-high walls that served as the kitchen for the mission. Heart racing from fear, Brother Fuster pressed as close to the adobe bricks of the back wall as possible while he reloaded the soldier's muskets. He had only the vaguest memory of how he and the others had come to be crowded together in this place, fighting for their lives.

The structure had been designed with one side completely open and three low walls with corner posts supporting a thatched roof high enough to allow the cooks to stand upright and the wind to clear away smoke. It was a practical design for a kitchen, but nearly useless for defense.

Two of the four soldiers recently assigned from the presidio to

serve as missions guards had sustained wounds, but they continued to fight despite their injuries.

Besides Fuster and the four soldiers, the kitchen held two boys:
Armando Ortega, son of the Presidio's commander, and Gilberto,
Armando's cousin. The pair had stayed overnight at the mission
rather than risk riding back to the presidio after dark. Both boys
had been excited by the unexpected adventure. Only, now their
lark had turned into a test of survival, thanks to the Indians
whose blood-chilling cries assaulted their ears between volleys
of arrows.

Corporal Rocha, the leader of the mission guard, ripped the
freshly-loaded weapon away from Fuster, trading it for his empty
gun. After so much practice, the Franciscan's hands moved deftly
through the routine of reloading. Everything went as usual until
he tapped powder into the firing chamber.

A hollow sound from the container told him what a glance
confirmed: they were out of powder.

"Corporal!"

Rocha's eyes hardened as Fuster held up the empty vessel.

"No more powder. We're dead." The words came from Armenta,
who had taken two arrows in the arm while working to build a
barricade across the kitchen structure's open side.

"Save your shots, men," Rocha said with resignation. "Don't
use them until the savages try to breach the wall."

Just then, a fresh shower of arrows came over the wall, putting
an end to conversation. One of the arrows struck Armenta in the
lower leg.

The sight jarred Fuster's memory. The mission had a small
supply of powder, apart from the soldiers'. Powder which was
used to celebrate the feast days of certain saints.

Aware that, of the five men, he was the only one available to go
for the spare powder, the Franciscan's heart set up a tattoo of fear.
He could not get his mouth to work in order to tell the corporal what
he had in mind, but, before panic could immobilize him, he vaulted
over the barricade and plunged into the fray.

Fuster scurried for the shadows of the outer adobe wall, expecting
at any moment to feel the sting of an arrow in his flesh.

Reaching the wall, he squinted into the smoke to get his bearings.
Everywhere he looked were native warriors, heads covered with
feathers, faces streaked with paint, hands bristling with weapons.
Incredibly, no one seemed to see him.

He sucked in a ragged breath and scuttled hunched over along
the wall, keeping to the shadows. Around him roiled a confusion

of terrifying smells and sounds that he mentally shoved aside in order to keep going.

The adobe wall surrounding the mission was only partially complete. When he reached the end of it, he had to stop.

Between him and the storeroom that held the powder lay an expanse of open ground.

His knees began to quiver. He knew he could not go on.

Then an arrow whistled past his ear, propelling him forward before he knew he was moving.

The storeroom's door was still closed. He forced it open with his shoulder.

The quiet inside the small space was eerie after the noise of the battle. He glanced around. Nothing seemed out of place.

Father Jayme had tucked the spare powder in a trunk of seasonal vestments. Fuster yanked open the top of the trunk and grabbed the bag. How small and light it felt. "Please, God, let it be enough."

Before he reopened the door, he dragged in another deep breath. Outside he darted glances left and right. Again none of the natives seemed to take notice of him. He bent into a crouch and sprinted across the open ground, clutching the bag to his chest. He had nearly reached the protection of the wall when a stone hurtled out of the night, striking him on the forehead.

For a fraction of an instant, the world tilted, staggering him. He caught himself on the wall. As he stood clutching the rough adobes and waited for the dizziness in his head to clear, four native men ran past, the closest less than an arm's length away from his position. Fuster held himself rigidly still, not daring to breathe until they were gone.

Opposite the kitchen he stopped again. Was he in time? Or had the natives killed all the soldiers and the two boys?

Thoughts of the two youngsters whose lives depended on him prodded him into a run. This time the attackers saw him. Desperate to escape capture, he dodged three warriors and dived headfirst over the barricade, coming down on his shoulder with a loud "oomph."

His sudden return surprised the soldiers. Not so the corporal. Immediately, Rocha ripped the bag out of Fuster's hands and set to reloading the guns.

Suddenly, Fuster felt drained of all energy. With difficulty, he crawled into the corner and closed his eyes against the pain in his wrenched shoulder.

When his heart finally stopped pounding and he could breathe freely again, he reopened his eyes to find that he had Amalia's glove clutched in his hands and that both boys were staring at it.

As casually as he could, he tucked it away as if it were normal for a priest to possess a woman's glove and focused on the corporal who was still busy reloading his men's weapons.

Rocha finished the last musket and smiled grimly. "The savages will drop back at dawn most likely. Let's keep alive till then, men."

Grunting, the soldiers turned back to their defense and Fuster resumed the task of reloading the muskets as they were emptied.

The hours of night stretched without end. The attack continued unabated. Behind the barricade no one spoke. Each man was busy with his own thoughts.

After what seemed like a month-long night, the corporal broke the silence. "Almost dawn." He nodded toward the eastern horizon as he handed Fuster his empty musket.

Rocha turned back to his post and Fuster set about reloading. Only, there was no more powder.

He put the bag down and swallowed against the lump that rose in his throat.

The corporal turned to him and held his hand out for his gun. All Fuster could do was shake his head.

Rocha looked to the sky. "Thy will be done."

Fuster also looked to the sky. "Amen."

IX

RETALIATION

November 6, 1775—August 15, 1776

Chapter 1—November 6, 1775

After taking her revenge on Twisted Face, Web left the mission and headed north for the river gorge where she hid the figure of the paleskin mother and baby in the rocks. Once the Spanish had been driven from the land, her husband and Casts No Shadow would perform rituals to neutralize the figure's power so that it could never again cast its spell over the Kumeyaay people. Her task done, she returned to Nipaguay to wait for the men to come back. She could not sleep. Instead, she prowled the village perimeter, keeping her ears tuned to the sounds issuing from the mission across the river.

At dawn, the noise of the attack escalated sharply. Web scrambled up on the defensive wall for a view of the mission. A thick pall of smoke hung over the scene. The few adobe walls that remained were charred where fire had burned away roofs and timbers. Crowds of warriors still occupied the mission grounds, but their chaotic movements gave her no clue as to the outcome of the attack. "May all the Spanish be gone, and may my men return safely," she prayed in a whisper.

After a time, the sounds from the mission diminished, and Kumeyaay men began to straggle across the river. She climbed off the wall and hurried to the river's edge. She scanned the returning faces, her body tense until she caught sight of Shadow Dancer and his father standing together near the destroyed mission gates, watching the warriors leave the compound. Her heart swelled with pride to see the deference the other warriors paid to her husband. Deference beyond that owed to an 'aww-kuseyaay. Deference of men to a leader they respected.

By now, other women and children had come down to the river. Shooting Star found her mother in the crowd and clutched at her skirts. "I want to see," she demanded.

Web lifted the little girl onto her shoulder.

"Mother, look," Shooting Star cried, pointing a small webbed finger over Web's shoulder. "The soldier place is still there."

Web could see the Spanish flag fluttering in the early morning wind at the mouth of the river valley. A flag that should not have been there if the attack led by Many Rains had succeeded.

Web carefully lowered Shooting Star to the ground and looked toward her husband. Something had gone wrong. Terribly wrong.

"They're gone." Corporal Rocha's voice cracked upon the words.

Brother Fuster put his forehead against the adobe wall of the mission's outside kitchen and closed his eyes, too overwhelmed with emotion to do more than issue a silent prayer of thanks to God for the respite. The natives' pre-dawn charge on their position had forever replaced his nebulous idea of hell with a concrete image of what awaited those who did not admit their sins and seek absolution.

Opening his hand, he stared blearily at the ball of damp lace resting on his palm. He had clutched Amalia's glove like a lifeline during the last wave of the attack. The glove and what it represented had sustained him through the fighting as much as his faith. After enduring a night in hell, he knew he could never give up this last physical link to his lost love.

Corporal Rocha's stifled groan yanked Fuster's thoughts back to his companions. The faint dawn light illuminated the toll the Indians' arrows and rocks had taken among their huddled group. The uniforms of all five soldiers sported rusty blood stains, and purpling bruised areas showed where rocks had struck exposed skin. After the night's noise, Fuster's ears rang with the silence left in the wake of the Indians' withdrawal.

"Can you see what it looks like out there, Padre?" Rocha asked hoarsely.

Fuster mustered the nerve to peek over the wall. What he saw knotted his insides. Debris littered the hard-packed earth of the main mission compound. The structure of wood and tules built to serve as the temporary mission church had been reduced to four charred uprights standing in a smoldering pile of ashes. The same fate had befallen the fourteen wood huts that had housed the community of converted Indians. Only the walls of the few adobe buildings had survived. Roofless, they stood like beheaded sentinels, smudged with black where tongues of fire had licked them.

As he watched, a pair of neophytes emerged from their hiding places to wander dazedly among the ruins.

It took a moment for the realization to sink in that the roof to the padres' quarters was still burning. "Dear God, Brother Jayme." He vaulted over the barricade and took off toward the river, yelling, "Buckets! To the river!"

At the river's edge, he came up short. A body lay face down in a pool of purple-red. Knives and arrows had punctured the pale skin in so many places that no span of flesh remained untouched. A brown robe lay on the wet sand so rent into shreds that it was scarcely recognizable.

But it was the sight of the poor missionary's lacerated hands that ripped a cry from Fuster's soul. He fell to his knees and beseeched the clear morning sky, "Oh, Lord, we commend Brother Jayme's soul into Your loving care. Forgive any sins that marred his life, for he dedicated his days to serving You. In everything, he did what he thought was best."

When his prayer was done, Fuster got wearily back to his feet and directed the converts to help him carry the body back to what was left of the mission. The fire at the padres' quarters had burned away the last of the roof. All that remained of the furnishings was a charred pallet. The neophytes righted it and helped Fuster lay the body out, then they left the missionary alone with his dead companion.

Fuster knelt beside the body, struggling to sort out the welter of confused thoughts that clogged his mind. Lost in the effort, he was only half-aware when one of the soldiers stuck his head into the room to report that Romero, the blacksmith, had been found dead.

While part of him wanted to believe that the Indian attack was in no way related to the blacksmith's maiming of the little native boy, he knew in his deepest heart that the crime had everything to do with what had happened. So many innocent people had been hurt, so much blood had been shed because he had not held his ground in seeing that Romero was punished for his atrocity. His priestly vow of obedience meant nothing compared to the lives that had been lost. All this was his fault. He did not deserve to wear the brown robe of a Franciscan.

Brother Jayme's crucifix hung askew on the blackened wall as if someone had stopped in the act of stealing it. Fuster spoke to it. "Forgive me, Father, for I am weak. I did what I thought was best, but I was wrong. Forgive, too, those who did this to my brother. They too did what they thought was best, and they too were wrong."

He paused and glanced around the little room. "Now the bloodshed must end. And I am the one who must see to ending it."

He held his steepled hands out toward the cross. "Holy Father, please give me the strength to do so in the face of the anger others will feel toward those who took my brother's life." He had to swallow against the lump that had formed in his throat before he could utter "Amen." Then he bowed his head and remained on his knees, rosary in hand, until he felt enough at peace to face the destruction outside.

Corporal Rocha and his four wounded privates had moved out of their stronghold into the open compound. There they sat in a ragged row, while one of the neophyte women tended their wounds. Fuster counted nine wounds in the corporal's body alone, but by some miracle, the two boys had escaped unharmed.

When Rocha attempted to get to his feet, Fuster hustled over to help. "Let me get what you need, corporal."

Anger contorted the normally kind features of Rocha's face. "I need an explanation. From the presidio, Padre. Where, in God's name, have they been all night?"

Fuster had been too preoccupied with the trials at hand to think about the fort.

"I'll have someone's head for this," Rocha growled.

He had moved only two steps when his knees buckled. Fuster succeeded in grabbing the man's arm and breaking his fall. Lowering the corporal to the ground, he said, "You stay here. I'll go to the presidio."

Grimacing in pain, Rocha nodded. "All right, but take my rifle."

"No, corporal. No guns."

"But the savages . . ."

"No guns. No more bloodshed."

"Have it your way then, Padre."

"I mean to."

By Sun Above the warriors from other villages had departed for their homes, taking their dead with them so the proper ceremonies could be performed by their families. Then it was time for the people of Nipaguay to care for their own dead.

While the men dug four cremation pits, one for each fallen warrior, women washed the bodies and laid them out. The personal possessions of each man went into the pit next to his corpse. One of the dead was Jackrabbit, one of Shadow Dancer's boyhood friends. From the time he could walk, Jackrabbit had never walked when he could run, never sat still when he could move, never frowned when he could smile, never let the other boys rest when he could play a prank on them. He had grown into a fine man with wisdom beyond his years. The kind of man destined to be chief one day.

Only, he would never be chief now.

Jackrabbit's family asked Casts No Shadow to preside over his burning. The wekuseyaay took his place beside the young man's pyre. Wailing and weeping their grief, the dead man's immediate family filled in around the pit where they sat down, facing away from the body, to sing their grief to the sky.

The same scene was repeated at the other three graves, and, as the tumult of mourning reached its pitch, the wekuseyaay touched a burning brand to the brush piled beneath Jackrabbit's corpse. The dry boughs caught with a force that caused the wekuseyaay to back away.

The other funeral leaders followed suit.

In only a moment, fire completely engulfed the four heaps of brush and the four bodies. In the heat, the dead men's muscles contracted, causing their arms and legs to jerk and writhe as if the warriors desperately sought to cling to the life they loved. Casts No Shadow and the other three attendants poked and prodded the corpses with long poles of green wood in order to keep the bodies in the hottest part of the flames. The smell of roasting flesh filled the air over Nipaguay. The wailing of the mourners rose ever higher.

In the heat and smoke and cacophony, Casts No Shadow's thoughts drifted back to last night's attack and elation replaced his sorrow over the loss of four young men. The Brown Robes' evil spell had been broken. Red Smoke had been wrong. The warriors of the Kumeyaay people had defeated the Spanish and driven away their deadly thunder sticks. Now the people would live on forever, free of the scourge of cruel, evil strangers.

He thought of that as the afternoon wore on, and the four bodies disintegrated into ashes under the flames' onslaught. Sun was about to enter Ocean for a night of rest when the fire had consumed Jackrabbit's corpse except for his heart. Using the sharpened point of his poking stick, Casts No Shadow punched holes in that mass of flesh causing the heart to sizzle and shrivel and finally vanish into the flames.

"The spirit of our brother is now free," he proclaimed. "Sing to the stars, my people. Sing our brother to the Land of the Ancestors. Sing loud so all the spirits will know of his coming."

The mourners around the pit broke off their wailing to join voices in the death song. The wekuseyaay remained at the pit to listen for a time, then walked away to cleanse himself of the taint of death in sage smoke fire from the sacred cremation lodge. The confidence of a victory won and deserved gave spring to his steps.

A figure darted out of the night shadows, startling him until he recognized Many Rains. "Ah, you have come just in time. My son will be here any moment. You can tell us of your victory as we purify ourselves."

Many Rains laughed, a short, angry sound. "What victory? We did not attack the fort."

Casts No Shadow started to protest but the younger man cut him off. "Your son owes me an explanation. Why did he attack first? That wasn't our plan," Many Rains said angrily.

The flap over the door to the cremation lodge moved aside and heads poked out to investigate the commotion.

Many Rains looked toward them and raised his voice as if seeking their support. "By the time we got into position, we could see the fires from the mission. If we could see them from where we were, certainly the soldiers in the fort could see them. I could not order a charge. Not knowing that all those thunder sticks would be aimed at us. I could not—I *would* not send dozens of men to certain death. By the soul of One Above, why did you not follow our plan?"

Big Nose ducked out of the purification lodge. He pointed to Casts No Shadow. "The wekuseyaay told us to attack."

Many Rains looked at Casts No Shadow. "Is that true?"

All eyes turned to the shaman. His mind reeled under the impact of Many Rains' revelation. The bearded ones had not been defeated. They—their sorcery and their thunder sticks— remained. Suddenly Red Smoke's dying warning took on an awful finality. Casts No Shadow answered with more confidence than he felt. "The gods gave the sign."

"The gods," snorted one of the men inside the sweat lodge.

"Yes, the gods!" Casts No Shadow thundered.

Many Rains glared at the shaman through narrowed eyes. "We had a plan, Wekuseyaay. A good plan."

"The gods had a different plan," Casts No Shadow said.

"Then the gods have forsaken us. Our cause is lost," Many Rains said, turning on his heel and disappearing into the darkness.

Casts No Shadow watched the young man stalk away. He felt the eyes of all the occupants of the sweat lodge on him. Without a word, he brushed past Big Nose and ducked into the lodge.

Then the gods have forsaken us. Many Rains' words rang in his mind.

Upon his entrance, two of the men rose to leave although they had not sweat long enough for their bodies and spirits to be clean of the contamination of battle. He leveled his sternest look at them.

Still, they left without offering an excuse. The other two men in the lodge would not meet his gaze. He tied down the flap and settled in, closing his eyes, retreating into silence.

The cremation fires had not yet died when Web stole away. At her 'ewaa, she checked on her sleeping children, then took a blanket off her pallet and went back out into the night air. With the dead and wounded from the attack to attend to, there had been no opportunity to ask Shadow Dancer about the presidio. Had there been a last minute change of plan? Had someone missed a signal, or had Many Rains' group failed to subdue the Spanish soldiers?

She had so many questions that would remain unanswered until Shadow Dancer returned from the sweat lodge. She wrapped the blanket around her and sat down beside the banked fire to wait.

Not long, after she heard a pair of angry voices approaching. She recognized them as her husband's and Many Rains' and scrambled to her feet to greet them. They walked past her, however, without acknowledgment.

"My father gave the order," Shadow Dancer said. "How could I refuse a message he brought from the spirits?"

Many Rains threw up his hands in disgust. "And I could not order my brothers to commit suicide."

So that was her answer: Many Rains had never attacked the fort. Web shivered and drew the blanket closer.

Abruptly Many Rains' tone turned fearful. "The Spanish are bound to come looking for us, my brother. We have to run away."

Shadow Dancer waved him off. Many Rains persisted. "You know how the Spanish work. They will find out who led the attack by beating the information out of the poor fool Kumeyaays who stayed at the mission. We were only runaways before and they came after us. Imagine what they will do now."

"I cannot go without my father," Shadow Dancer said.

"They don't know him. Leave him here," Many Rains said.

Web had to speak up though each word hurt. "Yes, you must go, Husband. Hide yourself until it is safe to return."

"Listen to her, Brother," Many Rains said.

"For the sake of our children, you must leave here," she pleaded. "Go now. Before the Spanish come."

Shadow Dancer looked from Many Rains to Web to the 'ewaa, then to the night sky. Web clung to the edges of the blanket as if it could keep her from drowning in the heartache filling the cavity of her chest. When he did not speak, she whispered. "Go. Please, my husband."

At last, he spoke. "Yes, you are right. Both of you."

Only then would she allow herself to touch him. He reciprocated, gathering her into his arms for a quick, fierce hug. "I will return soon," he murmured. Then he and Many Rains vanished into the night, leaving her with empty arms and a heart full of grief.

Chapter 2

Three days after the attack, soldiers from the presidio came to the ruined mission with orders from Lieutenant Ortega to evacuate all the survivors to the fort.

There had been no sign of more trouble from the Indians. Brother Fuster wanted to rebuild the mission, not abandon it, but with Brother Jayme dead and all the mission guards recovering from wounds, he had no choice. Leading a donkey burdened with the dead missionary's body, he walked the two leagues to the fort at the head of the column of dejected survivors.

Lieutenant Ortega and Brother Lasuen were in the front ranks of their welcoming party at the presidio. Lasuen was one of the missionaries assigned to found a new mission, San Juan Capistrano, twenty leagues north of San Diego. Ortega and Lasuen had both been at that location when the attack on Mission San Diego occurred, so the lieutenant had not witnessed the presidio soldiers close ranks when Fuster had arrived bearing the first news of the attack. Ortega had not heard the watchman claim that he had been awake all night. He had not seen the man's face when he lied about low clouds obscuring the view up the valley to the mission. He had not witnessed two other soldiers back up their lying friend. At the time Fuster had to swallow his anger and return to the mission, but now he intended to force out the truth.

He followed Ortega and Lasuen into the lieutenant's office. Taking a chair, he recounted the facts of the attack, keeping his voice as neutral as he could, emphasizing that the night had been clear and cloudless.

When he finished, he waited for the lieutenant to ask the obvious question. Instead, Ortega slammed his fist on the table and yelled for his corporals before saying, "You'll need to go along, Padre."

"Go? Go where?" asked Fuster.

"You'll need to go along with my men to identify the savages who took part in the attack."

"No, Lieutenant."

"What do you mean, no? They killed Brother Jayme. They must be punished."

Fuster came to his feet. "No, Lieutenant. No punishment. No retribution. They had their reasons for what they did. But the dead are dead, and we have the future to consider. Punishment will only create more problems."

Again Ortega's fist slammed onto the tabletop. "Nonsense, Padre. If we don't punish them, they'll attack this fort next, and that is something I mean to stop."

Fuster squared his shoulders. "You haven't asked about your guards, Lieutenant Ortega."

The change in direction of the conversation confused the man. "Guards?"

"The ones on duty during the attack. There is no way your men could have missed seeing the fires. That is, *if* they were awake," Fuster said.

Ortega sat back and looked at the missionary, then sent the guard at the door scurrying away for the private who had been on watch that night. The private arrived out of breath, his uniform disheveled. When he spotted Fuster, his expression hardened.

"You were on duty the night of the attack, Private?" Ortega asked.

"Yes, sir."

"What did you see?"

"Sir?"

The lieutenant's voice rose a notch. "Tell me what you saw, Private."

"N–nothing, sir. The fog was in, blocked my view."

At the lie, Fuster spoke more quickly than he intended. "As I have said, Lieutenant, the night was completely clear. No clouds anywhere."

"Out at the mission, perhaps," the private said. "But not here. If you don't believe me, sir, ask the others. They'll back me up."

The petulance in the man's tone bespoke his desperation. Instead of pressing, Ortega said, "Very well. Dismissed."

Fuster started to protest, but Lasuen's hand restrained him. "You want no retribution, remember?" Lasuen reminded him quietly. "What's done is done."

Fuster sank back to his seat, reining in his anger with great effort, hoping his restraint would change Ortega's mind.

It didn't. "If you won't go with me, Padre, I'll take as many of the mission guards as can ride," Ortega said. "Armenta, he has a good memory for faces. He'll be able to pick out the ones responsible."

Pressure from his fellow missionary's hand kept Fuster silent, though he had to bite his lips to do so. "May we excuse ourselves then, Lieutenant?" Lasuen asked. "We have funerals to prepare."

Ortega nodded, and the Franciscans left. When they were outside and alone, Lasuen said, "There's a rumor you ought to know about, Brother. Do you have a convert named Carlos?"

"He's one of our first. Our primary translator."

"According to the soldiers, Carlos led the attack."

Fuster started to refute the rumor, then stopped. Carlos had worked with Romero every day. Who better to avenge the blacksmith's attack on that little boy? A chill washed over him. He had never come up with a satisfactory explanation for why the little boy had been at the forge that day or why Carlos had vanished the day after. His mind had never put the two events together. Until now.

He looked the other missionary in the eye. "I was there, Brother. I saw a lot of Indians. Carlos was not one of them."

The rest of his words he kept to himself: *And I hope he's far away and stays there long enough for this trouble to die away.*

After Shadow Dancer disappeared into the night to hide from the Spanish soldiers, a deep sadness settled over Web. The attack on the mission had forced away the husband she had waited so long to reclaim. The future stretched ahead like a breadth of open ocean: terrifying, foreign, devoid of life as she knew it. Even sleep offered no respite from the weight that burdened her heart. Instead of forgetfulness, sleep brought dreams of her husband,

Cricket, and Hummingbird. Images too real to be fantasy and too painful to possess.

Two days after the attack, she sat under the *wisal*, legs stretched out in front of her, hands lying uselessly in her lap, eyes focused on but not seeing the willows along the river. Her mind seemed able to grasp only one fact: that Shadow Dancer would be gone for a long, long time. Every repetition of that thought sapped a bit more of her will to continue the unceasing struggle of daily living. She had not felt so alone since the day she left Hawi.

She was preoccupied with her troubles when a piercing whistle cut the air. Her leaden limbs moved awkwardly. In the time it took her to stand, people had emptied the lodges around hers, men heading for the defensive wall, women and children scattering into the safety of the overgrown river bottom.

Boom! Boom! Two explosions from Spanish thunder sticks stopped Web before she could make an escape.

Turning, she saw the village men, backing away from the picket wall, and a group of Spanish soldiers, mounted on their riding beasts, entering the breach. At the forefront of that group, just behind the leader, was the soldier who had violated her.

Seeing him overcame her lassitude. She sprinted for the river only to find her route blocked by one of the mounted Spanish. Using his riding beast to control her moves, he herded her back to his companions.

The soldiers' leader dismounted and began to speak. A Kumeyaay man dressed in the baggy clothing of a mission convert slid down from behind another soldier and translated the words. "This one is called Ortega. He is the war chief of the Spanish. He orders anyone who participated in the attack on the mission to step forward."

When none of the village men moved, the face of the Spaniard named Ortega darkened.

"He says to come forward or he will arrest you all," the interpreter said.

"What means this thing 'arrest'?" Casts No Shadow asked.

The convert's eyes darted nervously to Ortega. "They will lock you away in a dark room and they will beat you."

Web blanched. She had witnessed the bearded ones' beatings, but nothing filled her with more dread than the prospect of being locked away, unable to feel the breeze against her skin or see the sky or hear her children's laughter.

Casts No Shadow stepped forward. "We will never tell him what he wants." He waved his hand imperiously. "Tell these men to be gone from here. They are not welcome in our village."

Before the convert could start translating the wekuseyaay's words, a soldier with a wrapping of tan cloth covering wounds on his head began to speak excitedly to Ortega, pointing at both Big Nose and Casts No Shadow.

The Spanish war chief nodded and, within the space of a blink, soldiers grabbed both men.

Web had endured the deaths of Hummingbird and Cricket and the absence of her husband, but she could not bear standing by while the bearded ones took the grandfather of her children away. She leaped on the back of one of the captors, raking the man's face with her fingernails and screaming, "Let him go!"

The soldier uttered a surprised cry and tore her hands away from his face, wrenching her elbow in the process. Then he peeled her off his back and flung her aside as if she were no more trouble than an empty winnowing basket.

She landed on her back with a force that knocked the air from both lungs.

"Daughter!" Casts No Shadow cried, lunging to help her.

"No!" Her scream came too late.

The butt of a Spanish musket connected with the side of the wekuseyaay's skull, crumpling Casts No Shadow to the ground unconscious. The soldiers trussed the shaman's hands behind his back and heaved him face-down across the rump of one of the riding beasts.

Big Nose gave his captors no resistance, but they tied his hands anyway, attaching a rope to his wrists and leading him away like one of their pack animals.

Still struggling for breath, Web shrieked at the Nipaguay warriors, "Stop them! Do something!"

"There is nothing to do," one said. "Not now."

The others murmured agreement.

She stared up at the men in disbelief. "Those men are our leaders. You cannot let the Spanish take them."

The Kumeyaay men began to shuffle away dispiritedly. Web watched them helplessly until tears turned the figures into blurs. Then she put her head on her arm and wept.

Chapter 3

S ix nights later Web's own moaning woke her. Her heart was beating a furious tattoo against her ribs that placing a hand to her clammy chest would not calm.

The dream was the same one that had haunted her sleep every night since the Spanish took Casts No Shadow away: the wekuseyaay, his limbs thin and wasted as sticks, eyes glittering out of a cadaverous face like twin pools of black water, reached out for her with talon-like fingers and begged her for food. Food she could never seem to find.

Once awake, she dared not return to sleep for fear of the dream returning. She crawled out of the lodge and picked her way to the river in the pitch blackness of predawn. At the river's edge, she sank onto a shelf of rock and stared at the inky water.

The winter rains had not yet begun. West of the village, the riverbed was dry, but in this one place a few pools of water remained. For more summers than anyone could remember, the people of Nipaguay had depended on these same pools to sustain them during the dry times. And they had not failed to do so because every year around this time, Casts No Shadow led the village in a rite of thanks to the spirits of the river.

Yet, the Spanish had taken the wekuseyaay away. Now there was no one to lead the people in placating the gods. No one to teach the children about the spirits or tell them the stories of the Kumeyaay people. No one to journey into the spirit world and to bring back to the people the wisdom of the gods. No one for her to turn to in her grief over losing the two men she and her children depended on.

She did not need a dream to know the wekuseyaay was starving. He would starve rather than accept any food from the Spanish. But he must not starve. She needed him. Her children needed him. The village needed him. He was their link to the forces that shaped and controlled all their lives. He was their memory, their center, their essence. He must not die. He must not, but saving him required from her more bravery than she possessed. She hugged her knees to her chest and hid her face in them. Someone had to take food to him.

"I can't," she whispered. "Not to the fort. No."

Just above the eastern horizon, Morning Star twinkled as if to say, "You must. He needs you."

"No," Web sobbed, struggling to her feet and stumbling away from the river.

It was too dark to see the ground. Her foot caught and she went sprawling. Her cry of surprise touched off a chorus of barking among the village dogs.

She lay where she had fallen, hoping that no one would come

to investigate. She did not want to explain what caused her fall or her outcry.

Eventually the barking subsided, and she picked herself up. In the east, the offending star shown brighter against the light gray of Sun Awaking. "Go to him," the star seemed to say.

"I can't. I can't," she said, bowing her head and plodding back to her lodge in the ravine.

She watched Sun's rise from her *wisal*. The people of Nipaguay were still in their relocated village. They could not move back to the old site until a shaman purified it of the blood that had been spilled during the attack. Such a purification would have to wait for her husband or Casts No Shadow to return.

Watching the village come to life, she suddenly remembered that Casts No Shadow did not have his shaman's pouch. The soldiers had dragged him away before he could retrieve it. Immediately she understood the meaning of the dream. The dream image was not begging for food, but for the pouch containing the sacred objects that fed the wekuseyaay's spirit.

Web shivered at a sudden chill. Now it was doubly important for her to go to the fort, to find a way to see Casts No Shadow.

Shooting Star toddled out of the lodge, yawning and rubbing the sleep out of her eyes. She came to her mother and allowed herself to be hugged and kissed. "When is Grandfather coming back, mother? I miss him."

At that moment Sand Flea stepped into the morning light. "I had a dream last night, Mother."

Web glanced at her son, concerned that his nightmares of Twisted Face had returned. Instead of fear, his eyes showed worry. "It was about Grandfather. He needs his pouch, Mother. I must take it to him."

"No!" she shouted, then immediately felt remorse at the look on her son's face. The one time she had sent her sons into the Spanish lair on an errand she had been too afraid to do herself, that decision had cost her the life of one son and the mutilation of the other. She would breathe her last before her children got close to the Spanish again.

"But, in my dream, Grandfather was crying," Sand Flea insisted.

The troubled look on the boy's face broke through Web's own fear. "Then I will take it to him."

"But you can't touch it," her son said. "You are a woman."

"And I will not, if you will help me. Go to Grandfather's lodge and gather all the things you know he needs. Wrap them together in his blankets and make sure you tie the bundle tight so it will not come apart."

The boy nodded gravely and ran off to see to his task.

Shooting Star crawled off her mother's lap and trundled away in search of playmates. Left alone, Web's new-found courage wavered. How would she ever find the strength to step through the gates of the bearded ones' fort? How could she possibly put herself in a position that might lead to another rape? She looked toward the Spanish fort. "Father, I cannot do this."

Casts No Shadow's image appeared in her mind's eye. "You can, Daughter. You must. For the children."

She knew that she needed something more than entreaties to convince the suspicious Spanish to let her see Casts No Shadow. But what?

Brother Fuster was in the middle of his catechism lesson when a woman's scream pierced the mid-morning stillness of the presidio. Motioning the neophytes to stay where they were, he put down the missal and hurried out of the temporary church to see what had happened.

A group of soldiers milled about the gates, blocking the missionary's view. Then one of the men feinted sideways as if to escape a blow, and, in the opening, Fuster saw a small Indian woman struggling to throw off the grips of a pair of soldiers. The salacious tone of the men's laughter told him all he needed to know about their intentions toward the woman.

He strode into their midst bellowing "Unhand her!"

Their laughter died and the lust faded from their faces, replaced not by contrition but rather bitterness that their sport had been curtailed.

"Release her this instant!" he commanded.

The pair holding her exchanged a truculent glance. For a moment, the missionary feared he would be reduced to grappling for her release.

Instead they let her go. She sank to the ground. Fuster glared at the men until they dispersed, then bent to help her up. She grabbed his hands and pulled him down to her level. Once he was kneeling before her, she crossed herself and pointed to her burden net.

"I–I don't understand," he stammered.

Again she made the sign of the cross and pointed at the net, all the time pleading with fear-widened eyes for his understanding.

He made a wild guess at her meaning and mimed actions to go with his words. "You–have brought something–for the church?"

She uttered a small cry of success, popped to her feet and led him by the arm to a private corner where she took out one of the two bundles in her net and proceeded to unwrap it.

At the first glimpse of the figure of the Holy Virgin and Infant that had disappeared in the looting of the mission, Fuster uttered a cry of his own and clasped his hands in a prayer of thanks for its return.

The woman clutched the statue to her chest and unleashed a gush of native words.

"I don't speak your tongue," he stammered.

She switched to signs, taking a beautifully-made basket out of her net and pretending to eat from it.

"Food. Eat. What?"

More words, all incomprehensible.

"Use signs," he countered.

She pointed to the basket, then jabbed at the air. Fuster was completely stumped. Then she spoke, one word only. "Father."

Suddenly Fuster understood. The woman's father was among Lieutenant Ortega's prisoners. She had brought him some food.

For the last six days he had been praying for God to give him a way to help those imprisoned Indians. Now God had sent that answer in the form of this woman no taller than a ten-year-old boy.

At once he was up and pulling her along with him. The Indians had been thrown into an abandoned storeroom, and Lieutenant Ortega had ordered two guards to be posted on the cell at all times. At Fuster's approach, the sentries moved to block access to the door.

"Step aside, my sons," the missionary said calmly.

"You're not allowed, Padre. Lieutenant's orders," the taller of the guards said.

"This woman has come to visit her father. I don't recall any orders against that. Do you?"

This confused the taller man. The other soldier answered. "Padre's right, Ramón. We better let her in."

While the taller guard handed his musket to his partner and fumbled at the lock, Fuster gave the woman's hand a grateful squeeze.

She tried to smile, but the tense muscles in her face turned it into a grimace.

At the sound of voices outside, the six Kumeyaay men who had been crammed into the dark stinking room for almost a week came alert. Squeezed into the corner next to Big Nose, Casts No Shadow shifted position to ease the cramping in his legs. A crack at the top of the heavy door provided the room's only light. In the gloom he felt as much as saw the kwaipai's irritation at being jostled.

After much rattling and clanking, the door swung back, flooding the room with the light of the westering sun. The wekuseyaay shielded his eyes against the unaccustomed glare. Between his fingers, he saw two shapes backlit by the sun. The taller shape had to stoop to enter the low room. Casts No Shadow recognized him as the second Brown Robe from the mission, still very much alive. Because the ceiling was too low even for any of the shorter Kumeyaays to stand straight, once inside, the Brown Robe had to keep his head and upper body bent.

The second shape moved past the Brown Robe. Web! The sight of her infused the wekuseyaay with the energy to stand for the first time in days. His stiff legs prickled with the effort of supporting his weight.

She held out a basket to him. "I knew you would not eat what the bearded ones offered so I brought you this."

Casts No Shadow took it from her with a brief nod, too overcome by hunger and emotion to speak.

Shyly she held out another bundle. From the symbols painted on the leather, he recognized his sacred pouch. "I–I should not have touched it," she said. "But you need it and . . ."

Casts No Shadow darted a glance at the Brown Robe, fearing that, if he reached for the bundle, this paleskin witch would seize it. If that happened, the witch's touch would forever destroy the bundle's power, would destroy him.

"Don't be afraid, Father," Web said, recovering her voice. "The Brown Robe does not know what it is. Pretend it is more food."

Casts No Shadow took the pouch as nonchalantly as his anxiety would allow. Web covered the awkward silence by talking. "I would have come sooner but I–the woman's lodge."

Fingering the familiar leather of his sacred pouch, the wekuseyaay let the stammered falsehood pass without mention. He knew that his voice would break if he tried to tell her how much he respected the courage it took for her to come into the

Spanish stronghold after all she had endured at their hands. He
cleared his throat and said, "You did right to wait, my daughter."

A soldier's gruff voice sounded outside. Turning, the Brown
Robe replied in the sing-song paleskin tongue.

Casts No Shadow used the interruption to ask, "Why is he here
with you, Daughter?"

"The Spanish war chief allows none of our people inside the
fort. This Brown Robe convinced him to let me bring these
things to you."

Casts No Shadow searched the face of the Brown Robe,
searching for a clue as to why the man would help, rather than
hate, two of the people responsible for destroying the mission
and killing the other Brown Robe witch.

Big Nose interrupted. "My wife, when is she coming to see
me?"

Web hesitated as if weighing her answer. "She–she would not
come today. I–I don't know when she will come."

Big Nose's face darkened. "Tell her . . ."

The soldier outside barked a demand. The Brown Robe touched
Web's shoulder and motioned that they had to leave. She grasped
Casts No Shadow's wrist tightly, then released it quickly and
followed the white witch outside.

The guards slammed the door and relocked it. Casts No Shadow
stood holding the two precious bundles Web had brought to him,
waiting for his eyes to readjust to the darkness.

He groped back to his place on the floor and looked around at
the five men seated along the walls. None of them looked back at
him. Like Big Nose, they were all kwaipais from the villages
closest to the bearded ones' fort. All of them had been captured
by the Spanish on the same day and thrown together in this dark,
stinking room.

Thanks to Big Nose, they believed that the failure of the attack
and their subsequent imprisonment were both his fault. In the
beginning, Casts No Shadow had defended himself against their
accusations, citing the clear message he had received from the
spirits that night, but, after a time, he saw they did not believe him
and he stopped responding.

In the stench and darkness of the crowded cell, his soul festered
with doubt. Doubt about his powers. Doubt about his wisdom.
Doubt about his relationship with the gods. Three times since the
Spanish seized him, he had attempted to travel into the spirit
world. All three times he had failed.

He kneaded the leather of his medicine pouch. Of course the

gods had refused to talk with him. He had tried to come to them without the proper preparation. Thanks to Web, he could now remedy that situation. And, as soon as he ate, he would attempt another journey.

He removed the layer of dried grass from the top of the basket. The heady fragrance of Web's acorn cakes drifted into the room, warring with the stench from the slop bucket that stood in the corner. Five sets of eyes turned toward him.

He took out two small cakes and handed the basket to Big Nose. "Share these, my brothers."

Big Nose took the basket with a muttered thanks, the first kind words he had spoken to him since their capture. Casts No Shadow acknowledged the thanks with a nod. Inwardly he smiled. Someday the kwaipai would apologize for his lack of respect, but, for now, this was enough.

Chapter 4

Web carefully positioned her basket before raising the gate covering the feeder hole in the bottom of the communal acorn granary. As acorns dropped into her container, her thoughts turned again to Casts No Shadow.

Going to the fort to see him yesterday had taken all the fortitude she could muster. She had been so focused on her own problems that she had not been prepared for what she found. The reek of that awful cell and the woeful condition of those six proud men had nearly caused her to lose control of her stomach, but it was the doubt in the wekuseyaay's eyes that she could not erase from her mind.

Now that she had seen him, she could not let him languish. She had to return. That meant more trips to the fort and further dependence on the Brown Robe to help her. Suddenly her burden of responsibility seemed far too heavy for one person to bear.

Wearily, she shut the granary chute, hefted the basket and started toward the village mortars to grind the nuts. Sand Flea's hail stopped her.

The boy and his best friend trotted into the village from the east. Two plump rabbits dangled from both boy's right hands; in their left, *hempuus* throwing sticks.

Despite her fatigue, she smiled. Her son's increasing skill with the *hempuu* kept them in fresh meat. Even more important, his success as a hunter had allayed his nightmares about Twisted

Face.

He exchanged rabbits with his friend, then ran to Web, smiling proudly. "I will skin them and put them on to cook."

She aped shock. "But that is woman's work."

His small chest puffed out and he raised his chin in a show of pride that allowed her full view of his scars. "Today it is my work."

He walked off toward their 'ewaa, leaving her filled with equal parts of admiration for his courage and frustration that he would always wear Twisted Face's scars.

Although the people of Nipaguay could not yet move back to the original site of the village, the women had begun to use the old bedrock mortars again. A group of five were already there, each seated at a favorite grinding hole. The sound of crunching nutmeats underscored their chattering and laughter.

At Web's approach, they fell silent. Crooked Basket stared up at her. "You are not welcome here. Find another rock."

Thinking this was a joke, Web mustered a tight smile. "Where should I look for one, Sister?"

The lines of Crooked Basket's face hardened. "Why not ask your husband?"

With great effort, Web kept her facial expression friendly. "How can I? I do not know where he is."

Crooked Basket's eyes narrowed. "Well, I know where my husband is. Locked in a room at the paleskin's fort because of *you*. Your husband is a coward. You made him that way. You and your backward ways. You and your frog hands."

Anger rising, Web dropped all pretense of friendliness. She returned the woman's glare and deliberately displayed her hands. "I descend from Frog, Sister. That is something I am proud of. You can call me what you will, but you have no right to accuse anyone of cowardice. You who will not go to her husband. Do I need to remind you again that he asked for you yesterday?"

The stares of the other women shifted from Web to Crooked Basket.

"I told him that I did not know when you would come," Web said. "Now I see that I should have said 'if,' not 'when.'"

In the face of the truth, Crooked Basket broke off her glaring and began to gather her things.

Web took advantage of the opening. "My ways might be backward, but I care for those I love even if I must face fear to do so. Who, then, my sister, is the real coward: you or me?"

Crooked Basket vaulted to her feet and hurried away without

replying. While Web watched her go, two other women who had never been particular friends of the kwaipai's wife but who sided with her now also left, neither one meeting Web's gaze.

One of the remaining women glanced up at Web, a neutral look neither hostile nor friendly.

Web sat down at the deepest hole, her favorite. Instead of feeling good about besting Crooked Basket in a public argument, she felt drained. The chief's wife was gaining allies, turning others against her.

Since the day she arrived in Nipaguay, all she had ever wanted was to belong. For eight summers she thought she had succeeded. She had supported the attack on the mission in the belief that its success would avenge her son's death, drive out the Spanish and return life–hers and Shadow Dancer's–to normal. Instead, the attack had failed. Her husband had run off to avoid capture. And Casts No Shadow had ended up locked in a room unfit for garbage.

Every day that passed pulled her dream that much further out of reach. Where would it all end?

Chapter 5

A bone-chilling winter fog hung thick over the presidio. The sun had not shown for three weeks, since Christmas Day. Its absence weighed on everyone, banishing smiles and civility. With tempers shorter than ever, violence lay just beneath the surface of every exchange.

Inside the storeroom that had served as a church since the mission's destruction, Brother Fuster prepared for his first audience with Captain Rivera. Two of the six Indian prisoners had died of a mysterious fast-moving ailment that bloated their bodies and appeared to cause them to strangle on their own fluids. Fuster could do nothing to arrest the illness, and he feared that more of the Kumeyaays would die if he could not find some way to improve the conditions of their imprisonment.

Captain Rivera had led the first land expedition to San Diego in 1769. That service had earned him, in 1773, promotion to military commander of Upper California, replacing Don Pedro Fages, a change prompted by Father Serra who had traveled all the way to Mexico City to present to the Viceroy a list of complaints about Fages and the condition of the new missions in Upper California.

Although Fuster had questioned the few men who knew Rivera, he still had no clear picture of the man and no idea how best to approach him with the list of requests he had drawn up. Uncertainty added to the lethargy that weighted his limbs.

He knelt ponderously before the makeshift altar and bowed his head. "Please open the captain's eyes to the truth, and his ears and heart to mercy for those native peoples imprisoned here. May he grant Your servant a way to help those who have survived, and may he grant pardon to all the Indians who participated in the attack."

On this last, the image of Brother Jayme's broken body flashed through Fuster's mind. He waited for the image to clear before he rose and went to see the captain.

Lieutenant Ortega had temporarily vacated his office to Captain Rivera's use. The room seemed bigger without its normal cozy clutter. Bigger and colder.

Rivera sat behind a table, his back ramrod straight, scratching a quill pen across a piece of parchment. Even viewed upside down, his handwriting had authority. "Sit, Padre," he commanded, without missing a stroke or looking up from his work.

When he was done, he jabbed the quill into the bottle of ink and shoved the parchment toward Fuster. "Orders in writing leave nothing to chance. Go on, read it. It's for your benefit."

As Fuster scanned the page, his heart sank. The paper ordered more and harsher reprisals against the Indians.

"We need to teach them a lesson they will never forget," Rivera said.

Fuster looked straight into the man's hard eyes. "No, Captain."

The line of Rivera's mouth drew taut. "What do you mean, no?"

"More punishment will only create more hostility. The Lord commanded us to forgive our enemies."

The captain's mouth crooked into a condescending smile. "Fine words spoken by a man true to his faith. Only, the world doesn't work that way."

The missionary could not keep his voice from rising. "That is exactly the way the world works. If we let it. Stop the reprisals, Captain. Release those poor souls that Lieutenant Ortega has had locked in that storeroom the last two months. And let us put our energy into rebuilding the mission."

"No, no and no. This is a military matter, Father. The military will handle it. You tend to your affairs and we will restore order."

Fuster swallowed his frustration and tried another tack. "What about the sentries, Captain?"

"What sentries?"

"The ones who were on duty the night of the attack. We received no help from the presidio. None. Not until the next day–and only then because I walked all the way here to tell them what happened."

Rivera shot to his feet, yelling for Ortega. In short order, the men who had been at the presidio that night were standing at attention in front of the captain. Fuster stared at the wall while he endured all the lies he had heard before. Surely, the captain would see through these men and the stories they had concocted to save themselves from the punishment they deserved.

"Dismissed," Rivera ordered.

This time it was Fuster who shot off his seat. "But they're lying, Captain. All of them."

The door slammed behind the last soldier. "Those men might be a lot of things, Padre, but none of them would dare lie to me." The captain rolled up the parchment and thrust it at Ortega. "Lieutenant, here are your orders. You are to take your best men and make the rounds of all the Indian villages for ten leagues. Demand that the heathens hand over anyone who participated in the attack. If they do not cooperate, do anything necessary to get at the truth."

Lieutenant Ortega's eyes twinkled vindictively at the missionary as he strode outside.

"Is there anything else, Father?" Rivera asked, resuming his seat.

Fuster looked down at the hands lying in his lap. The useless hands of a useless man. He had accomplished nothing. If anything, he had made matters worse. The mission would continue to lie in ruins. The Indian prisoners would continue to sicken and die in their hellish cell. And now more natives would suffer at the hands of the military. "Dear God, help me," he murmured.

"What was that?" Rivera asked.

"A prayer–for guidance." Fuster came slowly to his feet and trudged to the door, his body and mind leaden with failure.

"Once we've established some order here, Padre, we can discuss the mission."

Fuster did not bother to acknowledge. He opened the door and stepped out into the fog.

Chapter 6

The gaze of the soldier at the gate moved slowly down Web's entire body. She stood stock still, enduring the leer, barely breathing, her eyes focused on a knot in a plank of wood.

At last, the man stepped aside just enough so that she could pass through the gates only if she brushed against him. She chose to stand her ground until he tired of the game. These Spanish were so predictable. In all the time she had been bringing food to Casts No Shadow, it was always the same: the wait, the leer, the same attempt to intimidate her.

How she despised these pale men! Everything about them was contemptible: the stench of their filthy bodies, the dirty hair bushing from their faces, the unhealthy color of their skin, their impatience, and their brutality toward all living creatures, especially each other.

The soldier finally moved back. She hurried through the gates, straight to the small building that was Casts No Shadow's prison. By now the guards were used to her visits. They lounged in the shade of another building and did not bother to acknowledge her passage.

Her heart skipped to see the door of the cell open. Immediately she feared the worst: that Casts No Shadow and Big Nose had survived the frightening sickness that had killed the other four prisoners only to face execution by the paleskin war chief.

She moved closer. Her heart skipped again, this time in relief at the sight of two pairs of brown legs stretched across the bare dirt floor of the interior.

She took three deep breaths to calm her hammering heart before stepping to the door. Two pairs of eyes turned her way and she saw why the door was open. Chains bound the men to the walls and to each other.

Against the heavy bonds, the wekuseyaay seemed more wasted than ever. His very bones seemed to have shrunk. The skin of his arms and legs sagged away from his frame. His dull eyes looked enormous in his sunken face. Bound as he was, he could not tend his hair, so his trademark horn of hair had come loose and fallen. Without it, he looked diminished and ordinary.

Web steeled herself and stooped to enter. With difficulty Big Nose moved to make room for her. She squatted beside Casts No Shadow, placed the basket of food in his lap, then turned her attention to reestablishing his distinctive hairstyle.

"What is the news, Daughter?" he asked. "We hear there is much trouble."

She had not wanted to say anything about recent events, but the concern in his voice changed her mind. "The soldiers are searching for those Kumeyaays who attacked the mission. There are many beatings, much . . . ."

He clutched her arm. "My son–have they found him?"

"No, Father. My husband is still safe."

He slumped in relief.

Big Nose snorted. "So, Wekuseyaay, it is true. The spirits no longer speak to you. You have to rely on this woman to feed you *and* to tell you what is going on with our people."

Web whirled to confront the chief. "You have no ri . . ."

"Daughter, no." Casts No Shadow cut her off.

"But, Father, he . . ."

"He speaks words. Words are made of air. Air can harm no one."

She searched the wekuseyaay's face for the strength that had always given her courage. But there was no strength. Only doubt. And defeat.

With trembling hands, she finished his hair in silence. She felt that her heart would crumble at his wan smile of thanks. "I will come again soon, my father. Is there anything you need?"

"Only the sight of you–and word that Shadow Dancer is safe."

As she ducked outside, the last thing she heard was another sarcastic snort from Big Nose. She needed to collect her scattered thoughts before she started back to Nipaguay. The only place she could think of where the soldiers would not bother her was the Brown Robe's church. She hurried there.

The interior was hushed and empty. She knelt on the hard-packed earth in the back corner. The church at the mission had been filled with the sacred objects of the Brown Robes. By contrast, this room was barren except for a rough table at the front. On it rested the joined sticks her husband called a cross, illuminated by two of the small torches called candles. She watched the candlelight flicker across the grains and angles of the cross, worrying over what she had just witnessed.

The changes in the wekuseyaay went far deeper than his skin. He was wasting away in spirit as well as body. Big Nose's open criticism was the first–and biggest–crack in the wall of trust that every shaman had to have in order to serve the people.

A village could not survive without a holy man to keep balance between the living and the spirits, to know the right time to burn the fields, and to teach the children the stories of their people. With Shadow Dancer in hiding, Nipaguay needed Casts No Shadow.

My husband, she thought. *I have to get word to him. He will know what I am to do.*

Chapter 7

B ack at Nipaguay, two men were preparing to head out to visit the Kumeyaay villages to the east in order to trade shells and salt for the goods from those groups. Web entrusted to them a message to her husband. Shadow Dancer and Many Rains had told no one where they were going when they left the village. All she could do was hope that these traveling men would find him and give him the message.

Many suns passed, one after another, with no word from Shadow Dancer. Each time Web carried food to Casts No Shadow, she witnessed more of the wekuseyaay's strength and assurance slipping away, and, with it, more of her hope for him and her village.

By the time Moon had rebloomed to again be gobbled up by Coyote, she still did not know if the traders had found Shadow Dancer. Discouraged, she prepared the food as usual and undertook the long walk to the fort, enduring yet another leering examination by the gate guard.

At the cell, Casts No Shadow scarcely acknowledged her presence. "The ceremony–sacred mountain–have to go," he said again and again, pulling and jerking in agitation at the chains that bound him to the wall and Big Nose.

Holding her breath against the reek of the room and the two unwashed men, she placed the food on the ground beside Casts No Shadow and turned to leave.

Casts No Shadow grabbed her skirt. "My son. Find my son. The ceremony–at Sun Awaking."

She glanced helplessly at Big Nose for an explanation.

"Someone must call Sun back from His winter's journey," the kwaipai said.

Instantly she understood. Squatting, she looked the wekuseyaay in the eye. "My husband will remember, and he will go to the sacred mountain. He will call Sun, as you have taught him."

Casts No Shadow ceased struggling then. His tremulous smile cracked her control. She hurried away from the cell before he could see her tears.

Would Shadow Dancer remember the ceremony? What terrible things would befall Nipaguay if he forgot? The questions haunted her for the rest of the way home.

That night, despite her fatigue, she could not sleep. She was sitting under the *wisal* starring up at the glittering stars worrying about the future when she sensed someone's presence. Before she could turn, arms grabbed her from behind.

She cried out, but a man's hand covered her mouth. "Shhh."

She knew that sound, that voice, the flesh of that hand. She leaned into the arms that held her. "My husband."

Shadow Dancer pressed her to him. "I came as soon as I got your message."

She turned to embrace him. He felt thin under her arms. Scores of new lines mapped the skin of his face. "Oh, how I've missed you," she half-sobbed, cupping his cheeks so that she could look deep into his eyes.

He turned away. "I have come to surrender to the Spanish."

"No, no, you can't!"

He put a finger to his lips to warn her to lower her voice. "I must. The Spanish imprisoned my father in my place. My surrender is the only way to put an end to the beatings."

Since the attack, Spanish soldiers had roamed the countryside, looking for Shadow Dancer. When they did not find him, they resorted to beatings–horrible beatings–that had left dozens of Kumeyaay men crippled and blinded. Too often the violence extended also to women and children.

Web pushed aside those thoughts. She had to find a way to save her husband, to change his mind. "But your children."

Shadow Dancer would not face her. "I will give myself up to the Brown Robes. They will protect me."

She had no reply. Of all the paleskins, the Brown Robes were the weakest. How could they possibly protect her husband from the cruel soldiers?

"Once I am inside their church, the soldiers cannot harm me," he said. "It is their law of sanctuary."

She found her voice. "The Spanish obey no laws."

He turned at last. "To the Spanish, the church is the 'ewaa of their god. They dare not violate it."

She could think of no argument to offer. "Where is Many Rains?"

Shadow Dancer bowed his head. "He would not come with me."

"Because he does not believe this sanctuary that you describe," Web said. "Nor do I. The Brown Robes will not protect you. The Spanish will kill you. Your children will grow up without a father."

The tears she had been holding back flooded out. Instead of offering comfort, Shadow Dancer again turned his back to her. "Too many of our people have suffered because of me. The only way to stop the punishment is to give myself up." He spun toward her, his voice a rasping whisper. "I am 'aww-kuseyaay. My duty is to all the people."

She knew that he spoke the truth, knew that she had to accept his decision, but that knowledge did not assuage her grief. He reached out to her and held her until she had no more tears to cry, then he scooped her into his arms and carried her into their 'ewaa.

There, to the sighs and murmurs of their two sleeping children, their bodies united.

The first hints of sunshine silhouetted the hills to the east when Brother Fuster left his room to enter the storeroom-turned-church. Since his disastrous interview with Captain Rivera two months ago, he had been unable to do anything to free the two remaining native prisoners or to stop the soldiers' brutal assaults on the Indians of the surrounding *rancherías*. In increasing desperation, he had turned to prayer.

Inside the church he genuflected and crossed himself, then moved forward to the altar where he bent to light the candles. On the periphery of his vision, something moved. His hands flew up in alarm.

When Carlos stepped out of the shadows, the missionary's alarm turned to joy. He put his hands out in welcome. "You have returned, my son."

Carlos made no move to approach him. "I led the attack on the mission, Padre. I came back to seek your protection."

He knows the law of sanctuary, Fuster thought exultantly. *Our teachings did get through.* "You have my protection and the Lord's. No one will harm you here."

When he turned to leave the church, Carlos's grip on his arm stopped him. "Where are you going, Padre?"

"I must tell Captain Rivera that you are here."

"No, Padre. No soldiers."

Fuster struggled to explain in terms that Carlos would understand. "Rivera is chief of all the soldiers. He will order them not to harm you."

Carlos looked baffled. "This is your god's house. You said your god would protect me."

"He will, he will. But I must speak with Rivera. It–it is our way."

For several moments Carlos studied him for signs of deceit.

Fuster held his tongue, silently beseeching the Almighty to help the Indian trust him.

At last Carlos turned loose of his sleeve and stepped aside. The missionary marched out of the church to the captain's quarters. With every step, his resolve hardened. God had given him this chance to right months of wrongs. He would not fail.

At first Casts No Shadow thought he was dreaming. His daughter had come to bring him food yesterday, hadn't she? She would not be here again today, would she? Yet he saw her as clearly as if she actually stood before him.

Big Nose spoke up. "Why didn't you bring food, woman?"

The vision bent down. The feel of its warm breath on his cheek convinced the wekuseyaay that this was indeed Web, not an apparition.

"Shadow Dancer has come back, my father," she said in a low voice.

He nodded. "He came to call Sun. A true son of his father."

Web shook her head. "He came to surrender–to the Brown Robes."

"No!" Casts No Shadow's voice carried the force of all the pain that surged up within him. "No, not that."

Web's lower lip quivered. "He is 'aww-kuseyaay. The people must have a shaman. He returned to restore one to them."

"But he cannot do this," Casts No Shadow insisted.

"He has done it already, my father. At this moment he is inside the Spanish church. He says that the Brown Robes will protect him in that place."

"The bearded ones will kill him. He must not trust them. He must not!" Casts No Shadow tried to stand but his legs were too weak from months of disuse to support his body plus the weight of his chains. He crumpled to the floor in despair.

Though the spirits would no longer show him the future, he knew that he was never going back to Nipaguay. Web was right: the people must have a shaman to guide them. A shaman called Shadow Dancer. He must find a way to stop his son's foolishness. Otherwise the world of his people would plunge into chaos, or worse.

"Don't let him do this thing, Daughter. Please. They will kill him." Casts No Shadow hated himself for begging, hated the weakness of his limbs, hated the long empty days away from his

people and his family, but he could do nothing else. There was no
time left to him to train another shaman. If Shadow Dancer died,
all the knowledge he had given his son died too–the history of
the people, the stories, the ceremonies to appease the gods and
cure ailments. Out of that void would come calamities no one
could imagine. The past would die and so would the future.

"Don't let him do it," Casts No Shadow demanded.

Web sat back on her heels. Her voice was low and filled with
profound sadness. "It is already done, my father. It is already
done."

Chapter 8

T o reassure Carlos, Brother Fuster spent that night in the
church with the Indian. Carlos promptly fell into the stuporous
sleep of one who is physically and emotionally exhausted. For a
long time, the missionary watched the play of light from the altar
candles on the man's face, filled with wonder at the ways of the
Divine Father. When he finally fell asleep, it was with a prayer of
thanksgiving on his lips.

The next morning, while Fuster sang the mass for the presidio
residents, Carlos crouched in the front corner like a frightened
animal, never taking his eyes off Captain Rivera and Lieutenant
Ortega who, as usual, occupied places in the front.

After the mass, Carlos still did not relax until the latest group
of native converts filed into the sanctuary for instruction. The
smiles and greetings exchanged showed that the Indians held Carlos
in high esteem. That discovery further strengthened Fuster's resolve
to protect this man, this treasure that had been so unexpectedly
delivered into his hands.

Without prompting, Carlos served as translator for the lesson,
and, for the first time in months, Fuster saw the glimmer of
understanding showing in the neophytes' eyes.

After the lesson, the converts went off to their assigned tasks–
the women to weave and cook; the men, to clear new fields,
make adobes and repair buildings. With only the two of them
remaining, the church was suddenly hushed.

That stillness was shattered by the entrance of one of the
soldiers. Carlos immediately backed against the wall. Fuster
moved to shield him from the intruder. "Yes, my son?"

"A note from the captain, Padre."

Fuster took the proffered page and scanned it. The smile he had worn all morning faded more with each terse sentence.

The law of sanctuary does not apply for crimes such as this man has committed. In addition, the law of sanctuary applies to churches. The room where mass is currently held is a warehouse, not a church. Therefore, you will surrender the prisoner to me before the bells ring sext tomorrow. If you refuse, you will leave me no choice but to take the man by force.

The brazen demand robbed Fuster of caution. "I will not!" The outburst startled both Carlos and the soldier. "Tell the captain that my answer is no."

The soldier stared back in disbelief, before turning on his heel and leaving the missionary and the native alone. Carlos looked expectantly at Fuster. The missionary smiled, hoping to hide his scattered wits. When he touched Carlos's arm, the man flinched. "There, there, my son. Don't worry. It's just a little misunderstanding. Everything will be all right."

There was little conviction in the native's voice when he said, "Yes, Father," and went back to his corner. Fuster lifted his eyes to the cross on the altar in a silent plea. *Dear God, don't make me a liar.*

Chapter 9

F irm in his conviction that he must protect Carlos and firmer in his belief that God would not give such a wondrous gift just to take it away from him, Fuster slept soundly that night again in the sanctuary. The next morning, he went through his normal routine, singing mass and teaching neophytes.

The day's lesson was on the Last Four Things: death, judgment, heaven, and hell, a coincidence that Fuster saw as further proof of God's support for his position.

The bells rang, signifying the office of sext. With every gong, the missionary's heart beat a little harder.

The last bell's echo still sounded as the syncopated tramp of a dozen pairs of boots approached the building. Fuster motioned Carlos behind the altar before moving to the door.

Captain Rivera marched at the head of a file of soldiers with Ortega immediately behind his commander. The captain drew up in front of Fuster. "You will now surrender the prisoner."

The Franciscan slid his hands into the sleeves of his habit. "This is God's house, Captain. You have no authority here."

"If you will not surrender him, then I will take him. By force, if necessary."

Fuster raised his head to mirror the tilt of the captain's. "Carlos is under God's protection, Captain. Any man who dares violate this sanctuary will suffer excommunication."

A vein in Rivera's reddening neck pulsed with angry blood. "Give him up, Padre."

"Such a thing I cannot do for he is not mine to surrender. Only God can do that."

"Men!" Rivera barked.

Fuster ripped his hands out of his sleeves and held them up. "I warn you: any man who crosses this threshold in violence forfeits forever the right to salvation and the solace of the Holy Mother Church!"

Lieutenant Ortega and his soldiers visibly blanched at the threat. Only Rivera remained unmoved. "Remove this man!" he bellowed.

No one moved.

"That's an order!"

This time a few of the soldiers reacted. One corpulent private nicknamed Puerco with smallpox pits covering his face and upper body ran at Fuster, knocking him backward, then pounced on him, pinning him to the dirt floor while Captain Rivera stormed into the church, followed by three of his men. With three muskets aimed at him, the unarmed Carlos submitted to the captain without a struggle.

Pinned under Puerco's abundant weight, Fuster's only weapon was words. "Lieutenant Ortega! Don't let this happen." Neither Ortega nor any of the others moved to intervene.

With the soldier on his back, Fuster could not get a deep breath. His voice lost power and volume, but he had to try. "You would give up salvation from eternal damnation, for this?"

Still no one moved.

Craning over his shoulder, Fuster saw Rivera shove Carlos over the threshold. "Captain, as of this moment, you are no longer welcome in God's house."

Rivera smirked at him, then stepped out after his prisoner.

Puerco rolled off the missionary. Fuster looked up at the man's pitted face and gasped, "Why, my son?"

Puerco shrugged. "I figure Hell can't be much worse than where I already am, Padre. Why not make this Hell easier if I have the chance?"

Fuster laid his forehead on the hard-packed dirt and closed his eyes. In one act of violence, everything he had believed in, everything he had worked for had died. There was nothing left to live for. Nothing.

"Mother!" Sand Flea's yell caused Web to drop her basket in alarm. She raced across the field to meet him on legs weak with fear that something had happened to Shooting Star.

Sand Flea fell into her arms breathless. "Father."

In a word, hope chased away her fear. "He is home?"

Sand Flea's head wagged and tears began to spill down his small face. "The soldiers took him."

Web stared at her son in shock. Shadow Dancer had been so sure that the Brown Robes would protect him. So sure that the Spanish soldiers would obey the law of their god's 'ewaa. She had given in to his arguments the way she always did, supporting his choices even if she did not agree with them. She should have argued more, should have convinced him to reconsider. Now it was too late. The worst had happened.

"What can we do, Mother?" Sand Flea sobbed.

Web looked slowly toward the fort. The adobe walls glowed golden in the rays of the setting sun. Her heart felt as void of feeling as her mind of answers to her son's question.

"We have to help him, Mother, but how?"

She looked down at her son's face. Her voice was raw with sorrow. "I don't know."

Sand Flea looked at her as if she had betrayed him. "But you have to know."

She shook her head. "I don't."

With a hate-filled glance, he dashed away, leaving her alone to struggle with her pain. She looked after her son and whispered again, "I don't know."

Chapter 10

B rother Fuster spent the next two days trying to persuade the captain to release Carlos. Nothing worked.

Finally Sunday came.

Frustration had honed the missionary's anger to a sharp edge by the time he entered the church to begin the mass. He paused at the threshold and squared his shoulders. As usual, Captain Rivera and Lieutenant Ortega fronted the congregation.

Fuster crossed himself and entered the room, pacing slowly and deliberately to the altar, then turned to face the captain. "Today the mass honors Our Lady of Sorrows."

Several people shifted, perplexed by the change in the routine they had come to expect.

Fuster continued. "However, there are among you men who chose to commit a grievous sin."

Rivera's mouth drew taut.

"Those men violated the sacred law of sanctuary, seizing by force of arms a man who had voluntarily placed himself under the protection of our Most Holy Father God." He paused to allow for the buzz of conversation.

Beside the captain, Lieutenant Ortega stared fixedly at the wall. All the color had drained from his face.

"As justification, they claimed that this room where we have all come together this day to worship God–they claimed that this room is only a warehouse. Not really a church."

A purplish flush oozed upward from the captain's neck to his face.

Fuster allowed silence to settle again before going on. "Those men knew the consequences of such an act, yet they went ahead."

Puerco appeared to shrink under the missionary's gaze. "For their sins, they must pay a heavy price. Henceforward, they are denied the sacraments of our Holy Mother Church."

Rivera glared at Fuster but made no move to leave.

"Captain Rivera, I cannot proceed with the mass until you and the men who helped you violate God's sanctuary leave this room."

The captain's head jerked at the mention of his name. Jumping to his feet, he yanked down on the bottom of his uniform jacket, spun on his heel and strode out the door. Ortega followed, along with a handful of soldiers. The last one out was Puerco, scuttling like a roach caught in the light of an opened door.

Rustling and throat clearing rippled through the congregation. At last Fuster turned to face the altar and began the holy ritual. "In nomine Patris, et Filii, et Spiritus Sancti. Amen."

Web spent the two days after Shadow Dancer's seizure too distraught to act. On the third day, she recovered enough to brave a trip to the fort. Since she no longer trusted the Brown Robe Fuster to intervene on her behalf, she feared what she would face among the Spanish soldiers.

Filled with anxiety, she halted where the path to the fort branched off the main trail in order to cover her breasts against the usual leers of the gate guards. Then, on unwilling legs, she started up the path.

Instead of guards, she found the gates wide open and the central compound empty. Immediately her senses came to the alert. From the nearby 'ewaa of the paleskin god came the eerie sounds of the Brown Robes' chanting. Off to the left, grumbling voices issued from another room whose door stood ajar. Besides those sounds, she detected no other noise or motion.

She moved cautiously past that partially-open door to avoid detection, then raced to Casts No Shadow's cell. When she did not see guards about, she pulled up, sure this was some kind of trick.

She hesitated until she made sure there were no bearded ones lurking about. Then she walked forward, scarcely believing her good luck.

Inside, the wekuseyaay was alone. No Big Nose. No Shadow Dancer.

Casts No Shadow looked up at her. "The bearded ones let Big Nose go."

Tension made it hard for her to talk. "And my husband?"

He blinked twice. "My son—they keep him in another place. They make him work."

Work, instead of chains or beatings. Hope sparked within her.

The shaman looked sadly up at her. "That is not good, Daughter. They do not let him rest, and they do not give him enough food or water."

"I have brought him food," she offered, handing over the basket she had prepared for him.

Casts No Shadow shook his head. "The bearded ones will not let you help my son. They will not let you see him, either."

"But I must try, Father. Where is he?"

He waved vaguely at the back wall of his prison. "No one sees him. Not even that Brown Robe witch."

Web went off in the direction the wekuseyaay indicated, passing three adjoining rooms before reaching piles of rubble that had once been a building. She stopped short. Where there had once been a floor, there was now a chest-deep pit. In the pit was Shadow Dancer with his hands and ankles draped in heavy chains, moving slowly and wearily, lifting one weighted leg, then the other in a lumbering kind of walk, going nowhere.

Edging closer, Web saw that mud filled the bottom of the pit. Mud and straw that her husband's movements mixed together to make the bricks the Spanish used to build their huts.

"Faster!" barked a voice, causing her to jump.

The moment she spotted the paleskin soldier squatting in the shade across the pit, he saw her. "Well, well, look who's here."

She put the food basket behind her and began to back away. That voice, those eyes—it was him, the one who had raped her.

Terror made her clumsy. The soldier caught up to her and grabbed her arm. "My, my, ain't you the answer to this man's prayers."

The feel of that despised flesh on hers threw her into action. She charged him, head lowered, butting him squarely in the midsection.

He staggered backward into a wall.

She attempted to dart to her husband, but the soldier caught her shoulder and dragged her back.

"Why you little . . ." His open palm connected with her cheek, stinging the flesh, violently wrenching her head to the side.

"Wife!" Shadow Dancer yelled, crawling out of the pit.

The soldier flung her to the ground and turned to defend against her husband. With an audible crack, the butt of his musket smashed into Shadow Dancer's forehead, driving him back into the pit unconscious.

"Now for you, woman. I have a little treat for you, just as hard as a rifle stock, aimed right between your legs."

Web did not need to understand the words to know his intentions. She unleashed a scream that echoed throughout the fort.

At that moment the door to the church slammed open and the Brown Robe Fuster appeared. Spotting her, the missionary yelled something to a nearby group of Spanish and sprinted to her, robes flapping, followed by the soldiers.

Her attacker threw her aside and retreated to the back lip of the pit.

Once free of her attacker, she climbed into the pit and knelt in the mud beside the inert body of her husband. She wiped the grime from his face and cradled his head against her chest, chafing his hands, willing him to revive.

A shadow fell across her. She looked up at the Brown Robe standing at the lip of the pit. She did not have the Spanish words for all the anger she felt toward the man, but she had to speak her heart. "Look what you have done to him. He trusted you. You betrayed him."

The Brown Robe stretched out a hand to her. She glared at him. "Traitor! Coward! Witch!"

As if he understood her words, the Brown Robe withdrew his hand and took a step backward.

"Wife?" came her husband's weak voice.

Looking down into eyes confused by the blow to his head, she had to swallow twice before she could speak in a loving tone. "I brought you food, my husband."

His weak smile tugged at the roots of her heart. She turned her face away from his view in order to get her emotions under control. She fumbled open the basket, took out an acorn cake, broke off a piece and put it to his lips.

Before he could take a bite, someone slapped the food away and wrenched the basket out of her hands.

Web had not heard anyone else enter the pit, but now she found herself locked by a pair of eyes of a flat gray so pale as to be nearly colorless, so hard as to be frightening. The man spoke in a tone as unforgiving as his eyes, brandishing the basket toward the soldiers gathered around the pit. "Who let this woman into this area?"

The Brown Robe answered. "God's mercy, Captain. She brought him food. Why not let her feed him?"

Gray Eyes tossed the basket to one of the soldiers and climbed out of the pit. Immediately one of the converts appeared and fell to cleaning the mud from the man's boots. Gray Eyes pointed at Web. "Remove her from the presidio grounds this instant."

"Mercy, Captain," the Brown Robe pleaded.

"Mercy, Padre? You speak of mercy when you will not allow me and these obedient men to attend mass?"

Fuster changed from pleading to anger. "You made your choice two days ago. The wrong choice."

"Remove her now!" Gray Eyes yelled.

It took two soldiers to drag the struggling Web away from her husband. She continued to fight them all the way to the presidio entrance where they shoved her bodily outside, slamming the gates behind her.

She stood there for a long time, too drained to move, too afraid to think. When she finally did move, she realized that there were sounds issuing from the other side of the wall. The thud of a lash falling on bare flesh followed by screams. Shadow Dancer's screams. She covered her ears against the terrible sound and stumbled down the trail.

Chapter 11

"**S**hip ho!" The fort lookout's cry pulled Brother Fuster out of his musings. More and more these days he turned to memories of his youth in Spain for comfort.

He sighed heavily. Too many ships had dropped anchor in San Diego since Captain Rivera had seized Carlos–all from the south.

"It's from Monterey!" came the cry.

Fuster sat up a little straighter. *Don't get your hopes up, Vicente. For all you know, Father Serra never received your letter.*

One of the neophyte women, a young female christened Ruth with a comely face despite the tattoos on her chin, appeared at the open door of his room. "Father, you come?"

"Yes, my child. I come. You run on ahead."

After she left, he got up wearily from his pallet and bowed his head toward the wall crucifix. "Dear Lord, please let this be the help that will save Carlos's life."

Not even excommunication and the humiliation of being publicly asked to leave the mass had made Captain Rivera relent on the issue of the native. The captain had assigned pairs of men to guard Carlos round-the-clock. Every day, all day those men worked their prisoner unmercifully, withholding water and food until he collapsed, then giving him only enough to revive him and get him back on his feet to work.

Every day Fuster tried to see Carlos. Every day the guards blocked his way. And every day Carlos grew thinner, weaker, more hollow-eyed.

In frustration at the stalemate, Fuster had written a letter to Father Serra begging for help. He had secretly entrusted the missive to the captain of the ship that left San Diego carrying Captain Rivera to Monterey three months ago. Three long months of waiting, hoping and praying for Carlos to endure until help could arrive to rescue him from the soldiers' clutches. Three months of standing firm on barring from the sacraments those men who had violated God's house.

Fuster had no doubt that, upon his arrival in Monterey, Captain Rivera had gone directly to Father Serra to plead for recision of that excommunication. So far, at San Diego, only one of the guilty soldiers had come to Fuster to discuss the matter: Lieutenant Ortega, who had sought an audience the moment the sails of Captain Rivera's ship had disappeared around Point Gijarros. Fuster's request to Ortega had been simple. Return Carlos to his protection and guarantee that none of Ortega's men would ever again violate the sanctuary.

"That I cannot do, Padre. I must obey my superior," Ortega had said.

"God comes first."

"God will not feed my family if I disobey my captain."

"So you will forsake the comfort of God's sacraments and deny yourself eternity in paradise in order to carry out the captain's immoral orders?"

Without answering, Ortega had stomped out, slamming the door behind him.

And there the situation had remained–the lieutenant angry and stubborn and the guilty soldiers melded by adversity into a surly group who passed their time getting drunk on the agave liquor they no longer bothered to hide.

Now the woman Ruth reappeared, out of breath and smiling. "Father Serra, he comes."

"You are certain?" Fuster asked.

"Yes, Father Serra." She pantomimed the mission president's tonsure and limp for emphasis.

"Dear God, thank you," Fuster whispered toward the crucifix before hurrying down the hill to join the crowd already waiting for the ship's shuttle craft to reach shore.

In the boat, Father Serra's bald pate gleamed in the intense mid-July sun. Fuster waited on the shore, his anxiety growing with every stroke of the oars. Had Father received his letter? Would he back the excommunication? More important, would Serra succeed where he had failed in winning Carlos's release?

He went forward to help drag the launch onto the sand and gave Father Serra a hand out of the boat.

The mission president immediately caught Fuster in an embrace. In a voice too low for anyone else to hear over the wash of the surf, he said, "I have come to help, if I can, Brother."

After months of despair, a small spark of hope flared in Fuster. Father Serra had received his letter. Now perhaps the stalemate would end.

Once the greetings were out of the way, the mission president asked Lieutenant Ortega to accompany him and Fuster to the presidio church. At the threshold, Serra paused and, holding out his hands, raised his face to the clear blue summer sky. "Thank you, most merciful Lord for the comfort of this, Your blessed house."

A glance sideways at Ortega showed that the words had hit the marks that Father Serra had doubtless aimed for.

"Would you wait outside a moment, Lieutenant?" Serra asked.

Ortega stepped aside, allowing Fuster to follow his superior inside the church. Serra shut the door, genuflected and walked to the altar. Fuster did likewise, his heart racing in anticipation of what he was about to hear.

Serra knelt at the altar. Fuster followed suit. In the silence, his agitated heart sounded in his own ears like the footfalls of a running man.

Serra finished his prayers with a bow, then turned to face Fuster. "Captain Rivera is not a man to cross, Brother."

"No, Father."

"I know that you did not make the decision to excommunicate him in haste."

Fuster's stomach began to flutter and his new-found hope began to fade. "No, Father."

Serra's voice shot up. "But no one, no one violates the house of God. Not even the King himself can seize by force a man who has sought the protection of the Almighty! For the captain and those who did his bidding, the excommunication stands until the native is returned to us."

Fuster did not know whether to laugh or cry. Serra turned toward the closed door. "Lieutenant, please join us."

The door creaked back to reveal Ortega, his face visibly paler from overhearing Serra's tirade. He walked forward with none of the verve normal to his stride.

"Lieutenant, I know you to be an honest man, a kind man who cares, physically and spiritually, for those in his charge," Serra said.

"Yes, Padre" Ortega said.

Some of the kindliness left the mission president's tone. "How long will your conscience allow you to deny yourself and your men the solace of God?"

"Padre, I . . ."

"How long will you–how long *can* you close your ears to the cries for mercy of that man you seized from this house of God? How long can you go on living with the knowledge that you have sinned against Him Who Gave You Life? How long before you admit that you must obey God first before any mortal?"

Ortega collapsed on his knees and put his hands over his face. While his shoulders heaved in silent weeping, Serra looked upon him with an expression of pity and understanding.

When Ortega could manage to speak again, Fuster had to strain to hear. "I will release the man immediately."

"And what about the mission?" Serra asked. "When can we count on your men to help us rebuild it?"

The lieutenant looked up. "Immediately, Padre."

Serra clapped his hands and hooted with joy that fit neither the time nor the circumstance. "Come, Brother," he said to Fuster. "Let us see to Carlos."

Fuster and the lieutenant had to hurry to keep up with Serra whose rapid stride was a legend despite his advanced age and pronounced limp. As usual the guards rose to block their way. "Lieutenant, tell them," Serra demanded.

Ortega had somehow recomposed his face. He stepped forward. "Stand aside."

The guards exchanged a disbelieving glance.

"Stand aside and release the prisoner," the lieutenant said.

The guards parted, giving Fuster his first close-up view in three months of the man he had worried about for so long. Carlos stood in the same mud pit where he had spent the last three-and-a-half backbreaking months, mixing mud and straw to make adobe bricks. Every minute of that time showed on his face; every minute of starvation, on his bent, skeletal frame.

As Fuster reached down to help the wasted native out of the pit, a lump of grief rose in his throat. Carlos's once strong arms were mere sticks. His proud round cheeks, sunken. His bright eager eyes, dull and without life.

Once out of the pit, Carlos fainted. When he came to again, he held a withered hand out toward Serra and rasped, "Father?"

"You are free now, my son. Return to your village," Serra said gently.

Carlos blinked weakly. "I can go–home?"

"Yes, my son. Home."

Carlos's old man's face crinkled into a grotesque imitation of a smile. "Home."

Movement near the bottom of the ravine drew Web's attention away from the rabbit hides she was scraping.

"What is it, Mother?" Shooting Star asked anxiously, seeing her mother come alert.

Web's eyes strained but picked up no more movement. She turned back to her daughter. "I thought I saw something moving. A wounded animal perhaps. But there is nothing there. Let me see your basket."

Shooting Star held out her work for approval. Barely six summers old, the girl surpassed most adult women in the beauty and quality of her baskets.

Suddenly Shooting Star sprang up. "Down there, Mother. I saw it too."

Web looked in the direction of her daughter's pointing finger to see what looked like a thin deer fallen beside the path.

"Why, Mother, it's Father!" cried Shooting Star, who sprinted off, leaving Web to chase after.

By the time she arrived, her daughter had Shadow Dancer sitting up. A gasp escaped Web's lips. Shadow Dancer was so very thin, almost a ghost.

He reached toward her, wincing with the effort. "I have come home, Wife."

She fell to her knees and gathered him into her arms. The feel of his bones under his too-loose skin filled her with anguish, robbing her of all speech. She held him and rocked him as if he were a child. With every sway, she sensed more tension desert his body.

What have they done to you? she cried silently.

For more than four moons she had made regular trips to the fort with food for him and Casts No Shadow. Although she had free and unlimited access now to Casts No Shadow, soldiers always barred her way to the part of the fort where her husband was held. More than once the food she had brought for him was confiscated and dumped in the dirt. Desperate to know her husband's condition, she had constantly prodded the mission converts for news about him. Their replies were always the same: only soldiers were allowed to see Shadow Dancer. The only thing that was left to her was prayer that the gods would watch over him.

Shadow Dancer's hand slid down to her rounded stomach. He looked up at her inquiringly.

She nodded. A new baby grew inside her now, the result of their last mating.

He sighed and sagged back against her.

"You are too skinny, Father," Shooting Star exclaimed. "You need to eat."

He granted his daughter a smile beyond weariness and leaned heavily on Web to get to his feet. She could feel how much pain the effort cost him. She supported him to their lodge fire.

"I–need to–lie down," he said hoarsely.

"Then I'll feed you in bed," Shooting Star declared.

"That would be good, my daughter."

Web helped him onto the pallet and tucked two fur blankets around his shivering body. He held onto her hand, looking at her as if he was afraid he would forget her face. She swallowed again and again against the constriction in her chest.

Shooting Star burst in with fresh soup and a horn spoon. Carefully, she fed her father one spoonful, then a second. He sipped slowly as if even that small effort hurt.

Shooting Star had just dipped the spoon into the soup for a third taste when Shadow Dancer stiffened, rolled onto his side and vomited in the dirt.

"Father, are you sick?" the girl asked with the restraint of a child who seeks to understand something that frightens her.

With effort, he turned his face toward her. "No, my child. Just tired."

"Then you must sleep, Father. And when you wake up I can show you my new baskets."

His smile flickered. "Oh, I would like that."

Shooting Star hugged him, then scampered out. Once they were alone, Web could not hold back. "Oh, my husband, look what they've done to you."

"Hush, my wife. That is in the past. I am home now. Home to stay."

Web embraced him, hiding her welling eyes against his matted hair. *I must not show him my fear.*

"I will sleep now," he whispered.

She nodded, knowing that any attempt to talk would betray her. When she bent to kiss him, a single tear fell on his arm.

He touched the wet spot gently. "Do not cry, my precious wife," he said in a faltering voice. "Everything will be all right now."

She brushed his cheek with unsteady fingers. She did not agree with him because she could not lie. "Sleep well, my husband."

Chapter 12

For the next thirteen suns, Shadow Dancer remained in the 'ewaa, too weak to do more than sleep. Web resented the many tasks that took her away from her husband, especially the long trips to the fort to take food to Casts No Shadow. Yet such trips were vital to keeping the wekuseyaay alive. She had to go.

On this morning, she finished packing the basket for Casts No Shadow, then, before leaving for the fort, she looked in on her husband on the chance that he might be awake. His eyes opened the moment she ducked inside. He flashed a tired smile

"I must take food to our father," she explained.

The smile sank. "It is not right that I am here and the Spanish still hold my father."

"They released you. No doubt they will release him, too," she said, putting as much hope in her voice as she could dredge up.

Shadow Dancer seemed to fall into thought for a moment. Then he said, "The chief Brown Robe Serra—he is the one."

"Which one, Husband?"

He reached for her hand, fervor lighting his face. "He is the one. You must go, Wife, to ask for our father's release."

"But I do not have the right words to do such a thing."

"I can teach you what to say. Just tell me that you will do it."

Under his fierce gaze, Web looked down at the basket of food. After all that had happened to him, how could he still trust the Brown Robes? Couldn't he see how difficult it was for her to leave him and go to the fort to take the food to Casts No Shadow? Approaching the Brown Robe was out of the question. Not after what the Spanish had done to the father of her children.

"Wife?"

She could not look at him.

"Please."

The plea in his voice tore away her defenses. She could not deny him. "Yes, I will go."

Shadow Dancer limply squeezed her hand. "I will wait for you—and our father—to return."

Brother Fuster pushed himself up from the table and trudged to the open door, rubbing at the stiffness that had developed in his neck and shoulders over the week of revising plans for rebuilding the mission. Since Father Serra's arrival two weeks ago, the presidio had hummed with preparations to begin the construction. In that atmosphere, Fuster's lethargy and doubt had fallen away. His confidence revived and, with it, his dreams.

He glanced over his shoulder toward Father Serra who was busy writing a letter to the Viceroy in the City of Mexico. The man was remarkable. He could work for hours on end without tiring.

Sensing another presence, Fuster faced forward to find the young native woman who had returned the statue of the Holy

Conception. He had not seen her since that painful day when she tried to bring food to Carlos. "Father Serra, we have a guest," he announced.

Behind him, the mission president sat back in his seat with the faint sigh of sackcloth.

Fuster beckoned the woman inside. "Come, my child."

She entered the room with halting steps and stopped just inside the door. "F–Father of C–Carlos, go home," she stammered.

Fuster's chin dropped to hear Spanish words–a complete sentence–come out of her mouth.

"Father of Carlos, go home," she repeated.

"Who is this father of Carlos, Brother?" Serra asked.

As if she understood the question, she repeated the statement, this time pointing outside.

"Do you understand her?" Serra asked.

"Why–the old man. I completely forgot about him," Fuster answered.

"What old man?" Serra asked.

"This woman's father."

"Carlos. Isn't that your neophyte? The one we just sent home?"

Quickly, pieces of the puzzle flew together in Fuster's mind. If the old man was her father and Carlos's father, she was either Carlos's sister or his wife.

"Where are you going, Brother?" Serra asked.

"To correct an oversight and have the lieutenant release this woman's father."

Serra's chair scraped back. "Wait, Brother. Shouldn't we discuss this first?"

The question coming from Serra stopped Fuster.

"Father of Carlos, go home," the woman insisted, plucking impatiently at Fuster's sleeve.

Serra came to the doorway. "Brother Fuster?"

It was a command, not a question. With a glance toward the storeroom where the old man was held, Fuster motioned for the woman to stay outside, then he reentered the room and closed the door.

"Come, sit down and let's discuss this thing," Serra said.

Fuster went back to his chair.

"Lieutenant Ortega is a fine man," Serra said. "He bears a heavy burden of responsibility. Not a small part of that load involves rebuilding our mission, wouldn't you agree?"

Fuster nodded.

"You have had to wait so long to see your mission rise from the ruins. Wouldn't it be better to get that task underway before we make any more requests of the lieutenant?"

Fuster looked down at his hands. "Yes, Father, you're right. That old man has been here a long time. A week or two won't make that much difference."

Serra nodded and resumed his seat. "Then you better tell her that."

Fuster returned to the door and opened it. The woman looked at him expectantly. He used his hands to make signs to go with his words. "Food, yes. Home, no."

The woman's face darkened. "Father of Carlos, go home."

He shook his head. "Home, no."

Such animosity filled her gaze that he had to turn away. When he looked back, she was on her way to the old man's cell. With a silent sigh, he took off after her.

The wekuseyaay was deep into memory when he sensed that someone was with him. He forced himself back to the present to find Web accompanied by a Brown Robe. The presence of the paleskin ignited the anger that had been smoldering in Casts No Shadow since his capture. He lunged at the man to the limit of his chains and his failing strength, snarling, "Sorcerer!"

The Brown Robe drew back, then touched Web's arm and signed that he would leave.

When they were alone, Web said, "I came to ask the Brown Robes to release you, Father."

His energy spent, Casts No Shadow slumped against the wall with a snort. "Why bother? The Brown Robes will never let me go. They know I have the power to destroy them." The words sounded hollow to his ears. He changed the subject. "How is my son?"

"He grows stronger with every sun."

Her eyes belied her words. This time the spirits had not misled him. Shadow Dancer needed a healer with the knowledge to counter the curses these bearded witches had laid on him. A powerful healer. A wekuseyaay.

"You have no need to lie, Daughter," Casts No Shadow said gently. "The spirits have told me the truth."

She turned her head but not fast enough to hide the tears welling into her eyes. Seeing tears in one so strong cinched his decision. "You must help me."

"I–I failed."

"No, here." He raised his chained ankle. "See the gap, there?"

She examined the chain and nodded.

"Help me pull it apart."

"No, Father. This is too strong. We will never budge it."

"We must try. I *must* get to my son."

A look of possibility spread slowly across her face, chasing her doubt before it. "I will return." She dashed out before he could protest.

He waited, yanking at the chain without effect until his hands grew numb. Where had she gone?

She returned, out of breath, excitement dancing in her eyes. In her hands, she hauled a tool that resembled a war club. "My husband calls this a hammer. And this is a wedge." She drew the object out of the folds of the blanket that covered her upper body. "They belonged to Twisted Face."

He searched her face for signs of the emotions she must be feeling to touch that hated man's tools. What he found in her eyes was hope.

She positioned the chain atop the cap of rock that formed part of the floor and showed him how to hold the wedge. Sitting back on her heels, she bit her lower lip. "This hammer is heavy. I might miss and hit your hands."

"But you will not miss, my daughter," Casts No Shadow said with as much confidence as his own flickering optimism would allow.

She looked at him doubtfully.

He spoke with a fervor he did not feel. "Shadow Dancer needs me. You will not miss."

She shifted into a crouch and rested the hammer head lightly on the wedge for position.

"You will not miss," he coaxed, keeping his voice soft to disguise his own doubt.

The head of the hammer moved upward, then hesitated. "I–I can't," she moaned softly.

"You must," he demanded.

Again she raised the hammer and, again, lowered it. "But your hands . . ."

"Daughter," he warned.

She swiped the back of her wrist across her eyes, then lifted the hammer again. With a grunt, she slammed it downward.

Casts No Shadow riveted his gaze on her face rather than witness the crushing of his hands. He expected her face to crumple in failure, expected lightning bolts of pain to jab through his brain. Instead, she laughed and dropped the hammer into the dirt.

He glanced down then to see the link split completely apart. Only a short length of chain still wrapped his ankle.

Her voice was breathy with relief. "My husband will know how to remove that piece, Father. I do not have the strength or the will to try."

"You have done all I need, my daughter. Now return to our village. I must wait until night when the bearded ones are asleep before I attempt to leave here. Tell my son that I will be there to help him soon."

She nodded and departed, taking the hammer and wedge with her. The wekuseyaay rearranged the chain to hide the open link from any guards who might happen by, then he opened the basket of food she had brought and ate with a relish he had not experienced since his capture.

The sounds of shouting ripped Brother Fuster out of a deep sleep. *Attack*, he thought, bolting from his pallet to the door.

The compound was filled with the moving shadows of firebrands. Light flickered across the faces of the soldiers grouped around Lieutenant Ortega who held the arm of a short thin naked man with long silver hair: the old prisoner, the father of Carlos, that the young Indian woman had come to see earlier.

Fuster let himself out into the compound to learn what had happened.

At his approach, Ortega whirled. "What do you know about this, Padre?"

"About what, Lieutenant?" The voice belonged to Father Serra who had just emerged from his room.

"Puerco here says he saw Brother Fuster in this one's cell today," Ortega said.

"Yes, the brother was there," Serra said. "He took this man's daughter to him. She had brought him food as I understand she does quite regularly."

Ortega glared at Fuster. "Did you leave them alone?"

Serra interrupted before Fuster could answer. "What's this all about, Lieutenant?"

"This one is a medicine man. According to your converts, the savages believe that he talks with the gods and he acts for their gods. A year before the attack on the mission, my men spotted this one at a dozen different native villages. There's only one reason he would be traveling around so much: he was stirring up the Indians to attack."

Hatred glittered in the gaze the old man riveted on Serra and Fuster. Yet, there was nothing unusual about the slender little man. No power. No mystery. But before Fuster could say so, Serra spoke up. "A medicine man, you say?"

Ortega nodded. "The guard caught him trying to escape just now. He got out of his chains somehow. That meant someone helped him. Someone meaning this daughter you took to see him, Brother Fuster."

"That's preposterous!" Fuster said. "She's pregnant. Besides you said all the prisoners had been released. There's no reason to hold him. Why not let him go?"

"Brother," Serra warned.

"He was carrying this." The lieutenant held out a pouch of hide, painted with various symbols.

The old man grabbed for the bag, but the officer whisked it out of reach.

When Serra reached for it, the old man shrieked and struggled, nearly breaking away from the lieutenant who needed two of his privates to help subdue him.

The instant the pouch rested in Serra's hands, the old man crumpled to the ground, keening at the top of his lungs. Serra had to raise his voice in order to be heard. "You are right to hold him, Lieutenant. My years in New Spain showed me the harm these medicine men can do. He and his kind are dangerous. They represent the ways and the superstition we are working so hard to erase."

Fuster could not believe his ears. "Father Serra, he's just an old man."

An angry glare from the mission president shut off his protest. "It's a blessing that you caught him, Lieutenant," Serra said. "Our deepest thanks."

Ortega smirked at Fuster. "Lock him up, Corporal," ordered the lieutenant. "In the strong room, and post a double guard."

Fuster could not stay silent. "I insist that this man's family be allowed to visit and bring him food. And no beatings."

Ortega looked at Serra as if seeking permission to deny the requests. Instead, the mission president said, "Reasonable requests, Lieutenant."

"All right," Ortega said after a long silence. "But there will be a guard present whenever anyone visits."

Fuster nodded. It was the best he could do, for now.

Chapter 13

On the way back to Nipaguay, Web decided not to tell Shadow Dancer about his father's planned escape. Instead, she assured him that the wekuseyaay would be back in the village the next day and left it at that, figuring there would be time later to explain everything once her husband was stronger.

Enlivened by her news, Shadow Dancer ate well and, for once, kept all the food down. Later he fell into the first deep sleep since his return.

While he slept, Web sat by the fire waiting for Casts No Shadow to arrive. For a time she worked at a new basket, but, as the night wore on without sign of him, worry began to nibble at the edges of her anticipation. She put the basket aside and stared toward the westward trail beside the river. What could be keeping him?

The first rays of sunlight beaming over the eastern hills found her up and pacing, too agitated to remain sitting after a night of waiting. There was still no sign of Casts No Shadow.

She went through the motions of feeding the children and sending them off to play with their friends. Finally she could stand the wait no more. She shook her husband awake. "I want to go to the fort to accompany our father home."

Shadow Dancer was too groggy to question her. She left him to sleep some more and hurried away.

At the fort, she found the gates open and unmanned. Even the center compound was deserted. Her disquiet began to turn to dread, but she forced herself to keep moving. Staying close to the walls of the hushed buildings, she went directly to the wekuseyaay's cell as she had so many times before.

The door was open. The room was empty. The chains were gone.

The bile of fear rose into her throat. It took some moments before she could rein in her racing thoughts to decide on a course of action. Her only option seemed to be to go to the Brown Robes. They would know where Casts No Shadow was, but could she trust them?

The need to know overrode her caution. She rushed to the church. Through the open door, she could see Kumeyaay converts seated on the floor, their backs to her, listening to the Brown Robe called Fuster who stood at the front. Each time he said something in Spanish, the converts repeated it in unison.

She positioned herself squarely in the doorway. "Father of Carlos," she said loudly.

A second Brown Robe stepped out of the shadows. In his hand, Casts No Shadow's medicine pouch.

At the sight, her voice lost strength. "Father of Carlos."

"She has come to see him," Fuster said to the other Brown Robe.

"Continue your lesson," said the second Brown Robe.

"She has the right to see him, Father Serra."

Web did not need to understand the words to hear the argument between the two men.

Before the second Brown Robe could answer, the one called Fuster came out to her. He reached as if to take her arm, but she jerked away, unwilling to risk his touch.

"Brother." The Second Brown Robe's voice issued from the interior of the church.

Ignoring him, Fuster took off out the door toward the opposite side of the compound. Web followed him to a sizable building with slits for windows. Two soldiers stood at attention in front of the stout door.

Fuster Brown Robe said something in a demanding voice. The guards stood impassive, eyes locked on the distance. Web scanned their faces for clues as to what the words meant.

For a long moment the two soldiers did not move. Then the taller one unlocked the door and allowed Fuster and Web to pass inside. It took a moment for her eyes to adjust to the gloom. When they did, the sight that met them caused her to draw in an audible breath.

In the corner Casts No Shadow lay curled into a fetal ball, moaning in grief.

Hands trembling, she faced Fuster. Her voice was hoarse with desperation. "Father of Carlos, go home."

The Brown Robe shook his head sadly. "No home."

Casts No Shadow's moans increased. She fell to her knees beside him. "Oh, my father, what have they done to you?"

The wekuseyaay's eyes fluttered open. "The witches have my sacred pouch."

"Yes, Father, I saw." She could not keep the sadness out of her voice.

"They have taken away my power. I have no more reason to live."

She could not trust her voice as she touched his arm.

"No more life," he whispered.

His eyes closed and he retreated into a place where she could not reach him. She got slowly to her feet and moved toward the door of the new prison. Fuster said something, but she was too preoccupied to listen, or care. There was no more to do here. Now she had to return to Nipaguay. What would she tell Shadow Dancer?

Chapter 14

W eb awoke at first light, feeling as if she had scarcely shut her eyes. She looked over at her husband. Good, he was still sleeping.

Slowly she sat up, passing a hand across her forehead as if to clear the fuzziness of her mind. Since her return from seeing Casts No Shadow three days ago, she had to force herself to perform even the simplest tasks. Not only was the wekuseyaay still locked in the bearded ones' prison, but also, when Casts No Shadow failed to return to Nipaguay as promised, Shadow Dancer had taken a turn for the worse. Now nothing would stay on his stomach, not even water.

In desperation she had plodded from one end of the river valley to the other, up slopes and down, searching for the funnel-shaped clusters of lavender flowers of the gum balm bush. Late yesterday, she had found some at last, but she was too exhausted to feel any elation. Although it was pitch dark when she made her way back to the village, she had used the last of her strength to brew a tea from the gathered leaves and coax her husband into three swallows. When that stayed down, she decided against pushing her luck and set the rest aside to give him this morning.

With great effort she rose from the pallet and stepped outside. The day was already warm. She got the fire going and put the cold gum balm tea on to heat. Straightening, she arched her back and massaged its stiff muscles. From inside the mound of her stomach, she felt the ripple of the new baby's movement. Wearily, she rested one hand there, a substitute for the words of endearment that she was too tired to utter.

She sighed. Today she had to go back to the fort, had to try to get food to Casts No Shadow.

If she had disliked going to the fort before, she hated the trips now, hated witnessing the disintegration of the wekuseyaay. For disintegrating he was. And there was nothing she could do to stop it. Once the Brown Robes took possession of his sacred pouch, they owned his power. Even taking the pouch back would not reverse the damage.

The tea began to steam. She dipped a gourdful and carried it into the lodge. Sand Flea rolled onto his back, yawned and stretched, then cast a worried glance toward his father.

Web was too tired to muster a smile to reassure her son. She squatted next to Shadow Dancer's pallet and touched his shoulder. "Husband."

He did not respond.

She raised her voice slightly. "Husband, wake up. I have more tea."

Still no movement.

Sand Flea slid off his pallet and came to squat beside her. "Father, wake up."

Shooting Star sat up. "Mother?"

Web touched Shadow Dancer's cheek. It felt waxy and too cool. A coldness crept over her. "Husband?"

Sand Flea looked at her. "Mother?"

A wail rose from deep within her soul. Shadow Dancer would never awaken again.

Chapter 15

Red Smoke walked into Casts No Shadow's dream with the same distinctive lumbering gait as when he had been alive. The face he turned to the wekuseyaay was creased with lines of mourning. "Cosoy is no more. My people are no more because we tried to fight the thunder sticks. The bearded ones will never go away. They have destroyed Cosoy. Soon they will destroy Nipaguay and . . ."

"No!" Casts No Shadow shouted back. "Shadow Dancer lives. The bearded ones cannot destroy Nipaguay." He leveled an accusing finger at the apparition. "I told you not to, but you led your people against the paleskins."

Red Smoke shook his head sadly. "I remember. It was seven summers ago this very day when you made the wrong choice, Wekuseyaay, not to join us. Together we would have destroyed the bearded ones. Now they will never leave. Never."

Voices outside the door shredded the image and dissolved the dream. The door opened. Web stepped inside.

Casts No Shadow's eyesight was still too sleep-blurred to recognize immediately the heaviness of her walk, her puffy face, her red-rimmed eyes.

Instead of coming over to him, she stood just inside the door. Her mouth worked for a time before any words came out. "My father, Shadow Dancer has gone to live among the spirits."

Casts No Shadow sat up, ignoring the creaking stiffness in his spine. He searched her face for signs of the joke she had to be playing on him.

Her voice was low and numb. "His body exists no more. Now his soul rests with Those Who Went Before."

He blinked, hoping that he had only been dreaming. She did not vanish. "No, no, it cannot be. I would have seen it," he rasped.

She raised her bowed head momentarily, revealing sad, swollen eyes. She did not speak. She didn't have to. Her look conveyed the truth: the Brown Robes had forever destroyed his shaman's power to see the future.

Casts No Shadow sat immobilized, the reality of her news seeping into his marrow like a chilling frost. To his son, he had imparted all his knowledge–the stories of his people stretching back to when One Above created them from mud; the way of the land, of growing things, of beasts and seasons; knowledge of the spirit world and how to communicate with the gods; and especially the ways to remove the curses and spells visited on the people by sorcerers. His power was gone and now his son was gone. He had lost everything that had brought meaning to his life.

Seven summers ago to this very day. Red Smoke's words echoed back to him from out of his dream. *You made the wrong choice not to join us.* With those words came the knowledge of what he now had to do. "Close the door, Daughter.

With a questioning glance, Web complied. No soldier came to open it again.

Weakly the wekuseyaay dragged himself to his feet using the wall for support until his knees stopped quivering and he could speak again. He pointed to the roof beam. "Toss the end of your carrying net over that, my daughter."

"Why, my father?"

"Just do as I say."

After three tries she succeeded, then turned to look at him. With one hand against the wall for balance, he stepped toward her. After months of sitting, he had to concentrate all his attention on the mechanics of walking: picking up one foot, moving it ahead, placing it on the floor and shifting his weight before picking up the other foot. Reaching her side, he took both ends of the net and centered it over the beam. It was a fine net, beautifully-woven and strong like everything his daughter's skillful hands made.

"My Father . . ."

His hand sliced through the air, silencing her. "You must witness my passing."

Recognition came slowly into her puffy eyes. She started to protest, but he cut her off. "You must, Daughter, so you can tell our people what you saw."

"No, Father, no. Don't do this."

Casts No Shadow put as much firmness into his tone as he could muster. "I have angered the gods and now I must pay."

Walking shakily back to the wall, he tied one end of the net to an iron ring and tested its hold. Then he took hold of her hand. "You were the right choice for my son, Daughter. No man could wish for a better wife. No child, a better mother. And no father, a better daughter."

"No, please. Don't do this thing," she pleaded.

Ignoring her, he dragged an empty wooden crate over under the beam and stood it on end. "Stand here to be my support."

Her eyes pleading for him to reconsider, she stood where he asked.

"You must not allow the bearded ones to bury me, my daughter. Take my body back to our village and set my spirit free."

"No, Father, no. I cannot."

"You must not disobey me."

She nodded numbly.

Using her shoulder to steady himself, he climbed onto the box and double-looped the loose end of the net around his neck.

"Not this way, Father," she whispered. "Anything but this."

He looked down at her. "Do not weep for me. I have lived too long. Now it is time to join my son and our ancestors."

With that, he stepped off the box.

Instantly he was aware of the pressure on his windpipe, aware of his body, his lungs screaming for air, but he would not allow his feet to kick or his hands to claw at the net or his mouth to open with a silent scream.

He would meet the spirits with bravery, without a struggle.

Web sank down on the dirt floor of the cell and stared at the far wall, trying to take in what had just happened. She did not look at the guard when he entered, did not notice his reaction to the

limp body dangling from the wooden beam or his shouts of
alarm. She did not respond to any of the Spanish who poured into
the room until one touched the wekuseyaay's body. Then she
hurled herself at the man, slapping away his hand, and stationed
herself between them and Casts No Shadow. "Father of Carlos,
go home!" she yelled at the circle of pale gaping faces.

The soldiers looked at each other. One hurried out and soon
brought the Brown Robe named Fuster who stopped inside the
doorway to cross himself.

The action infuriated Web and she screamed, "Father of Carlos,
go home!"

Fuster Brown Robe looked at her in surprise, then motioned for
the soldiers to cut the body down.

Casts No Shadow's form crumpled to the floor. She positioned
herself over the body and glared at the Spanish until they all left
the cell. Fuster Brown Robe was the last to go. He seemed on the
verge of saying something but did not.

Alone again, she refused to look at the wekuseyaay's contorted
face. She hefted the body onto her back, surprised at how light it
was. Every day she carried loads heavier. For a moment she
doubted that she could make it all the way to the village as
burdened with grief as she was.

Father of Carlos, go home. From deep within her soul, the words
rang like a command from the gods, tapping a hidden source of
strength that sent her out of the cell and out of the hated fort.

She arrived at Nipaguay in the late afternoon. She deposited the
wekuseyaay's body on the ground at the center of the village, laying
it out on its back with care. A small crowd began to gather.

She faced them, ignoring the horrified expressions of those
newcomers viewing the agonized face of the corpse, and announced
in a loud, formal voice. "Our brother lives no more. We must free
his spirit from this husk of flesh. We must raise our voices to the
sky so that the spirits will know he comes to join them."

Crooked Basket elbowed her way to the front of the watchers.
"Stand away from him!" she demanded, shoving Web. "The wekuseyaay brought you here, and now you must leave!"

In the face of the woman's vehemence, Web's confidence fled.
She scanned the other faces, searching for signs of disagreement.
She found none.

"You do not belong here," Crooked Basket said. "You never
have."

Among the crowd, heads nodded, though no one would meet
her eyes.

A lump gathered in Web's chest, rising to her throat.

Big Nose moved next to his wife. "Leave, woman."

Web swallowed to steady her voice. "What right have you to say I do not belong here?"

The kwaipai took a step forward. "You would challenge the decision of the people? Take your daughter and leave here so that we may mourn our brother."

Shooting Star burst out of the crowd and ran to Web. Wrapping her slender arms around her mother's legs, she buried her tears in Web's skirt.

On the edge of the crowd, Sand Flea looked at his mother but made no move to come forward.

"And my son?" Web asked.

"As the son of your husband, he must stay here with his band," Big Nose said.

Web looked down at her sobbing daughter. She did not need to ask why the village had rejected the little girl. All the shame she had ever felt when the children of Hawi used to tease her about her webbed hands came flooding out of the deep interior recesses where she had locked it away. And, behind it, the seething anger that had fueled her life until the Raven, shaman of Hawi, had told the story of the First Ancestor. Her torment by the other children had ended the moment the shaman had held up her hands as proof of the band's sacred link to the gods, but she never forgot or forgave their treatment.

Big Nose motioned for Sand Flea to come to his side.

Web watched her son obey. Despite his scars, Sand Flea's features wore the unmistakable stamp of Shadow Dancer. Soon he would undergo the ordeal of the passage to manhood. After that, he would move among the men of the village until he had proven himself as a warrior. Then he would take a wife and father children of his own.

In the strained silence, the kwaipai put a possessive hand on the boy's shoulder.

Web put her hand under Shooting Star's chin and raised the girl's face to hers. Through her tears, Shooting Star said, "Are we leaving, Mother?"

"Do you want to go, little one?"

The little head nodded.

"Then we shall."

Web smiled one last time at her son, then turned away, going home.

EPILOGUE

S hooting Star clutched the scratching stick and willed herself not
to feel the itch on her thigh. Through the holes in the woven
basket cap protecting her head and face from pestering flies, she
glimpsed her mother among the other women of Hawi, preparing
food for the dozens of *sh'mulq* members who clustered around
the four girls in the roasting pit.

Next to Shooting Star, Nedi, her best friend, sneezed.

The dancing and chanting stopped abruptly, while the adults
glared at the offender.

I will not move. Shooting Star repeated the silent order again
and again.

After a time, the dancing and singing resumed. A child darted to
the side of the pit and made a face at her, then raced off giggling.
Mourning Dove, her impish little sister, the child her mother had
been carrying when the two of them left Nipaguay.

Nipaguay. Her memories of that place and people were so
vague. She had a thousand questions about that time, none of
which she dared ask for fear of hurting her mother. She knew that
her brother Sand Flea lived there still, but she could not remember
him; a fact she would never admit to her mother.

The only thing about Nipaguay that she knew for certain was
that her mother had not smiled since the day they left. A dozen
times each day, her mother stopped what she was doing to gaze
toward the west. Shooting Star longed to know what she looked
for but never could work up the courage to ask.

The chanting stopped. She tensed. Now what?

Her mother broke away from the others and came to kneel at
the pit. She removed the protective cap from Shooting Star's
head. "It is over, my daughter."

"I did not move, Mother," Shooting Star said tiredly.

"I know, little one. I know. Now you are a woman–a fine, beautiful woman." With that, Web smiled at last.

GLOSSARY OF KUMEYAAY WORDS

'aakuull	yucca
'aanall	mesquite
'aww	fire
'aww-kuseyaay	fire shaman
'ehaasilth	ocean
'ehmuu	bedrock mortar
'ehpaa	prickly pear cactus
'ehpaa-kurraw	prickly pear cactus thorn
'empuul	loose-woven basket; fits over head
'empuun	large shallow basket
'emuukwin	pipe
'epilly	tule
esally	pestle
'eskwily	small round basket
'esnyaaw	live oak
'ewaa	hut, lodge
'ewii	rattle snake
haakwal	lizard
halypuusuutt	hummingbird
hantak	frog
hataayily	winnowing basket
hattepaa	coyote
hatupul	burden net
ha'waak	twins
hekwiin	acorn granary
hekwiir	rabbit's fur blanket
hellyaa	moon
hellyaach-temur	full moon
hellyaach-sekap-tewaa	half moon
hellyaaw	cottontail rabbit
hellyatai	summer solstice
hemach-kuseyaay	dream shaman
hemenyaaw	sandals
hempuu	throwing stick
hesill	manzanita
heyuly	skirt
'ihpaa	eagle
kalymuu	ritual mortar
kuseyay	strong witch with psychic powers

GLOSSARY OF KUMEYAAY WORDS (cont'd)

kusich-ne-awa	ceremonial enclosure
kwaipai	Chief
kwelmisp	hairy one
llehup	Cave
maaykaa	Daybreak
matsay	desert
metenyaally	tomorrow
neshaaw	black oak
nyemetaay	cougar
paat	duck
pellytaay	sage
shawii	acorn mush
shechaak	screech owl
sh'mulq	people descended from one ancestor; sib
shuullaw	thunder
shuuluk	lightning
sinkuseyaay	female healer and midwife
temshaa	shadow
tolvaach	jimsonweed
'uukwill	cradleboard
'up	tobacco
wekuseyaay	rattlesnake shaman
wisal	shade arbor

A SELECTED BIBLIOGRAPHY FOR *MISSION*

Almstedt, Ruth F., *Diegueño Curing Practices*, San Diego: Museum of Man, 1977

Aschmann, Homer, *Natural and Human History of Baja from Jesuit Missionaries Manuscripts*, Los Angeles: Dawson's Book Shop, 1966

Aschmann, Homer, *Central Desert of Baja California, Demography and Ecology*, Riverside, CA: Manessier Publishing Co., 1967

Balls, Edward K., *Early Uses of California Plants*, Berkley: University of California Press, 1962

Bean, Lowell John (ed.), *California Indian Shamanism*, Menlo Park, CA: Ballena Press, 1992

Bolton, Herbert Eugene, *Fray Juan Crespi, Missionary Explorer on the Pacific Coast*, Berkley: University of California Press, 1927

A SELECTED BIBLIOGRAPHY FOR *MISSION* (cont'd)

Carpenter, Kenneth J., *The History of Scurvy and Vitamin C*, Cambridge: Cambridge University Press, 1986

Carrico, Richard, *Strangers in a Stolen Land*, Newcastle, CA: Sierra Oaks Publishing, 1987

Chace, G. Earl, *Rattlesnakes*, New York: Dodd, Mead, 1984

Cline, Lora L., *Just Before Sunset*, Tombstone, AZ: LC Enterprises, 1984

Costanso, Miguel, *Costanso Narrative of the Portola Expedition*, Newhall, CA: Hogarth Press, 1970

Couro, Ted, *Dictionary of the Mesa Grande Diegueño*, Banning, CA: Malki Museum Press, 1973

Crosby, Alfred W. Jr., *The Columbian Exchange*, Westport, CT: Greenwood Press, 1972

Crosby, Harry, *The King's Highway in Baja*, La Jolla, CA: Copley Books, 1975

Davis, Edward H., *Early Cremation Ceremonies of the Luiseño and San Diegueño Indians*, New York: Museum of the American Indian (Heye Foundation), 1921

Davis, Edward H., *San Diegueño Ceremony of Death Images*, New York: Heye Foundation, 1919

DuBois, Constance G., "Mythology of the Diegueños", International Congress of Americanists, XIIIth session, New York, 1902

DuBois, Constance G., "Diegueño Mortuary Ollas", *American Anthropologist*, Vol. XI, 1907

Engelhardt, Fr. Zephyrin OFM, *The Missions and Missionaries of California*, San Francisco: Barry, 1912

Engelhardt, Fr. Zephyrin OFM, *San Diego Mission*, San Francisco: Barry, 1920

Fages, Pedro, *A Historical, Political and Natural Description of California*, Ramona, CA: Ballena Press, 1972

Fahy, Benin OFM, *The Writings of St. Francis of Assisi*, Chicago: Franciscan Herald, 1963

Freedman, Russell, *Rattlesnakes*, New York: Holiday House, 1984

Geiger, Maynard OFM, *Franciscan Missionaries in Hispanic California 1769-1848*, San Marino, CA: Huntington Library, 1969

Geiger, Maynard OFM, (trans. & ed.), *Letters of Luis Jayme OFM*, 1772, Los Angeles: Dawson's Book Shop, 1970

A SELECTED BIBLIOGRAPHY FOR *MISSION* (cont'd)

Gifford, E. W., *Clans and Moities in Southern California*, Berkley: University of California Press, 1918

Heizer, Robert F. and Elsasser, Albert, B., *The Natural World of the California Indians*, Berkley: University of California Press, 1980

James, George W., *In and Out of the Old Missions of California*, New York: Grosset & Dunlap, 1927

Johnson, Mary E., *Indian Legends of the Cuyamaca Mountains*, San Diego: 1914

Krell, Dorothy(ed.), *The California Missions*, Menlo Park, CA: Sunset Publishing Co., 1991

Kroeber, A.L., *Handbook of the Indians of California*, Dover Publications, 1976

Lee, Melicent, *Indians of the Oaks*, San Diego: San Diego Museum of Man, 1989

Lewis, Henry T., *Patterns of Indian Burning In California*, Ramona, CA: Ballena Books, 1973

Margolin, Malcolm(ed.), *The Way We Lived*, Berkley: Heyday Books, 1981

McDonald, Marquis, *Baja: Land of Lost Missions*, San Antonio: Naylor Co., 1968

McGown, Charlotte, *Ceremonial Fertility Sites in Southern California*, San Diego: Museum of Man, 1982

Minshall, Herbert, *The Broken Stones*, La Jolla, CA: Copley Books, 1976

Moriarty, James R., *Cosmogony, Rituals and Medical Practice Among the Diegueño Indians of Southern California*, Anthropological Journal of Canada, Vol. 3, #3, 1965

Niethammer, Carolyn, *American Indian Food and Lore*, New York: Collier Books, 1974

Pepper, Choral, *Baja California: Vanished Missions*, Los Angeles: Ward Ritchie Press, 1973

Pourade, Richard F., *The Explorers–The History of San Diego*, San Diego: Union-Tribune Publishing Co., 1960

Pourade, Richard F., *Time of the Bells*, San Diego: Union-Tribune Publishing Co., 1961

Robertson, Tomas, *Baja California and Its Missions*, Glendale, CA: La Siesta Press, 1978

A SELECTED BIBLIOGRAPHY FOR *MISSION* (cont'd)

Rogers, Malcolm, *Ancient Hunters of the Far West*, San Diego: Union-Tribune Publishing Co., 1966

Serra, Junípero OFM, *Diario, the Journal of Padre Serra*, San Diego: Don Diego's Libreria, 1964

Shipek, Florence C., *Delfina Cuero*, Menlo Park, CA: Ballena Press, 1991

Shipek, Florence C., *Pushed into the Rocks, Southern California Indian Land Tenure, 1769–1986*, Lincoln, NB: University of Nebraska Press, 1987

Spier, Leslie, *Southern Diegueño Customs*, Berkley: University of California Press, 1923

Strong, William D., *Aboriginal Society in Southern California*, Berkley: University of California Press, 1929

Taylor, Alexander S., *An Historical Summary of Lower California*, Pasadena: Socio-Technical, 1971

Treganza, Adan E.(check first name), *Possibilities of an Aboriginal Practice of Agriculture among the San Diegueño*, Berkley: University of California Press, 1947

Waterhouse, E.B., *Serra, California Conquistador*, Los Angeles: Parker & Son, 1968

Watson, Aldren A., *The Village Blacksmith*, New York: Norton, 1977

Weber, Francis J., *Missions and Missionaries of Baja*, Los Angeles: Dawson's Book Shop, 1968

Wiss, Winifred E., *Fray Junípero Serra and the California Conquest*, New York: Charles Scribner's Sons, 1967

The People Cabrillo Met, San Diego: Cabrillo Historical Association, 1976

The Impact of European Exploration and Settlement on Local Native Americans, San Diego: Cabrillo Historical Association, 1986

The Blacksmith in 18th Century Williamsburg, Williamsburg: Colonial Williamsburg, 1971